TROLLOPE THE TRAVELLER

Selections from Anthony Trollope's Travel Writings

Anthony Trollope, one of the best-loved novelists of nineteenth-century England, was born in 1815, went to school at Harrow and Winchester, and worked for thirty-three years in the General Post Office. A prolific writer, he is best known for his *Barsetshire* and *Palliser* novels, but he was also the quintessential Victorian traveler, adventurous and energetic.

Graham Handley is a writer, editor, and lecturer who has published widely on nineteenth-century fiction.

TROLLOPE THE TRAVELLER

Selections from Anthony Trollope's Travel Writings

Edited with an introduction by

GRAHAM HANDLEY

ELEPHANT PAPERBACKS
Ivan R. Dee, Publisher, Chicago

TROLLOPE THE TRAVELLER. Copyright ©1993 by Pickering & Chatto (Publishers) Limited. All rights reserved, including the right to reproduce this book or portions thereof in any form. First published in Great Britain by Pickering & Chatto (Publishers) Ltd.

First ELEPHANT PAPERBACK edition published 1995 by Ivan R. Dee, Inc., 1332 North Halsted Street, Chicago 60622. Manufactured in the United States of America and printed on acid-free paper.

Library of Congress Cataloging-in-Publication Data:
Trollope, Anthony, 1815–1882.
    Trollope the traveller : selections from Anthony Trollope's travel writings / edited with an introduction by Graham Handley. -- 1st Elephant pbk. ed.
        p.   cm.
    Includes bibliographical references (p. 243).
    ISBN 1-56663-074-6
    1. Trollope, Anthony, 1815–1882—Journeys.   2. Voyages and travels.
I. Handley, Graham.   II. Title.
PR5682.H38   1995
828'.803--dc20
    [B]   94-43052

For Robert Super

Most Distinguished Trollope Scholar

With Warm Regard

CONTENTS

ACKNOWLEDGEMENTS

I am grateful to Professor Robert Super and Dr James Gibson for reading my Introduction and making constructive comments on it.

I should like to thank my editor, Katherine Bright-Holmes, for her meticulous work, helpful advice and encouragement, Stephen Easton, Florence Hamilton, and Sara Marafini at the Senate, for the jacket design. I am grateful to Perry Birnbaum, Dennis Samuel and Kathleen Tillotson for help with the notes.

One debt is perhaps outside the usual prescription. In 1947 Oxford University Press published *The Trollope Reader: Selected and Edited by Esther Cloudman Dunn and Marion C. Dodd*. It has been my constant companion, and merits reissue. I have modelled some extract headings on those chosen by these sympathetic editors, and record my debt gratefully here.

A NOTE ON THE EXTRACTS

The texts used are first or early editions of the travel books: *The West Indies and the Spanish Main* (2nd edition, 1860): *North America* (1st edition, 1862); *Australia and New Zealand* (1st edition, 1873); *South Africa* (1st edition, 1878); *South Africa* (abridged from the 4th edition by the author, 1879). This contains a new chapter (xi), 'Zululand'. Errors and misprints have been silently corrected. I have also referred to the definitive edition of *Australia*, edited by P. D. Edwards and R. B. Joyce, University of Queensland Press, 1967, and to the abridged *North America*, edited by Robert Mason, with an introduction by John William Ward (Penguin 1968; reprinted 1992).

The extracts chosen follow the sequence of the original editions with one or two exceptions in the material on South Africa. Certain individual Trollope spellings and usages have been retained, for example *quaranteened, riggle, caldron, prospecter, demitted, wallabys* and *trowsers.*

CHRONOLOGY OF ANTHONY TROLLOPE

1815   (April 24) Born Bloomsbury, London
1823   Goes to Harrow as a day boy
1825   Moves to private school at Sunbury
1827   Attends Winchester
1831   Returns to Harrow
1834   Appointed Junior Clerk in the General Post Office at St
       Martin's-le-Grand, London
1835   Father dies
1841   Appointed Deputy Postal Surveyor, Banagher, Ireland
1844   (June) Marries Rose Heseltine. Transferred to
       Tipperary
1846   First son, Henry, born
1847   Second son, Frederic, born
       The MacDermots of Ballycloran published
1848   *The Kellys and the O'Kellys*
1850   *La Vendée*
1851   Transferred to Postal Mission in England and Wales
1853   Returns to Ireland – Surveyor in the Northern District
1855   Settles near Dublin
       The Warden
1857   *Barchester Towers*
       The Three Clerks
1858   *Dr Thorne*
       (February–March) Postal Mission to Suez
       (November) Postal Mission to West Indies
1859   *The Bertrams*
       THE WEST INDIES AND THE SPANISH MAIN
       Moves to Waltham Cross, Hertfordshire

(May) Leaves for Australia
1872   *The Golden Lion of Granpère*
        In Australia and New Zealand
1873   Moves to Montagu Square
        AUSTRALIA AND NEW ZEALAND
        The Eustace Diamonds
1874   *Phineas Redux*
        Lady Anna
        Harry Heathcote of Gangoil
1875   *The Way We Live Now*
        Visits Australia via Ceylon
        Begins *An Autobiography*
1876   Finishes *An Autobiography*
        The Prime Minister
1877   *The American Senator*
        (June) Sails for Cape Town
1878   SOUTH AFRICA
        Is He Popenjoy?
        'How "The Mastiffs" went to Iceland'
1879   *An Eye for An Eye*
        John Caldigate
        Thackeray
        Cousin Henry
1880   *The Duke's Children*
        The Life of Cicero
        Moves to South Harting, near Petersfield, Sussex
1881   *Dr Wortle's School*
        Ayala's Angel
1882   *The Fixed Period*
        Palmerston
        Marion Fay
        Kept in the Dark
        (May) Visits Ireland
        Moves to London
        Suffers a stroke

(December 6) Dies
1883   *Mr Scarborough's Family*
       An Autobiography
       The Landleaguers (unfinished)
1884   *An Old Man's Love*

Note   The dates given are those of the first book publication.
         Details of serial publication will be found in Mary
         Hamer's excellent *Writing by Numbers: Trollope's Serial
         Fiction* (Cambridge, 1987). Readers might also like to
         consult Michael Sadleir's *Trollope: A Bibliography*
         (Constable, 1928) and *Anthony Trollope: A Collector's
         Catalogue*, 1847–1990 (The Trollope Society, 1992) which
         incorporates Lance O. Tingay's *The Trollope Collector* (The
         Silverbridge Press, 1985).

INTRODUCTION

Anthony Trollope was born in 1815 some two months before the battle of Waterloo; he died in 1882 some two years before the passing of the Third Reform Bill which further increased the franchise. His mature years are therefore contemporaneous with the bulk of the Victorian period. He would have been aware of factory reform and the growth of industry, of political reform which extended the vote in 1832 and in 1867, and he certainly recorded the impact of the Oxford Movement with its High Church emphases (1833) in his Barchester novels (1855–67). He saw the terrible effects of the Irish famine in the late 1840s; attended the Great Exhibition in 1851. As a postal official he had seen the recommendations of the Northcote-Trevelyan report on the Civil Service of 1853–4 which suggested that the system of patronage should be replaced by competitive examination. He was politically aware, disliking what he considered the expediency of Sir Robert Peel over the Corn Laws in 1846, rejecting the Tory, Disraeli, greatly admiring Lord Palmerston.

Trollope described himself as a liberal conservative, stood for Parliament in the Whig cause at Beverley in 1868, and created his ideal politician of integrity and probity, Plantagenet Palliser. Foreign affairs greatly interested him (witness his devotion to Palmerston): the Crimean War (concluded by the Treaty of Paris in 1856) and the Indian Mutiny (1857) precede his first important journeys abroad. Trollope set forth his detailed knowledge of political affairs in their domestic and public interactions in what became known as the Palliser series (1864–80).

The nineteenth-century improvements in transport facilitated the expansion of travel in the Victorian period. The coming of the railways brought Europe within easier reach, and, before the middle of the century, the continental holiday and the cultural tour were well established for the upper classes. The vogue for travel meant the provision of a literature of travel, and guidebooks pioneered by the publisher John Murray began to appear regularly from 1836. The colonies and the powerful emergent democracy of the United States, as well as whole areas of Africa and South America, gave explorers, historians, geographers, scientists and amateurs further areas to negotiate. Charles Darwin voyaged for five years in the *Beagle* studying tropical regions, and his *Origin of Species* (1859), with its concept of evolution supported by natural selection, placed travel at the heart of significant scientific progress. Charles Dickens, Trollope's contemporary, visited the United States in 1842 and produced a travel book in the same year, *American Notes for General Circulation*. The reader can compare Dickens' views on institutions, slavery and manners with Trollope's, which appeared some twenty years later. By the time Trollope turned to travel, he was becoming an increasingly successful novelist, with a wide range of interests. *Barchester Towers* had been issued in 1857, a year before his official journeys began, but he brought to these journeys a voice which was both practical and independent.

Trollope's enthusiasm for travel perhaps derives from his mother's ability to turn her visit to America to literary (and popular) account. Her bestselling *Domestic Manners of the Americans* (1832) was the first of her spirited attempts in print to save her family from financial ruin: her husband suffered from melancholia and was impractical in business. She went to America in 1827 intent on making money, but she there showed her own ineptitude for business. In setting up a bazaar in Cincinnati to sell knick-knacks, she soon found herself bankrupt, but she had discovered a new world: she became a writer, successfully recording her American experiences in an independent and frequently abrasive way. Thereafter the name of Trollope was often associated with the offence her criticisms had given in America. Anthony was left at home during his mother's visit, but there is every reason to suppose that her achievements, both as travel writer and then as a novelist, influenced his own ambitions and later choices. The evidence of his *An Autobiography* (written 1875–6, but not published until 1883, after his death) indicates that he was habituated at least to insular travel from an early age. He was constantly on the move during his childhood and youth, from London, to Harrow, to Winchester, to Belgium, then back to London to begin his career in the Post Office in 1834. Here he was often restless, unhappy and slack in his work, but when the opportunity came for him to transfer to Ireland he changed the course of his life. He travelled the length and breadth of the country, achieved a high degree of what we may now call job satisfaction, and began to write fiction. Ireland had given him another career, travel in Ireland at least the initial inspiration for it and the settings to which he would often return. His first novels were *The MacDermots of Ballycloran* (1847) and *The Kellys and the O'Kellys* (1848), but he was to go back to the country he knew so well in some of his stories, and in novels such as *Castle Richmond* (1860), *An Eye for an Eye* (1879) and the uncompleted *The Landleaguers* (1883). The condition of Ireland in the mid-to-late 1840s prompted Trollope to write a series of letters to *The Examiner*.[1] The constant travelling in Ireland, the medium of his working life as a postal surveyor, provided him with a readily accessible context. He was always the acute observer, using the particularities of place, incident, anecdote as adhesives to the narrative imagination. He was often in Ireland from 1841–59, but spent some periods in England. Place fertilized his ideas, and he has left an account of how, wandering around the precincts of Salisbury, he conceived Barchester in all its immediacy and specificity.[2] English and Irish travel thus provided the basis for his career as a novelist. There is an ironic note on his early ambitions. He wanted to put his knowledge of Ireland to good effect by writing a guide book, which he sent to the publisher John Murray. Trollope feelingly records much later that his manuscript 'was never opened'. After a wait of nine months he 'insisted on having back my property – and got it. I need hardly say that my property has never been of the slightest use to me.'[3] This indication of his wish to write about travel comes before fiction had taken hold, and here his personal chronology follows that of his mother.

His circumstances were changing. Early in 1858 he was sent on a postal mission to Suez. His task was to evaluate the shipment of mails through Egypt to India (whether in bags or boxes), and then draft a fresh treaty with the Egyptians for the transfer between Alexandria and Suez of mails going to or from India and Australia. The treaty was drafted by February 23, and Trollope was able to spend ten days in the Holy Land, six days at Malta on the way home (he cast an eye on the efficiency of the Post Office there) as well as visiting Spain and Gibraltar. He reached London on May 10. He had finished *Dr Thorne* on March 31 and began *The Bertrams* the next day. His first significant and extended trip abroad did not result in a travel book, but the signs of the influence of travel on his writing career are there to be read in *The Bertrams*.

Certain chapters of this novel are steeped in the localised atmosphere; he described Cairo and the Holy Land particularly vividly. The novel was published in March 1859 (Trollope was in the West Indies at the time) and reflects his obvious wish to utilise the tandem of fiction and travel. In *The Bertrams* his own ironic commentary on tourists and tourism forms one of the most attractive sequences in the story. Trollope's characters 'do' the requisite places. There is an early chapter, 'Jerusalem', in which he combines the factual tracing of the route (he loves exactitude of itinerary and movement) with some guying of the conception of Middle Eastern travel. We have the impression that he is laughing at himself too:

> There is something enticing to an Englishman in the idea of riding off through the desert with a pistol girt about his waist, a portmanteau strapped on one horse before him . . . it is so un-English, oriental and inconvenient; so opposed to the accustomed haste and comfort of a railway; so out of his hitherto beaten way of life, that he is delighted to get into the saddle. But it may be a question whether he is not generally more delighted to get out of it; particularly if the saddle be a Turkish one.
>
> (Chapter VI)

Trollope is both participant and spectator here as in the travel books later, and the lightness of the tone is found in them too. He

ponders the opportunities, the situations, in which a traveller may
– fortuitously – find himself, observing 'When you have been up
the Great Pyramid with a lady, the chances are you know more
about her than you would do from a year's acquaintance fostered
by a dozen London parties' (Chapter VIII). Trollope's use of
place in *The Bertrams*, his ability to observe, describe, narrate and
to integrate his characters into their (and his) location make this
novel something of a bench-mark in his dual development. There
was also a registering of the possibility of contriving short
fictions out of this experience. On July 29 1860 he wrote to his
new publisher George Smith mentioning a story 'written within
the last ten days, about the Holy Land'.[4] At this stage it was
called 'The Banks of the Jordan'. It appeared in the *London Review*
in January 1861 and later in *Tales of All Countries* (2nd Series,
1863) as 'A Ride Across Palestine'. There are other examples of
his looking back and finding inspiration from what he had seen
on the postal mission to Suez, such as 'An Unprotected Female at
the Pyramids' and 'George Walker at Suez'.

If Trollope's trip to the Middle East whetted his appetite, gave
him the taste for ways of life other than his own and developed
further aspects of his creativity, these were enhanced by his
mission to the West Indies and the Spanish Main. He left Southampton on November 17 1858 on the *Atrato*, claiming in *An
Autobiography* that his task in the West Indies was to 'cleanse the
Augean stables of our Post Office system there,'.[5] He left the
ship at St Thomas, travelling to Jamaica on a smaller vessel, the
Derwent, which arrived at Kingston on December 6. Trollope's
first concern was to implement local control of the Post Offices in
Jamaica and British Guiana in line with a directive from the
General Post Office. He faced opposition in the shape of local
officials who feared that they would lose their jobs, and
moreover contended that costs would rise. He evaluated shipping
details, considering the problems of transfer across the isthmus of
Panama to the West Coast of America (particularly British Columbia), perhaps even to Australia and New Zealand. According
to R. H. Super, he had to persuade 'the Spanish islands of Cuba
and Puerto Rico' . . . to reduce their charges for local forwarding
of mail sent from the United Kingdom'.[6] These various concerns

enabled Trollope to travel the length and breadth of the Caribbean. Meticulously, he traversed the postal routes throughout
Jamaica, suggesting how economies might be effected. On January 24th 1859 he boarded the sailing brig *Linwood*. Like his
mother some twenty-eight years earlier, he began to write his
first travel book while he was actually on a journey. He recorded
his experience feelingly both in the book and in a letter to his
mother (January 27 1859): – 'Dearest mother . . . by way of
making a short cut across to Cuba, I got into this wretched
sailing vessel. But we have been becalmed half the time since
. . .'.[7] He was bent on calculating if mail could be sent on this
route, just as he had walked the beats of postmen in Ireland to
measure the time taken for their deliveries. He had to check on
procedures and individuals at Demerara and Grenada. While in
Panama he negotiated the carrying of British mail by train for an
annual payment and, after obtaining a tax reduction on postage
in New Granada, which then owned Panama, he was taken to
Costa Rica in the man-of-war *Vixen*. He was bent on observing
French activity towards the construction of a canal across Central
America, and some pages of his book were devoted to criticism
of these plans. Finally, in a stroke of irony worthy of his fiction,
he found himself taken back to Colon in the *Trent*, which was
later to be the focal point of an international incident in the
American Civil War.[8]

On July 16 1859, after he had returned to Dublin, Trollope
submitted his report. He advocated making Jamaica the centre for
mail distribution instead of the uneconomical and inconvenient
St Thomas. This meant a speeding up of deliveries and hence a
more quickly gathered profit. According to Super, 'His meticulous calculation indicated a saving of 3,300 miles a month over
the packet company's plan, or (at the rate at which mileage was
calculated) more than £15,000 a year'.[9] But as early as January
11 1859 he had written to the publishers Chapman and Hall
offering to write a book about the West Indies. The agreement
was signed by his brother Tom in April, as Anthony was just
about to set off from the Caribbean for Bermuda. He wrote about
the penal settlement at some length in his book, and later used
the location for one of his best stories, 'Aaron Trow', which was

published in *Public Opinion* in December 1861, and subsequently in *Tales of All Countries* (2nd Series, 1863). Trollope was certainly alert to one of the main chances that travel offered him, and while staying in New York on his way home he offered *Tales of All Countries* (before they were written) to Harper Brothers. He also offered them sheets of his forthcoming travel book, which they declined.

The West Indies and the Spanish Main was published in October 1859. Trollope later wrote that he thought it was one of his best books. It is a mixture of relaxed and informal writing on the one hand, with some self-mockery, and much anecdote and story; on the other there are serious sociological and moral commentaries which fairly reveal Trollope the man and his particular biases. He is concerned to evaluate the effect of the emancipation of the slaves (1833 in British colonies) on plantation owners, and the removal of tariff protection in the 1850s which further undermined their position. His attitudes towards race and slavery sometimes appal the modern reader. N. John Hall instances 'the insensitivity of Trollope's views on blacks', but insists, rightly, that he should be praised for having 'the honesty to write out his thoughts (however benighted they were) for any reader who wished to challenge him'.[10] Trollope's integrity is his own best apologia.

The last months of 1859 were fortuitous times for Trollope. In November he moved into his new home at Waltham House, and in the same month he signed an agreement to provide a full-length novel for the new and prestigious *Cornhill* magazine, with the first instalment to be ready near the beginning of December in time for the opening number in January 1860. The novel was *Framley Parsonage* and, while it was making his own success and the success of the *Cornhill* an established fact, he was still drawn towards his other writing. He proposed to his publisher George Smith that he might write a book on India, though he admits that he would not be heartbroken if he does not do it, adding 'Per se going to India is a bore, – but it would suit me professionally'.[11] This is a clear indication of his serious attitude towards another aspect of his authorial profession. With characteristic independence (and not a little obstinacy) he changed geographical direction and requested seven months leave of absence in order to go to America and write a book about it. He signed an agreement with his other publishers Chapman and Hall as early as March 20 1861. Sir Rowland Hill (of Penny Postage fame) as Secretary to the Postmaster General, Lord Stanley, objected to Trollope's having leave to go, but was rebuked by Lord Stanley, and Trollope obtained his release without any conditions attached to it. While he was making his preparations to leave, the open hostilities of the American Civil War began. Trollope wrote to his young American friend Kate Field on August 9 1861 commenting on the first significant engagement of the war (at Bull Run, July 21), 'The worst of it is, that by no event could a stronger presage of long bloodshed be given.'[12] A fortnight later he and his wife Rose left Liverpool, arriving in Boston on September 5, and, staying briefly at the virtually deserted Ocean Hotel at Newport, Rhode Island, where there were twenty-five guests in accommodation built for six hundred. But soon he came to meet a number of celebrities, among them Emerson, Lowell and Oliver Wendell Holmes. Intent on noting what he saw, he began the book on *North America* on September 16, a mere eleven days after he had landed, writing three pages that day and thirty within the week. He visited Canada, formed the view that ultimately it would cut its ties with Britain, and climbed Owl's Head Mountain with Rose, both exhibiting great delight in this shared adventure.

Trollope's self-imposed itinerary of observation and exploration was a wide one. Visiting Niagara for the second time (he had seen it briefly on his way home from the West Indies) enabled him to include in his book advice on how best to view and appreciate the area. He went westward by steamboat and train (he was full of praise for the sleeping cars), and took the opportunity to visit a woodcutter's cabin, noting approvingly the presence of a number of books. There is a marked independence and vividness about his impressions. He did not take notes, but it is clear that he took an active part in numerous experiences and situations. By October 31 he was in New York, investigating state schools and being duly impressed by them, and by November 12 he was back in Boston. Richard Mullen points out that

Trollope stored parts of conversations in the retrieval system he
used for his fiction, introducing a remark made to him by Oliver
Wendell Holmes into *The American Senator*, where he has Senator
Gotobed boast to his English host 'In the matter of wine, I don't
think I have happened to come across anything so good in this
country as our old Madeiras.'[13] His visit to America provided
him with much material for his fiction in the form of a number of
transatlantic characters. Certainly one of his stories, 'Miss Ophelia
Gledd', derives from his sleigh driving with a lady in Boston
(March 8 1862, see pp. 111–2 of this selection), when the horses
bolted but did not overturn them. Super describes the tale with
some justice as 'a very Henry Jamesian narrative of the conflict of
two cultures, Bostonian and English'.[14] In the previous November he had attended lectures in New York and Boston, on one
occasion hearing 'a rabid abolitionist discourse from Wendell
Phillips'.[15] On the same day his wife Rose sailed for England,
while Anthony went on to visit Concord, Cambridge, Lowell,
and then back to New York, then to Philadelphia, Baltimore and
Washington.

The seizure of the British vessel *Trent* on November 8 by the
Northern navy and the removal of the two confederate envoys
precipitated a crisis which is well documented by Trollope. He
heard of the coming release of the pair, Slidell and Mason, on
December 27. He went on to St Louis, visited his mother's one-
time bazaar in Cincinnati, and found the North–South confronta-
tion particularly repugnant in Baltimore, where 'Fathers were
divided from sons, and mothers from daughters'.[16] Once more
the situation provided him with the nucleus of a short story, 'The
Two Generals', which was first published in 1863 in the December number of *Good Words*.

By mid-February in 1862 in Cincinnati he had finished two-
thirds of his book, which was to be published on May 19. He
later said of it that it was 'tedious and confused, and will hardly,
I think, be of future value to those who wish to make themselves
acquainted with the United States'.[17] It is certainly true that he
tried to cover too much: his range included the length and
breadth of American culture, the nature of government and institutions. Above all, he was an important eye-witness of events

which could not properly be understood in England. He was at once specific, accurate and, as ever, independent in his reportage, describing frankly and vividly the conditions of American life in the often bewildering period which followed the Secession.

Trollope disliked Washington, nursed a carbuncle on his forehead (he drew a cartoon of it in a letter to Kate Field), was upset by the death of the Prince Consort (December 14 1861), and spent the first five days of 1862 in the army camps of Northern Virginia, bogged down in the fighting preparations and the mud. Possibly his travels in America encouraged him in his own political ambitions (he stood as one of the Liberal candidates for Beverley in 1868). Mullen reports him as telling an audience in England that 'slavery undermined the moral character of the master more than it hurt the slave',[18] but Trollope was always liable to articulate the unexpected and sometimes the unacceptable. Yet despite his dislikes (of women's dress, of children eating, of hot air pipes, of massive rooms, among others), he regarded America as a triumph for England.

Modern biographers disagree about the reception of the book. Hall feels it to have been well received in this country while Mullen thinks not. But Mullen himself has written persuasively and with insight on Trollope's achievement in *North America*. While recognising its faults of structure and diffuseness, he emphasises what it tells us of the man:

> It illustrates so many aspects of his character: his energy, his love of travel, his passionate concern for politics, his never-ending desire to be regarded as a serious writer and his peculiar blend of liberalism and conservatism. His time in America would influence his writing for the rest of his life ... *North America* is far from being the best portrait of its subject, but there is no better portrayal of its author.[19]

The evidence of his unfailing humanity and his adherence to principle is found so often in the book; in the aftermath of the visit he confided one strongly held belief in a letter to Kate Field. After jokingly implying that he wrote about his journeys so that he could cunningly insert his own political opinions, he makes a

radical statement which typifies his independence and conveys
his disgust of the war:

My feeling is that a man should die rather than be made
a soldier against his will. One's country has no right to
demand everything. There is much that is higher and
better and greater than one's country. One is patriotic
only because one is too small and too weak to be
cosmopolitan. If a country can not get along without a
military conscription, it had better give up – and let its
children seek other ties.[20]

Part of Trollope's greatness lies in the deep roots of his humanity, and these were nurtured by the American experience. His
views often contain sudden and unexpected revelations which at
first sight may seem to be paradoxical. He was capable of being
reactionary *and* enlightened, but without the taint of expediency
or hypocrisy.

Towards the end of 1870 Trollope and Rose determined that
they would pay a visit to their son Fred who was sheep-farming
at Mortray in New South Wales. Trollope signed a contract with
Chapman and Hall on January 12 1871 for a travel book about
Australia. He also negotiated terms with the *Daily Telegraph* that
he would write a series of letters from the Antipodes (eleven
were printed from December 1871 onwards). On May 24 the
Trollopes sailed via Suez and the Indian ocean. Characteristi-
cally, he began *Lady Anna* on the following day, completing it
before they reached Australia on July 27. Mullen deftly notes the
connection between the location and the end of the novel, when
'the newly-married couple decide to go "to the Antipodes" as a
place where titled ladies and radical tailors could dwell in democratic bliss'.[21] A visit to New Zealand was included in the itinerary,
and by the time the Trollopes started for home some seventeen
months later Anthony had completed three-quarters of the book.

In 1871 Australia consisted of six separate colonies, Victoria,
New South Wales, South Australia, Queensland, Tasmania and
Western Australia. Each had its own legislature and its own
governor was sent out from London. There were customs bar-
riers between each of these colonies, and Trollope had to obtain

a certificate which allowed him to travel freely through the
territories, and which stated that he was not a convict, nor had he
ever been one. The chapters on Australia are extensive, rambling,
occasionally statistical, reflecting his enthusiasm to see as much
as possible, to court experience, to pronounce, compare, evaluate. Throughout his travel writings analogies with England and
Ireland are his common measure. Sometimes these carry judg-
ments, but at others they are just loosely, even nostalgically,
comparative.

The New Zealand chapters, less prolix, more concise – perhaps
a reflection of a more compact terrain – contain in part another
comparison. His interest in the Maoris may be set against his
rejection of the Australian Aborigines. He felt that attempts to
convert the Maoris to Christianity were pointless and misguided,
and was greatly grieved by his own certainty of their destiny:

> But contact with Europeans does not improve them. At
> the touch of the higher race they are poisoned and melt
> away. There is scope for poetry in their past history.
> There is room for philanthropy as to their present
> condition. But in regard to their future, – there is hardly
> a place for hope.[22]

John Hall has rightly commented that Trollope's attitude towards
the aborigines makes 'disturbing reading':

> Of the Australian black man we may certainly say that
> he has to go. That he should perish without unneces-
> sary suffering should be the aim of all who are con-
> cerned in the matter.[23]

Hall adds that 'Trollope's moral sense, like that of most of his
contemporaries, simply did not register the horrors of this
analysis'.[24] The travel books show Trollope as a product of his
time, illustrating at once how strong were certain innate attitudes
in him and in his contemporaries. This should not diminish our
respect for him for he is capable of transcending the attitudes of
that time by his forthrightness and integrity.

Anthony and Rose met Fred's fiancée Susannah some weeks
after their arrival in Australia. The couple were married on

December 14 1871, but the Trollopes did not attend the wedding, probably because he did not like such ceremonies or perhaps because his itinerary was so crowded. The chapter 'Country Life in the Bush' derives from their stay at Mortray with Fred, which also provided him with material for his short novel, *Harry Heathcote of Gangoil* (1874). He wrote it in a period of four weeks in June 1873. It was Trollope's last story with a completely non-English setting, and later he observed 'The Harry Heathcote is my boy Frederic – or very much the same'.[25] His meeting with a young goldminer probably gave him the idea for *John Caldigate* (serialised in *Blackwood's* 1878–9), where four chapters of crucial importance to the plot are set in Australia, and where place and space are integral to the narrative. Among Trollope's experiences in Australia are his lowering himself into a gold mine (a statutory exercise for a man of his thoroughness), a visit to the Chudleigh stalactite caves, and taking a constant delight in the various scenery; there are some lovely vignettes, notably of sheep-shearing, while his determination to authenticate his account by historical detail and statistical evidence is characteristic. The approach is consistently sustained, the narrative frequently enlivened by eye-witness account, personal incident, something which obviously led the writer in the Brisbane *Courier* to refer ironically to *Australia* and *New Zealand* as 'Mr Trollope's Latest Work of Fiction', though the same writer immediately afterwards praises his 'truthfulness'.[26] Rose Trollope paid one domestic penalty for the trip, losing her cook, an efficient and loyal woman, in marriage to an Australian. Trollope enjoyed the fact that a mining company named the Disraeli apparently paid no dividends. Super slyly observes, 'In due course a new shaft at Ballarat was named "Sir Anthony Trollope" in honour of his visit; whether this shaft paid off is not disclosed'.[27] He took part in a stag hunt in Melbourne, where he suffered a mishap, investigated the degrading areas of the town at Ballarat, bought tobacco for the convicts after visiting a prison, camped out in conditions of extremity complete with billy-can and bad brandy, and went to an evening party in Perth 'in everyday clothes with a blue shirt',[28] acutely aware of his offence.

In 1875 Trollope returned to Australia in an attempt to sort out

Fred's affairs. He lost more than £4600 on Mortray, but during his two months' stay there he began work on *The American Senator*, again arranging to write letters about his travels which were published subsequently in the *Liverpool Mercury*.[29] For the first time, on this journey, there are signs of contracting time and space on his personal level: 'But I was 60 the other day, and at that age a man has no right to look forward to making many more voyages round the world'.[30]

Whatever the unevenness of *Australia and New Zealand* there are, as always with Trollope, profound compensations. Travel broadened him in the sense that his experiences were not only assimilated into his fiction, they entered his soul. Mullen believes that all Trollope's journeys after his visit to America were conditioned by his evaluation of the American way of life. He recognised clearly that 'colonies, like children, could not forever be ruled from home' and that 'structures like Empires were of secondary importance'.[31] This is a measure of Trollope's inner growth.

Although he felt his age on his second Australian visit, Trollope had not yet finished with travel. Ever susceptible to new motivation, and provoked by his own concern for particular issues then dominating South Africa, he made his final decision to go there in April 1877. South Africa at the time consisted of the Boer Republic and the British colonies, as well as powerful homelands such as those belonging to the Zulus (the latter under Cetywayo were defeated by the British in 1879). The Union of South Africa was not established until 1910. There is little doubt that the fertilising event which activated Trollope's visit was the entry of Sir Theophilus Shepstone into Pretoria in April 1877. He needed his accompanying force of a mere twenty-five mounted policemen to go beyond his brief and annexe the Transvaal. On June 29 Trollope embarked for Cape Town, determined to traverse with his usual thoroughness the main areas of the Boer Republic and the British colonies. He had, of course, concluded his customary deal with Chapman and Hall (though not as financially rewarding as the previous ones) to produce a two-volume travel book for £850, and fifteen letters to provincial newspapers for £175. Typically, his current fiction kept him well occupied. He completed *John Caldigate* on July 21, the day before he arrived at Cape Town. Prior to this, and just before he left for South Africa, *The American Senator* was published. Hall suggests that there is in Elias Gotobed's predilections in part an ironic self-portrait of Trollope the traveller:

> He had seen the miseries of a casual ward . . . He had measured the animal food consumed by the working classes, and knew the exact amount of alcohol swallowed by the average Briton. He had seen also the luxury of baronial halls, the pearl-drinking extravagances of commercial palaces, the unending labours of our pleasure-seekers . . .[32]

He began to write about what he saw on the day after his arrival. Super believes that Trollope's primary concern was to investigate the condition of the native populations, and that having been horrified by what he had seen of them and their accelerated decline in North America, Australia and New Zealand, he hoped that he would 'find something more creditable to England in South Africa'.[33] But initially he did his usual thing – he visited the public libraries and the botanical gardens and, of course, the Post Office. He observed wrily 'My advice is always received with attention and respect . . . But I never knew an instance yet in which any improvement recommended by me was ever carried out'.[34]

He inevitably visited the diamond mines and, in *An Old Man's Love* (1883), published after his death, wrote of Kimberley in Chapter 6, 'I know of no spot more odious'. But watching the scramble and the competition at Kimberley he also wrote – with a telling brevity that summarises his own creed – 'Who can doubt but that work is the great civilizer of the world – work and the growing desire for those good things which only work will bring?'[35] Hall points out that from time to time in *South Africa* Trollope 'With a novelist's talent . . . moves his account from generalities to particularities'.[36] There are many graphic incidents – consider the meetings with the various native chiefs – and Super recounts the amusing occasion when the young Rider Haggard arrived back in Pretoria from his duties elsewhere to find that Trollope was asleep in his bed; he was thoroughly rude when awakened.

Trollope was fascinated by ostrich farming and, despite the shortness of his visit – he was away for six months, just a little over a third of the time spent on his Australian/New Zealand trip – his excessive weight (sixteen stones) and poor eyesight, he was keenly observant. His experiences were different from those of his other travels and some of them were emotionally, sympathetically charged. He went over them in his mind afterwards, abridging *South Africa* into one volume (from the fourth edition in 1879) but adding a directly impassioned chapter called 'Zululand' which expressed his reaction to the Zulu War. He believed that Sir Bartle Frere (governor of the Cape and High Commissioner for the settlement of South African Affairs) had provoked the war. Interestingly, Frere was recalled in 1880. Trollope himself liked the Zulus, and this set him in opposition to the war, the new chapter showing clearly the nature of his commitment (an extract is included on pp. 211–2 of this selection).

His humour was often to the fore: he wrote 'In coming ages a Kafir may make as good a Prime Minister as Lord Beaconsfield', perhaps a whiplash tongue-in-cheek remark in view of Trollope's dislike of Disraeli – 'but he cannot do so now, – nor in this age, nor for many ages to come'.[37] He recorded that Englishmen in South Africa would not work alongside coloured men, and interrogated the problems with his usual directness: 'The difficult question meets one at every corner in South Africa. What is the duty of the white man in reference to the original inhabitant?' He concludes 'South Africa is a country of black men, – and not of white men'.[38] *South Africa* was finished the day before he arrived back in London on January 3 1878. Reviews were generally favourable. Trollope had told the truth as he saw it, and in doing so he may have undermined the prospects of emigration to that continent. But there is every evidence of a widening tolerance in his own attitudes, of his being able to take on board new ideas. He is able to balance the formal analysis and explication with the informal, relaxed, conversational tone which characterises so much of his writing. *South Africa* and its predecessors in Trollope's travelling preoccupations all share one particular quality, and this is the effortless, seamless – as they appear – sympathetic recognitions between the writer and the reader. Trollope confides and explains; he is not dogmatic without reason. We feel the strength of his feelings or the power of his thoughts, but even where we disagree we do not reject. Mullen is right in his emphasis that we learn much of Trollope the man from his reactions to the travels which were so important in his middle and later life.

In selecting extracts for this anthology I have tried to reflect the many-sidedness of Trollope, and this has meant the inclusion of some sequences which show a particular bias as well as those which have a literary quality, a moral perspective or both. Trollope is a man of the period essentially conditioned by some of its trends and its broad inheritance, but he is also a strikingly independent observer, sometimes enlightened beyond his time, reaching out with visionary hope to a future involving change. His 'many-sidedness' is seen in the striking range which these extracts cover. There is his love of story or anecdote, whether humorous or tragic (note the three in THE WEST INDIES); there is at times an endearing self-mocking quality, when he laughs at himself as he sees the figure he cuts (*He explores Mount Irazu*). Trollope, the civil servant, enjoys the accumulation of facts and the display of statistics (these latter have been kept to the bare minimum). Some extracts, perhaps particularly his appraisal of Niagara, show his capacity for natural description, and I suggest that this natural poetry is balanced by an 'urban poetry' when he is describing a city in America, or Melbourne, or Sydney Harbour. Everything is grist to the narrative mill: an incident, like the man getting into the coach with an outsized fish in South Africa, or the American porter who scatters Trollope's possessions, can light up his narration with an almost innocent delight in the happening for its own sake. He has an inquiring, probing, searching mind; his visits to convict settlements in Australia and Bermuda display this (*Convicts, He visits more Convicts*), and they also display his compassion and humanity on the one hand and entrenched views about the necessity for penal punishment on the other. The quality of honesty which his modern biographers

have noted to be so marked in his travel writings, is here exemplified in his unabashed opinions about aborigines or West Indian
negroes, American children (and a certain type of American
woman), but it is present too in his unqualified assertion that
South Africa is a black man's country (see p. 241). He loves to
weigh and judge cases, arguing secession and slavery, free-
selectors and squatters (see pp. 121–2). He likes to ponder the
quality of architecture in a town or the artistic, realistic effect of
a statue (see *Washington* and *The White House*), or a view, or the
machinations of Zulu chieftains. He is the great recorder of
localised affairs and recent history, as the extracts on diamonds
and gold demonstrate. In a sense we see his views developing as
he travels, as he argues for and against a particular question.
Mullen notes that Trollope reasons with himself as well as with
his readers, and 'That is why extracting the odd sentence on a
contentious topic and saying that it represents Trollope's view is
misleading'.[39] It is, and that is why the extracts are generally long
enough to let Trollope speak for himself, regardless of whether
what he says calls forth our anger or our appreciation. The
extracts reveal the man, his capacity for life and his interpretations of it in its various forms. Any selection is arbitrary, but
whatever is selected should show Trollope's narrative vibrancy.
In one sense each incident is to him a story, and his own natural
tendency towards embroidery takes over and informs the en-
suing account. As J. W. Ward has observed 'He had a fine eye for
the revelatory human gesture and the social significance of a
scene' as well as 'a tolerance for ways of life other than his
own!'[40] That travel to Trollope was a *raison d'être* there is no
doubt; that it fed into his fiction there is abundant proof. He
appraised and he evaluated with directness, settling in the cabin
or the train, sometimes with the portable desk or 'instrument
writer' which he used for sending back his letters from Australia.
To read the travel books is to become aware of the character of
the man and the qualities which make him one of the most
interesting literary personalities of his time. As he grew older, his
opinions became more tolerant. His enthusiasm for life, like his
enthusiasm for writing, was uncurbed to the end. He delighted in
probing to the heart of controversial matter. The span of his

mind, of his questing and questioning nature, will I hope be evident from the range of extracts which follow. The travel writings are not the poor relations in the prolific Trollopian literary output, but rather the index to the man and his concerns.

GRAHAM HANDLEY

NOTES

[1] See Lance O. Tingay ed., *The Irish Famine: Six Letters to the Examiner* 1849–50, Anthony Trollope, London, The Silverbridge Press, 1987.
[2] Anthony Trollope: *An Autobiography*, ed., Michael Sadleir and Frederick Page, with an introduction and notes by P. D. Edwards, Oxford, OUP 1980, 92–3.
[3] Ibid, 87.
[4] *The Letters of Anthony Trollope*, ed., N. John Hall, 2 vols, Stanford, Stanford University Press, 1983, I, 114. (Hereafter *Letters*.)
[5] *An Autobiography*, 127–8.
[6] R. H. Super, *The Chronicler of Barsetshire: A Life of Anthony Trollope*, Michigan, University of Michigan Press, 1988, 101. (Hereafter Super.)
[7] *Letters* I, 81.
[8] Super, 102.
[9] Ibid, 103.
[10] N. John Hall, *Trollope: A Biography*, Oxford, OUP 1991, 175. (Hereafter Hall.)
[11] *Letters* I, 107.
[12] *Letters* I, 158.
[13] Quoted by Richard Mullen, *Anthony Trollope: A Victorian in His World*, London, Duckworth, 1990, 400. (Hereafter Mullen.) (See *The American Senator*, ch. xlii.)
[14] Super, 143.
[15] Ibid, 139.
[16] *North America* (1862), I, 464. (See related extract, *The Probable Fate of the South*.)
[17] *An Autobiography*, 164.
[18] Quoted by Mullen, 411.
[19] Mullen, 418.
[20] *Letters* I, 192.
[21] Mullen, 535.
[22] *Australia and New Zealand*, II, ch. xxix. (See p. 183 of this selection.)
[23] Quoted by Hall, 374–5.
[24] Ibid, 375.
[25] *Letters* II, 693.

[26] Quoted in *Australia*, ed., Edwards and Joyce, Queensland, University of Queensland Press, 1967, 36.

[27] Super, 300.

[28] Ibid, 303.

[29] These were published as *Anthony Trollope: The Tireless Traveller: Twenty Letters to the Liverpool Mercury, 1875*, ed., Bradford Allen Booth, California, University of California Press, 1941 (reprinted 1978). They form an admirable supplement to the main travel books.

[30] *Letters* II, 659.

[31] Mullen, 537.

[32] Hall, 423 (see *The American Senator*, ch. lxxvii).

[33] Super, 369.

[34] *South Africa* I, ch. v. (See p. 189 of this selection.)

[35] *South Africa* II, ch. ix. (See p. 231 of this selection.)

[36] Hall, 431.

[37] Quoted by Super, 371.

[38] *South Africa* II, ch. xvii. (See p. 241 of this selection.)

[39] Mullen, 623.

[40] *North America*, ed., Robert Mason, with an Introduction by John William Ward, Harmondsworth, Penguin 1968, 1992, 9, 11.

TROLLOPE THE TRAVELLER

Selections from Anthony Trollope's Travel Writings

THE WEST INDIES
AND THE SPANISH MAIN

Introduction – He suffers at sea

I am beginning to write this book on board the brig ————,
trading between Kingston, in Jamaica, and Cien Fuegos, on the
southern coast of Cuba. At the present moment there is not a puff
of wind, neither land breeze nor sea breeze; the sails are flapping
idly against the masts; there is not motion enough to give us the
command of the rudder; the tropical sun is shining through upon
my head into the miserable hole which they have deluded me
into thinking was a cabin. The marine people – the captain and
his satellites – are bound to provide me; and all that they have
provided is yams, salt pork, biscuit, and bad coffee. I should be
starved but for the small ham – would that it had been a large one
– which I thoughtfully purchased in Kingston; and had not a kind
medical friend, as he grasped me by the hand at Port Royal,
stuffed a box of sardines into my pocket. He suggested two
boxes. Would that I had taken them!

It is now the 25th January, 1859, and if I do not reach Cien
Fuegos by the 28th, all this misery will have been in vain. I might
as well in such case have gone to St Thomas, and spared myself
these experiences of the merchant navy. Let it be understood by
all men that in these latitudes the respectable, comfortable, well-
to-do route from every place to every other place is viâ the little
Danish island of St Thomas. From Demerara to the Isthmus of
Panama, you go by St Thomas. From Panama to Jamaica and
Honduras, you go by St Thomas. From Honduras and Jamaica to
Cuba and Mexico, you go by St Thomas. From Cuba to the
Bahamas, you go by St Thomas – or did when this was written.

1

The Royal Mail Steam Packet Company dispense all their branches from that favoured spot.

But I was ambitious of a quicker transit and a less beaten path, and here I am lying under the lee of the land, in a dirty, hot, motionless tub, expiating my folly. We shall never make Cien Fuegos by the 28th, and then it will be eight days more before I can reach the Havana. May God forgive me all my evil thoughts!

Motionless, I said; I wish she were. Progressless should have been my word. She rolls about in a nauseous manner, disturbing the two sardines which I have economically eaten, till I begin to fear that my friend's generosity will become altogether futile. To which result greatly tends the stench left behind it by the cargo of salt fish with which the brig was freighted when she left St John, New Brunswick, for these ports. 'We brought but a very small quantity,' the skipper says. If so, that very small quantity was stowed above and below the very bunk which has been given up to me as a sleeping-place. Ugh!

'We are very poor,' said the blue-nosed skipper when he got me on board. 'Well; poverty is no disgrace,' said I, as one does when cheering a poor man.

'We are very poor indeed; I cannot even offer you a cigar.' My cigar-case was immediately out of my pocket. After all, cigars are but as coals going to Newcastle when one intends to be in Cuba in four days.

'We are very poor indeed, sir,' said the blue-nosed skipper again when I brought out my solitary bottle of brandy – for I must acknowledge to a bottle of brandy as well as to the small ham. 'We have not a drop of spirits of any kind on board.' Then I altered my mind, and began to feel that poverty was a disgrace. What business had this man to lure me into his stinking boat, telling me that he would take me to Cien Fuegos, and feed me on the way, when he had not a mouthful to eat, or a drop to drink, and could not raise a puff of wind to fill his sails? 'Sir,' said I, 'brandy is dangerous in these latitudes, unless it be taken medicinally; as for myself, I take no other kind of physic.' I think that poverty on shipboard is a disgrace, and should not be encouraged. Should I ever be on shore again, my views may become more charitable.

Oh, for the good ship 'Atrato,'[1] which I used to abuse with such objurgations because the steward did not come at my very first call; because the claret was only half iced; because we were forced to close our little whist at 11 P.M., the serjeant-at-arms at that hour inexorably extinguishing all the lights! How rancorous were our tongues! 'This comes of monopoly,' said a stern and eloquent neighbour at the dinner-table, holding up to sight a somewhat withered apple. 'And dis,' said a grinning Frenchman from Martinique with a curse, exhibiting a rotten walnut – 'dis, dis! They give me dis for my moneys – for my thirty-five pounds!' And glancing round with angry eye, he dropped the walnut on to his plate.

Apples! and walnuts!! What would I give for the 'Atrato' now; for my berth, then thought so small; for its awning; for a bottle of its soda water; for one cut from one of all its legs of mutton; for two hours of its steam movement! And yet it is only now that I am learning to forgive that withered apple and that ill-iced claret.

Having said so much about my present position, I shall be glad to be allowed to say a few words about my present person. There now exists an opportunity for doing so, as I have before me the Spanish passport, for which I paid sixteen shillings in Kingston the day before I left it. It is simply signed Pedro Badan. But it is headed Don Pedro Badan Calderon de la Barca,[2] which sounds to me very much as though I were to call myself Mr Anthony Trollope Ben Jonson.[3] To this will be answered that such might have been my name. But then I should not have signed myself Anthony Trollope. The gentleman, however, has doubtless been right according to his Spanish lights; and the name sounds very grand, especially as there is added to it two lines declaring how that Don Pedro Badan is a Caballero. He was as disguised a personage as a Spanish Don should be, and seemed somewhat particular about the sixteen shillings, as Spanish and other Dons generally are.

He has informed me as to my 'Talla,' that it is Alta. I rather like the old man on the whole. Never before this have I obtained in a passport any more dignified description of my body than robust. I certainly like the word 'Alta.' Then my eyes are azure.

This he did not find out by the unassisted guidance of personal inspection. 'Ojos, blue,' he suggested to me, trying to look through my spectacles. Not understanding 'Ojos,' I said 'Yes.' My 'cejas' are 'castañas,' and so is my cabello also. Castañas must be chestnut, surely – cejas may mean eyebrows – cabello is certainly hair. Now any but a Spaniard would have declared that as to hair, I was bald; and as to eyebrows, nothing in particular. My colour is sano. There is great comfort in that. I like the word sano. 'Mens sana in corpore sano.'[4] What has a man to wish for but that? I thank thee once more, Don Pedro Badan Calderon de la Barca.

But then comes the mystery. If I have any personal vanity, it is wrapped up in my beard. It is a fine, manly article of dandyism, that wears well in all climates, and does not cost much, even when new. Well, what has the Don said of my beard?

It is poblada. I would give five shillings for the loan of a Spanish dictionary at this moment. Poblada![5] Well, my first effort, if ever I do reach Cuba, shall be made with reference to that word.

(Chapter I)

Jamaica – Kingston

Kingston, on a map – for there is a map even of Kingston – looks admirably well. The streets all run in parallels. There is a fine large square, plenty of public buildings, and almost a plethora of places of worship. Everything is named with propriety, and there could be no nicer town anywhere. But this word of promise to the ear is strangely broken when the performance is brought to the test. More than half the streets are not filled with houses. Those which are so filled, and those which are not, have an equally ragged, disreputable, and bankrupt appearance. The houses are mostly of wood, and are unpainted, disjointed, and going to ruin. Those which are built with brick not unfrequently appear as though the mortar had been diligently picked out from the interstices.

But the disgrace of Jamaica is the causeway of the streets themselves. There never was so odious a place in which to move.

There is no pathway or trottoir to the streets, though there is very generally some such – I cannot call it accommodation – before each individual house. But as these are all broken from each other by steps up and down, as they are of different levels, and sometimes terminate abruptly without any steps, they cannot be used by the public. One is driven, therefore, into the middle of the street. But the street is neither paved nor macadamized, nor prepared for traffic in any way. In dry weather it is a bed of sand, and in wet weather it is a watercourse. Down the middle of this the unfortunate pedestrian has to wade, with a tropical sun on his head; and this he must do in a town which, from its position, is hotter than almost any other in the West Indies. It is no wonder that there should be but little walking.

But the stranger does not find himself naturally in possession of a horse and carriage. He may have a saddle-horse for eight shillings; but that is expensive as well as dilatory if he merely wishes to call at the post-office, or buy a pair of gloves. There are articles which they call omnibuses, and which ply cheap enough, and carry men to any part of the town for sixpence; that is, they will do so if you can find them. They do not run from any given point to any other, but meander about through the slush and sand, and are as difficult to catch as the musquitoes.

The city of Havana, in Cuba, is lighted at night by oil-lamps. The little town of Cien Fuegos, in the same island is lighted by gas. But Kingston is not lighted at all!

We all know that Jamaica is not thriving as once it throve, and that one can hardly expect to find there all the energy of a prosperous people. But still I think that something might be done to redeem this town from its utter disgrace. Kingston itself is not without wealth. If what one hears on such subjects contains any indications towards the truth, those in trade there are still doing well. There is a mayor, and there are aldermen. All the parapher-nalia for carrying on municipal improvements are ready. If the inhabitants have about themselves any pride in their locality, let them, in the name of common decency, prepare some sort of causeway in the streets; with some drainage arrangement, by which rain may run off into the sea without lingering for hours in every corner of the town. Nothing could be easier, for there is a fall towards the shore through the whole place. As it is now, Kingston is a disgrace to the country that owns it.

One is peculiarly struck also by the ugliness of the buildings – those buildings, that is, which partake in any degree of a public character – the churches and places of worship, the public offices, and such like. We have no right, perhaps, to expect good taste so far away from any school in which good taste is taught; and it may, perhaps, be said by some that we have sins enough of our own at home to induce us to be silent on this head. But it is singular that any man who could put bricks and stones and timber together should put them together in such hideous forms as those which are to be seen here.

I never met a wider and a kinder hospitality than I did in Jamaica, but I neither ate nor drank in any house in Kingston except my hotel, nor, as far as I can remember, did I enter any house except in the way of business. And yet I was there – necessarily there, unfortunately – for some considerable time. The fact is, that hardly any Europeans, or even white Creoles,[6] live in the town. They have country seats, pens as they call them, at some little distance. They hate the town, and it is no wonder they should do so.

(Chapter II)

The Scotchman embraces the Creole

The cotton-tree is almost as beautiful when standing alone. The trunk of this tree grows to a magnificent height, and with magnificent proportions: it is frequently straight; and those which are most beautiful throw out no branches till they have reached a height greater than that of any ordinary tree with us. Nature, in order to sustain so large a mass, supplies it with huge spurs at the foot, which act as buttresses for its support, connecting the roots immediately with the trunk as much as twenty feet above the ground. I measured more than one, which, including the buttresses, were over thirty feet in circumference. Then from its head the branches break forth in most luxurious profusion, covering an enormous extent of ground with their shade.

But the most striking peculiarity of these trees consists in the parasite plants by which they are enveloped, and which hang from their branches down to the ground with tendrils of wonderful strength. These parasites are of various kinds, the fig being the most obdurate with its embraces. It frequently may be seen that the original tree has departed wholly from sight, and I should imagine almost wholly from existence; and then the very name is changed, and the cotton-tree is called a fig-tree. In others the process of destruction may be observed, and the interior trunk may be seen to be stayed in its growth and stunted in its measure by the creepers which surround it. This pernicious embrace the natives describe as 'The Scotchman hugging the Creole.' The metaphor is sufficiently satirical upon our northern friends, who are supposed not to have thriven badly in their visits to the Western islands.

But it often happens that the tree has reached its full growth before the parasites have fallen on it, and then, in place of being strangled, it is adorned. Every branch is covered with a wondrous growth – with plants of a thousand colours and a thousand sorts. Some droop with long and graceful tendrils from the boughs, and so touch the ground; while others hang in a ball of leaves and flowers, which swing for years, apparently without changing their position.

(Chapter III)

Love Sorrows

Nevertheless, there was a decent little inn at Port Antonio, which will always be memorable to me on account of the love sorrows of a young maiden whom I chanced to meet there. The meeting was in this wise:

I was sitting in the parlour of the inn, after dinner, when a young lady walked in, dressed altogether in white. And she was well dressed, and not without the ordinary decoration of crinoline and ribbons. She was of the coloured race; and her jet black, crisp, yet wavy hair was brushed back in a becoming fashion. Whence she came or who she was I did not know, and never

learnt. That she was familiar in the house I presumed from her
moving the books and little ornaments on the table, and arranging the cups and shells upon a shelf. 'Heigh-ho!' she ejaculated,
when I had watched her for about a minute.

I hardly knew how to accost her, for I object to the word Miss,
as standing alone; and yet it was necessary that I should accost
her. 'Ah, well: heigh-ho!' she repeated. It was easy to perceive
that she had a grief to tell.

'Lady,' said I – I felt that the address was somewhat stilted, but
in the lack of any introduction I knew not how else to begin –
'Lady, I fear that you are in sorrow?'

'Sorrow enough!' said she. 'I'se in de deepest sorrow. Heigh-
ho me! Well, de world will end some day,' and turning her face
full upon me, she crossed her hands. I was seated on a sofa, and
she came and sat beside me, crossing her hands upon her lap, and
looking away to the opposite wall. I am not a very young man;
and my friends have told me that I show strongly that steady
married appearance of a paterfamilias which is so apt to lend
assurance to maiden timidity.

'It will end some day for us all,' I replied. 'But with you, it has
hardly yet had its beginning.'

''Tis a very bad world, and sooner over de better. To be
treated so's enough to break any girl's heart; it is! My heart's
clean broke, I know dat.' And as she put both her long, thin dark
hands to her side, I saw that she had not forgotten her rings.

'It is love then that ails you?'

'No!' She said this very sharply, turning full round upon me,
and fixing her large black eyes upon mine. 'No, I don't love him
one bit; not now, and never again. No, not if he were down dere
begging.' And she stamped her little foot upon the ground as
though she had an imaginary neck beneath her heel.

'But you did love him?'

'Yes.' She spoke very softly now, and shook her head gently.
'I did love him – oh, so much! He was so handsome, so nice! I
shall never see such a man again: such eyes; such a mouth! and
then his nose! He was a Jew, you know.'

I had not known it before, and received the information
perhaps with some little start of surprise.

'Served me right; didn't it? And I'se a Baptist, you know. They'd have read me out,[7] I know dat. But I didn't seem to mind it den.' And then she gently struck one hand with the other, as she smiled sweetly in my face. The trick is customary with the coloured women in the West Indies when they have entered upon a nice familiar, pleasant bit of chat. At this period I felt myself to be sufficiently intimate with her to ask her name.

'Josephine; dat's my name. D'you like dat name?'

'It's as pretty as its owner – nearly.'

'Pretty! no; I'se not pretty. If I was pretty, he'd not have left me so. He used to call me Feeny.'

'What! the Jew did.' I thought it might be well to detract from the merit of the lost admirer. 'A girl like you should have a Christian lover.'

'Dat's what dey all says.'

'Of course they do: you ought to be glad it's over.'

'I ain't tho'; not a bit; tho' I do hate him so. Oh, I hate him; I hate him! I hate him worse dan poison.' And again her little foot went to work. I must confess that it was a pretty foot; and as for her waist, I never saw one better turned, or more deftly clothed. Her little foot went to work upon the floor, and then clenching her small right hand, she held it up before my face as though to show me that she knew how to menace.

I took her hand in mine, and told her that those fingers had not been made for threats. 'You are a Christian,' said I, 'and should forgive.'

'I'se a Baptist,' she replied; 'and in course I does forgive him: I does forgive him; but – ! He'll be wretched in this life, I know; and she – she'll be wretcheder; and when he dies – oh-h-h-h!'

In that prolonged expression there was a curse as deep as any that Ernulphus[8] ever gave. Alas! such is the forgiveness of too many a Christian!

'As for me, I wouldn't demean myself to touch de hem of her garment! Poor fellow! What a life he'll have; for she's a virgo with a vengeance.' This at the moment astonished me; but from the whole tenor of the lady's speech I was at once convinced that no satirical allusion was intended. In the hurry of her fluttering thoughts she had merely omitted the letter 'a.' It was her rival's temper, not her virtue, that she doubted.

'The Jew is going to be married then?'

'He told her so; but p'raps he'll jilt her too, you know.' It was easy to see that the idea was not an unpleasant one.

'And then he'll come back to you?'

'Yes, yes; and I'll spit at him;' and in the fury of her mind she absolutely did perform the operation. 'I wish he would; I'd sit so, and listen to him;' and she crossed her hands and assumed an air of dignified quiescence which well became her. 'I'd listen every word he say; just so. Every word till he done; and I'd smile' – and she did smile – 'and den when he offer me his hand' – and she put out her own – 'I'd spit at him, and leave him so.' And rising majestically from her seat she stalked out of the room.

As she fully closed the door behind her, I thought that the interview was over, and that I should see no more of my fair friend; but in this I was mistaken. The door was soon reopened, and she again seated herself on the sofa beside me.

'Your heart would permit of your doing that?' said I; 'and he with such a beautiful nose?'

'Yes; it would. I'd 'spise myself to take him now, if he was ever so beautiful. But I'se sure of this, I'll never love no oder man – never again. He did dance so genteelly.'

'A Baptist dance!' I exclaimed.

'Well; it wasn't de ting, was it? And I knew I'd be read out; oh, but it was so nice! I'll never have no more dancing now. I've just taken up with a class now, you know, since he's gone.'

'Taken up with a class?'

'Yes; I teaches the nigger children; and I has a card for the minister. I got four dollars last week, and you must give me something.'

Now I hate Baptists – as she did her lover – like poison; and even under such pressure as this I could not bring myself to aid in their support.

'You very stingy man! Caspar Isaacs' – he was her lost lover – 'gave me a dollar.'

'But perhaps you gave him a kiss.'

'Perhaps I did,' said she. 'But you may be quite sure of this, quite; I'll never give him anoder,' and she again slapped one hand upon the other, and compressed her lips, and gently shook her head as she made the declaration. 'I'll never give him anoder kiss – dat's sure as fate.'

I had nothing further to say, and began to feel that I ought not to detain the lady longer. We sat together, however, silent for a while, and then she arose and spoke to me standing. 'I'se in a reg'lar difficulty now, however; and it's just about that I am come to ask you.'

'Well, Josephine, anything that I can do to help you – '

'"Tain't much; I only want your advice. I'se going to Kingston, you see.'

'Ah, you'll find another lover there.'

'It's not for dat den, for I don't want none; but I'se going anyways, 'cause I live dere.'

'Oh, you live at Kingston?'

'Course I does. And I'se no ways to go but just in de droger' – the West Indian coasting vessels are so called.

'Don't you like going in the droger?' I asked.

'Oh, yes; I likes it well enough.'

'Are you sea-sick?'

'Oh, no.'

'Then what's the harm of the droger?'

'Why, you see' – and she turned away her face and looked towards the window – 'why you see, Isaacs is the captain of her, and 'twill be so odd like.'

'You could not possibly have a better opportunity for recovering all that you have lost.'

'You tink so?'

'Certainly.'

'Den you know noting about it. I will never recover noting of him, never. Bah! But I tell you what I'll do. I'll pay him my pound for my passage; and den it'll be a purely 'mercial transaction.'

On this point I agreed with her, and then she offered me her hand with the view of bidding me farewell.

'Good-bye, Josephine,' I said; 'perhaps you would be happier with a Christian husband.'

'P'raps I would; p'raps better with none at all. But I don't tink

I'll ever be happy no more. 'Tis so dull: good-bye.' Were I a girl, I doubt whether I also would not sooner dance with a Jew than pray with a Baptist.

'Good-bye, Josephine'. I pressed her hand, and so she went, and I neither saw nor heard more of her.

There was not about my Josephine all the pathos of Maria;[9] nor can I tell my story as Sterne told his. But Josephine in her sorrow was I think more true to human nature than Maria. It may perhaps be possible that Sterne embellished his facts. I, at any rate, have not done that.

I had another adventure at Port Antonio. About two o'clock in the morning there was an earthquake, and we were all nearly shaken out of our beds. Some one rushed into my room, declaring that not a stone would be left standing of Port Royal. There were two distinct blows, separated by some seconds, and a loud noise was heard. I cannot say that I was frightened, as I had not time to realise the fact of the earthquake before it was all over. No harm was done, I believe, anywhere, beyond the disseverance of a little plaster from the walls.

(Chapter III)

He climbs the Blue Mountain

I have nothing remarkable to tell of the ascent. We soon got into a cloud, and never got out of it. But that is a matter of course. We were soon wet through up to our middles, but that is a matter of course also. We came to various dreadful passages, which broke our toes and our nails and our hats, the worst of which was called Jacob's ladder[10] – also a matter of course. Every now and then we regaled the negroes with rum, and the more rum we gave them the more they wanted. And every now and then we regaled ourselves with brandy and water, and the oftener we regaled ourselves the more we required to be regaled. All which things are matters of course. And so we arrived at the Blue Mountain Peak.

Our first two objects were to construct a hut and collect wood for firing. As for any enjoyment from the position, that, for that evening, was quite out of the question. We were wet through and through, and could hardly see twenty yards before us on any side. So we set the men to work to produce such mitigation of our evil position as was possible.

We did build a hut, and we did make a fire; and we did administer more rum to the negroes, without which they refused to work at all. When a black man knows that you want him, he is apt to become very impudent, especially when backed by rum; and at such times they altogether forget, or at any rate disregard, the punishment that may follow in the shape of curtailed gratuities.

Slowly and mournfully we dried ourselves at the fire; or rather did not dry ourselves, but scorched our clothes and burnt our boots in a vain endeavour to do so. It is a singular fact, but one which experience has fully taught me, that when a man is thoroughly wet he may burn his trousers off his legs and his shoes off his feet, and yet they will not be dry – nor will he. Mournfully we turned ourselves before the fire – slowly, like badly-roasted joints of meat; and the result was exactly that: we were badly roasted – roasted and raw at the same time.

And then we crept into our hut, and made one of these wretched repasts in which the collops of food slip down and get sat upon; in which the salt is blown away and the bread saturated in beer; in which one gnaws one's food as Adam probably did, but as men need not do now, far removed as they are from Adam's discomforts. A man may cheerfully go without his dinner and feed like a beast when he gains anything by it; but when he gains nothing, and has his boots scorched off his feet into the bargain, it is hard then for him to be cheerful. I was bound to be jolly, as my companion had come there merely for my sake; but how it came to pass that he did not become sulky, that was the miracle. As it was, I know full well that he wished me – safe in England.

Having looked to our fire and smoked a sad cigar, we put ourselves to bed in our hut. The operation consisted in huddling on all the clothes we had. But even with this the cold prevented us from sleeping. The chill damp air penetrated through two shirts, two coats, two pairs of trousers. It was impossible to believe that we were in the tropics.

And then the men got drunk and refused to cut more firewood, and disputes began which lasted all night; and all was cold, damp, comfortless, wretched, and endless. And so the morning came.

That it was morning our watches told us, and also a dull dawning of muddy light through the constant mist; but as for sunrise ——! The sun may rise for those who get up decently from their beds in the plains below, but there is no sunrising on Helvellyn, or Righi, or the Blue Mountain Peak. Nothing rises there; but mists and clouds are for ever falling.

And then we packed up our wretched traps, and again descended. While coming up some quips and cranks had passed between us and our sable followers; but now all was silent as grim death. We were thinking of our sore hands and bruised feet; were mindful of the dirt which clogged us, and the damp which enveloped us; were mindful also a little of our spoilt raiment, and ill-requited labours. Our wit did not flow freely as we descended.

(Chapter III)

Problems of freedom

But to return to our sable friends. The first desire of a man in a state of civilization is for property. Greed and covetousness are no doubt vices; but they are the vices which have grown from cognate virtues. Without a desire for property, man could make no progress. But the negro has no such desire; no desire strong enough to induce him to labour for that which he wants. In order that he may eat to-day and be clothed tomorrow, he will work a little; as for anything beyond that, he is content to lie in the sun.

Emancipation and the last change in the sugar duties have made land only too plentiful in Jamaica, and enormous tracts have been thrown out of cultivation as unprofitable. And it is also only too fertile. The negro, consequently, has had unbounded facility of squatting, and has availed himself of it freely. To recede from civilization and become again savage – as savage as the laws of the community will permit – has been to his taste. I believe that he would altogether retrograde if left to himself.

I shall now be asked, having said so much, whether I think that emancipation was wrong. By no means. I think that emancipation was clearly right; but I think that we expected far too great and far too quick a result from emancipation.

These people are a servile race, fitted by nature for the hardest physical work, and apparently at present fitted for little else. Some thirty years since they were in a state when such work was their lot; but their tasks were exacted from them in a condition of bondage abhorrent to the feelings of the age, and opposed to the religion which we practised. For us, thinking as we did, slavery was a sin. From that sin we have cleansed ourselves. But the mere fact of doing so has not freed us from our difficulties. Nor was it to be expected that it should. The discontinuance of a sin is always the commencement of a struggle.

(Chapter IV)

The position of white men

It seems to us natural that white men should hold ascendancy over those who are black or coloured. Although we have emancipated our own slaves, and done so much to abolish slavery elsewhere, nevertheless we regard the negro as born to be a servant. We do not realize it to ourselves that it is his right to share with us the high places of the world, and that it should be an affair of individual merit whether we wait on his beck or he on ours. We have never yet brought ourselves so to think, and probably never shall. They still are to us a servile race. Philanthropical abolitionists will no doubt deny the truth of this; but I have no doubt that the conviction is strong with them – could they analyze their own convictions – as it is with others.

Where white men and black men are together, the white will order and the black will obey, with an obedience more or less implicit according to the terms on which they stand. When those terms are slavery, the white men order with austerity, and the black obey with alacrity. Both such terms have been found to be prejudicial to both. Each is brutalized by the contact.

(Chapter VI)

Gentlemen and the old country

A better fellow cannot be found anywhere than a gentleman of Jamaica, or one with whom it is easier to live on pleasant terms. He is generally hospitable, affable, and generous; easy to know, and pleasant when known; not given perhaps to much deep erudition, but capable of talking with ease on most subjects of conversation; fond of society, and of pleasure, if you choose to call it so; but not generally addicted to low pleasures. He is often witty, and has a sharp side to his tongue if occasion be given him to use it. He is not generally, I think, a hard-working man. Had he been so, the country perhaps would not have been in its present condition. But he is bright and clever, and in spite of all that he has gone through, he is at all times good-humoured.

No men are fonder of the country to which they belong, or prouder of the name of Great Britain than these Jamaicans. It has been our policy – and, as regards our larger colonies, the policy I have no doubt has been beneficial – to leave our dependencies very much to themselves; to interfere in the way of governing as little as might be; and to withdraw as much as possible from any participation in their internal concerns. This policy is anything but popular with the white aristocracy of Jamaica. They would fain, if it were possible, dispense altogether with their legislature, and be governed altogether from home. In spite of what they have suffered, they are still willing to trust the statesmen of England, but are most unwilling to trust the statesmen of Jamaica.

Nothing is more peculiar than the way in which the word 'home' is used in Jamaica, and indeed all through the West Indies. With the white people, it always signifies England, even though the person using the word has never been there. I could never trace the use of the word in Jamaica as applied by white men or white women to the home in which they lived, not even though that home had been the dwelling of their fathers as well as of themselves. The word 'home' with them is sacred, and means something holier than a habitation in the tropics. It refers always to the old country.

(Chapter VI)

Sugar production

But I would wish this much to be understood, that the sugar planter, as things at present are, must attend to and be master of, and practically carry out three several trades. He must be an agriculturist, and grow his cane; and like all agriculturists must take his crop from the ground and have it ready for use; as the wheat grower does in England, and the cotton grower in America. But then he must also be a manufacturer, and that in a branch of manufacture which requires complicated machinery. The wheat grower does not grind his wheat and make it into bread. Nor does the cotton grower fabricate calico. But the grower of canes must make sugar. He must have his boiling-houses and trash-houses;[11] his water power and his steam power; he must dabble in machinery, and, in fact, be a Manchester manufacturer as well as a Kent farmer. And then, over and beyond this, he must be a distiller. The sugar leaves him fit for your puddings, and the rum fit for your punch – always excepting the slight article of adulteration which you are good enough to add afterwards yourselves. Such a complication of trades would not be thought very alluring to a gentleman farmer in England.

And yet the Jamaica proprietor holds faithfully by his sugar-canes.

It has been said that sugar is an article which for its proper production requires slave labour. That this is absolutely so is certainly not the fact, for very good sugar is made in Jamaica without it. That thousands of pounds could be made with slaves where only hundreds are made – or, as the case may be, are lost – without it, I do not doubt. The complaint generally resolves itself to this, that free labour in Jamaica cannot be commanded; that it cannot be had always, and up to a certain given quantity at a certain moment; that labour is scarce, and therefore high priced, and that labour being high priced, a negro can live on half a day's wages, and will not therefore work the whole day – will not always work any part of the day at all, seeing that his yams, his breadfruit, and his plantains are ready to his hands. But the slaves! – Oh! those were the good times!

I have in another chapter said a few words about the negroes as at present existing in Jamaica, I also shall say a few words as to slavery elsewhere; and I will endeavour not to repeat myself. This much, however, is at least clear to all men, that you cannot eat your cake and have it. You cannot abolish slavery to the infinite good of your souls, your minds, and intellects, and yet retain it for the good of your pockets. Seeing that these men are free, it is worse than useless to begrudge them the use of their freedom.

(Chapter VII)

Cuba – Cuban sugar and hospitality

The works at the Cuban sugar estate were very different from those I had seen at Jamaica. They were on a much larger scale, in much better order, overlooked by a larger proportion of white men, with a greater amount of skilled labour. The evidences of capital were very plain in Cuba; whereas, the want of it was frequently equally plain in our own island.

Not that the planters in Cuba are as a rule themselves very rich men. The estates are deeply mortgaged to the different merchants at the different ports, as are those in Jamaica to the merchants of Kingston. These merchants in Cuba are generally Americans, Englishmen, Germans, Spaniards from the American republics – anything but Cubans; and the slave-owners are but the go-betweens, who secure the profits of the slave-trade for the merchants.

My friend at the estate invited us to a late breakfast after having shown me what I came to see. 'You have taken me so unawares,' said he, 'that we cannot offer you much except a welcome.' Well, it was not much – for Cuba perhaps. A delicious soup, made partly of eggs, a bottle of excellent claret, a paté dè foie gras, some game deliciously dressed, and half a dozen kinds of vegetables; that was all. I had seen nothing among the slaves which in any way interfered with my appetite, or with the cup of coffee and cigar which came after the little nothings above mentioned.

(Chapter X)

Filibustering[12]

We reprobate the name of filibuster, and have a holy horror of the trade. And it is perhaps fortunate that with us the age of individual filibustering is well-nigh gone by. But it may be fair for us to consider whether we have not in our younger days done as much in this line as have the Americans – whether Clive, for instance, was not a filibuster – or Warren Hastings.[13] Have we not annexed, and maintained, and encroached; protected, and assumed, and taken possession in the East – doing it all of course for the good of humanity? And why should we begrudge the same career to America?

That we do begrudge it is certain. That she purchased California and took Texas went at first against the grain with us; and Englishmen, as a rule, would wish to maintain Cuba in the possession of Spain. But what Englishman who thinks about it will doubt that California and Texas have thriven since they were annexed, as they never could have thriven while forming part of the Mexican empire – or can doubt that Cuba, if delivered up to the States, would gain infinitely by such a change of masters?

Filibustering, called by that or some other name, is the destiny of a great portion of that race to which we Englishmen and Americans belong. It would be a bad profession probably for a scrupulous man. With the unscrupulous man, what stumbling-blocks there may be between his deeds and his conscience is for his consideration and for God's judgment. But it will hardly suit us as a nation to be loud against it. By what other process have poor and weak races been compelled to give way to those who have power and energy? And who have displaced so many of the poor and weak, and spread abroad so vast an energy, such an extent of power as we of England?

(Chapter X)

He savours Cuban hotels

But let it not be supposed that I speak in praise of the hotels at the Havana. Far be it from me to do so. I only say that they are not dear. I found it impossible to command the luxury of a bedroom to myself. It was not the custom of the country they told me. If I chose to pay five dollars a day, just double the usual price, I could be indulged as soon – as circumstances would admit of it; which was intended to signify that they would be happy to charge me for the second bed as soon as the time should come that they had no one else on whom to levy the rate. And the dirt of that bedroom!

I had been unable to get into either of the hotels at the Havana to which I had been recommended, every corner in each having been appropriated. In my grief at the dirt of my abode, and at the too near vicinity of my Spanish neighbour – the fellow-occupant of my chamber was from Spain – I complained somewhat bitterly to an American acquaintance, who had as I thought been more lucky in his inn.

'One companion!' said he; 'why, I have three; one walks about all night in a bed-gown, a second snores, and the other is dying!'

(Chapter X)

Flirting

There is a feminine accomplishment so much in vogue among the ladies of the West Indies, one practised there with a success so specially brilliant, as to make it deserving of special notice. This art is one not wholly confined to ladies, although, as in the case with music, dancing, and cookery, it is to be looked for chiefly among the female sex. Men, indeed, do practice it in England, the West Indies, and elsewhere; and as Thalberg and Soyer[14] are greatest among pianists and cooks, so perhaps are the greatest adepts in this art to be found among the male practitioners; – elsewhere, that is, than in the West Indies. There are to be found ladies never equalled in this art by any effort of manhood. I speak of the science of flirting.

And be it understood that here among these happy islands no idea of impropriety – perhaps remembering some of our starched people at home, I should say criminality – is attached to the pursuit. Young ladies flirt, as they dance and play, or eat and drink, quite as a matter of course. There is no undutiful, unfilial idea of waiting till mamma's back be turned; no uncomfortable fear of papa; no longing for secluded corners, so that the world should not see. The doing of anything that one is ashamed of is bad. But as regards flirting, there is no such doing in the West Indies. Girls flirt not only with the utmost skill, but with the utmost innocence also. Fanny Grey,[15] with her twelve admirers, required no retired corners, no place apart from father, mother, brothers, or sisters. She would perform with all the world around her as some other girl would sing, conscious that in singing she would neither disgrace herself nor her masters.

It may be said that the practice of this accomplishment will often interfere with the course of true love. Perhaps so, but I doubt whether it does not as often assist it. It seemed to me that young ladies do not hang on hand in the West Indies. Marriages are made up there with apparently great satisfaction on both sides; and then the flirting is laid aside – put by, at any rate, till the days of widowhood, should such evil days come. The flirting is as innocent as it is open, and is confined to ladies without husbands.

It is confined to ladies without husbands, but the victims are not bachelors alone. No position, or age, or state of health secures a man from being drawn, now into one and now into another Circean circle,[16] in which he is whirled about, sometimes in a most ridiculous manner, jostled amongst a dozen neighbours, left without power to get out or to plunge further in, pulled back by a skirt at any attempt to escape, repulsed in the front at every struggle made to fight his way through.

Rolling about in these Charybdis pools[17] are, perhaps, oftenest to be seen certain wearers of red coats; wretches girt with tight sashes, and with gilding on their legs and backs. To and fro they go, bumping against each other without serious injury, but apparently in great discomfort. And then there are black-coated stragglers, with white neck-ties, very valiant in their first efforts, but often to be seen in deep grief, with heads thoroughly submersed. And you may see gray-haired sufferers with short necks, making little useless puffs, puffs which would be so impotent were not Circe merciful to those short-necked gray-haired sufferers.

If there were, as perhaps there should be, a college in the West

Indies, with fellowships and professorships, – established with the view of rewarding proficiency in this science – Fanny Grey should certainly be elected warden, or principal, or provost of that college. Her wondrous skill deserves more than mere praise, more than such slight glory as my ephemeral pages can give her. Pretty, laughing, brilliant, clever Fanny Grey! Whose cheeks ever were so pink, whose teeth so white, whose eyes so bright, whose curling locks so raven black! And then who ever smiles as she smiled? or frowned as she can frown? Sharply go those brows together, and down beneath the gurgling pool sinks the head of the red-coated wretch, while with momentary joy up pops the head of another, who is received with a momentary smile.

Yes; oh my reader! it is too true, I also have been in that pool, making, indeed, no wilful struggles, attempting no Leander[18] feat of swimming, sucked in as my steps unconsciously strayed too near the dangerous margin; sucked in and then buffeted about, not altogether unmercifully when my inaptitude for such struggling was discovered. Yes; I have found myself choking in those Charybdis waters, have glanced into the Circe cave. I have been seen in my insane struggles. But what shame of that? All around me, from the old patriarch dean of the island to the last subaltern fresh from Chatham, were there as well as I.

(Chapter XI)

British Guiana – In praise of Demerara

If there were but a snug secretaryship vacant there – and these things in Demerara are very snug – how I would invoke the goddess of patronage; how I would nibble round the officials of the Colonial Office; how I would stir up my friends' friends to write little notes to their friends! For Demerara is the Elysium[19] of the tropics – the West Indian happy valley of Rasselas[20] – the one true and actual Utopia of the Caribbean Seas – the Transatlantic Eden.

The men in Demerara are never angry, and the women are never cross. Life flows along on a perpetual stream of love, smiles, champagne, and small-talk. Everybody has enough of everything. The only persons who do not thrive are the doctors; and for them, as the country affords them so little to do, the local government no doubt provides liberal pensions.

The form of government is a mild despotism, tempered by sugar. The Governor is the father of his people, and the Governor's wife the mother. The colony forms itself into a large family, which gathers itself together peaceably under parental wings. They have no noisy sessions of Parliament as in Jamaica, no money squabbles as in Barbados. A clean bill of health, a surplus in the colonial treasury, a rich soil, a thriving trade, and a happy people – these are the blessings which attend the fortunate man who has cast his lot on this prosperous shore. Such is Demerara as it is made to appear to a stranger.

That custom which prevails there, of sending to all new comers a deputation with invitations to dinner for the period of his sojourn, is an excellent institution. It saves a deal of trouble in letters of introduction, economizes one's time, and puts one at once on the most-favoured-nation footing. Some may fancy that they could do better as to the bestowal of their evenings by individual diplomacy; but the matter is so well arranged in Demerara that such people would certainly find themselves in the wrong.

If there be a deficiency in Georgetown – it is hardly necessary to explain that Georgetown is the capital of the province of Demerara, and that Demerara is the centre province in the colony of British Guiana; or that there are three provinces, Berbice, Demerara, and Essequibo, so called from the names of the three great rivers of the country – But if there be a deficiency in Georgetown, it is in respect to cabs. The town is extensive, as will by-and-by be explained; and though I would not so far militate against the feelings of the people as to say that the weather is ever hot – I should be ungrateful as well as incredulous were I to do so – nevertheless, about noonday one's inclination for walking becomes subdued. Cabs would certainly be an addition to the luxuries of the place. But even these are not so essential as might at the first sight appear, for an invitation to dinner always includes an offer of the host's carriage. Without a carriage no one dreams of dragging on existence in British Guiana.

In England one would as soon think of living in a house without
a fireplace, or sleeping in a bed without a blanket.

For those who wander abroad in quest of mountain scenery it
must be admitted that this colony has not much attraction. The
country certainly is flat. By this I mean to intimate, that go where
you will, travel thereabouts as far as you may, the eye meets no
rising ground. Everything stands on the same level. But then, what
is the use of mountains? You can grow no sugar on them, even
with ever so many Coolies. They are big, brown, valueless things,
cumbering the face of the creation; very well for autumn idlers
when they get to Switzerland, but utterly useless in a colony which
has to count its prosperity by the number of its hogsheads.

(Chapter XII)

New Amsterdam

Late at night we did reach New Amsterdam, and crossed the broad
Berbice after dark in a little ferryboat which seemed to be perilously near the water. At ten o'clock I found myself at the hotel,
and pronounce it to be, without hesitation, the best inn, not only in
that colony, but in any of these Western colonies belonging to
Great Britain. It is kept by a negro, one Mr Paris Brittain, of which
I was informed that he was once a slave. 'O, si sic omnes!'[21] But as
regards my experience, he is merely the exception which proves
the rule. I am glad, however, to say a good word for the energies
and ambition of one of the race, and shall be glad if I can obtain for
Mr Paris Brittain an innkeeper's immortality.

His deserts are so much the greater in that his scope for displaying them is so very limited. No man can walk along the broad
strand street of New Amsterdam, and then up into its parallel
street, so back towards the starting-point, and down again to the
sea, without thinking of Knickerbocker and Rip van Winkle.[22]
The Dutchman who built New Amsterdam and made it once a
thriving town must be still sleeping, as the New York Dutchman
once slept, waiting the time when an irruption from Paramaribo
and Surinam shall again restore the place to its old possessors.

At present life certainly stagnates at New Amsterdam. Three

persons in the street constitute a crowd, and five collected for any purpose would form a goodly club. But the place is clean and orderly, and the houses are good and in good repair. They stand, as do the houses in Georgetown, separately, each surrounded by its own garden or yard, and are built with reference to the wished-for breeze from the windows.

The estates up the Berbice river, and the Canje creek which runs into it, are, I believe, as productive as those on the coast, or on the Demerara or Essequibo rivers, and are as well cultivated; but their owners no longer ship their sugars from New Amsterdam. The bar across the Berbice river is objectionable, and the trade of Georgetown has absorbed the business of the colony. In olden times Berbice and Demerara were blessed each with its own Governor, and the two towns stood each on its own bottom as two capitals. But those halcyon days – halcyon for Berbice – are gone; and Rip van Winkle, with all his brethren, is asleep.

(Chapter XII)

Trinidad – Beyond the Agenda?

The 'peculiar institution' of slavery is, I imagine, quite as little likely to find friends in England now as it was when the question of its abolition was so hotly pressed some thirty years since. And God forbid that I should use either the strength or the weakness of my pen in saying a word in favour of a system so abhorrent to the feelings of a Christian Englishman. But may we not say that that giant has been killed? Is it not the case that the Anti-Slavery Society has done its work? – has done its work at any rate as regards the British West Indies? What should we have said of the Anti-Corn-Law League,[23] had it chosen to sit in permanence after the repeal of the obnoxious tax, with the view of regulating the fixed price of bread?

Such is the attempt now being made by the Anti-Slavery Society with reference to the West Indian negroes. If any men are free, these men are so. They have been left without the slightest constraint or bond over them. In the sense in which they are free, no English labourer is free. In England a man cannot select whether he will work or whether he will let it alone. He, the poor Englishman, has that freedom which God seems to have intended as good for man; but work he must. If he do not do so willingly, compulsion is in some sort brought to bear upon him. He is not free to be idle; and I presume that no English philanthropists will go so far as to wish to endow him with that freedom.

But that is the freedom which the negro has in Jamaica, which he still has in many parts of Trinidad, and which the Anti-Slavery Society is so anxious to secure for him. It – but no; I will give the Society no monopoly of such honour. We, we Englishmen, have made our negroes free. If by further efforts we can do anything towards making other black men free – if we can assist in driving slavery from the earth, in God's name let us still be doing. Here may be scope enough for an Anti-Slavery Society. But I maintain that these men are going beyond their mark – that they are minding other than their own business, in attempting to interfere with the labour of the West Indian colonies. Gentlemen in the West Indies see at once that the Society is discussing matters which it has not studied, and that interests of the utmost importance to them are being played with in the dark.

(Chapter XIV)

New Granada, and the Isthmus of Panama

From Cartagena I went on to the isthmus; the Isthmus of Panamá, as it is called by all the world, though the American town of Aspinwall will gradually become the name best known in connexion with the passage between the two oceans.

This passage is now made by a railway which has been opened by an American company between the town of Aspinwall, or Colon, as it is called in England, and the city of Panamá. Colon is the local name for this place, which also bears the denomination of Navy Bay in the language of sailors. But our friends from Yankee-land like to carry things with a high hand, and to have a nomenclature of their own.

Here, as their energy and their money and their habits are undoubtedly in the ascendant, they will probably be successful; and the place will be called Aspinwall in spite of the disgust of the

New Granadians, and the propriety of the English, who choose to adhere to the names of the existing government of the country.

A rose by any other name would smell as sweet,[24] and Colon or Aspinwall will be equally vile however you may call it. It is a wretched, unhealthy, miserably situated but thriving little American town, created by and for the railway and the passenger traffic which comes here both from Southampton and New York. That from New York is of course immensely the greatest, for this is at present the main route to San Francisco and California.

I visited the place three times, for I passed over the isthmus on my way to Costa Rica, and on my return from that country I went again to Panamá, and of course back to Colon. I can say nothing in its favour. My only dealing there was with a washerwoman, and I wish I could place before my readers a picture of my linen in the condition in which it came back from that artist's hands. I confess that I sat down and shed bitter tears. In these localities there are but two luxuries of life, iced soda-water and clean shirts. And now I was debarred from any true enjoyment of the latter for more than a fortnight.

The Panamá railway is certainly a great fact, as men now-a-days say when anything of importance is accomplished. The necessity of some means of passing the isthmus, and the question as to the best means, has been debated since, I may say, the days of Cortes.[25] Men have foreseen that it would become a necessity to the world that there should be some such transit, and every conceivable point of the isthmus has, at some period or by some nation, been selected as the best for the purpose. This railway is certainly the first that can be regarded as a properly organized means of travelling; and it may be doubted whether it will not remain as the best, if not the only permanent mode of transit.

Very great difficulty was experienced in erecting this line. In the first place, it was necessary that terms should be made with the government of the country through which the line should pass, and to effect this it was expedient to hold out great inducements. Among the chief of these is an understanding that the whole line shall become the absolute property of the New Granadian government when it shall have been opened for forty-nine years. But who can tell what government will prevail in New

Granada in forty-nine years? It is not impossible that the whole district may then be an outlying territory belonging to the United States. At any rate, I should imagine that it is very far from the intention of the American company to adhere with rigid strictness to this part of the bargain. Who knows what may occur between this and the end of the century?

And when these terms were made there was great difficulty in obtaining labour. The road had to be cut through one continuous forest, and for the greater part of the way along the course of the Chagres river. Nothing could be more unhealthy than such work, and in consequence the men died very rapidly. The high rate of wages enticed many Irishmen here, but most of them found their graves amidst the works. Chinese were tried, but they were quite inefficacious for such labour, and when distressed had a habit of hanging themselves. The most useful men were to be got from the coast round Cartagena, but they were enticed thither only by very high pay.

The whole road lies through trees and bushes of thick tropical growth, and is in this way pretty and interesting. But there is nothing wonderful in the scenery, unless to one who has never before witnessed tropical forest scenery. The growth here is so quick that the strip of ground closely adjacent to the line, some twenty yards perhaps on each side, has to be cleared of timber and foliage every six months. If left for twelve months the whole would be covered with thick bushes, twelve feet high. At intervals of four and a half miles there are large wooden houses – prettylooking houses they are, built with much taste, – in each of which a superintendent with a certain number of labourers resides. These men are supplied with provisions and all necessaries by the company. For there are no villages here in which workmen can live, no shops from which they can supply themselves, no labour which can be hired as it may be wanted.

(Chapter XVI)

Central America – Panama to San José

I had intended to embark at Panamá in the American steam-ship 'Columbus' for the coast of Central America. In that case I should have gone to San Juan del Sur, a port in Nicaragua, and made my way from thence across the lake, down the river San Juan to San Juan del Norte, now called Greytown, on the Atlantic. But I learnt that the means of transit through Nicaragua had been so utterly destroyed – as I shall by-and-by explain – that I should encounter great delay in getting across the lake; and as I found that one of our men-of-war steamers, the 'Vixen,' was immediately about to start from Panamá to Punta-arenas, on the coast of Costa Rica, I changed my mind, and resolved on riding through Costa Rica to Greytown. And accordingly I did ride through Costa Rica.

My first work was to make petition for a passage in the 'Vixen,' which was accorded to me without difficulty. But even had I failed here, I should have adhered to the same plan. The more I heard of Costa Rica, the more I was convinced that that republic was better worth a visit than Nicaragua. At this time I had in my hands a pamphlet written by M. Belly, a Frenchman, who is, or says that he is, going to make a ship canal from the Atlantic to the Pacific. According to him the only Paradise now left on earth is in this republic of Costa Rica. So I shipped myself on board the 'Vixen.'

I had never before been on the waters of the Pacific. Now when one premeditates one's travels, sitting by the domestic fireside, one is apt to think that all those advancing steps into new worlds will be taken with some little awe, some feeling of amazement at finding oneself in very truth so far distant from Hyde Park Corner. The Pacific! I was absolutely there, on the ocean in which lie the Sandwich Islands, Queen Pomare,[26] and the Cannibals! But no; I had no such feeling. My only solicitude was whether my clean shirts would last me on to the capital of Costa Rica.

And in travelling these are the things which really occupy the mind. Where shall I sleep? Is there anything to eat? Can I have my clothes washed? At Panamá I did have my clothes washed in a very short space of time; but I had to pay a shilling apiece for them all round. In all these ports, in New Granada, Central America, and even throughout the West Indies, the luxury which is the most expensive in proportion to its cost in Europe is the washing of clothes – the most expensive, as it is also the most essential.

(Chapter XVII)

Costa Rica – He dresses for a long journey

I am not much given to the sins of dandyism, but I must own I was not a little proud of my costume as I left Punta-arenas. We had been told that according to the weather our ride would be either dusty or muddy in no ordinary degree, and that any clothes which we might wear during the journey would be utterly useless as soon as the journey was over. Consequently we purchased for ourselves, in an American store, short canvas smock-frocks, which would not come below the saddle, and coarse holland trousers. What class of men may usually wear these garments in Costa Rica I cannot say; but in England I have seen navvies look exactly as my naval friends looked; and I flatter myself that my appearance was quite equal to theirs. I had procured at Panamá a light straw hat, with an amazing brim, and had covered the whole with white calico. I have before said that my beard had become 'poblada,' so that on the whole I was rather gratified than otherwise when I was assured by the store-keeper that we should certainly be taken for three filibusters. Now the name of filibuster means something serious in those localities, as I shall in a few pages have to explain.

We started on our journey by railroad, for there is a tramway that runs for twelve miles through the forest. We were dragged along on this by an excellent mule, till our course was suddenly impeded by a tree which had fallen across the road. But in course of time this was removed, and in something less than three hours we found ourselves at a saw-mill in the middle of the forest.

The first thing that met my view on stepping out of the truck was a solitary Englishman seated on a half-sawn log of wood. Those who remember Hood's Whims and Oddities[27] may bear in mind a heart-rending picture of the last man. Only that the times do not agree, I should have said that this poor fellow must have sat for the picture. He was undeniably an English labourer. No man of any other nation would have had that face, or worn those clothes, or kicked his feet about in that same awkward, melancholy humour.

He was, he said, in charge of the saw-mill, having been induced to come out into that country for three years. According to him, it was a wretched, miserable place. 'No man,' he said, 'ever found himself in worse diggings.' He earned a dollar and a half a day, and with that he could hardly buy shoes and have his clothes washed. 'Why did he not go home?' I asked. 'Oh, he had come for three years, and he'd stay his three years out – if so be he didn't die.' The saw-mill was not paying, he said; and never would pay. So that on the whole his account of Costa Rica was not encouraging.

(Chapter XVII)

He enters San José

In the neighbourhood of San José we began to come across the coffee plantations. They certainly give the best existing proof of the fertility and progress of the country. I had seen coffee plantations in Jamaica, but there they are beautifully picturesque, placed like hanging gardens on the steep mountain-sides. Some of these seem to be almost inaccessible, and the plant always has the appearance of being a hardy mountain shrub. But here in Costa Rica it is grown on the plain. The secret, I presume, is that a certain temperature is necessary, and that this is afforded by a certain altitude from the sea. In Jamaica this altitude is only to be found among the mountains, but it is attained in Costa Rica on the high plains of the interior.

And then we jogged slowly into San José on the third day after our departure from Punta-arenas. Slowly, sorely, and with minds much preoccupied, we jogged into San José. On leaving the saw-mill at the end of the tramway my two friends had galloped gallantly away into the forest, as though a brave heart and a sharp pair of spurs would have sufficed to carry them right through to their journey's end. But the muleteer with his pony and the baggage-mule then lingered far behind. His heart was not so brave, nor were his spurs apparently so sharp. The luggage, too, was slipping every ten minutes, for I unfortunately had a portmanteau, of which no muleteer could ever make anything. It has been condemned in Holy Land, in Jamaica, in Costa Rica, wherever it has had to be fixed upon any animal's back. On this occasion it nearly broke both the heart of the muleteer and the back of the mule.

But things were changed as we crept into San José. The muleteer was all life, and led the way, driving before him the pack-mule, now at length reconciled to his load. And then, at straggling intervals, our jibes all silenced, our showy canters all done, rising wearily in our stirrups at every step, shifting from side to side to ease the galls 'That patient merit of the unworthy takes'[28] – for our merit had been very patient, and our saddles very unworthy – we jogged into San José.

(Chapter XVII)

San José scenery

The scenery round San José is certainly striking but not suffi-ciently so to enable one to rave about it. I cannot justly go into an ecstasy and sing of Pelion or Ossa;[29] nor can I talk of deep ravines to which the Via Mala is as nothing. There is a range of hills, respectably broken into prettinesses, running nearly round the town, though much closer to it on the southern than on the other sides. Two little rivers run by it, which here and there fall into romantic pools, or pools which would be romantic if they were not so very distant from home; if having travelled so far, one did not expect so very much. There are nice walks too, and pretty rides; only the mules do not like fast trotting when the weight upon them is heavy. About a mile and a half from the town, there is a Savanah, so-called, or large square park, the Hyde Park of San José; and it would be difficult to imagine a more pleasant place for a gallop. It is quite large enough for a race-course, and is open to everybody. Some part of the mountain range as seen from here is really beautiful.

The valley of San José, as it is called, is four thousand five hundred feet above the sea; and consequently, though within the tropics, and only ten degrees north of the line, the climate is good, and the heat, I believe, never excessive. I was there in April, and at that time, except for a few hours in the middle of the day, and that only on some days, there was nothing like tropical heat. Within ten days of my leaving San José I heard natives at Panamá complaining of the heat as being altogether unendurable. But up there, on that high plateau, the sun had no strength that was inconvenient even to an Englishman.

Indeed, no climate can, I imagine, be more favourable to fertility and to man's comfort at the same time than that of the interior of Costa Rica.

(Chapter XVIII)

The Costa Ricans

Generally speaking, the inhabitants of Costa Rica are of course Spanish by descent, but here, as in all these countries, the blood is very much mixed: pure Spanish blood is now, I take it, quite an exception. This is seen more in the physiognomy than in the colour, and is specially to be noticed in the hair. There is a mixture of three races, the Spanish, the native Indian, and the Negro; but the traces of the latter are comparatively light and few. Negroes, men and women, absolutely black, and of African birth or descent, are very rare; and though traces of the thick lip and the woolly hair are to be seen – to be seen in the streets and market-places – they do not by any means form a staple of the existing race.

The mixture is of Spanish and of Indian blood, in which the Spanish no doubt much preponderates. The general colour is that of a white man, but of one who is very swarthy. Occasionally this becomes so marked that the observer at once pronounces the man or woman to be coloured. But it is the colouring of the Indian, and not of the negro; the hue is rich, and to a certain extent bright, and the lines of the face are not flattened and blunted. The hair also is altogether human, and in no wise sheepish.

I do not think that the inhabitants of Costa Rica have much to boast of in the way of personal beauty. Indeed, the descendant of the Spaniard, out of his own country, seems to lose both the manly dignity and the female grace for which old Spain is still so noted. Some pretty girls I did see, but they could boast only the ordinary prettiness which is common to all young girls, and which our friends in France describe as being the special gift of the devil. I saw no fine, flaming, flashing eyes; no brilliant figures, such as one sees in Seville around the altar-rails in the churches: no profiles opening upon me struck me with mute astonishment.

The women were humdrum in their appearance, as the men are in their pursuits. They are addicted to crinoline, as is the nature of women in these ages; but so long as their petticoats stuck out, that seemed to be everything. In the churches they squat down on the ground, in lieu of kneeling, with their dresses and petticoats arranged around them, looking like huge turnips with cropped heads – like turnips that, by their persevering growth, had got half their roots above the ground. Now women looking like turnips are not specially attractive.

(Chapter XVIII)

He explores Mount Irazu

This huge excavation, which I take to be the extent of the crater, for it has evidently been all formed by the irruption of volcanic matter, is divided into two parts, a broken fragment of a mountain now lying between them; and the smaller of these two has lost all volcanic appearance. It is a good deal covered with bush and scrubby forest trees, and seems to have no remaining connection with sulphur and brimstone.

The other part, in which the crater now absolutely in use is situated, is a large hollow in the mountain-side, which might perhaps contain a farm of six hundred acres. Not having been able to measure it, I know no other way of describing what appeared to me to be its size. But a great portion of this again has lost all its volcanic appendages; except, indeed, that lumps of lava are scattered over the whole of it, as they are, though more sparingly, over the mountain beyond. There is a ledge of rock running round the interior of this division of the excavation, half-way down it, like a row of seats in a Roman amphitheatre, or an excrescence, if one can fancy such, half-way down a teacup. The ground above this ledge is of course more extensive than that below, as the hollow narrows towards the bottom. The present working mouth of the volcanic, and all those that have been working for many a long year – the eight in number of which I have spoken – lie at the bottom of this lowest hollow. This I should say might contain a farm of about two hundred acres.

Such was the form of the land on which we looked down. The descent from the top to the ledge was easy enough, and was made by myself and my friend with considerable rapidity. I started at a pace which convinced him that I should break my neck, and he followed, gallantly resolving to die with me. 'You'll surely kill yourself, Mr Trollope; you surely will,' said the mild voice. And yet he never deserted me.

'Sir William got as far as this,' said he, when we were on the ledge, but he got no further. 'We will do better than Sir William,' said I. 'We will go down into that hole where we see the sulphur.' 'Into the very hole?' 'Yes. If we get to windward, I think we can get into the very hole. Look at the huge column of white smoke; how it comes all in this direction! On the other side of the crater we should not feel it.'

The descent below the ledge into my smaller farm was not made so easily. It must be understood that our guide was left above with the mules. We should have brought two men, whereas we had only brought one; and had therefore to perform our climbing unassisted. I at first attempted it in a direct line, down from where we stood; but I soon found this to be impracticable, and was forced to reascend. The earth was so friable that it broke away from me at every motion that I made; and after having gone down a few feet I was glad enough to find myself again on the ledge.

We then walked round considerably to the right, probably for more than a quarter of a mile, and there a little spur in the hillside – a buttress as it were to the ledge of which I have spoken – made the descent much easier, and I again tried.

'Do not you mind following me,' I said to my companion, for I saw that he looked much aghast. 'None of Sir William's party went down there,' he answered. 'Are you sure of that?' I asked. Quite sure,' said the mild voice. 'Then what a triumph we will

have over Sir William!' and so saying I proceeded. 'I think I'll
come too,' said the mild voice. 'If I do break my neck nobody'll
be much the worse;' and he did follow me.

There was nothing very difficult in the clambering, but, unfortunately, just as we got to the bottom the mist came pouring
down upon us, and I could not but bethink me that I should find
it very difficult to make my way up again without seeing any of
the landmarks. I could still see all below me, but I could see
nothing that was above. It seemed as though the mist kept at our
own level, and that we dragged it with us.

We were soon in one of the eight small craters or mouths of
which I have spoken. Looking at them from above, they seemed
to be nearly on a level, but it now appeared that one or two were
considerably higher than the others. We were now in the one
that was the highest on that side of the excavation. It was a
shallow basin, or rather saucer, perhaps sixty yards in diameter,
the bottom of which was composed of smooth light-coloured
sandy clay. In dry weather it would partake almost of the nature
of sand. Many many years had certainly rolled by since this
mouth had been eloquent with brimstone.

The place at this time was very cold. My friend had brought a
large shawl with him, with which over and over again he attempted to cover my shoulders. I, having meditated much on the
matter, had left my cloak above. At the present moment I regret-
ted it sorely; but, as matters turned out, it would have half
smothered me before our walk was over.

We had now nothing for it but to wait till the mist should go
off. There was but one open mouth to this mountain – one
veritable crater from which a column of smoke and sulphur did
then actually issue, and this, though the smell of the brimstone
was already oppressive, was at some little distance. Gradually
the mist did go off, or rather it shifted itself continually, now
ascending far above us, and soon returning to our feet. We then
advanced between the other mouths, and came to that which was
nearest to the existing crater.

Here the aperture was of a very different kind. Though no
smoke issued from it, and though there was a small tree growing
at the bottom of it, – showing, as I presume, that there had been

no eruption from thence since the seed of that tree had fallen to the ground, – yet the sides of the crater were as sharp and steep as the walls of a house. Into those which we had hitherto visited we could walk easily; into this no one could descend even a single foot, unless, indeed, he descended somewhat more than a foot so as to dash himself to pieces at the bottom. They were, when compared together, as the interior of a plate compared to that of a tea-caddy. Now a traveller travelling in such realms would easily extricate himself from the plate, but the depths of the tea-caddy would offer him no hope.

(Chapter XIX)

The sad tale of Mrs X

The reader would not care that I should repeat it at length, for it would make this chapter too long. Her husband had been engaged in mining operations, and she had come out to Guatemala with him in search of gold. From thence, after a period of partial success, he was enticed away into Costa Rica. Some speculation there, in which he or his partners were concerned, promised better than that other one in Guatemala, and he went, leaving his young wife and children behind him. Of course he was to return very soon, and of course he did not return at all. Mrs X—— was left with her children searching for gold herself. 'Every evening,' she said, 'I saw the earth washed myself, and took up with me to the house the gold that was found.' What an occupation for a young Englishwoman, the mother of three children! At this time she spoke no Spanish, and had no one with her who spoke English.

And then tidings came from her husband that he could not come to her, and she made up her mind to go to him. She had no money, the gold-washing having failed; her children were without shoes to their feet; she had no female companion; she had no attendant but one native man; and yet, starting from the middle of Guatemala, she made her way to the coast, and thence by ship to Costa Rica.

After that her husband became engaged in what, in those

countries, is called 'transit.' Now 'transit' means the privilege of making money by transporting Americans of the United States over the isthmus to and from California, and in most hands has led to fraud, filibustering, ruin, and destruction. Mr X——, like many others, was taken in, and according to his widow's account, the matter ended in a deputation being sent, from New York I think, to murder him. He was struck with a life-preserver in the streets of San José, never fully recovered from the blow, and then died.

He had become possessed of a small estate in the neighbourhood of Cartago, on the proceeds of which the widow was now living. 'And will you not return home?' I said. 'Yes; when I have got my rights. Look here – ' and she brought down a ledger, showing me that she had all manner of claims to all manner of shares in all manner of mines. 'Aurum irrepertum et sic melius situm!'[30] As regards her, it certainly would have been so.

(Chapter XIX)

Another sad story

A few days before I reached San José, a gentleman resident there had started for England with his wife, and they had decided upon going by the San Juan. It seems that the lady had reached San José, as all people do reach it, by Panamá and Punta-arenas, and had suffered on the route. At any rate, she had taken a dislike to it, and had resolved on returning by the San Juan and the Serapiqui rivers, a route which is called the Serapiqui road.

To do this it is necessary for the traveller to ride on mules for four, five, or six days, according to his or her capability. The Serapiqui river is then reached, and from that point the further journey is made in canoes down the Serapiqui river till it falls into the San Juan, and then down that river to Greytown.

This gentleman with his wife reached the Serapiqui in safety; though it seems that she suffered greatly on the road. But when once there, as she herself said, all her troubles were over. That weary work of supporting herself on her mule, through mud and thorns and thick bushes, of scrambling over precipices and through rivers, was done. She had been very despondent, even from before the time of her starting; but now, she said, she believed that she should live to see her mother again. She was seated in the narrow canoe, among cloaks and cushions, with her husband close to her, and the boat was pushed into the stream. Almost in a moment, within two minutes of starting, not a hundred yards from the place where she had last trod, the canoe struck against a snag or upturned fragment of a tree and was overset. The lady was born by the stream among the entangled branches of timber which clogged the river, and when her body was found life had been long extinct.

This had happened on the very day that I reached San José, and the news arrived two or three days afterwards. The wretched husband, too, made his way back to the town, finding himself unable to go on upon his journey alone, with such a burden on his back. What could he have said to his young wife's mother when she came to meet him at Southampton, expecting to throw her arms round her daughter?

(Chapter XX)

Mainly mules and mud

We came at last to a track that was divided crossways by ridges, somewhat like the ridge of ploughed ground. Each ridge was perhaps a foot and a half broad, and the mules invariably stepped between them, not on them. Stepping on them they could not have held their feet. Stepping between them they came at each step with their belly to the ground, so that the rider's feet and legs were trailing in the mud. The struggles of the poor brutes were dreadful. It seemed to me frequently impossible that my beast should extricate himself, laden as he was. But still he went on patiently, slowly, and continuously; splash, splash, slosh, slosh! Every muscle of his body was working; and every muscle of my body was working also.

For it is not very easy to sit upon a mule under such circumstances. The bushes were so close upon me that one hand was required to guard my face from the thorns; my knees were constantly in contact with the stumps of trees, and when my knees were free from such difficulties, my shins were sure to be in the wars. Then the poor animal rolled so from side to side in his incredible struggles with the mud that it was frequently necessary to hold myself on by the pommel of the saddle. Added to this, it was essentially necessary to keep some sort of guide upon the creature's steps, or one's legs would be absolutely broken. For the mule cares for himself only, and not for his rider. It is nothing to him if a man's knees be put out of joint against the stump of a tree.

Splash, splash, slosh, slosh! on we went in this way for hours, almost without speaking. On such occasions one is apt to become mentally cross, to feel that the world is too hard for one, that one's own especial troubles are much worse than those of one's neighbours, and that those neighbours are unfairly favoured.... and then, again, on we went, slosh, slosh, splash, splash! My shins by this time were black and blue, and I held myself on to my mule chiefly by my spurs. Our way was still through dense forest, and was always either up or down hill. And here we came across the grandest scenery that I met with in the western world; scenery which would admit of raving, if it were given to me to rave on such a subject.

We were travelling for the most part along the side of a volcanic mountain, and every now and then the declivity would become so steep as to give us a full view down into the ravine below, with the prospect of the grand, steep, wooded hill on the other side, one huge forest stretching up the mountain for miles. At the bottom of the ravine one's eye would just catch a river, looking like a moving thread of silver wire. And yet, though the descent was so great, there would be no interruption to it. Looking down over the thick forest trees which grew almost from the side of a precipice, the eye would reach the river some thousand feet below, and then ascend on the other side over a like unbroken expanse of foliage.

Of course we both declared that we had never seen anything to equal it. In moments of ecstasy one always does so declare. But there was a monotony about it, and a want of grouping which forbids me to place it on an equality with scenery really of the highest kind, with the mountains, for instance, round Colico, with the head of the Lake of the Four Cantons, or even with the views of the upper waters of Killarney.

And then, to speak the truth, we were too much engulfed in mud, too thoughtful as to the troubles of the road, to enjoy it thoroughly. 'Wonderful that; isn't it?' 'Yes, very wonderful; fine break; for heaven's sake do get on.' This is the tone which men are apt to adopt under such circumstances. Five or six pounds of thick mud clinging round one's boots and inside one's trousers do not add to one's enjoyment of scenery.

Mud, mud; mud, mud! At about five o'clock we splashed into another pasture farm in the middle of the forest, a place called San Miguel, and there we rested for that night. Here we found that our beef also must be thrown away, and that our bread was all gone. We had picked up some more hard-boiled eggs at ranchos on the road, but hard-boiled eggs to my companion were no more than grains of gravel to a barn-door fowl; they merely enabled him to enjoy his regular diet. At this place, however, we were able to purchase fowls – skinny old hens which were shot for us at a moment's warning. The price being, here and else-where along the road, a dollar a head. Tea and candles a minis-tering angel had given to me at the moment of my departure from San José. But for them we should have indeed been com-fortless, thirsty, and in utter darkness. Towards evening a man gets tired of brandy and water, when he has been drinking it since six in the morning.

Our washing was done under great difficulties, as in these districts neither nature nor art seems to have provided for such emergencies. In this place I got my head into a tin pot, and could hardly extricate it. But even inside the houses and ranchos every-thing seemed to turn into mud. The floor beneath one's feet became mud with the splashing of the water. The boards were begrimed with mud. We were offered coffee that was mud to the taste and touch. I felt that the blood in my veins was becoming muddy.

(Chapter XX)

He goes by canoe

That passage down the Serapiqui was not without interest, though it was somewhat monotonous. Here, for the first time in my life, I found my bulk and size to be of advantage to me. In the after part of the canoe sat the master boatman, the captain of the expedition, steering with a paddle. Then came the mails and our luggage, and next to them I sat, having a seat to myself, being too weighty to share a bench with a neighbour. I therefore could lean back among the luggage; and with a cigar in my mouth, with a little wooden bicher[31] of weak brandy and water beside me, I found that the position had its charms.

On the next thwart sat, check by jowl, the lieutenant and the distressed Britisher. Unfortunately they had nothing on which to lean, and I sincerely pitied my friend, who, I fear, did not enjoy his position. But what could I do? Any change in our arrangements would have upset the canoe. And then close in the bow of the boat sat the two natives paddling; and they did paddle without cessation all that day, and all the next till we reached Greytown.

The Serapiqui is a fine river; very rapid, but not so much so as to make it dangerous, if care be taken to avoid the snags. There is not a house or hut on either side of it; but the forest comes down to the very brink. Up in the huge trees the monkeys hung jabbering, shaking their ugly heads at the boat as it went down, or screaming in anger at this invasion of their territories. The macaws flew high over head, making their own music, and then there was the constant little splash of the paddle in the water. The boatmen spoke no word, but worked on always, pausing now and again for a moment to drink out of the hollow of their hands. And the sun became hotter and hotter as we neared the sea; and the musquitoes began to bite; and cigars were lit with greater frequency. 'Tis thus that one goes down the waters of the Serapiqui.

(Chapter XX)

He gives offence

We landed at one such place to dine, and at another to sleep, selecting in each place some better class of habitation. At neither place did we find the owner there, but persons left in charge of the place. At the first the man was a German; a singularly handsome and dirty individual, who never shaved or washed himself, and lived there, ever alone, on bananas and muskmelons. He gave us fruit to take into the boat with us, and when we parted we shook hands with him. Out here every one always does shake hands with every one. But as I did so I tendered him a dollar. He had waited upon us, bringing water and plates; he had gathered fruit for us; and he was, after all, no more than the servant of the river squatter. But he let the dollar fall to the ground, and that with some anger in his face. The sum was made up of the small silver change of the country, and I felt rather little as I stooped under the hot sun to pick it up from out the mud of the garden. Better that than seem to leave it there in anger. It is often hard for a traveller to know when he is wished to pay, and when he is wished not to pay. A poorer-looking individual in raiment and position than that German I have seldom seen; but he despised my dollar as though it had been dirt.

(Chapter XX)

The Bermudas – The sleepy isles

The sleepiness of the people appeared to me the most prevailing characteristic of the place. There seemed to be no energy among the natives, no idea of going ahead, none of that principle of constant motion which is found so strongly developed among their great neighbours in the United States. To say that they live for eating and drinking would be to wrong them. They want the energy for the gratification of such vicious tastes. To live and die would seem to be enough for them. To live and die as their fathers and mothers did before them, in the same houses, using the same furniture, nurtured on the same food, and enjoying the same immunity from the dangers of excitement.

I must confess that during the short period of my sojourn there, I myself was completely overtaken by the same sort of lassitude. I could not walk a mile without fatigue. I was always anxious to be supine, lying down whenever I could find a sofa; ever anxious for a rocking-chair, and solicitous for a quick arrival of the hour of bed, which used to be about half-past nine o'clock. Indeed this feeling became so strong with me that I feared I was ill, and began to speculate as to the effects and pleasures of a low fever and a Bermuda doctor. I was comforted, however, by an assurance that everybody was suffering in the same way. 'When the south wind blows it is always so.' 'The south wind must be very prevalent then,' I suggested. I was told that it was very prevalent. During the period of my visit it was all south wind.

(Chapter XXII)

Their attractions

These islands are certainly very pretty; or I should perhaps say that the sea, which forms itself into bays and creeks by running in among them, is very pretty. The water is quite clear and transparent, there being little or no sand on those sides on which the ocean makes its entrance; and clear water is in itself so beautiful. Then the singular way in which the land is broken up into narrow necks, islands, and promontories, running here and there in a capricious, half-mysterious manner, creating a desire for amphibiosity, necessarily creates beauty. But it is mostly the beauty of the sea, and not of the land. The islands are flat, or at any rate there is no considerable elevation in them. They are covered throughout with those scrubby little trees; and, although the trees are green, and therefore when seen from the sea give a freshness to the landscape, they are uninteresting and monotonous on shore.

I must not forget the oleanders, which at the time of my visit were in full flower; which, for aught I know, may be in full flower during the whole year. They are so general through all the islands, and the trees themselves are so covered with the large straggling, but bright blossoms, as to give quite a character

to the scenery. The Bermudas might almost be called the olean-
der isles.

(Chapter XXII)

Convicts

We have the will, the determination as well as the wish, to do
well by our rogues, even if we have not as yet found the way;
and this is much. In this, as in everything else, the way will
follow the will, sooner or later.

But in the mean time we have been trying various experi-
ments, with more or less success; forgiving men half their terms
of punishment on good behaviour; giving them tickets of leave;
crank-turning; solitary confinement; pietising – what may be
called a system of gaol sanctity, perhaps the worst of all schemes,
as being a direct advertisement for hypocrisy; work without
result, the most distressing punishment going, one may say, next
to that of no work at all; enforced idleness, which is horrible for
human nature to contemplate; work with result, work which
shall pay; good living, pound of beef, pound of bread, pound of
potatoes, ounce of tea, glass of grog, pipe of tobacco, resulting in
much fat, excellent if our prisoners were stalled oxen to be eaten;
poor living, bread and water, which has its recommendations
also, though it be so much opposed to the material humanity of
the age; going to school, so that life if possible may be made to
recommence; very good also, if life would recommence; corporal
punishment, flogging of the body, horrible to think of, impossible to be looked at; spirit punishment, flogging of the soul, best
of all if one could get at the soul so as to do it effectually.

All these schemes are being tried; and as I believe that they are
tried with an honest intent to arrive at that which is best, so also
do I believe that we shall in time achieve that which is, if not
heavenly best, at any rate terrestrially good; – shall at least get
rid certainly of all that is hellishly bad. At present, however, we
are still groping somewhat uncertainly. Let us try for a moment
to see what the Bermuda groping has done.

I do not in the least doubt that the intention here also has been good; the intention, that is, of those who have been responsible for the management of the establishment. But I do not think that the results have been happy. . . .

As to the second object, that of divesting these rogues of their roguery, the best way of doing that is the question as to which there is at the present moment so much doubt. As to what may be the best way I do not presume to give an opinion; but I do presume to doubt whether the best way has as yet been found at Bermuda. The proofs at any rate were not there. Shortly before my arrival a prisoner had been killed in a row. After that an attempt had been made to murder a warder. And during my stay there one prisoner was deliberately murdered by two others after a faction fight between a lot of Irish and English, in which the warders were for some minutes quite unable to interfere. Twenty-four men were carried to the hospital dangerously wounded, as to the life of some of whom the doctor almost despaired. This occurred on a day intervening between two visits which I made to the establishment. Within a month of the same time three men had escaped, of whom two only were retaken; one had got clear away, probably to America. This tells little for the discipline, and very little for the moral training of the men. . . .

The two murderers will I presume be tried, and if found guilty probably hanged; but the usual punishment for outbreaks of this kind seems to be, or to have been, flogging. A man would get some seventy lashes; the Governor of the island would go down and see it done; and then the lacerated wretch would be locked up in idleness till his back would again admit of his bearing a shirt. 'But they'll venture their skin,' said the officer; 'they don't mind that till it comes.' 'But do they mind being locked up alone?' I asked. He admitted this, but said that they had only six – I think six – cells, of which two or three were occupied by madmen; they had no other place for lunatics. Solitary confinement is what these men do mind, what they do fear; but here there is not the power of inflicting that punishment.

What a piece of work for a man to step down upon; – the amendment of the discipline of such a prison as this! Think what the feeling among them will be when knives and razors are again taken from them, when their grog is first stopped, their liberty first controlled. They sleep together, a hundred or more within talking distance, in hammocks slung at arm's length from each other, so that one may excite ten, and ten fifty. Is it fair to put warders among such men, so well able to act, so ill able to control their actions? . . .

Among the lower classes, from which these convicts do doubtless mostly come, the goods of life are chiefly reckoned as being food, clothing, warm shelter, and hours of idleness. It may seem harsh to say so thus plainly; but will any philanthropical lover of these lower classes deny the fact? I regard myself as a philanthropical lover of those classes, and as such I assert the fact; nay, I might go further and say that it is almost the same of some other classes. That many have knowledge of other good things, wife-love and children-love – heart-goods, if I may so call them; knowledge of mind-goods, and soul-goods also, I do not deny. That such knowledge is greatly on the increase I verily believe; but with most among us back and belly, or rather belly and back, are still supreme. On belly and back must punishment fall, when sinners such as these are to be punished.

But with us – very often I fear elsewhere, but certainly at that establishment of which we are now speaking – there is no such punishment at all. In scale of dietary among subjects of our Queen, I should say that honest Irish labourers stand the lowest; they eat meat twice a year, potatoes and milk for six months, potatoes without milk for six, and fish occasionally if near the shore. Then come honest English labourers; they generally have cheese, sometimes bacon. Next above them we may probably rank the inhabitants of our workhouses; they have fresh meat perhaps three times a week. Whom shall we name next? Without being anxious to include every shade of English mankind, we may say soldiers, and above them sailors; then, perhaps, ordinary mechanics. There must be many another ascending step before we come to the Bermuda convict, but it would be long to name them; but now let us see what the Bermuda convict eats and drinks every day.

He has a pound of meat; he has good meat too, lucky dog, while those wretched Bermudians are tugging out their teeth against tough carcasses! He has a pound and three ounces of bread; the amount may be of questionable advantage, as he cannot eat it all; but he probably sells it for drink. He has a pound of fresh vegetables; he has tea and sugar; he has a glass of grog – exactly the same amount that a sailor has; and he has an allowance of tobacco-money, with permission to smoke at mid-day and evening, as he sits at his table or takes his noontide pleasant saunter. So much for belly.

Then as to back, under which I include a man's sinews. The convict begins the day by going to chapel at a quarter-past seven: his prayers do not take him long, for the chaplain on the occasion of my visit read small bits out of the Prayer-book here and there, without any reference to church rule or convict-establishment reason. At half-past seven he goes to his work, if it does not happen to rain, in which case he sits till it ceases. He then works till five, with an hour and a half interval for his dinner, grog, and tobacco. He then has the evening for his supper and amusements. He thus works for eight hours, barring the rain, whereas in England a day labourer's average is about ten. As to the comparative hardness of their labour there will of course be no doubt. The man who must work for his wages will not get any wages unless he works hard. The convict will at any rate get his wages, and of course spares his sinews.

As to clothes, they have, and should have exactly what is best suited to health. Shoes when worn out are replaced. The straw hat is always decent, and just what one would wish to wear oneself in that climate. The jacket and trousers have the word 'Boaz'[32] printed over them in rather ugly type; but one would get used to that. The flannel shirts, etc., are all that could be desired.

Their beds are hammocks like those of sailors, only not subject o be swung about by the winds, and not hung quite so closely as hose of some sailors. Did any of my readers ever see the beds of ın Irish cotter's establishment in county Cork? Ah! or of some English cotter's establishments in Dorsetshire, Wiltshire, and Somersetshire?

The hospital arrangements and attendance are excellent as regards the men's comfort; though the ill-arrangement of the buildings is conspicuous, and must be conspicuous to all who see them.

And then these men, when they take their departure, have the wages of their labour given to them, – so much as they have not spent either licitly in tobacco, or illicitly in extra grog. They will take home with them sixteen pounds, eighteen pounds, or twenty pounds. Such is convict life in Bermuda, – unless a man chance to get murdered in a faction fight.

As to many of the comforts above enumerated, it will of course be seen that they are right. The clothes, the hospital arrangements, and sanitary provision are, and should be, better in a prison than they can, unfortunately, be at present among the poor who are not prisoners. But still they must be reckoned among the advantages which convicted crime enjoys.

It seems to be a cruel task, that of lessening the comforts of men who are, at any rate, in truth not to be envied – are to be pitied rather, with such deep, deep pity! But the thing to look to, the one great object, is to diminish the number of those who must be sent to such places. Will such back and belly arrangements as those I have described deter men from sin by the fear of its consequences?

Why should not those felons – for such they all are, I presume, till the term of their punishment be over – why should they sleep after five? why should their diet be more than strong health requires? why should their hours of work be light? Why that drinking of spirits and smoking of tobacco among men whose term of life in that prison should be a term of suffering? Why those long twelve hours of bed and rest, spent in each other's company, with noise, and singing, and jollity? Let them eat together, work together, walk together if you will; but surely at night they should be separated! Faction fights cannot take place unless the fighters have time and opportunity to arrange them.

I cannot but think that there should be great changes in this establishment, and that gradually the punishment, which undoubtedly is intended, should be made to fall on the prisoners. 'Look at the prisoners' rations!' the soldiers say in Bermuda when they complain of their own; and who can answer them?

(Chapter XXII)

Conclusion

From Bermuda I took a sailing vessel to New York, in company with a rather large assortment of potatoes and onions. I had declared during my unlucky voyage from Kingston to Cuba that no consideration should again tempt me to try a sailing vessel, but such declarations always go for nothing. A man in his misery thinks much of his misery; but as soon as he is out of it it is forgotten, or becomes matter for mirth. Of even a voyage in a sailing vessel one may say that at some future time it will perhaps be pleasant to remember that also. And so I embarked myself along with the potatoes and onions on board the good ship 'Henrietta.'

Indeed, there is no other way of getting from Bermuda to New York; or of going anywhere from Bermuda except to Halifax and St Thomas, to which places a steamer runs once a month. In going to Cuba I had been becalmed, starved, shipwrecked, and very nearly quaranteened. In going to New York I encountered only the last misery. The doctor who boarded us stated that a vessel had come from Bermuda with a sick man, and that we must remain where we were till he had learnt what was the sick man's ailment. Our skipper, who knew the vessel in question, said that one of their crew had been drunk in Bermuda for two or three days, and had not yet worked it off. But the doctor called again in the course of the day, and informed us that it was intermittent fever. So we were allowed to pass. It does seem strange that sailing vessels should be subjected to such annoyances. I hardly think that one of the mail steamers going into New York would be delayed because there was a case of intermittent fever on board another vessel from Liverpool.

It is not my purpose to give an Englishman's ideas of the United States, or even of New York, at the fag end of a volume treating about the West Indies. On the United States I should like to write a volume, seeing that the government and social life of the people there – of that people who are our children – afford the most interesting phenomena which we find as to the new world; – the best means of prophesying, if I may say so, what the world will next be, and what men will next do. There, at any rate, a new republic has become politically great and commercially active; whereas all other new republics have failed in those points, as in all others. But this cannot be attempted now.

(Chapter XXIII)

NORTH AMERICA

Introduction

It has been the ambition of my literary life to write a book about the United States, and I had made up my mind to visit the country with this object before the intestine troubles of the United States Government had commenced. I have not allowed the division among the States and the breaking out of civil war to interfere with my intention; but I should not purposely have chosen this period either for my book or for my visit. I say so much, in order that it may not be supposed that it is my special purpose to write an account of the struggle as far as it has yet been carried. My wish is to describe as well as I can the present social and political state of the country. This I should have attempted, with more personal satisfaction in the work, had there been no disruption between the North and South; but I have not allowed that disruption to deter me from an object which, if it were delayed, might probably never be carried out. I am therefore forced to take the subject in its present condition, and being so forced I must write of the war, of the causes which have led to it, and of its probable termination. But I wish it to be understood that it was not my selected task to do so, and is not now my primary object.

Thirty years ago my mother wrote a book about the Americans,[1] to which I believe I may allude as a well known and successful work without being guilty of any undue family conceit. That was essentially a woman's book. She saw with a woman's keen eye, and described with a woman's light but graphic pen, the social defects and absurdities which our near relatives had adopted into their domestic life. All that she told was worth the telling, and the telling if done successfully, was sure to produce a good result. I am satisfied that it did so. But she did not regard it as a part of her work to dilate on the nature and operation of those political arrangements which had produced the social absurdities which she saw, or to explain that though such absurdities were the natural result of those arrangements in their newness, the defects would certainly pass away, while the political arrangements, if good, would remain. Such a work is fitter for a man than for a woman. I am very far from thinking that it is a task which I can perform with satisfaction either to myself or to others. It is a work which some man will do who has earned a right by education, study, and success to rank himself among the political sages of his age. But I may perhaps be able to add something to the familiarity of Englishmen with Americans. The writings which have been most popular in England on the subject of the United States have hitherto dealt chiefly with social details; and though in most cases true and useful, have created laughter on one side of the Atlantic, and soreness on the other. If I could do anything to mitigate the soreness, if I could in any small degree add to the good feeling which should exist between two nations which ought to love each other so well, and which do hang upon each other so constantly, I should think that I had cause to be proud of my work.[2]

But it is very hard to write about any country a book that does not represent the country described in a more or less ridiculous point of view. It is hard at least to do so in such a book as I must write. A De Tocqueville[3] may do it. It may be done by any philosophico-political or politico-statistical, or statistico-scientific writer; but it can hardly be done by a man who professes to use a light pen, and to manufacture his article for the use of general readers. Such a writer may tell all that he sees of the beautiful; but he must also tell, if not all that he sees of the ludicrous, at any rate the most piquant part of it. How to do this without being offensive is the problem which a man with such a task before him has to solve. His first duty is owed to his readers, and consists mainly in this: that he shall tell the truth, and shall so tell that truth that what he has written may be readable. But a second duty is due to those of whom he writes; and he does not perform that duty well if he gives offence to those, as to whom, on the

summing up of the whole evidence for and against them in his
own mind, he intends to give a favourable verdict.

(Vol. One, Chapter 1)

Boston and politics

Boston is not in itself a fine city, but it is a very pleasant city.
They say that the harbour is very grand and very beautiful. It
certainly is not so fine as that of Portland in a nautical point of
view, and as certainly it is not as beautiful. It is the entrance from
the sea into Boston of which people say so much; but I did not
think it quite worthy of all I had heard. In such matters, however,
much depends on the peculiar light in which scenery is seen. An
evening light is generally the best for all landscapes; and I did not
see the entrance to Boston harbour by an evening light. It was
not the beauty of the harbour of which I thought the most; but of
the tea that had been sunk there,[4] and of all that came of that
successful speculation. Few towns now standing have a right to
be more proud of their antecedents than Boston.

But as I have said, it is not specially interesting to the eye –
what new town, or even what simply adult town, can be so?
There is an Athenæum, and a State Hall, and a fashionable street,
– Beacon Street, very like Piccadilly as it runs along the Green
Park, – and there is the Green Park opposite to this Piccadilly,
called Boston Common. Beacon Street and Boston Common are
very pleasant. Excellent houses there are, and large churches, and
enormous hotels; but of such things as these a man can write
nothing that is worth the reading. The traveller who desires to
tell his experience of North America must write of people rather
than of things.

As I have said, I found myself instantly involved in discussions
on American politics, and the bearing of England upon those
politics. 'What do you think, you in England – what do you all
believe will be the upshot of this war?' That was the question
always asked in those or other words. 'Secession, certainly,' I
always said, but not speaking quite with that abruptness. 'And
you believe, then, that the South will beat the North?' I explained

that I, personally, had never so thought, and that I did not believe that to be the general idea. Men's opinions in England, however, were too divided to enable me to say that there was any prevailing conviction on the matter. My own impression was, and is, that the North will, in a military point of view, have the best of the contest, – will beat the South; but that the Northerners will not prevent secession, let their success be what it may. Should the North prevail after a two years' conflict, the North will not admit the South to an equal participation of good things with themselves, even though each separate rebellious State should return suppliant, like a prodigal son, kneeling on the floor of Congress, each with a separate rope of humiliation round its neck. Such was my idea as expressed then, and I do not know that I have since had much cause to change it.

(Vol. One, Chapter II)

Children

And then the children, – babies, I should say if I were speaking of English bairns of their age; but seeing that they are Americans, I hardly dare to call them children. The actual age of these perfectly civilized and highly educated beings may be from three to four. One will often see five or six such seated at the long dinner-table of the hotel, breakfasting and dining with their elders, and going through the ceremony with all the gravity, and more than all the decorum of their grandfathers. When I was three years old I had not yet, as I imagine, been promoted beyond a silver spoon of my own wherewith to eat my bread and milk in the nursery, and I feel assured that I was under the immediate care of a nursemaid, as I gobbled up my minced mutton mixed with potatoes and gravy. But at hotel life in the States the adult infant lisps to the waiter for everything at table, handles his fish with epicurean delicacy, is choice in his selection of pickles, very particular that his beef-steak at breakfast shall be hot, and is instant in his demand for fresh ice in his water. But perhaps his, or in this case her, retreat from the room when the meal is over, is the *chef d'œuvre*[5] of the whole performance. The little precocious, full-

blown beauty of four signifies that she has completed her meal, –
or is 'through' her dinner, as she would express it, – by carefully
extricating herself from the napkin which has been tucked around
her. Then the waiter, ever attentive to her movements, draws
back the chair on which she is seated, and the young lady glides
to the floor. A little girl in Old England would scramble down,
but little girls in New England never scramble. Her father and
mother, who are no more than her chief ministers, walk before
her out of the saloon, and then she, – swims after them. But
swimming is not the proper word. Fishes in making their way
through the water assist, or rather impede, their motion with no
dorsal riggle. No animal taught to move directly by its Creator
adopts a gait so useless, and at the same time so graceless. Many
women, having received their lessons in walking from a less
eligible instructor, do move in this way, and such women this
unfortunate little lady has been instructed to copy. The peculiar
step to which I allude is to be seen often on the Boulevards in
Paris. It is to be seen more often in second rate French towns,
and among fourth rate French women. Of all signs in women
betokening vulgarity, bad taste, and aptitude to bad morals, it is
the surest. And this is the gait of going which American mothers,
– some American mothers I should say, – love to teach their
daughters! As a comedy at an hotel, it is very delightful, but in
private life I should object to it.

(Vol. One, Chapter II)

Railway cars

And here I beg, once for all, to enter my protest loudly against
the manner in which these conveyances are conducted. The one
grand fault – there are other smaller faults – but the one grand
fault is that they admit but one class. Two reasons for this are
given. The first is that the finances of the companies will not
admit of a divided accommodation; and the second is that the
republican nature of the people will not brook a superior or
aristocratic classification of travelling. As regards the first, I do
not in the least believe in it. If a more expensive manner of

railway travelling will pay in England, it would surely do so here. Were a better class of carriages organized, as large a portion of the population would use them in the United States as in any country in Europe. And it seems to be evident that in arranging that there shall be only one rate of travelling, the price is enhanced on poor travellers exactly in proportion as it is made cheap to those who are not poor. For the poorer classes, travelling in America is by no means cheap, – the average rate being, as far as I can judge, fully three-halfpence a mile. It is manifest that dearer rates for one class would allow of cheaper rates for the other; and that in this manner general travelling would be encouraged and increased.

But I do not believe that the question of expenditure has had anything to do with it. I conceive it to be true that the railways are afraid to put themselves at variance with the general feeling of the people. If so the railways may be right. But then, on the other hand, the general feeling of the people must in such case be wrong. Such a feeling argues a total mistake as to the nature of that liberty and equality for the security of which the people is so anxious, and that mistake the very one which has made shipwreck so many attempts at freedom in other countries. It argues that confusion between social and political equality which has led astray multitudes who have longed for liberty fervently, but who have not thought of it carefully. If a first-class railway carriage should be held as offensive, so should a first-class house, or a first-class horse, or a first-class dinner. But first-class houses, first-class horses, and first-class dinners are very rife in America. Of course it may be said that the expenditure shown in these last-named objects is private expenditure, and cannot be controlled; and that railway travelling is of a public nature, and can be made subject to public opinion. But the fault is in that public opinion which desires to control matters of this nature. Such an arrangement partakes of all the vice of a sumptuary law, and sumptuary laws are in their very essence mistakes. It is well that a man should always have all for which he is willing to pay. If he desires and obtains more than is good for him, the punishment, and thus also the preventive, will come from other sources.

It will be said that the American cars are good enough for all purposes. The seats are not very hard, and the room for sitting is sufficient. Nevertheless I deny that they are good enough for all purposes. They are very long, and to enter them and find a place often requires a struggle and almost a fight. There is rarely any person to tell a stranger which car he should enter. One never meets an uncivil or unruly man, but the women of the lower ranks are not courteous. American ladies love to lie at ease in their carriages, as thoroughly as do our women in Hyde Park, and to those who are used to such luxury, travelling by railroad in their own country must be grievous. I would not wish to be thought a Sybarite[6] myself, or to be held as complaining because I have been compelled to give up my seat to women with babies and bandboxes who have accepted the courtesy with very scanty grace. I have borne worse things than these, and have roughed it much in my days from want of means and other reasons. Nor am I yet so old but what I can rough it still. Nevertheless I like to see things as well done as is practicable, and railway travelling in the States is not well done. I feel bound to say as much as this, and now I have said it, once for all.

(Vol. One, Chapter III)

He turns guide

The great beauty of the autumn, or fall, is in the brilliant hues which are then taken by the foliage. The autumnal tints are fine with us. They are lovely and bright wherever foliage and vegetation form a part of the beauty of scenery. But in no other land do they approach the brilliancy of the fall in America. The bright rose colour, the rich bronze which is almost purple in its richness, and the glorious golden yellows must be seen to be understood. By me at any rate they cannot be described. These begin to show themselves in September, and perhaps I might name the latter half of that month as the best time for visiting the White Mountains.

I am not going to write a guide-book, feeling sure that Mr Murray[7] will do New England, and Canada, including Niagara and the Hudson river, with a peep into Boston and New York before many more seasons have passed by. But I cannot forbear to tell my countrymen that any enterprising individual with a hundred pounds to spend on his holiday, – a hundred and twenty would make him more comfortable in regard to wine, washing, and other luxuries, – and an absence of two months from his labours, may see as much and do as much here for the money as he can see or do elsewhere. In some respects he may do more; for he will learn more of American nature in such a journey than he can ever learn of the nature of Frenchmen or Americans by such an excursion among them. Some three weeks of the time, or perhaps a day or two over, he must be at sea, and that portion of his trip will cost him fifty pounds, – presuming that he chooses to go in the most comfortable and costly way; – but his time on board ship will not be lost. He will learn to know much of Americans there, and will perhaps form acquaintances of which he will not altogether lose sight for many a year. He will land at Boston, and staying a day or two there will visit Cambridge, Lowell, and Bunker Hill; and, if he be that way given, will remember that here live, and occasionally are to be seen alive, men such as Longfellow, Emerson, Hawthorne,[8] and a host of others whose names and fames have made Boston the throne of Western Literature. He will then, – if he take my advice and follow my track, – go by Portland up into the White Mountains. At Gorham, a station on the Grand Trunk line, he will find an hotel as good as any of its kind, and from thence he will take a light waggon, so called in these countries; – and here let me presume that the traveller is not alone; he has his wife or friend, or perhaps a pair of sisters, – and in his waggon he will go up through primeval forests to the Glen House. When there he will ascend Mount Washington on a pony. That is *de rigueur*,[9] and I do not, therefore, dare to recommend him to omit the ascent. I did not gain much myself by my labour. He will not stay at the Glen House, but will go on to – Jackson's I think they call the next hotel; at which he will sleep. From thence he will take his waggon on through the Notch to the Crawford House, sleeping there again; and when here let him of all things remember to go up Mount Willard. It is but a walk of two hours, up and down, if so much. When reaching the top he will be startled to find that he looks down into the ravine without an inch of fore-ground. He will come out suddenly on a ledge of rock, from whence, as it seems, he might leap down at once into the valley below. Then going on from the Crawford House he will be driven through the woods of Cherry Mount, passing, I fear without toll of custom, the house of my excellent friend Mr Plaistead, who keeps an hotel at Jefferson. 'Sir,' said Mr Plaistead, 'I have everything here that a man ought to want; air, sir, that ain't to be got better nowhere; trout, chickens, beef, mutton, milk, – and all for a dollar a day. A top of that hill, sir, there's a view that ain't to be beaten this side of the Atlantic, or I believe the other. And an echo, sir! – We've an echo that comes back to us six times, sir; floating on the light wind, and wafted about from rock to rock till you would think the angels were talking to you. If I could raise that echo, sir, every day at command I'd give a thousand dollars for it. It would be worth all the money to a house like this.' And he waved his hand about from hill to hill, pointing out in graceful curves the lines which the sounds would take. Had destiny not called on Mr Plaistead to keep an American hotel, he might have been a poet.

(Vol. One, Chapter III)

He becomes ironic

I cannot say that I like the hotels in those parts, or indeed the mode of life at American hotels in general. In order that I may not unjustly defame them, I will commence these observations by declaring that they are cheap to those who choose to practise the economy which they encourage, that the viands are profuse in quantity and wholesome in quality, that the attendance is quick and unsparing, and that travellers are never annoyed by that grasping greedy hunger and thirst after francs and shillings which disgrace in Europe many English and many continental inns. All this is, as must be admitted, great praise; and yet I do not like the American hotels.

One is in a free country and has come from a country in which one has been brought up to hug one's chains, – so at least the English traveller is constantly assured – and yet in an American inn one can never do as one likes. A terrific gong sounds early in the morning, breaking one's sweet slumbers, and then a second gong sounding some thirty minutes later, makes you understand that you must proceed to breakfast, whether you be dressed or no. You certainly can go on with your toilet and obtain your meal after half an hour's delay. Nobody actually scolds you for so doing, but the breakfast is, as they say in this country, 'through.' You sit down alone, and the attendant stands immediately over you. Probably there are two so standing. They fill your cup the instant it is empty. They tender you fresh food before that which has disappeared from your plate has been swallowed. They begrudge you no amount that you can eat or drink; but they begrudge you a single moment that you sit there neither eating nor drinking. This is your fate if you're too late, and therefore as a rule you are not late. In that case you form one of a long row of eaters who proceed through their work with a solid energy that is past all praise. It is wrong to say that Americans will not talk at their meals. I never met but few who would not talk to me, at any rate till I got to the far west; but I have rarely found that they would address me first. Then the dinner comes early; at least it always does so in New England, and the ceremony is much of the same kind. You came there to eat, and the food is pressed on you almost *ad nauseam*.[10] But as far as one can see there is no drinking. In these days, I am quite aware, that drinking has become improper, even in England. We are apt at home to speak of wine as a thing tabooed, wondering how our fathers lived and swilled. I believe that as a fact we drink as much as they did; but nevertheless that is our theory. I confess, however, that I like wine. It is very wicked, but it seems to me that my dinner goes down better with a glass of sherry than without it. As a rule I always did get it at hotels in America. But I had no comfort with it. Sherry they do not understand at all. Of course I am only speaking of hotels. Their claret they get exclusively from Mr Gladstone,[11] and looking at the quality, have a right to quarrel even with Mr Gladstone's price. But it is not the quality of the wine that I hereby intend to subject to ignominy, so much as the want of any opportunity for it. After dinner, if all that I hear be true, the gentleman occasionally drop into the hotel bar and 'liquor up.' Or rather this is not done specially after dinner, but without prejudice to the hour at any time that may be found desirable. I also have 'liquored up,' but I cannot say that I enjoy the process. I do not intend hereby to accuse Americans of drinking much, but I maintain that what they do drink, they drink in the most uncomfortable manner that the imagination can devise.

The greatest luxury at an English inn is one's tea, one's fire, and one's book. Such an arrangement is not practicable at an American hotel. Tea, like breakfast, is a great meal, at which meat should be eaten, generally with the addition of much jelly, jam, and sweet preserve; but no person delays over his tea-cup. I love to have my tea-cup emptied and filled with gradual pauses, so that time for oblivion may accrue, and no exact record be taken. No such meal is known at American hotels. It is possible to hire a separate room and have one's meals served in it; but in doing so a man runs counter to all the institutions of the country, and a woman does so equally. A stranger does not wish to be viewed askance by all around him; and the rule which holds that men at Rome should do as Romans do, if true anywhere, is true in America. Therefore I say that in an American inn one can never do as one pleases.

(Vol. One, Chapter III)

He enters Canada

I must confess that in going from the States into Canada, an Englishman is struck by the feeling that he is going from a richer country into one that is poorer, and from a greater country into one that is less. An Englishman going from a foreign land into a land which is in one sense his own, of course finds much in the change to gratify him. He is able to speak as the master, instead of speaking as the visitor. His tongue becomes more free, and he is able to fall back to his national habits and national expressions. He no longer feels that he is admitted on sufferance, or that he must be careful to respect laws which he does not quite under-stand. This feeling was naturally strong in an Englishman in passing from the States into Canada at the time of my visit. English policy at that moment was violently abused by Americans, and was upheld as violently in Canada. But, nevertheless, with all this, I could not enter Canada without seeing, and hearing, and feeling that there was less of enterprise around me there than in the States – less of general movement, and less of commercial success. To say why this is so would require a long and very difficult discussion, and one which I am not prepared to hold. It may be that a dependent country, let the feeling of dependence be ever so much modified by powers of self-governance, cannot hold its own against countries which are in all respects their own masters. Few, I believe, would now maintain that the Northern States of America would have risen in commerce as they have risen, had they still remained attached to England as colonies. If this be so, that privilege of self-rule which they have acquired, has been the cause of their success. It does not follow as a consequence that the Canadas fighting their battle alone in the world could do as the States have done. Climate, or size, or geographical position might stand in their way. But I fear that it does follow, if not as a logical conclusion at least as a natural result, that they never will do so well unless some day they shall so fight their battle. It may be argued that Canada has in fact the power of self-governance; that she rules herself and makes her own laws as England does; that the Sovereign of England has but a veto on those laws, and stands in regard to Canada exactly as she does in regard to England. This is so, I believe, by the letter of the Constitution, but is not so in reality, and cannot, in truth, be so in any colony, even of Great Britain. In England the political power of the Crown is nothing. The Crown has no such power, and now-a-days makes no attempt at having any. But the political power of the Crown, as it is felt in Canada, is everything. The Crown has no such power in England because it must change its ministers whenever called upon to do so by the House of Commons. But the Colonial Minister in Downing Street is the Crown's Prime Minister as regards the Colonies, and he is changed not as any Colonial House of Assembly may wish, but in accordance with the will of the British Commons. Both the Houses in Canada – that, namely, of the Representatives, or

Lower House, and of the Legislative Council, or Upper House –
are now elective, and are filled without direct influence from the
Crown. The power of self-government is as thoroughly developed as perhaps may be possible in a colony. But after all it is a
dependent form of government, and as such may perhaps not
conduce to so thorough a development of the resources of the
country as might be achieved under a ruling power of its own, to
which the welfare of Canada itself would be the chief if not the
only object.

I beg that it may not be considered from this that I would
propose to Canada to set up for itself at once and declare itself
independent. In the first place I do not wish to throw over Canada;
and in the next place I do not wish to throw over England. If such
a separation shall ever take place, I trust that it may be caused, not
by Canadian violence but by British generosity. Such a separation,
however, never can be good till Canada herself shall wish it. That
she does not wish it yet is certain. If Canada ever should wish it,
and should ever press for the accomplishment of such a wish, she
must do so in connection with Nova Scotia and New Brunswick. If
at any future time there be formed such a separate political power,
it must include the whole of British North America.

(Vol. One, Chapter IV)

A professional interest

From Sherbrooke we went with the mails on a pair-horse waggon to Magog. Cross country mails are not interesting to the
generality of readers, but I have a professional liking for them
myself. I have spent the best part of my life in looking after and
I hope in improving such mails, and I always endeavour to do a
stroke of work when I come across them. I learned on this
occasion that the conveyance of mails with a pair of horses in
Canada costs little more than half what is paid for the same work
in England with one horse, and something less than what is paid
in Ireland, also for one horse. But in Canada the average pace is
only five miles an hour. In Ireland it is seven, and the time is
accurately kept, which does not seem to be the case in Canada. In

England the pace is eight miles an hour. In Canada, and in Ireland these conveyances carry passengers; but in England they are prohibited from doing so. In Canada the vehicles are much better got up than they are in England, and the horses too look better. Taking Ireland as a whole they are more respectable in appearance there than in England. From all which it appears that pace is the article that costs the highest price, and that appearance does not go for much in the bill. In Canada the roads are very bad in comparison with the English or Irish roads; but to make up for this, the price of forage is very low.

I have said that the cross mail conveyances in Canada did not seem to be very closely bound as to time; but they are regulated by clock-work in comparison with some of them in the United States. 'Are you going this morning?' I said to a mail-driver in Vermont. 'I thought you always started in the evening.' 'Wa'll; I guess I do. But it rained some last night, so I jist stayed at home.' I do not know that I ever felt more shocked in my life, and I could hardly keep my tongue off the man. The mails, however, would have paid no respect to me in Vermont, and I was obliged to walk away crestfallen.

(Vol. One, Chapter IV)

Mr and Mrs Trollope ascend Owl's Head

'I doubt if the lady can do it,' one man said to me. I asked if ladies did not sometimes go up. 'Yes; young women do, at times,' he said. After that my wife resolved that she would see the top of the Owl's Head, or die in the attempt, and so we started. They never think of sending a guide with one in these places, whereas in Europe a traveller is not allowed to go a step without one. When I asked for one to show us the way up Mount Washington, I was told that there were no idle boys about that place. The path was indicated to us, and off we started with high hopes.

I have been up many mountains, and have climbed some that were perhaps somewhat dangerous in their ascent. In climbing the Owl's Head there is no danger. One is closed in by thick trees the whole way. But I doubt if I ever went up a steeper ascent. It was very hard work, but we were not beaten. We reached the top, and there sitting down thoroughly enjoyed our victory. It was then half-past five o'clock, and the sun was not yet absolutely sinking. It did not seem to give us any warning that we should especially require its aid, and as the prospect below us was very lovely we remained there for a quarter of an hour. The ascent of the Owl's Head is certainly a thing to do, and I still think, in spite of our following misfortune, that it is a thing to do late in the afternoon. The view down upon the lakes and the forests around, and on the wooded hills below, is wonderfully lovely. I never was on a mountain which gave me a more perfect command of all the country round. But as we arose to descend we saw a little cloud coming towards us from over Newport.

The little cloud came on with speed, and we had hardly freed ourselves from the rocks of the summit before we were surrounded by rain. As the rain became thicker, we were surrounded by darkness also, or if not by darkness by so dim a light that it became a task to find our path. I still thought that the daylight had not gone, and that as we descended and so escaped from the cloud we should find light enough to guide us. But it was not so. The rain soon became a matter of indifference, and so also did the mud and briars beneath our feet. Even the steepness of the way was almost forgotten as we endeavoured to thread our path through the forest before it should become impossible to discern the track. A dog had followed us up, and though the beast would not stay with us so as to be our guide, he returned ever and anon and made us aware of his presence by dashing by us. I may confess now that I became much frightened. We were wet through, and a night out in the forest would have been unpleasant to us. At last I did utterly lose the track. It had become quite dark, so dark that we could hardly see each other. We had succeeded in getting down the steepest and worst part of the mountain, but we were still among dense forest-trees, and up to our knees in mud. But the people at the Mountain House were Christians, and men with lanterns were sent hallooing after us through the dark night. When we were thus found we were not many yards from the path, but unfortunately on the wrong side of a stream. Through that we waded and then made our way in

safety to the inn. In spite of which misadventure I advise all
travellers in Lower Canada to go up the Owl's Head.

(Vol. One, Chapter IV)

The glory of Ottawa

But the glory of Ottawa will be – and, indeed, already is – the set
of public buildings which is now being erected on the rock which
guards as it were the town from the river. How much of the
excellence of these buildings may be due to the taste of Sir
Edmund Head,[12] the late Governor, I do not know. That he has
greatly interested himself in the subject is well known: and as the
style of the different buildings is so much alike as to make one
whole, though the designs of different architects were selected,
and these different architects employed, I imagine that considerable alterations must have been made in the original drawings.
There are three buildings, forming three sides of a quadrangle;
but they are not joined, the vacant spaces at the corner being of
considerable extent. The fourth side of the quadrangle opens
upon one of the principal streets of the town. The centre building
is intended for the Houses of Parliament, and the two side
buildings for the Government offices. Of the first Messrs Fuller
and Jones are the architects, and of the latter Messrs Stent and
Laver. I did not have the pleasure of meeting any of these
gentlemen; but I take upon myself to say that as regards purity
of art and manliness of conception their joint work is entitled to
the very highest praise. How far the buildings may be well
arranged for the required purposes, how far they may be econo-
mical in construction, or specially adapted to the severe climate
of the country, I cannot say; but I have no hesitation in risking
my reputation for judgment in giving my warmest commenda-
tion to them as regards beauty of outline and truthful nobility of
detail.

(Vol. One, Chapter V)

Toronto

But the University is the glory of Toronto. This is a Gothic building and will take rank after, but next to the buildings at Ottawa. It will be the second piece of noble architecture in Canada, and as far as I know on the American continent. It is, I believe, intended to be purely Norman, though I doubt whether the received types of Norman architecture have not been departed from in many of the windows. Be this as it may the College is a manly, noble structure, free from false decoration, and infinitely creditable to those who projected it. I was informed by the head of the College that it has been open only two years, and here also I fancy that the colony has been much indebted to the taste of the late Governor, Sir Edmund Head.

Toronto as a city is not generally attractive to a traveller. The country around it is flat; and, though it stands on a lake, that lake has no attributes of beauty. Large inland seas such as are these great Northern lakes of America never have such attributes. Picturesque mountains rise from narrow valleys, such as form the beds of lakes in Switzerland, Scotland, and Northern Italy. But from such broad waters as those of Lake Ontario, Lake Erie, and Lake Michigan, the shores shelve very gradually, and have none of the materials of lovely scenery.

The streets in Toronto are framed with wood, or rather planked, as are those of Montreal and Quebec; but they are kept in better order. I should say that the planks are first used at Toronto, then sent down by the lake to Montreal, and when all but rotted out there, are again floated off by the St Lawrence to be used in the thoroughfares of the old French capital. But if the streets of Toronto are better than those of the other towns, the roads round it are worse. I had the honour of meeting two distinguished members of the Provincial Parliament at dinner some few miles out of town, and, returning back a short while after they had left our host's house, was glad to be of use in picking them up from a ditch into which their carriage had been upset. To me it appeared all but miraculous that any carriage should make its way over that road without such misadventure. I may perhaps be allowed to hope that the discomfiture of those worthy legislators may lead to some improvement in the thoroughfare.

I had on a previous occasion gone down the St Lawrence, through the thousand isles, and over the rapids in one of those large summer steamboats which ply upon the lake and river. I cannot say that I was much struck by the scenery, and therefore did not encroach upon my time by making the journey again. Such an opinion will be regarded as heresy by many who think much of the thousand islands. I do not believe that they would be expressly noted by any traveller who was not expressly bidden to admire them.

From Toronto we went across to Niagara, re-entering the States at Lewiston in New York.

(Vol. One, Chapter V)

Canadian independence

Why should the colonies remain true to us as children are true to their parents, if we grudge them the assistance which is due to a child? They raise their own taxes, it is said, and administer them. True; and it is well that the growing son should do something for himself. While the father does all for him the son's labour belongs to the father. Then comes a middle state in which the son does much for himself, but not all. In that middle state now stand our prosperous colonies. Then comes the time when the son shall stand alone by his own strength; and to that period of manly self-respected strength let us all hope that those colonies are advancing. It is very hard for a mother country to know when such a time has come; and hard also for the child-colony to recognize justly the period of its own maturity. Whether or no such severance may ever take place without a quarrel, without weakness on one side and pride on the other, is a problem in the world's history yet to be solved. The most successful child that ever yet has gone off from a successful parent and taken its own path into the world, is without doubt the nation of the United States. Their present troubles are the result and the proofs of their success. The people that were too great to be dependent on any nation have now spread till they are themselves too great for a single nationality. No one now thinks that that daughter should have remained longer subject to her mother. But the severance was not made in amity, and the shrill notes of the old family quarrel are still sometimes heard across the waters.

From all this the question arises whether that problem may ever be solved with reference to the Canadas. That it will never be their destiny to join themselves to the States of the Union, I feel fully convinced. In the first place it is becoming evident from the present circumstances of the Union, – if it had never been made evident by history before, – that different people with different habits living at long distances from each other cannot well be brought together on equal terms under one Government. That noble ambition of the Americans that all the continent north of the isthmus should be united under one flag, has already been thrown from its saddle. The North and South are virtually separated, and the day will come in which the West also will secede. As population increases and trades arise peculiar to those different climates, the interests of the people will differ, and a new secession will take place beneficial alike to both parties. If this be so, if even here be any tendency this way, it affords the strongest argument against the probability of any future annexation of the Canadas. And then, in the second place, the feeling of Canada is not American, but British. If ever she be separated from Great Britain, she will be separated as the States were separated. She will desire to stand alone, and to enter herself as one among the nations of the earth.

She will desire to stand alone; – alone, that is without dependence either on England or on the States. But she is so circumstanced geographically that she can never stand alone without amalgamation with our other North American provinces. She has an outlet to the sea at the Gulf of St Lawrence, but it is only a summer outlet. Her winter outlet is by railway through the States, and no other winter outlet is possible for her except through the sister provinces. Before Canada can be nationally great, the line of railway which now runs for some hundred miles below Quebec to Rivière du Loup, must be continued on through New Brunswick and Nova Scotia to the port of Halifax.

(Vol. One, Chapter VI)

Niagara

The falls are, as I have said, made by a sudden breach in the level
of the river. All cataracts are, I presume, made by such breaches;
but generally the waters do not fall precipitously as they do at
Niagara, and never elsewhere, as far as the world yet knows, has
a breach so sudden been made in a river carrying in its channel
such or any approach to such a body of water. Up above the falls,
for more than a mile, the waters leap and burst over rapids, as
though conscious of the destiny that awaits them. Here the river
is very broad, and comparatively shallow, but from shore to
shore it frets itself into little torrents, and begins to assume the
majesty of its power. Looking at it even here, in the expanse
which forms itself over the greater fall, one feels sure that no
strongest swimmer could have a chance of saving himself, if fate
had cast him in even among those petty whirlpools. The waters,
though so broken in their descent, are deliciously green. This
colour as seen early in the morning, or just as the sun has set, is
so bright as to give to the place of its chiefest charms.

This will be best seen from the further end of the island, –
Goat Island, as it is called, which, as the reader will understand,
divides the river immediately above the falls. Indeed the island is
a part of that precipitously broken ledge over which the river
tumbles; and no doubt in process of time will be worn away and
covered with water. The time, however, will be very long. In the
meanwhile it is perhaps a mile round, and is covered thickly with
timber. At the upper end of the island the waters are divided, and
coming down in two courses, each over its own rapids, form two
separate falls. The bridge by which the island is entered is a
hundred yards or more above the smaller fall. The waters here
have been turned by the island, and make their leap into the body
of the river below at a right angle with it, – about two hundred
yards below the greater fall. Taken alone this smaller cataract
would, I imagine, be the heaviest fall of water known, but taken
in conjunction with the other it is terribly shorn of its majesty.
The waters here are not green as they are at the larger cataract,
and though the ledge has been hollowed and bowed by them so
as to form a curve, that curve does not deepen itself into a vast

abyss as it does at the horseshoe up above. This smaller fall is again divided, and the visitor passing down a flight of steps and over a frail wooden bridge finds himself on a smaller island in the midst of it.

But we will go at once on to the glory, and the thunder, and the majesty, and the wrath of that upper hell of waters. We are still, let the reader remember, on Goat Island, still in the States, and on what is called the American side of the main body of the river. Advancing beyond the path leading down to the lesser fall, we come to that point of the island at which the waters of the main river begin to descend. From hence across to the Canadian side the cataract continues itself in one unabated line. But the line is very far from being direct or straight. After stretching for some little way from the shore, to a point in the river which is reached by a wooden bridge at the end of which stands a tower upon the rock, – after stretching to this, the line of the ledge bends inwards against the flood, – in, and in, and in, till one is led to think that the depth of that horse-shoe is immeasurable. It has been cut with no stinting hand. A monstrous cantle has been worn back out of the centre of the rock, so that the fury of the waters converges, and the spectator as he gazes into the hollow with wishful eyes fancies that he can hardly trace out the centre of the abyss.

Go down to the end of that wooden bridge, seat yourself on the rail, and there sit till all the outer world is lost to you. There is no grander spot about Niagara than this. The waters are absolutely around you. If you have that power of eye-control which is so necessary to the full enjoyment of scenery you will see nothing but the water. You will certainly hear nothing else; and the sound, I beg you to remember, is not an ear-cracking, agonizing crash and clang of noises; but is melodious, and soft withal, though loud as thunder. It fills your ears, and as it were envelopes them, but at the same time you can speak to your neighbour without an effort. But at this place, and in these moments, the less of speaking I should say the better. There is no grander spot than this. Here, seated on the rail of the bridge, you will not see the whole depth of the fall. In looking at the grandest works of nature, and of art too, I fancy, it is never well to see all.

There should be something left to the imagination, and much should be half concealed in mystery. The greatest charm of a mountain range is the wild feeling that there must be strange unknown desolate worlds in those far-off valleys beyond. And so here, at Niagara, that converging rush of waters may fall down, down at once into a hell of rivers for what the eye can see. It is glorious to watch them in their first curve over the rocks. They come green as a bank of emeralds; but with a fitful flying colour, as though conscious that in one moment more they would be dashed into spray and rise into air, pale as driven snow. The vapour rises high into the air, and is gathered there, visible always as a permanent white cloud over the cataract; but the bulk of the spray which fills the lower hollow of that horse-shoe is like a tumult of snow. This you will not fully see from your seat on the rail. The head of it rises ever and anon out of that caldron below, but the caldron itself will be invisible. It is ever so far down, – far as your own imagination can sink it. But your eyes will rest full upon the curve of the waters. The shape you will be looking at is that of a horse-shoe, but of a horse-shoe miraculously deep from toe to heel; – and this depth becomes greater as you sit there. That which at first was only great and beautiful, becomes gigantic and sublime till the mind is at loss to find an epithet for its own use. To realize Niagara you must sit there till you see nothing else than that which you have come to see. You will hear nothing else, and think of nothing else. At length you will be at one with the tumbling river before you. You will find yourself among the waters as though you belonged to them. The cool liquid green will run through your veins, and the voice of the cataract will be the expression of your own heart. You will fall as the bright waters fall, rushing down into your new world with no hesitation and with no dismay; and you will rise again as the spray rises, bright, beautiful, and pure. Then you will flow away in your course to the uncompassed, distant, and eternal ocean.

(Vol. One, Chapter VII)

The Maid of the Mist

But I will beg you to take notice of those rapids from the bridge and to ask yourself what chance of life would remain to any ship, craft, or boat required by destiny to undergo navigation beneath the bridge and down into that whirlpool. Heretofore all men would have said that no chance of life could remain to so ill-starred a bark. The navigation, however, has been effected. But men used to the river still say that the chances would be fifty to one against any vessel which should attempt to repeat the experiment.

The story of that wondrous voyage was as follows. A small steamer called the *Maid of the Mist* was built upon the river, between the falls and the rapids, and was used for taking adventurous tourists up amidst the spray, as near to the cataract as was possible. *The Maid of the Mist* plied in this way for a year or two, and was, I believe, much patronized during the season. But in the early part of last summer an evil time had come. Either the *Maid* got into debt, or her owner had embarked in other and less profitable speculations. At any rate he became subject to the law, and tidings reached him that the Sheriff would seize the *Maid.* On most occasions the Sheriff is bound to keep such intentions secret, seeing that property is moveable, and that an insolvent debtor will not always await the officers of justice. But with the poor *Maid* there was no need of such secrecy. There was but a mile or so of water on which she could ply, and she was forbidden by the nature of her properties to make any way upon land. The Sheriff's prey therefore was easy and the poor *Maid* was doomed.

In any country in the world but America such would have been the case, but an American would steam down Phlegethon[13] to save his property from the Sheriff; he would steam down Phlegethon or get some one else to do it for him. Whether or no in this case the captain of the boat was the proprietor, or whether, as I was told, he was paid for the job, I do not know; but he determined to run the rapids, and he procured two others to accompany him in the risk. He got up his steam, and took the *Maid* up amidst the spray according to his custom. Then suddenly turning on his course, he with one of his companions fixed himself at the wheel, while the other remained at his engine. I wish I could look into the mind of that man and understand what his thoughts were at that moment; what were his thoughts and what his beliefs. As to one of the men I was told that he was carried down, not knowing what he was about to do, but I am inclined to believe that all the three were joined together in the attempt.

I was told by a man who saw the boat pass under the bridge, that she made one long leap down as she came thither, that her funnel was at once knocked flat on the deck by the force of the blow, that the waters covered her from stem to stern, and that then she rose again and skimmed into the whirlpool a mile below. When there she rode with comparative ease upon the waters, and took the sharp turn round into the river below without a struggle. The feat was done, and the *Maid* was rescued from the Sheriff. It is said that she was sold below at the mouth of the river, and carried from thence over Lake Ontario and down the St Lawrence to Quebec.

(Vol. One, Chapter VII)

Return to the States – the Northern army

I have endeavoured to explain the circumstances of the Western command in Missouri, as they existed at the time when I was in the North-Western States, in order that the double action of the North and West may be understood. I, of course, was not in the secret of any official persons, but I could not but feel sure that the Government in Washington would have been glad to have removed Fremont[14] at once from the command, had they not feared that by doing so they would have created a schism, as it were, in their own camp, and have done much to break up the integrity or oneness of Northern loyalty. The western people almost to a man desired abolition. The States there were sending out their tens of thousands of young men into the army with a prodigality as to their only source of wealth which they hardly recognized themselves, because this to them was a fight against slavery. The western population has been increased to a wonderful degree by a

German infusion; – so much so that the western towns appear to have been peopled with Germans. I found regiments of volunteers consisting wholly of Germans. And the Germans are all abolitionists. To all the men of the West the name of Fremont is dear. He is their hero, and their Hercules. He is to cleanse the stables[15] of the southern king, and turn the waters of emancipation through the foul stalls of slavery. And, therefore, though the Cabinet in Washington would have been glad for many reasons to have removed Fremont in October last, it was at first scared from committing itself to so strong a measure. At last, however, the charges made against him were too fully substantiated to allow of their being set on one side, and early in November, 1861, he was superseded. I shall be obliged to allude again to General Fremont's career as I go on with my narrative.

At this time the North was looking for a victory on the Potomac; but they were no longer looking for it with that impatience which in the summer had led to the disgrace at Bull's Run.[16] They had recognized the fact that their troops must be equipped, drilled, and instructed; and they had also recognized the perhaps greater fact, that their enemies were neither weak, cowardly, nor badly officered. I have always thought that the tone and manner with which the North bore the defeat at Bull's Run was creditable to it. It was never denied, never explained away, never set down as trifling. 'We have been whipped!' was what all Northerners said, – 'We've got an almighty whipping, and here we are.' I have heard many Englishmen complain of this, saying that the matter was taken almost as a joke, – that no disgrace was felt, and the licking was owned by a people who ought never to have allowed that they had been licked. To all this, however, I demur. Their only chance of speedy success consisted in their seeing and recognizing the truth. Had they confessed the whipping and then sat down with their hands in their pockets, – had they done as second-rate boys at school will do, declare that they had been licked, and then feel that all the trouble is over, – they would indeed have been open to reproach.

(Vol. One, Chapter VIII)

American ingenuity

The great glory of the Americans is in their wondrous contrivances, – in their patent remedies for the usually troublous operations of life. In their huge hotels all the bell-ropes of each house ring on one bell only, but a patent indicator discloses a number, and the whereabouts of the ringer is shown. One fire heats every room, passage, hall, and cupboard, – and does it so effectually that the inhabitants are all but stifled. Soda-water bottles open themselves without any trouble of wire or strings. Men and women go up and down stairs without motive power of their own. Hot and cold water are laid on to all the chambers; – though it sometimes happens that the water from both taps is boiling, and that when once turned on it cannot be turned off again by any human energy. Everything is done by a new and wonderful patent contrivance; and of all their wonderful contrivances that of their railroad beds is by no means the least. For every four seats the negro builds up four beds, – that is, four half-beds or accommodation for four persons. Two are supposed to be below on the level of the ordinary four seats, and two up above on shelves which are let down from the roof. Mattresses slip out from one nook and pillows from another. Blankets are added, and the bed is ready. Any over particular individual – an islander, for instance, who hugs his chains – will generally prefer to pay the dollar for the double accommodation. Looking at the bed in the light of a bed, – taking as it were an abstract view of it, – or comparing it with some other bed or beds with which the occupant may have acquaintance, I cannot say that it is in all respects perfect. But distances are long in America, and he who declines to travel by night will lose very much time. He who does so travel will find the railway bed a great relief. I must confess that the feeling of dirt on the following morning is rather oppressive.

(Vol. One, Chapter IX)

The frontier man

The western American has no love for his own soil, or his own house. The matter with him is simply one of dollars. To keep a farm which he could sell at an advantage from any feeling of affection, – from what we should call an association of ideas, – would be to him as ridiculous as the keeping of a family pig would be in an English farmer's establishment. The pig is a part of the farmer's stock in trade, and must go the way of all pigs. And so is it with house and land in the life of the frontier man in the western States.

But yet this man has his romance, his high poetic feeling, and above all his manly dignity. Visit him, and you will find him without coat or waistcoat, unshorn, in ragged blue trousers and old flannel shirt, too often bearing on his lantern jaws the signs of ague and sickness; but he will stand upright before you and speak to you with all the ease of a lettered gentleman in his own library. All the odious incivility of the republican servant has been banished. He is his own master, standing on his own threshold, and finds no need to assert his equality by rudeness. He is delighted to see you, and bids you sit down on his battered bench without dreaming of any such apology as an English cottier offers to a Lady Bountiful when she calls. He has worked out his independence, and shows it in every easy movement of his body. He tells you of it unconsciously in every tone of his voice. You will always find in his cabin some newspaper, some book, some token of advance in education. When he questions you about the old country he astonishes you by the extent of his knowledge. I defy you not to feel that he is superior to the race from whence he has sprung in England or in Ireland. To me I confess that the manliness of such a man is very charming. He is dirty and perhaps squalid. His children are sick and he is without comforts. His wife is pale, and you think you see shortness of life written in the faces of all the family. But over and above it all there is an independence which sits gracefully on their shoulders, and teaches you at the first glance that the man has a right to assume himself to be your equal. It is for this position that the labourer works, bearing hard words and the indignity of tyranny, – suffering also too often the dishonest ill-usage which his superior power enables the master to inflict.

(Vol. One, Chapter IX)

Soldiers from Minnesota

I got out upon the quay and stood close by the plank, watching each man as he left the vessel and walked across towards the railway. Those whom I had previously seen in tents were not equipped, but these men were in uniform and each bore his musket. Taking them all together they were as fine a set of men as I ever saw collected. No man could doubt on seeing them that they bore on their countenances the signs of higher breeding and better education than would be seen in a thousand men enlisted in England. I do not mean to argue from this that Americans are better than English. I do not mean to argue here that they are even better educated. My assertion goes to show that the men generally were taken from a higher level in the community than that which fills our own ranks. It was a matter of regret to me, here and on many subsequent occasions, to see men bound for three years to serve as common soldiers, who were so manifestly fitted for a better and more useful life. To me it is always a source of sorrow to see a man enlisted. I feel that the individual recruit is doing badly with himself – carrying himself and the strength and intelligence which belongs to him to a bad market. I know that there must be soldiers; but as to every separate soldier I regret that he should be one of them. And the higher is the class from which such soldiers are drawn, the greater the intelligence of the men so to be employed, the deeper with me is that feeling of regret. But this strikes one much less in an old country than in a country that is new. In the old countries population is thick, and food sometimes scarce. Men can be spared, and any employment may be serviceable, even though that employment be in itself so unproductive as that of fighting battles or preparing for them. But in the western States of America every arm that can guide a plough is of incalculable value. Minnesota was admitted as a State about three years before this time, and its whole population is not much above 150,000. Of this number perhaps 40,000 may be working men. And now this infant State with its huge territory and scanty population is called upon to send its heart's blood out to the war.

(Vol. One, Chapter X)

Boats on the Mississippi

For these reasons I must say that life on board these steam-boats was not as pleasant as I had hoped to find it, but for our discomfort in this respect we found great atonement in the scenery through which we passed. I protest that of all the river scenery that I know, that of the Upper Mississippi is by far the finest and the most continued. One thinks of course of the Rhine; but, according to my idea of beauty, the Rhine is nothing to the Upper Mississippi. For miles upon miles, for hundreds of miles, the course of the river runs through low hills, which are there called bluffs. These bluffs rise in every imaginable form, looking sometimes like large, straggling, unwieldy castles, and then throwing themselves into sloping lawns which stretch back away from the river till the eye is lost in their twists and turnings. Landscape beauty, as I take it, consists mainly in four attributes: in water, in broken land, in scattered timber, – timber scattered as opposed to continuous forest timber, – and in the accident of colour. In all these particulars the banks of the Upper Mississippi can hardly be beaten. There are no high mountains; but high mountains themselves are grand rather than beautiful. There are no high mountains, but there is a succession of hills which group themselves for ever without monotony. It is perhaps the ever-variegated forms of these bluffs which chiefly constitute the wonderful loveliness of this river. The idea constantly occurs that some point on every hillside would form the most charming site ever yet chosen for a noble residence. I have passed up and down rivers clothed to the edge with continuous forest. This at first is grand enough, but the eye and feeling soon become weary. Here the trees are scattered so that the eye passes through them, and ever and again a long lawn sweeps back into the country, and up the steep side of a hill, making the traveller long to stay there and linger through the oaks, and climb the bluffs, and lie about on the bold but easy summits. The boat, however, steams quickly up against the current, and the happy valleys are left behind, one quickly after another. The river is very various in its breadth, and is constantly divided by islands. It is never so broad that the beauty of the banks is lost in the distance or injured by it. It is rapid, but has not the beautifully bright colour of some European rivers, – of the Rhine for instance, and the Rhone. But what is wanting in the colour of the water is more than compensated by the wonderful hues and lustre of the shores. We visited the river in October, and I must presume that they who seek it solely for the sake of scenery should go there in that month. It was not only that the foliage of the trees was bright with every imaginable colour, but that the grass was bronzed, and that the rocks were golden. And this beauty did not last only for a while and then cease. On the Rhine there are lovely spots and special morsels of scenery with which the traveller becomes duly enraptured. But on the Upper Mississippi there are no special morsels.

(Vol. One, Chapter X)

He visits woodcutters

I spoke to the master of the house, whom I met outside, and he at once asked me to come in and sit down. I found his father there and his mother, his wife, his brother, and two young children. The wife, who was cooking, was a very pretty, pale young woman, who, however, could have circulated round her stove more conveniently had her crinoline been of less dimensions. She bade me welcome very prettily, and went on with her cooking, talking the while, as though she were in the habit of entertaining guests in that way daily. The old woman sat in a corner knitting – as old women always do. The old man lounged with a grandchild on his knee, and the master of the house threw himself on the floor while the other child crawled over him. There was no stiffness or uneasiness in their manners, nor was there anything approaching to that republican roughness which so often operates upon a poor, well-intending Englishman like a slap on the cheek. I sat there for about an hour, and when I had discussed with them English politics and the bearing of English politics upon the American war, they told me of their own affairs. Food was very plenty, but life was very hard. Take the year through each man could not earn above half a dollar a day by cutting wood. This, however, they owned, did not take up all their time. Working on favourable wood on favourable days they could each earn two dollars a day; but these favourable circumstances did not come together very often. They did not deal with the boats themselves, and the profits were eaten up by the middleman. He, the middleman, had a good thing of it, because he could cheat the captains of the boats in the measurement of the wood. The chopper was obliged to supply a genuine cord of logs,[17] – true measure. But the man who took it off in the barge to the steamer could so pack it that fifteen true cords would make twenty-two false cords. 'It cuts up into a fine trade, you see, sir,' said the young man, as he stroked back the little girl's hair from her forehead. 'But the captains of course must find it out,' said I. This he acknowledged, but argued that the captains on this account insisted on buying the wood so much cheaper, and that the loss all came upon the chopper. I tried to teach him that the remedy lay in his own hands, and the three men listened to me quite patiently while I explained to them how they should carry on their own trade. But the young father had the last word. 'I guess we don't get above the fifty cents a day any way.' He knew at least where the shoe pinched him. He was a handsome, manly, noble-looking fellow, tall and thin, with black hair and bright eyes. But he had the hollow look about his jaws, and so had his wife, and so had his brother. They all owned to fever and ague. They had a touch of it most years, and sometimes pretty sharply. 'It was a coarse place to live in,' the old woman said, 'but there was no one to meddle with them, and she guessed that it suited.' They had books and newspapers, tidy delf, and clean glass upon their shelves, and undoubtedly provisions in plenty.

(Vol. One, Chapter X)

Elevators at Buffalo

An elevator is as ugly a monster as has been yet produced. In uncouthness of form it outdoes those obsolete old brutes who used to roam about the semi-aqueous world, and live a most uncomfortable life with their great hungering stomachs and huge unsatisfied maws. The elevator itself consists of a big moveable

trunk, – moveable as is that of an elephant, but not pliable, and
less graceful even than an elephant's. This is attached to a huge
granary or barn; but in order to give altitude within the barn for
the necessary moving up and down of this trunk, – seeing that it
cannot be curled gracefully to its purposes as the elephant's is
curled, – there is an awkward box erected on the roof of the barn,
giving some twenty feet of additional height, up into which the
elevator can be thrust. It will be understood, then, that this big
moveable trunk, the head of which, when it is at rest, is thrust up
into the box on the roof, is made to slant down in an oblique
direction from the building to the river. For the elevator is an
amphibious institution, and flourishes only on the banks of
navigable waters. When its head is ensconced within its box, and
the beast of prey is thus nearly hidden within the building, the
unsuspicious vessel is brought up within reach of the creature's
trunk, and down it comes, like a mosquito's proboscis, right
through the deck, in at the open aperture of the hole, and so into
the very vitals and bowels of the ship. When there, it goes to
work upon its food with a greed and an avidity that is disgusting
to a beholder of any taste or imagination. And now I must
explain the anatomical arrangement by which the elevator still
devours and continues to devour, till the corn within its reach has
all been swallowed, masticated, and digested. Its long trunk, as
seen slanting down from out of the building across the wharf and
into the ship, is a mere wooden pipe; but this pipe is divided
within. It has two departments; and as the grain-bearing troughs
pass up the one on a pliable band, they pass empty down the
other. The system therefore is that of an ordinary dredging
machine; only that corn, and not mud is taken away, and that the
buckets or troughs are hidden from sight. Below, within the
stomach of the poor bark, three or four labourers are at work
helping to feed the elevator. They shovel the corn up towards its
maw, so that at every swallow he should take in all that he can
hold. Thus the troughs, as they ascend, are kept full, and when
they reach the upper building they empty themselves into a
shoot, over which a porter stands guard, moderating the shoot by
a door, which the weight of his finger can open and close.
Through this doorway the corn runs into a measure, and is

weighed. By measures of forty bushels each, the tale is kept. There stands the apparatus, with the figures plainly marked, over against the porter's eye; and as the sum mounts nearly up to forty bushels he closes the door till the grains run thinly through, hardly a handful at a time, so that the balance is exactly struck. Then the teller standing by marks down his figure, and the record is made. The exact porter touches the string of another door, and the forty bushels of corn run out at the bottom of the measure, disappear down another shoot, slanting also towards the water, and deposit themselves in the canal-boat. The transit of the bushels of corn from the larger vessel to the smaller will have taken less than a minute, and the cost of that transit will have been – a farthing.

(Vol. One, Chapter XI)

New York – Money

But not on this account can I, nor on this account will any Englishman, reconcile himself to the savour of dollars which pervades the atmosphere of New York. The *ars celare artem*[18] is wanting. The making of money is the work of man; but he need not take his work to bed with him, and have it ever by his side at table, amidst his family, in church, while he disports himself, as he declares his passion to the girl of his heart in the moments of his softest bliss, and at the periods of his most solemn cere-monies. That many do so elsewhere than in New York, – in London, for instance in Paris, among the mountains of Switzer-land, and the steppes of Russia, I do not doubt. But there is generally a veil thrown over the object of the worshipper's idolatry. In New York one's ear is constantly filled with the fanatic's voice as he prays, one's eyes are always on the familiar altar. The frankincense from the temple is ever in one's nostrils. I have never walked down Fifth Avenue alone without thinking of money. I have never walked there with a companion without talking of it. I fancy that every man there in order to maintain the spirit of the place, should bear on his forehead a label stating how many dollars he is worth, and that every label should be expected to assert a falsehood.

I do not think that New York has been less generous in the use of its money than other cities, or that the men of New York generally are so. Perhaps I might go farther and say that in no city has more been achieved for humanity by the munificence of its richest citizens than in New York. Its hospitals, asylums, and institutions for the relief of all ailments to which flesh is heir, are very numerous, and beyond praise in the excellence of their arrangements. And this has been achieved in a great degree by private liberality. Men in America are not as a rule anxious to leave large fortunes to their children. The millionaire when making his will very generally gives back a considerable portion of the wealth which he has made to the city in which he made it. The rich citizen is always anxious that the poor citizen shall be relieved. It is a point of honour with him to raise the character of his municipality, and to provide that the deaf and dumb, the blind, the mad, the idiots, the old, and the incurable shall have such alleviation in their misfortune as skill and kindness can afford.

Nor is the New Yorker a hugger-mugger[19] with his money. He does not hide up his dollars in old stockings and keep rolls of gold in hidden pots. He does not even invest it where it will not grow but only produce small though sure fruit. He builds houses, he speculates largely, he spreads himself in trade to the extent of his wings, – and not seldom somewhat further. He scatters his wealth broadcast over strange fields, trusting that it may grow with an increase of an hundred-fold, but bold to bear the loss should the strange field prove itself barren. His regret at losing his money is by no means commensurate with his desire to make it. In this there is a living spirit which to me divests the dollar-worshipping idolatry of something of its ugliness. The hand when closed on the gold is instantly reopened. The idolator is anxious to get, but he is anxious also to spend. He is energetic to the last, and has no comfort with his stock unless it breeds with transatlantic rapidity of procreation.

(Vol. One, Chapter XIV)

New York – street cars

The street cars are manned with conductors, and therefore are free from many of the perils of the omnibus, but they have perils of their own. They are always quite full. By that I mean that every seat is crowded, that there is a double row of men and women standing down the centre, and that the driver's platform in front is full, and also the conductor's platform behind. That is the normal condition of a street car in the Third Avenue. You, as a stranger in the middle of the car, wish to be put down at, let us say, 89th Street. In the map of New York now before me the cross streets running from east to west are numbered up northwards as far as 154th Street. It is quite useless for you to give the number as you enter. Even an American conductor, with brains all over him, and an anxious desire to accommodate as is the case with all these men, cannot remember. You are left therefore in misery to calculate the number of the street as you move along, vainly endeavouring through the misty glass to decipher the small numbers which after a day or two you perceive to be written on the lamp posts.

But I soon gave up all attempts at keeping a seat in one of these cars. It became my practice to sit down on the outside iron rail behind, and as the conductor generally sat in my lap I was in a measure protected. As for the inside of these vehicles, the women of New York, were, I must confess, too much for me. I would no sooner place myself on a seat, than I would be called on by a mute, unexpressive, but still impressive stare into my face, to surrender my place. From cowardice if not from gallantry I would always obey; and as this led to discomfort and an irritated spirit, I preferred nursing the conductor on the hard bar in the rear.

(Vol. One, Chapter XIV)

New York – American women

The woman, as she enters, drags after her a misshapen, dirty mass of battered wirework, which she calls her crinoline, and which adds as much to her grace and comfort as a log of wood does to a donkey when tied to the animal's leg in a paddock. Of this she takes much heed, not managing it so that it may be conveyed up the carriage with some decency, but striking it about against men's legs, and heaving it with violence over people's knees. The touch of a real woman's dress is in itself delicate; but these blows from a harpy's fins are loathsome. If there be two of them they talk loudly together, having a theory that modesty has been put out of court by women's rights. But, though not modest, the woman I describe is ferocious in her propriety. She ignores the whole world around her, and as she sits with raised chin and face flattened by affectation, she pretends to declare aloud that she is positively not aware that any man is even near her. She speaks as though to her, in her womanhood, the neighbourhood of men was the same as that of dogs or cats. They are there, but she does not hear them, see them, or even acknowledge them by any courtesy of motion. But her own face always gives her the lie. In her assumption of indifference she displays her nasty consciousness, and in each attempt at a would-be propriety is guilty of an immodesty. Who does not know the timid retiring face of the young girl who when alone among men unknown to her feels that it becomes her to keep herself secluded? As many men as there are around her, so many knights has such a one, ready bucklered for her service, should occasion require such services. Should it not, she passes on unmolested, – but not, as she herself will wrongly think, unheeded. But as to her of whom I am speaking, we may say that every twist of her body, and every tone of her voice is an unsuccessful falsehood. She looks square at you in the face, and you rise to give her your seat. You rise from a deference to your own old convictions, and from that courtesy which you have ever paid to a woman's dress, let it be worn with ever such hideous deformities. She takes the place from which you have moved without a word or a bow. She twists herself round, banging your shins with her wires, while her chin is still raised, and her face is still flattened, and she directs her friend's attention to another seated man, as though that place were also vacant, and necessarily at her disposal. Perhaps the man opposite has his own ideas about chivalry. I have seen such a thing, and have rejoiced to see it.

(Vol. One, Chapter XIV)

New York – *institutions*

'Have you seen any of our great institootions, sir?' That of course is a question, which is put to every Englishman who has visited New York, and the Englishman who intends to say that he has seen New York, should visit many of them. I went to schools, hospitals, lunatic asylums, institutes for deaf and dumb, water works, historical societies, telegraph offices, and large commercial establishments. I rather think that I did my work in a thorough and conscientious manner, and I owe much gratitude to those who guided me on such occasions. Perhaps I ought to describe all these institutions; but were I to do so, I fear that I should inflict fifty or sixty very dull pages on my readers. If I could make all that I saw as clear and intelligible to others as it was made to me who saw it, I might do some good. But I know that I should fail. I marvelled much at the developed intelligence of a room full of deaf and dumb pupils, and was greatly astonished at the perform-ance of one special girl, who seemed to be brighter and quicker, and more rapidly easy with her pen than girls generally are who can hear and talk; but I cannot convey my enthusiasm to others. On such a subject a writer may be correct, may be exhaustive, may be statistically great; but he can hardly be entertaining, and the chances are that he will not be instructive.

In all such matters, however, New York is pre-eminently great. All through the States suffering humanity receives so much attention that humanity can hardly be said to suffer. The daily recurring boast of 'our glorious institootions, sir,' always provokes the ridicule of an Englishman. The words have become ridiculous, and it would, I think, be well for the nation if the term 'Institution' could be excluded from its vocabulary. But, in truth, they are glorious. The country in this respects boasts, but it has done that which justifies a boast. The arrangements for sup-plying New York with water are magnificent. The drainage of the new part of the city is excellent. The hospitals are almost alluring. The lunatic asylum which I saw was perfect, – though I did not feel obliged to the resident physician for introducing me to all the worst patients as countrymen of my own. 'An English lady, Mr Trollope. I'll introduce you. Quite a hopeless case. Two

old women. They've been here fifty years. They're English.
Another gentleman from England, Mr Trollope. A very interesting case! Confirmed inebriety.'

(Vol. One, Chapter XIV)

New York – the city

New York is built upon an island, which is I believe about ten
miles long, counting from the southern point at the battery up to
Carmansville, to which place the city is presumed to extend
northwards. This island is called Manhattan, – a name which I
have always thought would have been more graceful for the city
than that of New York. It is formed by the Sound or East river,
which divides the continent from Long Island, by the Hudson
river which runs into the Sound or rather joins it at the city foot,
and by a small stream called the Haarlem river which runs out of
the Hudson and meanders away into the Sound at the north of
the city, thus cutting the city off from the main land. The breadth
of the island does not much exceed two miles, and therefore the
city is long, and not capable of extension in point of breadth. In
its old days it clustered itself round about the Point, and stretched
itself up from there along the quays of the two waters. The
streets down in this part of the town are devious enough, twist-
ing themselves about with delightful irregularity; but as the city
grew there came the taste for parallelograms, and the upper
streets are rectangular and numbered. Broadway, the street of
New York with which the world is generally best acquainted,
begins at the southern point of the town and goes northward
through it. For some two miles and a half it walks away in a
straight line, and then it turns to the left towards the Hudson, and
becomes in fact a continuation of another street called the Bow-
ery, which comes up in a devious course from the south-east
extremity of the island. From that time Broadway never again
takes a straight course, but crosses the various Avenues in an
oblique direction till it becomes the Bloomingdale road, and
under that name takes itself out of town. There are eleven so-
called Avenues, which descend in absolutely straight lines from

the northern, and at present unsettled, extremity of the new town, making their way southward till they lose themselves among the old streets. These are called First Avenue, Second Avenue, and so on. The town had already progressed two miles up northwards from the Battery before it had caught the parallelogrammic fever from Philadelphia, for at about that distance we find, 'First Street.' First Street runs across the Avenues from water to water, and then Second Street. I will not name them all, seeing that they go up to 154th Street! They do so at least on the map, and I believe on the lamp-posts. But the houses are not yet built in order beyond 50th or 60th Street. The other hundred streets, each of two miles long, with the Avenues which are mostly unoccupied for four or five miles, is the ground over which the young New Yorkers are to spread themselves. I do not in the least doubt that they will occupy it all, and that 154th Street will find itself too narrow a boundary for the population.

(Vol. One, Chapter XIV)

Lectures

The most popular lectures are given by big people, whose presence is likely to be attractive; and the whole thing, I fear we must confess, is not pre-eminently successful. In the Northern States of America the matter stands on a very different footing. Lectures there are more popular than either theatres or concerts. Enormous halls are built for them. Tickets for long courses are taken with avidity. Very large sums are paid to popular lecturers, so that the profession is lucrative, – more so, I am given to understand, than is the cognate profession of literature. The whole thing is done in great style. Music is introduced. The lecturer stands on a large raised platform, on which sit around him the bald and hoary-headed and superlatively wise. Ladies come in large numbers; especially those who aspire to soar above the frivolities of the world. Politics is the subject most popular, and most general. The men and women of Boston could no more do without their lectures, than those of Paris could without their theatres. It is the decorous diversion of the best ordered of her citizens. The fast young men go to clubs, and the fast young women to dances, as fast young men and women do in other places that are wicked; but lecturing is the favourite diversion of the steady-minded Bostonian. After all, I do not know that the result is very good. It does not seem that much will be gained by such lectures on either side of the Atlantic, – except that respectable killing of an evening which might otherwise be killed less respectably. It is but an industrious idleness, an attempt at a royal road to information, that habit of attending lectures. Let any man or woman say what he has brought away from any such attendance. It is attractive, that idea of being studious without any of the labour of study; but I fear it is illusive. If an evening can be so passed without ennui, I believe that they may be regarded as the best result to be gained. But then it so often happens that the evening is not passed without ennui!

(Vol. One, Chapter XVI)

He socializes in Boston

I shall always look back to social life in Boston with great pleasure. I met there many men and women whom to know is a distinction, and with whom to be intimate is a great delight. It was a Puritan city, in which strict old Roundhead sentiments and laws used to prevail but now-a-days ginger is hot in the mouth there and in spite of the war there were cakes and ale.[20] There was a law passed in Massachusetts in the old days that any girl should be fined and imprisoned who allowed a young man to kiss her. That law has now, I think, fallen into abeyance, and such matters are regulated in Boston much as they are in other large towns further eastward. It still, I conceive, calls itself a Puritan city, but it has divested its Puritanism of austerity, and clings rather to the politics and public bearing of its old fathers than to their social manners and pristine severity of intercourse. The young girls are, no doubt, much more comfortable under the new dispensation, – and the elderly men also, as I fancy. Sunday, as regards the outer streets, is sabbatical. But Sunday evenings within doors I always found to be, what my friends in that country call 'quite a good time.' It is not the thing in Boston to smoke in the streets during the day; but the wisest, the sagest, and the most holy, – even those holy men whom the lecturer saw around him, – seldom refuse a cigar in the dining-room as soon as the ladies have gone. Perhaps even the wicked weed would make its appearance before that sad eclipse, thereby postponing, or perhaps absolutely annihilating, the melancholy period of widowhood to both parties, and would light itself under the very eyes of those who in sterner cities will lend no countenance to such lightings. Ah me, it was very pleasant! I confess I like this abandonment of the stricter rules of the more decorous world. I fear that there is within me an aptitude to the milder debaucher- ies which makes such deviations pleasant. I like to drink and I like to smoke, but I do not like to turn women out of the room. Then comes the question whether one can have all that one likes together. In some small circles in New England I found people simple enough to fancy that they could. In Massachusetts the Maine Liquor Law[21] is still the law of the land, but, like that other law to which I have alluded, it has fallen very much out of use. At any rate it had not reached the houses of the gentlemen with whom I had the pleasure of making acquaintance. But here I must guard myself from being misunderstood. I saw but one drunken man through all New England, and he was very respect- able. He was, however, so uncommonly drunk that he might be allowed to count for two or three. The Puritans of Boston are, of course, simple in their habits and simple in their expenses. Cham- pagne and canvas-back ducks I found to be the provisions most in vogue among those who desired to adhere closely to the manners of their forefathers. Upon the whole I found the ways of life which had been brought over in the 'Mayflower'[22] from the stern sects of England, and preserved through the revolutionary war for liberty, to be very pleasant ways, and I made up my mind that a Yankee Puritan can be an uncommonly pleasant fellow. I wish that some of them did not dine so early; for when a man sits down at half-past two, that keeping up of the after-dinner recreations till bedtime becomes hard work.

(Vol. One, Chapter XVII)

The rights of women

As for the women in America especially, I must confess that I think they have a 'good time.' I make them my compliments on their sagacity, intelligence, and attractions, but I utterly refuse to them any sympathy for supposed wrongs. *O fortunatas sua si bona nôrint!*[23] Whether or no, were I an American married man and father of a family, I should not go in for the rights of man – that is altogether another question.

This question of the rights of women divides itself into two heads, – one of which is very important, worthy of much consideration, capable perhaps of much philanthropic action, and at any rate affording matter for grave discussion. This is the question of women's work; how far the work of the world, which is now borne chiefly by men, should be thrown open to women further than is now done. The other seems to me to be worthy of no consideration, to be capable of no action, to admit of no grave discussion. This refers to the political rights of women; how far the political working of the world, which is now entirely in the hands of men, should be divided between them and women. The first question is being debated on our side of the Atlantic as keenly perhaps as on the American side. As to that other question, I do not know that much has ever been said about it in Europe.

'You are doing nothing in England towards the employment of females,' a lady said to me in one of the States soon after my arrival in America. 'Pardon me,' I answered, 'I think we are doing much, perhaps too much. At any rate we are doing something.' I then explained to her how Miss Faithfull[24] had instituted a printing establishment in London; how all the work in that concern was done by females, except such heavy tasks as those for which women could not be fitted, and I handed to her one of Miss Faithfull's cards. 'Ah,' said my American friend, 'poor creatures! I have no doubt their very flesh will be worked off their bones.' I thought this a little unjust on her part; but nevertheless it occurred to me as an answer not unfit to be made by some other lady, – by some woman who had not already advocated the increased employment of women. Let Miss Faithfull look to that. Not that she will work the flesh off her young women's bones, or allow such terrible consequences to take place in Coram-street; not that she or that those connected with her in that enterprise will do aught but good to those employed therein. It will not even be said of her individually, or of her partners, that they have worked the flesh off women's bones; but may it not come to this, that when the tasks now done by men have been shifted to the shoulders of women, women themselves will so complain. May it not go further, and come even to this, that women will have cause for such complaint. I do not think that such a result will come, because I do not think that the object desired by those who are active in the matter will be attained. Men, as a general rule among civilized nations, have elected to earn their own bread and the bread of the women also, and from this resolve on their part I do not think that they will be beaten off.

(Vol. One, Chapter XVIII)

A chastening incident

It is not that I, who, at any rate, can read and write, have cause to wish that I had been an American. But it is this; – if you and I can count up in a day all those on whom our eyes may rest, and learn the circumstances of their lives, we shall be driven to conclude that nine-tenths of that number would have had a better life as Americans than they can have in their spheres as Englishmen. The States are at a discount with us now, in the beginning of this year of grace 1862; and Englishmen were not very willing to admit the above statement, even when the States were not at a discount. But I do not think that a man can travel through the States with his eyes open and not admit the fact. Many things will conspire to induce him to shut his eyes and admit no conclusion favourable to the Americans. Men and women will sometimes be impudent to him; – the better his coat, the greater the impudence. He will be pelted with the braggadocio[25] of equality. The corns of his Old-World conservatism will be trampled on hourly by the purposely vicious herd of uncouth democracy. The fact that he is paymaster will go for nothing, and will fail to insure civility. I shall never forget my agony as I saw and heard my desk fall from a porter's hand on a railway station, as he tossed it from him seven yards off on to the hard pavement. I heard its poor weak intestines rattle in their death-struggle, and knowing that it was smashed I forgot my position on American soil and remonstrated. 'It's my desk, and you have utterly destroyed it,' I said. 'Ha! ha! ha!' laughed the porter. 'You've destroyed my property,' I rejoined, 'and it's no laughing matter.' And then all the crowd laughed. 'Guess you'd better get it glued,' said one. So I gathered up the broken article and retired mournfully and crestfallen into a coach. This was very sad, and for the moment I deplored the ill-luck which had brought me to so savage a country. Such and such like are the incidents which make an Englishman in the States unhappy, and rouse his gall against the institutions of the country; – these things and the continued appliance of the irritating ointment of American braggadocio with which his sores are kept open. But though I was badly off on that railway platform, – worse off than I should have been in England, – all that crowd of porters round me were better off than our English porters.

(Vol. One, Chapter XIX)

Washington

I have a strong idea, which I expressed before in speaking of the capital of the Canadas, that no man can ordain that on such a spot shall be built a great and thriving city. No man can so ordain even though he leave him behind him, as was the case with Washington,[26] a prestige sufficient to bind his successors to his wishes. The political leaders of the country have done what they could for Washington. The pride of the nation has endeavoured to sustain the character of its chosen metropolis. There has been no rival, soliciting favour on the strength of other charms. The country has all been agreed on the point since the father of the country first commenced the work. Florence and Rome in Italy have each their pretensions; but in the States no other city has put itself forward for the honour of entertaining Congress. And yet Washington has been a failure. It is commerce that makes great cities, and commerce has refused to back the General's choice. New York and Philadelphia, without any political power, have become great among the cities of the earth. They are beaten by none except by London and Paris. But Washington is but a ragged, unfinished collection of unbuilt broad streets, as to the completion of which there can now, I imagine, be but little hope.

Of all places that I know it is the most ungainly and most unsatisfactory; – I fear I must also say the most presumptuous in its pretensions. There is a map of Washington accurately laid down; and taking that map with him in his journeyings a man may lose himself in the streets, not as one loses oneself in London between Shoreditch and Russell Square, but as one does so in the deserts of the Holy Land, between Emmaus and Arimathea. In the first place no one knows where the places are, or is sure of their existence, and then between their presumed localities the country is wild, trackless, unbridged, uninhabited, and desolate. Massachusetts Avenue runs the whole length of the city, and is inserted on the maps as a full-blown street, about four miles in length. Go there, and you will find yourself not only out of town, away among the fields, but you will find yourself beyond the fields, in an uncultivated, undrained wilderness. Tucking your trousers up to your knees you will wade through the bogs, you will lose yourself among rude hillocks, you will be out of the reach of humanity. The unfinished dome of the Capitol will loom before you in the distance, and you will think that you approach the ruins of some western Palmyra.[27] If you are a sportsman, you will desire to shoot snipe within sight of the President's house. There is much unsettled land within the States of America, but I think none so desolate in its state of nature as three-fourths of the ground on which is supposed to stand the city of Washington.

(Vol. Two, Chapter I)

The White House

The President's house – or the White House as it is now called all the world over – is a handsome mansion fitted for the chief officer of a great Republic, and nothing more. I think I may say

that we have private houses in London considerably larger. It is
neat and pretty, and with all its immediate outside belongings
calls down no adverse criticism. It faces on to a small garden,
which seems to be always accessible to the public, and opens out
upon that everlasting Pennsylvania Avenue, which has now
made another turn. Here in front of the White House is President's Square, as it is generally called. The technical name is, I
believe, La Fayette Square.[28] The houses round it are few in
number, – not exceeding three or four on each side, but they are
among the best in Washington, and the whole place is neat and
well kept. President's Square is certainly the most attractive part
of the city. The garden of the square is always open, and does not
seem to suffer from any public ill-usage; by which circumstance
I am again led to suggest that the gardens of our London squares
might be thrown open in the same way. In the centre of this one
at Washington, immediately facing the President's house, is an
equestrian statue of General Jackson.[29] It is very bad; but that it
is not nearly as bad as it might be is proved by another equestrian
statue, – of General Washington, – erected in the centre of a
small garden-plat at the end of Pennsylvania Avenue, near the
bridge leading to Georgetown. Of all the statues on horseback
which I ever saw, either in marble or bronze, this is by far the
worst and most ridiculous. The horse is most absurd, but the man
sitting on the horse is manifestly drunk. I should think the time
must come when this figure at any rate will be removed.[30]

(Vol. Two, Chapter I)

Congress and the army

There is a building in Washington, built by private munificence
and devoted, according to an inscription which it bears, 'To the
Arts.' It has been turned into an army clothing establishment.
The streets of Washington, night and day, were thronged with
army waggons. All through the city military huts and military
tents were to be seen, pitched out among the mud and in the
desert places. Then there was the chosen locality of the teamsters
and their mules and horses – a wonderful world in itself; and all

within the city! Here horses and mules lived, – or died, – sub dio,[31] with no slightest apology for a stable over them, eating their provender from off the waggons to which they were fastened. Here, there, and everywhere large houses were occupied as the head-quarters of some officer, or the bureau of some military official. At Washington and round Washington the army was everything. While this was so, is it to be conceived that Congress should ask questions about military matters with success?

All this, as I say, filled me with sorrow. I hate military belongings, and am disgusted at seeing the great affairs of a nation put out of their regular course. Congress to me is respectable. Parliamentary debates, be they ever so prosy, – as with us, or even so rowdy, as sometimes they have been with our cousins across the water, – engage my sympathies. I bow inwardly before a Speaker's chair, and look upon the elected representatives of any nation, as the choice men of the age. Those muddy, clattering dragoons, sitting at the corners of the streets with dirty woollen comforters round their ears, were to me hideous in the extreme. But there at Washington, at the period of which I am writing, I was forced to acknowledge that Congress was at a discount, and that the rough-shod generals were the men of the day. 'Pack them up and send them in boxes to their several States.' It would come to that, I thought, or to something like that unless Congress would consent to be submissive. 'I have yet to learn – !' said indignant members, stamping with their feet on the floor of the house. One would have said that by that time the lesson might almost have been understood.

(Vol. Two, Chapter II)

His views on abolition

I confess that this cry of abolition has been made peculiarly displeasing to me, by the fact that the northern abolitionist is by no means willing to give even to the negro who is already free that position in the world which alone might tend to raise him in the scale of human beings, – if anything can so raise him and make him fit for freedom. The abolitionists hold that the negro is the white man's equal. I do not. I see, or think that I see, that the negro is the white man's inferior through laws of nature. That he is not mentally fit to cope with white men, – I speak of the full-blooded negro, – and that he must fill a position simply servile. But the abolitionist declares him to be the white man's equal. But yet, when he has him at his elbow, he treats him with a scorn which even the negro can hardly endure. I will give him political equality, but no social equality, says the abolitionist. But even in this he is untrue. A black man may vote in New York, but he cannot vote under the same circumstances as a white man. He is subjected to qualifications which in truth debar him from the poll. A white man votes by manhood suffrage, providing he has been for one year an inhabitant of his State; but a man of colour must have been for three years a citizen of the State, and must own a property qualification of 50% free of debt. But political equality is not what such men want, nor indeed is it social equality. It is social tolerance and social sympathy; and these are denied to the negro. An American abolitionist would not sit at table with a negro. He might do so in England at the house of an English duchess; but in his own country the proposal of such a companion would be an insult to him. He will not sit with him in a public carriage if he can avoid it. In New York I have seen special street-cars for coloured people. The abolitionist is struck with horror when he thinks that a man and a brother should be a slave; but when the man and the brother has been made free, he is regarded with loathing and contempt. All this I cannot see with equanimity. There is falsehood in it from the beginning to the end. The slave as a rule is well treated, – gets all he wants and almost all he desires. The free negro as a rule is ill treated, and does not get that consideration which alone might put him in the worldly position for which his advocate declares him to be fit. It is false throughout, – this preaching. The negro is not the white man's equal by nature. But to the free negro in the northern States his inequality is increased by the white man's hardness to him.

(Vol. Two, Chapter III)

A nostalgic visit

I had some little personal feeling in visiting Cincinnati, because my mother had lived there for some time, and had there been concerned in a commercial enterprise, by which no one, I believe, made any great sum of money.[32] Between thirty and forty years ago she built a bazaar in Cincinnati, which I was assured by the present owner of the house, was at the time of its erection considered to be the great building of the town. It has been sadly eclipsed now, and by no means rears its head proudly among the great blocks around it. It had become a 'Physico-medical Institute' when I was there, and was under the dominion of a quack doctor on one side, and of a college of rights-of-women female medical professors on the other. 'I believe, sir, no man or woman ever yet made a dollar in that building; and as for rent, I don't even expect it.' Such was the account given of the unfortunate bazaar by the present proprietor.

(Vol. Two, Chapter IV)

Kentucky slaves

A gentleman in Kentucky does not sell his slaves. To do so is considered to be low and mean, and is opposed to the aristocratic traditions of the country. A man who does so willingly, puts himself beyond the pale of good-fellowship with his neighbours. A sale of slaves is regarded as a sign almost of bankruptcy. If a man cannot pay his debts, his creditors can step in and sell his slaves; but he does not himself make the sale. When a man owns more slaves than he needs, he hires them out by the year; and when he requires more than he owns, he takes them on hire by the year. Care is taken in such hirings not to remove a married man away from his home. The price paid for a negro's labour at the time of my visit was about a hundred dollars, or twenty pounds, for the year; but this price was then extremely low in consequence of the war disturbances. The usual price had been about fifty or sixty per cent above this. The man who takes the negro on hire feeds him, clothes him, provides him with a bed,

and supplies him with medical attendance. I went into some of
their cottages on the estate which I visited, and was not in the
least surprised to find them preferable in size, furniture, and all
material comforts to the dwellings of most of our own agricultural labourers. Any comparison between the material comfort of a
Kentucky slave and an English ditcher and delver would be
preposterous. The Kentucky slave never wants for clothing fitted
to the weather. He eats meat twice a day, and has three good
meals; he knows no limit but his own appetite; his work is light;
he has many varieties of amusement; he has instant medical
assistance at all periods of necessity for himself, his wife, and his
children. Of course he pays no rent, fears no baker, and knows
no hunger. I would not have it supposed that I conceive slavery
with all these comforts to be equal to freedom without them; nor
do I conceive that the negro can be made equal to the white man.
But in discussing the condition of the negro, it is necessary that
we should understand what are the advantages of which abolition would deprive him, and in what condition he has been
placed by the daily receipt of such advantages. If a negro slave
wants new shoes, he asks for them, and receives them, with the
undoubting simplicity of a child. Such a state of things has its
picturesquely patriarchal side; but what would be the state of
such a man if he were emancipated to-morrow?

(Vol. Two, Chapter IV)

Political dishonesty

Who has not known that hour of misery when in the sullenness
of the heart all help has been refused, and misfortune has been
made welcome to do her worst? So is it now with those once
United States. The man who can see without inward tears the
self-inflicted wounds of that American people can hardly have
within his bosom the tenderness of an Englishman's heart.

But the strong runner will rise again to his feet, even though
he be stunned by his fall. He will rise again, and will have learned
something by his sorrow. His anger will pass away, and he will
again brace himself for his work. What great race has ever been

won by any man, or by any nation, without some such fall during
its course? Have we not all declared that some check to that
career was necessary? Men in their pursuit of intelligence had
forgotten to be honest; in struggling for greatness they had
discarded purity. The nation has been great, but the statesmen of
the nation have been little. Men have hardly been ambitious to
govern, but they have coveted the wages of governors. Corruption has crept into high places, – into places that should have
been high, – till of all holes and corners in the land they have
become the lowest. No public man has been trusted for ordinary
honesty. It is not by foreign voices, by English newspapers or in
French pamphlets, that the corruption of American politicians
has been exposed, but by American voices and by the American
press. It is to be heard on every side. Ministers of the cabinet,
senators, representatives, State legislatures, officers of the army,
officials of the navy, contractors of every grade, – all who are
presumed to touch, or to have the power of touching public
money, are thus accused. For years it has been so. The word
politician has stunk in men's nostrils. When I first visited New
York, some three years since, I was warned not to know a man,
because he was a 'politician.' We in England define a man of a
certain class as a black-leg. How has it come about that in
American ears the word politician has come to bear a similar
signification?

(Vol. Two, Chapter V)

The army at Rolla

Those in front are divided, not into separate huts, but into
chambers capable of containing nearly two hundred men each.
They were surrounded on the inside by great wooden trays, in
three tiers, – and on each tray four men were supposed to sleep.
I went into one or two while the crowd of soldiers was in them,
but found it inexpedient to stay there long. The stench of those
places was foul beyond description. Never in my life before had
I been in a place so horrid to the eyes and nose as Benton
barracks. The path along the front outside was deep in mud. The

whole space between the two rows of sheds was one field of mud, so slippery that the foot could not stand. Inside and outside every spot was deep in mud. The soldiers were mud-stained from head to foot. These volunteer soldiers are in their nature dirty, as must be all men brought together in numerous bodies without special appliances for cleanliness, or control and discipline as to their personal habits. But the dirt of the men in the Benton barracks surpassed any dirt that I had hitherto seen. Nor could it have been otherwise with them. They were surrounded by a sea of mud, and the foul hovels in which they were made to sleep and live were fetid with stench and reeking with filth. I had at this time been joined by another Englishman, and we went through this place together. When we inquired as to the health of the men, we heard the saddest tales, – of three hundred men gone out of one regiment, of whole companies that had perished, of hospitals crowded with fevered patients. Measles had been the great scourge of the soldiers here, – as it had also been in the army of the Potomac. I shall not soon forget my visits to Benton barracks. It may be that our own soldiers were as badly treated in the Crimea; or that French soldiers were treated worse on their march into Russia.[33] It may be that dirt, and wretchedness, disease and listless idleness, a descent from manhood to habits lower than those of the beasts, are necessary in warfare. I have sometimes thought that it is so; but I am no military critic and will not say. This I say, – that the degradation of men to the state in which I saw the American soldiers in Benton barracks, is disgraceful to humanity.

(Vol. Two, Chapter V)

The men of the west

No men love money with more eager love than these western men, but they bear the loss of it as an Indian bears his torture at the stake. They are energetic in trade, speculating deeply whenever speculation is possible; but nevertheless they are slow in motion, loving to loaf about. They are slow in speech, preferring to sit in silence, with the tobacco between their teeth. They drink, but are seldom drunk to the eye; they begin at it early in the morning, and take it in a solemn, sullen, ugly manner, standing always at a bar; swallowing their spirits, and saying nothing as they swallow it. They drink often, and to great excess; but they carry if off without noise, sitting down and ruminating over it with the everlasting cud within their jaws. I believe that a stranger might go into the West, and passing from hotel to hotel through a dozen of them, might sit for hours at each in the large everlasting public hall, and never have a word addressed to him. No stranger should travel in the western States, or indeed in any of the States, without letters of introduction. It is the custom of the country, and they are easily procured. Without them everything is barren; for men do not travel in the States of America as they do in Europe, to see scenery and visit the marvels of old cities which are open to all the world. The social and political life of the Americans must constitute the interest of the traveller, and to these he can hardly make his way without introductions.

(Vol. Two, Chapter V)

The bank of the Ohio

I never saw a sadder picture, or one which did more to awaken pity for those whose fate had fixed their abodes in such a locality. And yet there was a beauty about it too, – a melancholy, death-like beauty. The disordered ruin and confused decay of the forest was all gemmed with particles of ice. The eye reaching through the thin underwood could form for itself picturesque shapes and solitary bowers of broken wood, which were bright with the opaque brightness of the hoar-frost. The great river ran noise-lessly along, rapid, but still with an apparent lethargy in its waters. The ground beneath our feet was fertile beyond compare, but as yet fertile to death rather than to life. Where we then trod man had not yet come with his axe and his plough; but the railroad was close to us, and within a mile of the spot thousands of dollars had been spent in raising a city which was to have been rich with the united wealth of the rivers and the land. Hitherto fever and ague, mud and malaria, had been too strong for man, and the

dollars had been spent in vain. The day, however, will come
when this promontory between the two great rivers will be a fit
abode for industry. Men will settle there, wandering down from
the North and East, and toil sadly, and leave their bones among
the mud. Thin, pale-faced, joyless mothers will come there, and
grow old before their time; and sickly children will be born,
struggling up with wan faces to their sad life's labour. But the
work will go on, for it is God's work; and the earth will be
prepared for the people, and the fat rottenness of the still living
forest will be made to give forth its riches.

(Vol. Two, Chapter VI)

The Green River

But perhaps the greatest charm of the place to me was the beauty
of the scenery. The Green River at this spot is as picturesque a
stream as I ever remember to have seen in such a country. It lies
low down between high banks, and curves hither and thither,
never keeping a straight line. Its banks are wooded; but not, as is
so common in America, by continuous, stunted, uninteresting
forest, but by large single trees standing on small patches of
meadow by the water-side, with the high banks rising over them,
with glades through them open for the horseman. The rides here
in summer must be very lovely. Even in winter they were so, and
made me in love with the place in spite of that brown, dull,
barren aspect which the presence of an army always creates. I
have said that the railway bridge which crossed the Green River
at this spot had been destroyed by the secessionists. This had
been done effectually as regarded the passage of trains, but only
in part as regarded the absolute fabric of the bridge. It had been,
and still was when I saw it, a beautifully light construction, made
of iron and supported over a valley, rather than over a river, on
tall stone piers. One of these piers had been blown up; but when
we were there, the bridge had been repaired with beams and
wooden shafts. This had just been completed, and an engine had
passed over it. It looked to me most perilously insecure; but the
eye uneducated in such mysteries is a bad judge of engineering

work. I passed with a horse backwards and forwards on it, and it did not tumble down then; but I confess that on the first attempt I was glad enough to lead the horse by the bridle.

(Vol. Two, Chapter VI)

The army of the Potomac

I have been informed by those who professed to know that it contained over 200,000 men, and by others who also professed to know, that it did not contain 100,000. To me the soldiers seemed to be innumerable, hanging like locusts over the whole country, – a swarm desolating everything around them. Those pomps and circumstances are not glorious in my eyes. They affect me with a melancholy which I cannot avoid. Soldiers gathered together in a camp are uncouth and ugly when they are idle; and when they are at work their work is worse than idleness. When I have seen a thousand men together, moving their feet hither at one sound and thither at another, throwing their muskets about awkwardly, prodding at the air with their bayonets, trotting twenty paces here and backing ten paces there, wheeling round in uneven lines, and looking, as they did so, miserably conscious of the absurdity of their own performances, I have always been inclined to think how little the world can have advanced in civilization, while grown-up men are still forced to spend their days in such grotesque performances. Those to whom the 'pomps and circumstances' are dear – nay, those by whom they are considered simply necessary – will be able to confute me by a thousand arguments. I readily own myself confuted. There must be soldiers, and soldiers must be taught. But not the less pitiful is it to see men of thirty undergoing the goose-step, and tortured by orders as to the proper mode of handling a long instrument which is half-gun and half-spear. In the days of Hector and Ajax,[34] the thing was done in a more picturesque manner, and the songs of battle should, I think, be confined to those ages.

(Vol. Two, Chapter VII)

Baltimore revisited

I passed again through Pittsburg, and over the Alleghany mountains by Altoona, and down to Baltimore, – back into civilization,
secession, conversation, and gastronomy. I never had secessionist sympathies and never expressed them. I always believed in the
North as a people, – discrediting, however, to the utmost the
existing northern Government, or, as I should more properly say,
the existing northern Cabinet; but nevertheless, with such feelings and such belief, I found myself very happy at Baltimore.
Putting aside Boston, which must, I think, be generally preferred
by Englishmen to any other city in the States, I should choose
Baltimore as my residence if I were called upon to live in America. I am not led to this opinion, if I know myself, solely by the
canvas-back ducks; and as to the terrapins, I throw them to the
winds. The madeira, which is still kept there with a reverence
which I should call superstitious were it not that its free circulation among outside worshippers prohibits the just use of such a
word, may have something to do with it; as may also the beauty
of the women, – to some small extent. Trifles do bear upon our
happiness in a manner that we do not ourselves understand, and
of which we are unconscious. But there was an English look
about the streets and houses which I think had as much to do
with it as either the wine, the women, or the ducks; and it seemed
to me as though the manners of the people of Maryland were
more English than those of other Americans.

(Vol. Two, Chapter VIII)

Mud!

During my second visit to Baltimore I went over to Washington
for a day or two, and found the capital still under the empire of
King Mud. How the élite of a nation – for the inhabitants of
Washington consider themselves to be the élite – can consent to
live in such a state of thraldom, a foreigner cannot understand.
Were I to say that it was intended to be typical of the condition
of the government, I might be considered cynical; but undoubtedly

the sloughs of despond[35] which were deepest in their despond-
ency were to be found in localities which gave an appearance of
truth to such a surmise. The Secretary of State's office in which
Mr Seward[36] was still reigning, though with diminished glory,
was divided from the Head-Quarters of the Commander-in-
Chief, which are immediately opposite to it, by an opaque river
which admitted of no transit. These buildings stand at the corner
of President Square, and it had been long understood that any
close intercourse between them had not been considered desirable by the occupants of the military side of the causeway. But
the Secretary of State's office was altogether unapproachable
without a long circuit and begrimed legs. The Secretary-at-War's
department was, if possible, in a worse condition. This is situated on the other side of the President's house, and the mud lay,
if possible, thicker in this quarter than it did round Mr Seward's
chambers. The passage over Pennsylvania Avenue, immediately
in front of the War Office, was a thing not to be attempted in
those days. Mr Cameron, it is true, had gone, and Mr Stanton[37]
was installed; but the labour of cleansing the interior of that
establishment had hitherto allowed no time for a glance at the
exterior dirt, and Mr Stanton should, perhaps, be held as excused.
That the Navy Office should be buried in mud, and quite debarred from approach, was to be expected. The space immediately in
front of Mr Lincoln's own residence was still kept fairly clean,
and I am happy to be able to give testimony to this effect. Long
may it remain so. I could not, however, but think that an energetic and careful President would have seen to the removal of the
dirt from his own immediate neighbourhood. It was something
that his own shoes should remain unpolluted; but the foul mud
always clinging to the boots and leggings of those by whom he
was daily surrounded must, I should think, have been offensive
to him. The entrance to the Treasury was difficult to achieve by
those who had not learned by practice the ways of the place; but
I must confess that a tolerably clear passage was maintained on
that side which led immediately down to the halls of Congress.
Up at the Capitol the mud was again triumphant in the front of
the building; this however was not of great importance, as the
legislative chambers of the States are always reached by the

back-door. I, on this occasion, attempted to leave the building by the grand entrance, but I soon became entangled among rivers of mud and mazes of shifting sand. With difficulty I recovered my steps, and finding my way back to the building was forced to content myself by an exit among the crowd of senators and representatives who were thronging down the back-stairs.

Of dirt of all kinds it behoves Washington and those concerned in Washington to make themselves free. It is the Augean stables[38] through which some American Hercules must turn a purifying river before the American people can justly boast either of their capital or of their government. As to the material mud, enough has been said. The presence of the army perhaps caused it, and the excessive quantity of rain which had fallen may also be taken as a fair plea. But what excuse shall we find for that other dirt? It also had been caused by the presence of the army, and by that long-continued down-pouring of contracts which had fallen like Danaë's golden shower[39] into the laps of those who understood how to avail themselves of such heavenly waters.

(Vol. Two, Chapter VIII)

The probable fate of the South

Such is the light in which the struggle is regarded by the two parties, and such the hopes and feelings which have been engendered. It may therefore be surmised with what amount of neighbourly love secessionist and northern neighbours regarded each other in such towns as Baltimore and Washington. Of course there was hatred of the deepest dye; of course there were muttered curses, or curses which sometimes were not simply muttered. Of course there were wretchedness, heart-burnings, and fearful divisions in families. That, perhaps, was the worst of all. The daughter's husband would be in the northern ranks, while the son was fighting in the South; or two sons would hold equal rank in the two armies, sometimes sending to each other frightful threats of personal vengeance. Old friends would meet each other in the street, passing without speaking; or, worse still, would utter words of insult for which payment is to be demanded when a southern gentleman may again be allowed to quarrel in his own defence.

And yet society went on. Women still smiled, and men were happy to whom such smiles were given. Cakes and ale were going and ginger was still hot in the mouth.[40] When many were together no words of unhappiness were heard. It was at those small meetings of two or three that women would weep instead of smiling, and that men would run their hands through their hair and sit in silence, thinking of their ruined hopes and divided children.

I have spoken of southern hopes and northern fears, and have endeavoured to explain the feelings of each party. For myself I think that the Southerners have been wrong in their hopes, and that those of the North have been wrong in their fears. It is not better to rule in hell than serve in heaven.[41] Of course a southern gentleman will not admit the premises which are here by me taken for granted. The hell to which I allude is, the sad position of a low and debased nation. Such, I think, will be the fate of the Gulf States, if they succeed in obtaining secession, – of a low and debased nation, or, worse still, of many low and debased nations. They will have lost their cotton monopoly by the competition created during the period of the war, and will have no material of greatness on which either to found themselves or to flourish. That they had much to bear when linked with the North, much to endure on account of that slavery from which it was all but impossible that they should disentangle themselves, may probably be true. But so have all political parties among all free nations much to bear from political opponents, and yet other free nations do not go to pieces.

(Vol. Two, Chapter VIII)

A Boston story

During my last week there the world of Boston was moving itself on sleighs. There was not a wheel to be seen in the town. The omnibuses and public carriages had been dismounted from their axles and put themselves upon snow runners, and the private world had taken out its winter carriages, and wrapped itself up in buffalo robes. Men now spoke of the coming thaw as of a misfortune which must come, but which a kind Providence might perhaps postpone, – as we all, in short, speak of death. In the morning the snow would have been hardened by the night's frost, and men would look happy and contented. By an hour after noon the streets would be all wet, and the ground would be slushy and men would look gloomy and speak of speedy dissolution. There were those who would always prophesy that the next day would see the snow converted into one dull, dingy river. Such I regarded as seers of tribulation, and endeavoured with all my mind to disbelieve their interpretations of the signs. That sleighing was excellent fun. For myself I must own that I hardly saw the best of it at Boston, for the coming of the end was already at hand when I arrived there, and the fresh beauty of the hard snow was gone. Moreover when I essayed to show my prowess with a pair of horses on the established course for such equipages, the beasts ran away, knowing that I was not practised in the use of snow chariots, and brought me to grief and shame. There was a lady with me on the sleigh whom, for a while, I felt that I was doomed to consign to a snowy grave, – whom I would willingly have overturned into a drift of snow, so as to avoid worse consequences, had I only known how to do so. But Providence, even though without curbs and assisted only by simple snaffles, did at last prevail; and I brought the sleigh, horses, and lady alive back to Boston, whether with or without permanent injury I have never yet ascertained.

(Vol. Two, Chapter VIII)

He takes more professional interest

It is, I think, undoubtedly true that the amount of accommodation given by the Post-office of the States is small, – as compared with that afforded in some other countries, and that that accommodation is lessened by delays and uncertainty. The point which first struck me was the inconvenient hours at which mails were brought in and despatched. Here, in England, it is the object of our Post-office to carry the bulk of our letters at night; to deliver them as early as possible in the morning, and to collect them and take them away for despatch as late as may be in the day; – so that the merchant may receive his letters before the beginning of his day's business, and despatch them after its close. The bulk of our letters is handled in this manner, and the advantage of such an arrangement is manifest. But it seemed that in the States no such practice prevailed. Letters arrived at any hour in the day miscellaneously, and were despatched at any hour, and I found that the postmaster at one town could never tell me with certainty when letters would arrive at another. If the towns were distant, I would be told that the conveyance might take about two or three days; if they were near, that my letter would get to hand, 'some time to-morrow.' I ascertained, moreover, by painful experience that the whole of a mail would not always go forward by the first despatch. As regarded myself this had reference chiefly to English letters and newspapers. – 'Only a part of the mail has come,' the clerk would tell me. With us the owners of that part which did not 'come,' would consider themselves greatly aggrieved and make loud complaint. But, in the States, complaints made against official departments are held to be of little moment.

Letters also in the States are subject to great delays by irregularities on railways. One train does not hit the town of its destination before another train, to which it is nominally fitted, has been started on its journey. The mail trains are not bound to wait; and thus, in the large cities, far distant from New York, great irregularity prevails. It is owing to this, – at any rate partly to this, – that the system of telegraphing has become so prevalent. It is natural that this should be so between towns which are in the due course of post perhaps forty-eight hours asunder; but the uncertainty of the post increases the habit, to the profit, of course, of the companies which own the wires, – but to the manifest loss of the Post-office.

But the deficiency which struck me most forcibly in the American Post-office, was the absence of any recognized official delivery of letters. The United States Post-office does not assume to itself the duty of taking letters to the houses of those for whom they are intended, but holds itself as having completed the work for which the original postage has been paid, when it has brought them to the window of the Post-office of the town to which they are addressed. It is true that in most large towns, – though by no means in all, – a separate arrangement is made by which a delivery is afforded to those who are willing to pay a further sum for that further service; but the recognized official mode of delivery is from the office window. The merchants and persons in trade have boxes at the windows, for which they pay. Other old-established inhabitants in towns, and persons in receipt of a considerable correspondence, receive their letters by the subsidiary carriers and pay for them separately. But the poorer classes of the community, those persons among which it is of such paramount importance to increase the blessing of letter writing, obtain their letters from the Post-office windows.

(Vol. Two, Chapter XIII)

Hotel food

How I did learn to hate those little dishes and their greasy contents! At a London eating-house things are often not very nice, but your meat is put on a plate and comes before you in an edible shape. At these hotels it is brought to you in horrid little oval dishes, and swims in grease. Gravy is not an institution at American hotels, but grease has taken its place. It is palpable, undisguised grease, floating in rivers, – not grease caused by accidental bad cookery, but grease on purpose. A beef-steak is not a beef-steak unless a quarter of a pound of butter be added to it. Those horrid little dishes! If one thinks of it how could they have been made to contain Christian food? Every article in that long list is liable to the call of any number of guests for four hours. Under such circumstances how can food be made eatable? Your roast mutton is brought to you raw; – if you object to that you are supplied with meat that has been four times brought before the public. At hotels on the continent of Europe different dinners are cooked at different hours, but here the same dinner is kept always going. The house breakfast is maintained on a similar footing. Huge boilers of tea and coffee are stewed down and kept hot. To me those meals were odious. It is of course open to any one to have separate dinners and separate breakfasts in his own room; but by this little is gained and much is lost. He or she who is so exclusive pays twice over for such meals, – as they are charged as extras on the bill; and, after all, receives the advantage of no exclusive cooking. Particles from the public dinners are brought to the private room, and the same odious little dishes make their appearance.

(Vol. Two, Chapter XIV)

Newspapers

The newspapers of the States generally may not only be said to have reached none of the virtues here named, but to have fallen into all the opposite vices. In the first place they are never true. In requiring truth from a newspaper the public should not be anxious to strain at gnats. A statement setting forth that a certain gooseberry was five inches in circumference, whereas in truth its girth was only two and a half, would give me no offence. Nor would I be offended at being told that Lord Derby was appointed to the premiership, while in truth the Queen had only sent for his lordship, having as yet come to no definite arrangement.[42] The demand for truth which may reasonably be made upon a newspaper amounts to this, – that nothing should be stated not believed to be true, and that nothing should be stated as to which the truth is important, without adequate ground for such belief. If a newspaper accuse me of swindling, it is not sufficient that the writer believe me to be a swindler. He should have ample and sufficient ground for such belief; – otherwise in making such a statement he will write falsely. In our private life we all recognize the fact that this is so. It is understood that a man is not a whit the less a slanderer because he believes the slander which he promulgates. But it seems to me that this is not sufficiently recognized by many who write for the public press. Evil things are said, and are probably believed by the writers; they are said with that special skill for which newspaper writers have in our days become so conspicuous, defying alike redress by law or redress by argument;

but they are too often said falsely. The words are not measured when they are written, and they are allowed to go forth without any sufficient inquiry into their truth. But if there be any ground for such complaint here in England, that ground is multiplied ten times – twenty times – in the States. This is not only shown in the abuse of individuals, in abuse which is as violent as it is perpetual, but in the treatment of every subject which is handled. All idea of truth has been thrown overboard. It seems to be admitted that the only object is to produce a sensation, and that it is admitted by both writer and reader that sensation and veracity are incompatible. Falsehood has become so much a matter of course with American newspapers that it has almost ceased to be falsehood. Nobody thinks me a liar because I deny that I am at home when I am in my study. The nature of the arrangement is generally understood. So also is it with the American newspapers.

But American newspapers are also unreadable. It is very bad that they should be false, but it is very surprising that they should be dull. Looking at the general intelligence of the people, one would have thought that a readable newspaper, put out with all pleasant appurtenances of clear type, good paper, and good internal arrangement, would have been a thing specially within their reach. But they have failed in every detail. Though their papers are always loaded with sensation headings, there are seldom sensation paragraphs to follow. The paragraphs do not fit the headings. Either they cannot be found, or if found they seem to have escaped from their proper column to some distant and remote portion of the sheet. One is led to presume that no American editor has any plan in the composition of his newspaper. I never know whether I have as yet got to the very heart's core of the daily journal, or whether I am still to go on searching for that heart's core. Alas, it too often happens that there is no heart's core! The whole thing seems to have been put out at haphazard. And then the very writing is in itself below mediocrity; – as though a power of expression in properly arranged language was not required by a newspaper editor, either as regards himself or as regards his subordinates. One is driven to suppose that the writers for the daily press are not chosen with any view to such capability. A man ambitious of being on the staff of an American newspaper should be capable of much work, should be satisfied with small pay, should be indifferent to the world's good usage, should be rough, ready, and of long sufferance; but, above all, he should be smart. The type of almost all American newspapers is wretched – I think I may say of all; – so wretched that that alone forbids one to hope for pleasure in reading them. They are ill-written, ill-printed, ill-arranged, and in fact are not readable. They are bought, glanced at, and thrown away.

(Vol. Two, Chapter XV)

A backward glance

I know that I shall never again be at Boston, and that I have said that about the Americans which would make me unwelcome as a guest if I were there. It is in this that my regret consists; – for this reason that I would wish to remember so many social hours as though they had been passed in sleep. They who will expect blessings from me, will say among themselves that I have cursed them. As I read the pages which I have written I feel that words which I intended for blessings when I prepared to utter them have gone nigh to turn themselves into curses.

I have ever admired the United States as a nation. I have loved their liberty, their prowess, their intelligence, and their progress. I have sympathized with a people who themselves have had no sympathy with passive security and inaction. I have felt confidence in them, and have known, as it were, that their industry must enable them to succeed as a people, while their freedom would insure to them success as a nation. With these convictions I went among them wishing to write of them good words, – words which might be pleasant for them to read, while they might assist perhaps in producing a true impression of them here at home. But among my good words there are so many which are bitter, that I fear I shall have failed in my object as regards them. And it seems to me, as I read once more my own pages, that in saying evil things of my friends, I have used language stronger than I intended; whereas I have omitted to express myself with emphasis when I have attempted to say good things. Why need I have told of the mud of Washington, or have exposed the nakedness of Cairo? Why did I speak with such eager enmity of those poor women in the New York cars, who never injured me, now that I think of it? Ladies of New York, as I write this, the words which were written among you, are printed and cannot be expunged; but I tender to you my apologies from my home in England. And as to that Van Wyck committee![43] Might I not have left those contractors to be dealt with by their own Congress, seeing that that Congress committee was by no means inclined to spare them? I might have kept my pages free from gall, and have sent my sheets to the press unhurt by the conviction that I was hurting those who had dealt kindly by me! But what then? Was any people ever truly served by eulogy; or an honest cause furthered by undue praise?

(Vol. Two, Chapter XVI)

Second thoughts

And now had come the end of my adventures, and as I set my foot once more upon the deck of the Cunard steamer I felt that my work was done. Whether it were done ill or well, or whether indeed any approach to the doing of it had been attained, all had been done that I could accomplish. No further opportunity remained to me of seeing, hearing, or of speaking. I had come out thither, having resolved to learn a little that I might if possible teach that little to others; and now the lesson was learned, or must remain unlearned. But in carrying out my resolution I had gradually risen in my ambition, and had mounted from one stage of inquiry to another, till at last I had found myself burdened with the task of ascertaining whether or not the Americans were doing their work as a nation well or ill; and now if ever, I must be prepared to put forth the result of my inquiry. As I walked up and down the deck of the steamboat I confess I felt that I had been somewhat arrogant. . . .

But again I put in my slight plea. In doing as I have done, I have at least done my best. I have endeavoured to judge without prejudice, and to hear with honest ears, and to see with honest eyes. The subject, moreover, on which I have written, is one which, though great, is so universal in its bearings, that it may be said to admit of being handled without impropriety by the unlearned as well as the learned; – by those who have grown gray in the study of constitutional lore, and by those who have simply looked on at the government of men as we all look on at those matters which daily surround us. There are matters as to which a man should never take a pen in hand unless he has given to them much labour. The botanist must have learned to trace the herbs and flowers before he can presume to tell us how God has formed them. But the death of Hector is a fit subject for a boy's verses though Homer also sang of it.[44] I feel that there is scope for a book on the United States' form of government as it was founded, and as it has since framed itself, which might do honour to the life-long studies of some one of those great constitutional pundits whom we have among us; but, nevertheless, the plain words of a man who is no pundit need not disgrace the subject, if they be honestly written, and if he who writes them has in his heart an honest love of liberty. Such were my thoughts as I walked the deck of the Cunard steamer. Then I descended to my cabin, settled my luggage, and prepared for the continuance of my work. It was fourteen days from that time before I reached London, but the fourteen days to me were not unpleasant. The demon of seasickness usually spares me, and if I can find on board one or two who are equally fortunate – who can eat with me, drink with me, and talk with me – I do not know that a passage across the Atlantic is by any means a terrible evil. . . .

It is right that all this should be acknowledged by us. When we speak of America and of her institutions we should remember that she has given to our increasing population rights and privileges which we could not give; – which as an old country we probably can never give. That self-asserting, obtrusive independence which so often wounds us, is, if viewed aright, but an outward sign of those good things which a new country has produced for its people. Men and women do not beg in the States; – they do not offend you with tattered rags; they do not complain to heaven of starvation; they do not crouch to the ground for halfpence. If poor, they are not abject in their poverty.

They read and write. They walk like human beings made in God's form. They know that they are men and women, owing it to themselves and to the world that they should earn their bread by their labour, but feeling that when earned it is their own. If this be so, – if it be acknowledged that it is so, – should not such knowledge in itself be sufficient testimony of the success of the country and of her institutions?

(Vol. Two, Chapter XVI)

AUSTRALIA AND NEW ZEALAND

Queensland – Free selectors and squatters

The term 'free-selectors' used above is one with which the traveller soon finds himself very intimately acquainted in the Australian colonies, and if he be fortunate enough to become hand and glove with the squatters, he always hears it as a term of reproach. The normal squatter hates the 'free-selector' almost as thoroughly as the English country gentleman hates the poacher. As I shall speak at large in another chapter of Queensland squatters and Queensland sheep-runs, I will not say much of them here; but to explain the condition of the free-selector, it is necessary to state that a considerable portion of a squatter's run within the settled districts is always open to be selected by any human being above twenty-one years of age. You, oh reader ignorant of your privilege, may go at once and select no less than 10,280 acres on the run of any Queensland squatter within the line of settled districts who has so much as yet unselected and unprotected by the present laws from immediate selection. You may take not less than 210 or more than 640 acres of agricultural land at 15*s*. an acre; also if you please not less than 80 or more than 2,560 of first-class pastoral land at 10*s*. an acre; – and also, if you are so minded, not less than 80 or more than 7,680 acres of second-class pastoral land at 10*s*. an acre; and for these purchases you need only pay a tenth of the price in the first year, and so on for ten years when the whole estate will be your own. Or, if you be more humble, – and are not a married woman, – you may free-select a nice little farm of 80 acres of agricultural land, or 160 of pastoral, on still easier terms. This you do under the homestead clause; – but as to this you are bound down to residence. This you have at 9*d.* an acre per annum for agricultural land, or

6*d.* for pastoral, and if at the end of five years you shall have lived on it continually, and have either fenced it in or cultivated the tenth of it, it is yours for ever with an undefeasible title-deed without further payment. Now 80 acres out of a squatter's run is nothing. Even 10,280 acres out of a larger run is not much. But one squatter may be subject to many free selectors; and when the free-selector makes his selection with the express object of stealing the squatter's cattle, – as the squatter often believes to be the case, – the squatter of course omits to love his neighbour as himself.

It must be understood that from this order of things arises a very different condition of feeling with regard to land from that to which we are subject at home. With us the owner of the land, the freeholder, is the big man, and he who holds by lease is the little man. In the Australian colonies the squatter who holds his run by lease from the Crown, and who only purchases in order to keep others from puchasing, and who is half ruined by being compelled thus to become the owner of the soil, is the big man; whereas the free-holder, who has free-selected his holding, is the little man. But he is in no degree dependent on the squatter, and their interests are altogether at variance.

There has, however, latterly arisen a point of junction between the classes which does to a certain degree bring them together. The squatter when he washes and shears his sheep, – during the period that is of his harvest, – requires a great deal of temporary labour. Now the free-selectors cannot live on their farms, and are consequently glad to hire themselves out during three or four months of the year as washers and shearers. For this work they receive high wages, – and rations, which enable them to take their earnings home with them. It is always for the advantage both of the employed and of employers that they should think well of each other, and hence some kindly feeling does spring up tending to allay the irritation as to cattle-stealing on the one side, and the anger produced by contempt and perhaps by false accusation on the other. The squatter's money is necessary to the free-selector, and the free-selector's labour is necessary to the squatter, and in this way the two classes amalgamate. Nor do they often quarrel over their work, though the laws laid down by the squatter for the governance of his men are somewhat peremptory. Order must be kept in the wool-shed. There must be no drinking there, and no smoking except at stated intervals. And shearers must be subject to fines if they shear badly, – as to which the squatter's superintendents are the judge. But peace usually prevails, and the contracts made are carried out to an end. Occasionally a shearer may be dismissed, who will then leave the shed in disgust, – not always without some expression. A squatter, who will allow me to call him my friend, found the following plaintive melody nailed up on one of his gates no doubt by a melancholy free-selector from a distance, who had been found to be unequal to his work:-

> 'Farewell to the wild emu.
> Farewell to the kangaroo.
> Farewell to the squatter of the plain.
> I hope I may never see that —— rascal again!!'

In this great question between the squatter and the free-selector of land, – for with its different ramifications in regard to immigration, agricultural produce, and pastoral success, it is the greatest of all questions in Australian life, – it is almost impossible for the normal traveller not to sympathize with the squatter. The normal traveller comes out with introductions to the gentlemen of the colony, and the gentlemen of the colony are squatters. The squatters' houses are open to him. They introduce the traveller to their clubs. They lend their horses and buggies. Their wives and daughters are pretty and agreeable. They exercise all the duties of hospitality with a free hand. They get up kangaroo hunts and make picnics. It is always pleasant to sympathize with an aristocracy when an aristocracy will open its arms to you. We still remember republican Mrs Beecher Stowe with her sunny memories of duchesses.[1] But the traveller ought to sympathize with the free-selector, – always premising that the man keep his hands from picking and stealing his neighbour's cattle.

(Vol. One, Chapter II)

An Aboriginal trial

When at Gladstone I found that an 'aboriginal' negro was to be tried for breaking into a shop, and I walked through the woods to the little court-house, which stands about a mile from the wharf, in order that I might see the ceremony. There I found a magistrate, four policemen, a young woman who attended as a witness, and the prisoner. The black man was described in the sheet as 'Aboriginal Boney.' He had taken away a slab from the corner of a wooden store in the hope of getting a bit of tobacco. He had been disturbed before making good his booty, and had left behind him a small pouch which he had taken from his waist to enable him the better to get through the hole. In this pouch there was elevenpence in silver, – for even a black man will not condescend to carry copper in the colonies, – and a lock of hair. Let us hope that it was a lock from the head of his favourite gin[2] or wife. There was no evidence against him except his own, – for the woman had only seen the form of a man escaping. Boney, when taxed by the sergeant, had confessed at once, seeming to have been more willing to bear the brunt of the offence than the loss of his purse. I wished I could have learned how much of his regret was sordid as attaching to the money, and how much tender as attaching to the lock of hair. He had gone, he said, for tobacco, but had got none, and had escaped when disturbed, leaving behind him his little property. The sergeant of police had it all his own way, – examining the witnesses, putting himself into the box and giving his own evidence, taking the statement of the prisoner, and managing the matter in a manner that would be very serviceable if introduced at the Old Bailey. Aboriginal Boney was sentenced to six months' imprisonment, and seemed to be perfectly satisfied. He had, in fact, pleaded guilty, – but had probably done so without comprehending much of the nature of the proceeding. I saw him afterwards in the prison at Rockhampton, and he seemed to be enjoying life in that retreat.

(Vol. One, Chapter III)

Speculation

An Englishman cannot be a month in Australia without finding himself driven to speculate, – almost driven to come to some conclusion as to the future destinies of the colonies. At present they are loyal to England with an expressive and almost violent loyalty of which we hear and see little at home. There may be causes of quarrel on this or that subject of custom duties and postal subsidies. One colony may expostulate with a Secretary of State at home in language a little less respectful than another, in accordance with the temperament of the minister of the moment. But the feeling of the people is one of the affectionate adherence to England, with some slight anger caused by a growing idea that England is becoming indifferent. The withdrawal of our troops, especially from New Zealand, has probably done more than anything else to produce an apprehension which is certainly unnecessary and, to my thinking, irrational. But the love of the colonies for England, and the Queen, and English government, – what may best probably be described as the adherence of the colonies to the mother country, – cannot be doubted. An Australian of the present day does not like to be told of the future independence of Australia. I think that I met no instance in which the proposition on my part was met with an unqualified assent. And yet it can hardly be doubted that the independence of Australia will come in due time. But other things must come first. Before that day shall arrive the bone and sinews of the colonies must be of colonial produce. The leading men must not only have lived but have been born in Australia, so as to have grown up into life without the still existing feeling that England is their veritable 'home.' And I venture to express an opinion that another great change must have come first, as to the coming of which there is at present certainly no sign. The colonies will join themselves together in some Australian federation, as has been done with our North American provinces, and will learn the political strength and commercial advantage of combined action.

(Vol. One, Chapter III)

Miners

And it may be well to remark here that Australian miners are almost invariably courteous and civil. A drunken man is never agreeable; but even a drunken miner is rarely quarrelsome. They do not steal, and are rough rather than rowdy. It seemed to me that very little care was taken, or was necessary, in the preservation of gold, the men trusting each other with great freedom. There are quarrels about claims for land, – and a claim is sometimes unjustly 'jumped.' The jumping of a claim consists in taking possession of the land and works of absent miners, who are presumed by their absence to have deserted their claims. But such bickerings rarely lead to personal violence. The miners do not fight and knock each other about. They make constant appeals to the government officer, – the police magistrate, or, above him, to the gold commissioner of the district, – and they not unfrequently go to law. They do not punch each other's heads.

At the beginning of a rush the work consists, I think always, in alluvial washing. Some lucky man or set of men, – three or four together probably, – 'prospecting' about the country, came upon gold. This they are bound to declare to the government, and it is now thoroughly understood by miners that it is for their interest to declare it. The 'prospecter' is then rewarded by being allowed to take up two or three men's ground, as the case may be. And every miner is allowed to take up a certain fixed share of ground on the sole condition that it has not already been taken up by any other miner, and that gold has been found in the neighbourhood. But the 'prospecter' has the double advantage of choosing his ground where gold has certainly been found, and of having more ground than any of his neighbours.

– – – –

And probably the class of miners which as a class does worst is that composed of young gentlemen who go to the diggings, led away, as they fancy, by a spirit of adventure, but more generally, perhaps, by a dislike of homely work at home. An office-stool for six or eight hours a day is disagreeable to them, or the profession of the law requires too constant a strain, or they are sick of attending lectures, or they have neglected the hospitals; – and so they go away to the diggings. They soon become as dirty as genuine diggers, but they do not quickly learn anything but the dirt. They strive to work, but they cannot work alongside of experienced miners, and consequently they go to the wall. They are treated with no contempt, for all men at the diggings are free and equal. As there is no gentility, such men are not subject to any reproach or ill-usage on that score. The miner does not expect that any airs will be ⁻ssumed, and takes it for granted that the young man will not sin in that direction. Our 'gentleman,' therefore, is kindly treated; but, nevertheless, he goes to the wall, and becomes little better than the servant, or mining hodsman, of some miner who knows his work. Perhaps he has a little money, and makes things equal with a partner in this way; but they will not long be equal, – for his money will go quicker than his experience will come. On one gold-field I found a young man whom I had known at home, who had been at school with my sons, and had frequented my house. I saw him in front of his little tent, which he occupied in partnership with an experienced working miner, eating a beefsteak out of his frying-pan with his clasp-knife. The occupation was not an alluring one, but it was the one happy moment of his day. He was occupied with his companion on a claim, and his work consisted in trundling a rough windlass, by which dirt was drawn up out of a hole. They had found no gold as yet, and did not seem to expect to find it. He had no friend near him but his mining friend, – or mate, as he called him. I could not but think what would happen to him if illness came, or if his mate should find him too far removed from mining capability. He had been softly nurtured, well educated, and was a handsome fellow to boot; and there he was eating a nauseous lump of beef out of a greasy frying-pan with his pocket-knife, just in front of the contiguous blankets stretched on the ground, which constituted the beds of himself and his companion.

(Vol. One, Chapter V)

A dramatic incident

The only man about the place was a coolie cook, and this man was not very manly. She had babies, – or a baby, and a nurse and so forth. And things being in this condition, a black man made his way into the lady's kitchen and there took up his quarters. She asked him to go, but he declined to go, and there he remained, – I forget whether it was one or two nights. He committed no great violence, but grinned, and demanded food, and gradually made himself very much at home. 'What on earth did you do?' I asked. 'My husband had a revolver,' she said, 'and I walked up to him with it and pointed it at him.' 'Well, and what then?' 'I did it two or three times, and he didn't seem to mind it much.' 'And what next?' 'I couldn't bring myself to shoot him, you know,' she said. I quite sympathized with her there, remarking that it would be difficult to shoot a man who only grinned and asked for food. I went on to ask again what she did do; – for an aboriginal who gets with ease all that he demands is likely in the end to ask for a good deal, and it may be a question whether, after all, the shooting him might not be the least of the possible evils. 'I remembered,' she said, 'that my husband had a sword-stick. I went and got that, and drew it out before him. When he retreated I ran on at him and pricked him. He did not like it at all, so I pricked him again. When I pricked him the third time he ran away and never came back any more.' It was a happy and in some sort a glorious termination; – but then the lady might have had no sword-stick at her command, or might have lacked the courage to make upon a savage an attack so merciful and yet so persistent.

(Vol. One, Chapter VII)

Station life

It was a very pleasant life that I led at these stations. I like tobacco and brandy and water, with an easy-chair out on a verandah, and my slippers on my feet. And I like men who are energetic and stand up for themselves and their own properties. I like having horses to ride and kangaroos to hunt, and sheep become quite a fascination to me as a subject of conversation. And I liked that roaming from one house to another, – with a perfect conviction that five minutes would make me intimate with the next batch of strangers. Men are never ashamed of their poverty; nor are they often proud of their wealth. In all country life in Australia there is an absence of any ostentation or striving after effect, – which is delightful. Such as their life is, the squatters share it with you, giving you, as is fitting for a stranger, the best they have to give. Upon the Darling Downs the stations are large and the accommodation plentiful; but I have been on many sheep-runs which were not so well found, – at which bedrooms were scarce, and things altogether were less well arranged. But there is never any shame as to the inferiority, never any pretence at superiority. What there is, is at your service. If there be not a whole bedroom for you, there is half a bedroom. If there be not wine, there is brandy or rum; – if no other meat, there is at least mutton. If the house be full, some young man can turn out and go to the barracks, or sleep on the verandah. If all the young men have been turned out the old men can follow them. It is a rule of life on a sheep-run that the station is never so full that another guest need be turned away.

These houses, – stations as they are called, – are built after a very simple and appropriate fashion. There is not often any upper storey. Every room is on the ground floor. There is always a verandah, running the length of the house, and not unfrequently continued round the ends. The rooms all open out upon the verandah, and generally have no communication with each other. The kitchen is invariably a separate building, usually attached to the house by a covered way. When first building his residence the squatter probably has had need for but small accommodation, and has constructed his house with perhaps three rooms. Children have come, and guests, and increased demands, and increased house-room has been wanted. Another little house has therefore been joined on to the first, and then perhaps a third added. I have seen an establishment consisting of seven such little houses. Many hours are passed in the verandah, in which old people sit in easy-chairs and young men lie about, seeming to find the boards soft enough for luxurious ease. Attached to the station there is always a second home called the barracks, or the cottage, in which the young men have their rooms. There are frequently one or two such young men attached to a sheep-station, either learning their business or earning salaries as superintendents. According to the terms of intimacy existing, or to the arrangements made, these men live with the squatter's family or have a separate table of their own. They live a life of plenty, freedom, and hard work, but one which is not surrounded by the comforts which young men require at home. Two or three share the same room, and the washing apparatus is chiefly supplied by the neighbouring creek. Tubs are scarce among them, but bathing is almost a rule of life. They are up and generally on horseback by daylight, and spend their time in riding about after sheep. The general idyllic idea of Arcadian shepherd-life, which teaches us to believe that Tityrus[3] lies under a beech-tree most of his hours, playing on his reed and 'spooning' Phyllis, is very unlike the truth in Australian pastures. Corin is nearer the mark when he tells Touchstone[4] of his greasy hands. It is a life, even for the upper shepherd of gentle birth and sufficient means, of unremitting labour amidst dust and grease, amidst fleeces and carcasses. The working squatter, or the squatter's working assistant, must be a man capable of ignoring the delicacies of a soft way of living. He must endure clouds of dust, and be not averse to touch tar and oil, wool and skins. He should be able to catch a sheep and handle him almost as a nurse does a baby. He should learn to kill a sheep, and wash a sheep, and shear a sheep. He should tell a sheep's age by his mouth, – almost by his look. He should know his breeding, and the quality of his wool. He should be able to muster sheep, – collect them in together from the vast pastures on which they feed, and above all he should be able to count them. He must be handy with horses, – doing anything which has to be done for himself. He must catch his own horse, – for the horses live on grass, turned out in paddocks, – and saddle him. The animal probably is never shod, never groomed, and is ignorant of corn. And the young man must be able to sit his horse, – which perhaps is more than most young men could do in England, for it may be that the sportive beast will buck with the young man, jumping up into the air with his head between his legs, giving his rider as he does so such a blow by the contraction of his loins as will make any but an Australian young man sore all over for a week, even if he be not made sore for a much longer time by being sent far over the brute's head. This young man on a station must have many accomplishments, much knowledge, great capability; and in return for these things he gets his rations, and perhaps £100 per annum, perhaps £50, and perhaps nothing. But he lives a free, pleasant life in the open air.

(Vol. One, Chapter VII)

Sheep washing

Many declare that sheep should not be washed at all, and that the wool should be shorn 'in the grease.' My opinion will not, I fear, be valued much by the great Queensland squatters, but, such as it is, it goes with the non-washers. Presuming that my own outside garniture required to be cleansed, I should not like to have it done on my back; – and if I knew that it was to be taken off immediately after the operation, I should think that to be an additional reason for deferring the washing process. There are various modes of washing, – but on the stations which I saw on the Darling Downs the sheep were all 'spouted.' I will endeavour to explain to the ordinary non-pastoral reader this system of spouting, premising that perhaps some 200,000 sheep have to undergo the process on one station, and at the same set of spouts.

But before we get to the spouting there is a preliminary washing to be undergone, and as to that also there are fierce contests. Shall this preliminary washing be performed with warm or with cold water? And then again there is, so to say, an anti-preliminary washing in vogue, which some call 'raining.' If I remember rightly sheep were 'rained on' in Queensland only at those stations in which warm water was in demand. The sheep by thirties and forties were driven into long narrow pens, over which pipes were supported, pierced with holes from end to end. Into these pipes water is forced by a steam-engine, and pours itself right and left, in the guise of rain, over the sheep below. In this way the wool is gently saturated with moisture, and then the sheep are driven out of the pens into long open tanks filled with water, just lukewarm. Here they are soaked for a few minutes, – and this practice is matter for fierce debate among squatters. I have heard a squatter declare with vehement gesture that he hoped every squatter would be ruined who was mad enough to use warm water in his washpool. I have heard others declare with equal vehemence that no wool could be really clean which had not been subjected to the process. For myself, I am dead against washing altogether; but if sheep are to be washed then I am dead against warm water. The sheep becomes cold after it and chill during the three or four days necessary for drying, and in that condition of the animal the yolk which is necessary to the excellence of the wool does not rise, and the fleece when taken off, though cleaner than it would otherwise have been, is less rich in its quality and less strong in its fibre.

But whether out of tanks with warm water or tanks with cold water, the sheep are passed on, one by one, into the hands of the men at the spouts. At one washpool I saw fourteen spouts at work, with two men at each spout. These twenty-eight men are quite amphibious for the time, standing up to their middles in a race of running water. But this race is not a natural stream. High over their heads are huge iron cisterns which are continually filled by a steam pump, and which empty themselves by spouts from the bottom, through which the water comes with great force, – a force which can of course be moderated by the weight of water thrown in. The water is kept at a certain height according to the force wanted, and falls with the required weight, in obedience to the law of gravitation, on a board between the two rough water-spirits below. Now the tanks, of which I have spoken, are high above the water-spirits, and the sheep are brought out from them on to a small intermediate pen or platform, from which they are dropped one by one down a steep inclined trap, – each sheep by a separate trap, – into the very hands of the washers. The fall may be about twelve or fifteen feet. Then the animal undergoes the real work of washing, – the bad quarter of an hour of his life. He is turned backwards and forwards under the spout with great violence, – for great violence is necessary, – till the fury of the water shall have driven the dirt from his fleece. The bad quarter of an hour lasts, at some washpools, half a minute, – at others as long as a minute and a half; and I think I am justified in saying that the sheep does not like it. He goes out of the spouter's hands, not into the water, but on to steep boards, arranged so as to give him every facility for travelling up to the pen which is to receive him. But I have seen sheep so weak with what they have endured as to be unable to raise themselves on to their feet. Indeed at some washpools such was the normal condition of the sheep when they came from the spouts. It is impossible that there should not be rough handling. That, and the weight of the water together, prostrates them. This is so much the case that no squatter dares to wash his rams, – the pride of his flock, – for fear of injuring them. But, as a rule, sheep are washed in Queensland, and this is the fashion of their washing.

(Vol. One, Chapter VII)

Sheep shearing

In Queensland the washpool, as at present arranged, is the squatter's great hobby, and next to it his wool-shed. They are generally at some distance from each other, – perhaps seven or eight miles, – for the sheep must have time to dry, and it is well that they should travel a little over the pastures, feeding as they go, as being less likely to become again dirty with their own dust, as they would do if they were left together in large numbers. They are mustered and kept apart with infinite care, as ewes with their lambs must not be shorn with hoggetts,[5] or hoggetts with old wethers. And there are sheep of different breeding and various qualities of wool which must not be mixed. In different flocks the sheep make their way from the washpool to the wool-shed, and then are shorn on about the fourth day. It is essentially necessary that they should be dry, so that rain during the double process is very detrimental to the squatter.

The wool-shed is a large building open on every side, with a high-pitched roof, – all made of wood and very rough. The sheep are driven in either at one end or both, or at three sides, according to the size of the station and the number of sheep to be shorn. They are then assorted into pens, from which the shearers take them on to the board; – two, three, or four shearers selecting their sheep from each pen. The floor, on which the shearers absolutely work, is called 'the board.' I have seen as few as four or five shearing together, and I have seen as many as seventy-six. I have watched a shearer take the wool off his sheep in five minutes, and I have seen a man occupied nearly fifteen in the same operation. As they are paid by the score or by the hundred, and not by the day, the great object is to shear as many as possible. I have known a man to shear ninety-five in a day. I have heard of a man shearing one hundred and twenty. From sixty to seventy may be taken as a fair day's work. But as rapidity of work is so greatly to the workman's interest, and as too rapid a hand either leaves the wool on the sheep's back or else cuts skin and fleece together, there is often a diversity of opinion between the squatter and the shearer. 'Shear as quick as you can,' says the squatter, who is very anxious to get his work out of hand; – 'but let me have all my wool, – and let it not be cut mincemeat-fashion, but with its full length of staple; – and above all do not mutilate and mangle my poor sheep.' But the poor sheep are mutilated and mangled by many a sore wound, and from side to side about the shed the visitor hears the sound of 'Tar.' When a sheep has been wounded the shearer calls for tar, and a boy with a tar-pot rushes up and daubs the gory wound. Each shearer has an outside pen of his own to which the sheep when shorn is demitted, and so the tally is kept.

The shearer does nothing but shear. When one sheep has left his hand he seizes at once another, being very careful to select that which will be the easiest shorn. The fleece, when once separated from the animal's back, is no longer a care to him. Some subordinate picks it up and makes away with it, when folded, to the sorter's table. The sorter is a man of mark, and should be a man of skill, who gives himself airs and looks grand. It is his business to allot the wool to its proper sphere, – combing or clothing, first combing or second combing, first clothing or second clothing, broken wool, greasy, ram's-wool, hoggett's-wool, lamb's-wool, and the like. He stands immovable, and does his work with a touch, while ministers surround him, unfolding and folding, and carrying the assorted fleeces to their proper bins. But I am told that in England very little is thought of this primary sorting, and that all wools are re-sorted as they are scoured. The squatter, however, says that unless he sorted his wool in his own shed he could not realise a good price for a good article.

(Vol. One, Chapter VII)

New South Wales – Woolhara

It is so inexpressibly lovely that it makes a man ask himself whether it would not be worth his while to move his household goods to the eastern coast of Australia, in order that he might look at it as long as he can look at anything. There are certain spots, two or three miles out of the town, now occupied generally by villas, or included in the grounds of some happy resident, which have nothing for the imagination to add. Greenoaks and Mount Adelaide, belonging to two brothers, Mr Thomas and Mr Henry Mort, are perfect. Sir James Martin,[6] who was the prime minister when I was first there, and who, I hope may soon be so again, has a garden falling down to the sea, which is like fairyland. There is a rock outside, – or probably inside, – the grounds of Woolhara, belonging to Mr Cooper, on which the blacks in the old days, when they were happy and undisturbed, used to collect themselves for festive, political, and warlike purposes. I wonder whether they enjoyed it as I did! How they must have hated the original Cooper when he came and took it, – bought it for 20s. an acre, out of which they got no dividend, or had a grant of it from the English Crown! Woolhara is a magnificent property, covered with villas and gardens, all looking down upon the glorious sea. In England it would be worth half a million of money, and as things go on, it will soon be worth as much in New South Wales; and perhaps some future Cooper will be Duke Cooper or Marquis Cooper, and Woolhara will be as famous as Lowther or Chatsworth.[7] It is infinitely more lovely than either. I envied the young man, and almost hated him for having it, – although he had just given me an excellent dinner.

(Vol. One, Chapter XIII)

Sydney Harbour

I doubt whether I ever read any description of scenery which gave me an idea of the place described, and I am not sure that such effect can be obtained by words. Scott in prose, and Byron[8] in verse, are both eloquent in declaring that this or that place is romantic, picturesque, or charming; and their words have been powerful enough to send thousands to see the spots which they have praised. But the charm conveyed has been in the words of the writer, not in the beauty of the place. I know that the task would be hopeless were I to attempt to make others understand the nature of the beauty of Sydney Harbour. I can say that it is lovely, but I cannot paint its loveliness. The sea runs up in various bays or coves, indenting the land all around the city, so as to give a thousand different aspects of the water, – and not of water, broad, unbroken, and unrelieved, – but of water always with jutting corners of land beyond it, and then again of water and then again of land. And you, the resident, – even though you be a lady not over strong, though you be a lady, if possible, not over young, – will find, unless you choose your residence most unfortunately, that you have walks within your reach as deliciously beautiful as though you had packed up all your things and travelled days and spent pounds to find them.

(Vol. One, Chapter XIII)

Country towns

In England it is sometimes very difficult to discover the *raison d'être* of a community called a town. One cannot understand why that especial lot of human beings have formed themselves together and determined to live in that particular place. It seems that the tailor lives on the butcher, the butcher on the baker, the baker on the publican, and so on. In many of our towns, probably in all the greater cities, there is some particular industry, – but in others, especially in the South and East, there is no such cause. I never could understand why Wincanton or Ilminster should continue to exist, or Chelmsford or Bury St Edmunds. There were causes when the towns were new, and in new countries the causes are still to be recognised. In New South Wales many of the towns have been absolutely created by the gold-fields, and are still being created. Some of the gold-field towns are already in a state of decay, and are almost passing away. Still something of life remains, but of all the sad places I ever saw they are the most melancholy. They are 'bush' towns. Readers who desire to understand anything of Australian life should become acquainted with the technical meaning of the word 'bush.' The bush is the gum-tree forest, with which so great a part of Australia is covered, that folk who follow a country life are invariably said to live in the bush. Squatters who look after their own runs always live in the bush, even though their sheep are pastured on plains. Instead of a town mouse and a country mouse in Australia, there would be a town mouse and a bush mouse, – but mice living in the small country towns would still be bush mice. A young lady when she becomes engaged to a gentleman whose avocations call upon him to live far inland always declares that she prefers 'bush life.' The mining towns are comprised of the sudden erections which spring from the finding of gold in the neighbourhood, and are generally surrounded by thick forest. But in their immediate vicinity the trees have been cut down either for firewood or for use under ground; – but have not been altogether cleared away, so that the hideous stumps remain above the surface. Around on all sides the ground has been stirred in the search for gold, and ugly bare heaps of clay are left. The road to and from such a place will meander causelessly between yawning holes, in each of which some desponding miner has probably buried his high hopes, – and which he has then abandoned. One wonders that every child in the neighbourhood does not perish by falling into them. At different points around the centre which have once been supposed to be auriferous, there are the skeleton remains of wooden habitations, with here and there the tawdry sign-boards of deserted shops from which high profits were once expected. In some few of these skeleton habitations there are still inhabitants, – men and women who having a house have been unwilling to leave it, even when the dreadful fact that gold is not to be found in paying quantities has been acknowledged. In the centre there is still the town, though day by day its right to the name is passing from it.

(Vol. One, Chapter XVI)

Travel

This travelling through the endless forest of gum-trees is very peculiar, and at first attractive. After a while it becomes monotonous in the extreme. There is a great absence of animal life. One may go all day through a pastoral country without seeing a sheep or a kangaroo. Now and again one hears the melancholy note of the magpie, or the unmelodious but cheerful gobble of the laughing jackass, and sometimes the scream of a cockatoo; but even birds are not common. Travellers one meets occasionally, – a man on horseback, with his swag before him on his saddle, or a line of drays drawn by bullocks, or perhaps a squatter in his buggy, – but they are few and far between. The road, such as it is, consists of various tracks, running hither and thither, and very puzzling at first to a 'new chum' – till he learns that all these tracks in the bush are only deviations of one road. When the bullock-drays have so cut up a certain passage that the ruts are big enough and deep enough to swallow up a buggy or to overset the stage-coach, the buggies and the stage-coach make another passage, from which they move again when the inevitable bullock-drays have followed them. The government shows its first care on these roads in making bridges over the streams; but even bridges are not absolutely essential. With some rough contrivance, when any contrivance is absolutely necessary, the vehicles descend and ascend the banks, though the wheels be down to the nave in mud. Over many of these bush roads, Cobb's coaches travel day and night, passing in and out through the trees, up and down across the creeks, sticking here and there in the mud, in a rough, uneasy, but apparently not very insecure fashion. Now and then one hears that a coach has been upset, and that the passengers have been out in the bush all night; but one very rarely hears that any one has been hurt, unless it be the coachman. The average pace of the travelling in New South Wales is about six miles an hour.

But more go in their own buggies than by coach, and perhaps more on horseback than in buggies. In Australia every one keeps horses; – every squatter keeps horses by the dozen; and a buggy is as necessary a part of his establishment as a dinner-table. These vehicles are either American, or are built on the American plan, and are admirably adapted for bush work. They are very light, and go over huge logs and across unfathomable ruts almost without feeling them. To upset them seems to be an impossibility. They are constantly being broken, – hopelessly broken to the mind of an ignorant stranger; but they go on apparently as well without a pole as with one, and are indifferent to bent axles and injured wheels. There are always yards of rope at hand, and supplementary timber can be cut from the next tree. Many scores of miles through the bush I have travelled in these buggies, – and have sometimes felt the hours to pass by very slowly; but though there have been no roads, – nothing that in England would be called a road, – I have encountered no injury, nor have I been aware of any danger.

But the pleasantest mode of bush travelling is on horseback. It is open to this objection, – that you can carry nothing with you but what can be strapped on to your saddle before you. Two changes of linen, a night-shirt, a pair of trousers, with hair-brushes, tooth-brush, and a pair of slippers, is about as much as can be taken. But, on the other hand, bush-life requires but little in the way of dress, and a man travelling on horseback is held to be exempt from rules which he should observe if he travelled in a buggy. The squatter travelling alone through the country generally takes two horses, leading one and riding the other, and in this way makes very long journeys. The work which Australian horses will do when immediately taken off the grass is very surprising. I have ridden forty, fifty, and even as much as sixty-four miles a day, – the whole weight on the animal's back being over seventeen stone, and have come to the end of the day's work without tiring the horse. According to the distance to be done, and the number of consecutive days during which you require your steed to travel, will be your pace. The fastest which I ever did from morning to evening was eight miles an hour throughout, resting two hours and journeying eight; but six miles an hour will perhaps be the average rate. The stories, however, that we hear are very wonderful, – for in matters of horseflesh, gentlemen in Australia do not hide their lights under bushels. I have heard men boasting of doing ten miles an hour for ten hours running; and one very enterprising horseman assured me that he had ridden seventy-five miles in four hours.

(Vol. One, Chapter XVI)

Life in the Bush[9]

Those rides through the forest either when I was alone, or when I could get my host to go with me, – which was rarely, unless on a Sunday afternoon, – were very pleasant. The melancholy note of the magpie was almost the only sound that was heard. Occasionally kangaroos would be seen, – two or three staring about them after a half-tame fashion, as though they had not as yet made up their mind whether it would be necessary for them to run. When approached they would move, – always in a line, and with apparent leisure till pursued. Then they would bound away, one here and one there, at a pace which made it impossible for a single horseman to get near them in a thickly timbered country. It was all wood. There arose at last a feeling that go where one might through the forest, one was never going anywhere. It was all picturesque, – for there was rocky ground here and there, and hills in the distance, and the trees were not too close for the making of pretty vistas through them; – but it was all the same. One might ride on, to the right or to the left, or might turn back, and there was ever the same view. And there were no objects to reach, unless it was the paddock fence. And when the paddock fence was jumped, then it was the same thing again. Looking around, one could tell by no outward sign, whether one was inside or outside the boundary, – whether one was two miles or ten miles from the station.

Perhaps the most astonishing phenomenon on these runs is the apparent paucity of sheep. As a fact, there are thousands all around; – but unless looked for they are never seen; and even when looked for by inexperienced eyes are often missed. If the reader will bear in mind that an enclosure of 12,000 acres contains more than eighteen square miles, he will understand how unlike to anything in England must be even the enclosed country in Australia. One seems to ride for ever and to come to nothing, and to relinquish at last the very idea of an object. Nevertheless, it was very pleasant. Of all the places that I was ever in this place seemed to be the fittest for contemplation. There was no record of the hours but by the light. When it was night work would be over. The men would cease as the sun was setting, – but the masters would continue till the darkness had come upon them.

– – – –

My wife had brought a cook with her from England who was invaluable, – or would have been had she not found a husband for herself when she had been about a month in the bush. But in spite of her love, and her engagement to a man who was considerably above her in position, she was true to us while she remained at M——, and did her best to make us all comfortable. She was a good-looking, strong woman, of excellent temper, who could do anything she put her hand to, from hairdressing and confectionery up to making butter and brewing beer. I saw her six months afterwards, – 'quite the lady,' but ready for any kind of work that might come in her way. When I think of her, I feel that no woman of that kind ought, as regards herself, to stay in England if she can take herself or get herself taken to the colonies. I mention our cook because her assistance certainly tended very greatly to our increased comfort. The viands provided were mutton, bread, vegetables, and tea. Potatoes were purchased as an ordinary part of the station stores, and the opossums had left us lettuce, tomatoes, and a few cabbages.

Dinner was always dignified with soup and salad, – which must not, however, be regarded as being within the ordinary bush dietary. In other respects the meals were all alike. There was mutton in every shape, and there was always tea. Tea at a squatter's table, – at the table of a squatter who has not yet advanced himself to a man-cook or butler and a two-storied house, – is absolutely indispensable. At this squatter's table there was colonial wine and there was brandy, – produced chiefly to supply my wants; but there was always tea. The young men when they came in, hot and fagged with their day's work, would take a glass of brandy and water standing, as a working man with us takes his glass of beer at a bar. But when they sat down with their dinners before them, the tea-cup did for them what the wine-glass does for us. The practice is so invariable that any shepherd whose hut you may visit will show his courtesy by asking you to take a pannikin of tea. In supplying stores to men, tea and sugar, flour and meat, are the four things which are included as matters of course. The tea is always bought by the chest, and was sold by the merchant at the rate of 1s. 6d. a pound. There was but one class of tea at the station, which I found to be preferable to very much that I am called upon to drink in England.

The recreations of the evening consisted chiefly of tobacco in the verandah. I did endeavour to institute a whist table, but I found that my friends, who were wonderfully good in regard to the age and points of a sheep, and who could tell to the fraction of a penny what the wool of each was worth by the pound, never could be got to remember the highest card of the suit. I should not have minded that had they not so manifestly despised me for regarding such knowledge as important. They were right, no doubt, as the points of a sheep are of more importance than the pips of a card, and the human mind will hardly admit of the two together. Whist is a jealous mistress; – and so is a sheep-station.

I have been at very many bush houses, – at over thirty different stations in the different colonies, – but at not one, as I think, in which I have not found a fair provision of books. It is universally recognised among squatters that a man who settles down in the bush without books is preparing for himself a miserable future life. That the books are always used when they are there I will not say. That they are used less frequently than they should be used I do not doubt. When men come in from physical work, hungry, tired, – with the feeling that they have earned an hour or two of ease by many hours of labour, – they are apt to claim the right to allow their minds to rest as well as their limbs. Who does not know how very much this is the case at home, even among young men and women in our towns, who cannot plead the same excuse of real bodily fatigue? That it should be so is a pity of pities, – not on the score chiefly of information lost or of ignorance perpetuated; but because the power of doing that which should be the one recreation and great solace of our declining years perishes from desuetude, and cannot be renewed when age has come upon us. But think that this folly is hardly more general in the Australian Bush than in English cities. There are books to be read, – and the young squatter, when the evening comes upon him, has no other recreation to entice him. He has no club, no billiard table, no public-house which he can frequent. Balls and festivities are very rare. He probably marries early, and lives the life of a young patriarch, lord of everything around him, and the master of every man he meets on his day's ride. Of course there are many who have risen to this from lower things, – who have become squatters without any early education, who have been butchers, drovers, or perhaps shepherds themselves. That they should not be acquainted with books is a matter of course. They have lacked the practice in youth of which I have just spoken. But among those who have had the advantage of early nurture, and have been taught to handle books familiarly when young, I think that reading is at least as customary as it is with young men in London.

(Vol. One, Chapter XX)

The Blue Mountains

The railway from Sydney to Bathurst passes through the Blue Mountains, which form a portion of the same dividing range. They presented a cruel, awful barrier to the earlier settlers, and for a long time debarred them from the land beyond, which they hoped to find flowing with all the requisites for milk and honey. The eastern strip, where Sydney is built and Paramatta, was singularly barren, though a little farther to the north and west there were river valleys, the soil of which was as singularly rich. It was felt by all the settlers that the Blue Mountains hemmed them in, making, as it were, a prison for them on the shores of Port Jackson. With infinite suffering and indefatigable energy, a way was at last found through the dark defiles of the hills, and the colonists made their way down to those plains, which are now called the Plains of Bathurst. Now a railway passes up and down through the wildest parts of the mountains, crossing their very summit, and passengers go from Sydney to Bathurst, thinking nothing of the struggles of their forefathers, – and thinking very little of the wonders around them.

Close to the highest part of the range, with a fall to it so slight as to be hardly more than perceptible, and at a distance of about two miles from the railway, there is a ravine called Govatt's Leap. Mr Govatt was, I believe, simply a government surveyor, who never made any leap into the place at all. Had he done so, it would certainly have been effectual for putting an end to his earthly sorrows. I had hoped, when I heard the name, to find that some interesting but murderous bushranger had on that spot baffled his pursuers and braved eternity; – but I was informed that a government surveyor had visited the spot, had named it, and had gone home again. No one seeing it could fail to expect better things from such a spot and such a name.

It consists of a ravine probably more than a mile wide. I had no means of ascertaining the distances or heights of the place, – but the whole was on so gigantic a scale as to deceive the eye greatly at the first sight. The only approach to it from the railway leads the visitor to the head of the ravine, at which he is stopped by a precipitous wall of rock, which runs round, in various huge curves, till on each side it loses itself in the distance. As you stand there, looking down, you see a world below you, – a valley, but certainly not a happy valley, dark, awful, and inaccessible. Nowhere round these curves and lines of the rock can the eye find a spot at which it would be possible to descend. It is as though the ocean were below, and you were standing on the edge of a lofty cliff; – but in lieu of the ocean there is this black valley, densely filled with forest timber, filled so densely that you see nothing but the continuous tops of the black foliage, which, though the wind is blowing hard above, never seemed to move. In looking down from cliffs upon the sea, one is conscious that the foot of the rocks may be reached. A boat, at any rate, will place you there, if the weather be fair. But here the mind becomes aware of no mode of entering the abyss. On reaching the edge it seems as though you had come upon a spot of earth which defied you to touch it, and which forbad the possibility of escape should you succeed in doing so. The idea is common to us when we look up at snowy peaks, – and is not the less common because we know that men have learned the way to climb them. But to look down on a place which cannot be reached, – into a valley full of trees, through which a stream runs, a green, dark, crowded valley, – and to feel that you are debarred from reaching it by a sheer descent of four or five hundred feet of cliff all round, is uncommon. I would say double that descent only that I do not quite believe in their entirety some accounts of the place that I have heard. I never saw before so vast a gaping hole on the earth's surface.

(Vol. One, Chapter XXI)

Victoria – gold

But it is necessary to point out that the entire condition of the colony was changed by the success of the gold-finders, and that Victoria, as she is now and has been since we first began to talk about Melbourne at home as one of the great cities of the earth, was made out of gold. Gold made Melbourne. Gold made the other cities of Victoria. Gold made her railways; gold brought to her the population which demanded and obtained that democratic form of government which is her pride. Gold gave its special value to her soil, – not only or chiefly from its own intrinsic value, not only or chiefly to that soil which contains it, – but to surrounding districts, far and wide, by the increased demand for its product and the increasing population which required it for their homes.

But this success was achieved by no means without a struggle, nor did the good things come without bringing for a while many ill things in their train. There is this peculiarity in gold, as an object of industry, that the quest of it disturbs all other adjacent industries. It is natural of course that men should seek that work in which they can earn the best wages, and that any new calling offering high pay will to a certain degree derange the supply of labour ordinarily forthcoming for ordinary occupations. But in all other trades than that of gold-seeking, the customary working of commerce soon brings matters to a level. Wages rise a little on one side and fall a little on the other. Skill, and power, and intelligence hold their own, and the disruptions that occur are those of a passing storm. But gold upheaves everything, and its disruptions are those of an earthquake. The workman rushes away from his old allotted task, not to higher wages, not to 3s. a day instead of 2s., or 6s. instead of 5s., – but to untold wealth and unlimited splendour, – to an unknown, fabulous, but not the less credited realm of the riches. All that he has seen of worldly grandeur, hitherto removed high as the heavens above his head, may with success be his. All that he has dreamed of the luxurious happiness of those whom he has envied seems to be brought within his reach. It seems to him that the affairs of the world generally are to be turned over and reversed, and that thus at last justice is to be done to him who has hitherto been kept cruelly too near the bottom of the wheel. His imagination is on fire, and he is unable any longer to listen to reason. He is no longer capable of doing a plain day's work for a plain day's wages. There is gold to be had by lifting it from the earth, and he will be one of the happy ones to lift it. The presence of gold is a fact. All the corollaries of the fact might be plain to him also, if he would open his ears to them, – but, in regard to himself, he is deaf as an adder to them. In regard to other men he does open his ears, and does believe in them. That all the world around him is rushing to the diggings, he can see; – and he knows that there are not princely fortunes for them all. In some rough way he knows that were there fortunes for them all, the fortunes would cease to be

princely. But 'something tells him,' – as he explains to the friend
of his bosom, – 'something tells him' that he is to be the lucky
man. There is a something telling the same lie to every man in
that toil-worn crowd, as with sore feet and heavy burden on his
shoulders he hurries on to the diggings. In truth he has become a
gambler. . . .

(Vol. One, Chapter XXIV)

He considers Melbourne and 'blowing'

Melbourne is not a city beautiful to the eye from the charms of
the landscape surrounding it, as are Edinburgh and Bath with us,
and as are Sydney and Hobart Town in Australia, and Dunedin
in New Zealand. Though it stands on a river which has in itself
many qualities of prettiness in streams, – a tortuous, rapid little
river with varied banks, – the Yarra Yarra by name, it seems to
have but little to do with the city. It furnishes the means of
rowing to young men, and waters the Botanical Gardens. But it
is not 'a joy for ever'[10] to the Melbournites, as the Seine is to the
people of Paris, or the Inn to the people of Innsbruck. You might
live in Melbourne all your life and hardly know that the Yarra
Yarra was running by your door. Nor is Melbourne made graceful with neighbouring hills. It stands indeed itself on two hills,
and on the valley which separates them; and these afford rising
ground sufficient to cause considerable delay to the obese and
middle-aged pedestrian when the hot winds are blowing, – as hot
winds do blow at summer-time in Melbourne. But there are no
hills to produce scenery, or scenic effect. Though you go up and
down the streets, the country around is flat, – and for the most
part uninteresting. I know no great town in the neighbourhood
of which there is less to see in the way of landscape beauty.

– – – –

At present the city, in all the pride of youthful power, looks as
though she were boasting to herself hourly that she is not as are
other cities.

And she certainly does utter many such boasts. Her population is not given to hide its light under a bushel. I do not think that I said a pleasant word about the town to any inhabitant of it during my sojourn there, driven into silence on the subject by the calls which were made upon me for praise. 'We like to be cracked up, sir,' says the American. I never heard an American say so, but such are the words which we put into his mouth, and they are true as to his character. They are equally true as to the Australian generally, as to the Victorian specially, and as to the citizen of Melbourne in a more especial degree. He likes to be 'cracked up,' and he does not hesitate to ask you to 'crack him up.' He does not proceed to gouging or bowie knives if you decline, and therefore I never did crack him up.

I suppose that a young people falls naturally into the fault of self-adulation. I must say somewhere, and may as well say here as elsewhere, that the wonders performed in the way of riding, driving, fighting, walking, working, drinking, love-making, and speech-making, which men and women in Australia told me of themselves, would have been worth recording in a separate volume had they been related by any but the heroes and heroines themselves. But reaching one as they do always in the first person, these stories are soon received as works of a fine art much cultivated in the colonies, for which the colonial phrase of 'blowing' has been created. When a gentleman sounds his own trumpet he 'blows.' The art is perfectly understood and appreciated among the people who practise it. Such a gentleman or such a lady was only 'blowing!' You hear it and hear of it every day. They blow a good deal in Queensland; – a good deal in South Australia. They blow even in poor Tasmania. They blow loudly in New South Wales, and very loudly in New Zealand. But the blast of the trumpet as heard in Victoria is louder than all the blasts, – and the Melbourne blast beats all the other blowing of that proud colony. My first, my constant, my parting advice to my Australian cousins is contained in two words – 'Don't blow.'

But if a man must blow it is well that he should have something to blow about beyond his own prowess, and I do not know that a man can have a more rational source of pride than the well-being of the city in which he lives. It is impossible for a man to

walk the length of Collins Street up by the churches and the club
to the Treasury Chambers, and then round by the Houses of
Parliament away into Victoria Parade, without being struck by
the grandeur of the dimensions of the town.

————

Were I to finish my account of Melbourne as a city without
speaking of the Yan Yean water, I should be thought to have
omitted the greatest glory of the glorious town. Melbourne is
supplied from a distance of about twenty miles with millions of
gallons of water, – with so many millions that every one says
that the supply cannot be exhausted. It is laid on to every house
in the town and suburbs, and is supposed to be the most perfect
water supply ever produced for the use of man. Ancient Rome
and modern New York have been less blessed in this respect than
is Melbourne with its Yan Yean. I do believe that the supply is
almost as inexhaustible as it is described to be. But the method of
bringing it into the city is not as yet by any means perfect.
During the very heart of the summer of 1871, when the hot
winds were blowing as they blow only in Melbourne, I moved
from a house in the town to a friend's residence in the country;
and neither at the one nor the other could a bath be filled. The
Yan Yean was not 'running.' In those days the Water Commis-
sioners must, I think, have had a bad time. I will also add that the
Yan Yean water is not pleasant to drink; – a matter of comparatively small consideration in a town in which brandy is so
plentiful.

(Vol. One, Chapter XXV)

A mine at Ballaarat

I went down one such mine called 'Winter's Freehold,' descending 450 feet in an iron cage. I was then taken 4,000 feet along an
underground tramway in a truck drawn by a horse. At the end of
that journey I was called upon to mount a perpendicular ladder
about 20 feet high, and was then led along another tramway

running apparently at right angles to the first. From this opened out the cross passages in which the miners were at work. Here we saw the loose alluvial grit, so loose that a penknife would remove it, lying on the solid rock, – on it and under it, – to the breadth I was told of some four feet; though I saw the bottom of the grit, where it lay on its bed, I could not see the top where it was covered. Here and there among the grit, with candle held up, and some experienced miner directing my eye, I could see the minute specks of gold, in search of which these vast subterranean tunnels had been made. It seemed to be but a speck here and there, – so inconsiderable as to be altogether unworth the search. – But the mining men who were with us, the manager, deputy-manager, or shareholders, – for on such occasions one hardly knows who are the friends who accompany one, – expressed themselves highly satisfied.

I was told that £150,000 had been expended on this single mine up to the present time, and that the machinery was the finest in the colony. Perhaps the finest machinery in the colony may be seen at more than one mine in the colony. But I was informed that hitherto the results had not been magnificent. There was, however, a good time coming, and all the money expended would certainly come back with copious interest. I hope that it may be so. We were two hours in seeing the mine, – and I must say that as regards immediate enjoyment the two hours were not well spent. The place was wet and dirty and dark, the progress was tedious, and the result to the eye very poor. But such is the result to all amateur inspectors of mines. When we had extricated ourselves from the bowels of the earth we ascended to a platform on the top of the machinery, to which the wash-dirt is carried that it may there be puddled and the gold extracted. The height enables the water and mud to run off. The dirt is placed in a round flat receptacle or trough, into which water runs, and an instrument somewhat like a harrow is worked through it. The water and mud are amalgamated, and the height enables them to run off together. The gold by its own weight falls to the bottom mixed with stones or shingle. This is after-wards sent down to an open spout below, through which water runs, a man the while working it with a fork prepared for the purpose. Again the stones and mud pass off with the water, and again the gold remains behind sinking to the bottom by its own weight. When all has escaped that will escape, and the stones that will not fall have been thrown out, then the specks of gold are seen lying thick, collected in the little furrows which are marked on the bottom of the spout. To the uninitiated eye the product of all this costly labour still seems to be small.

After all this the gold is smelted into bars and sold to the merchants or bankers. We went to the offices of another company, – the Band of Hope and Albion Consols, – to see the smelting. In this operation there is nothing wonderful. The small gold, – for it is all small in comparison with the nuggets of which we have heard so much and which are now very rare in Australia, – is poured into an earthen pot, is melted, is poured out into moulds, is then washed so that it may have a clean face, and is straightway sent to the bank. At present the greater part of the gold found at Ballaarat when thus prepared is worth something over £4 an ounce. At this Band of Hope mine they raise about 3,000 ounces of gold a month, at an expense of about half its value. The other half is divided among the shareholders, and gives an average interest of £12 15*s.* per cent. on the capital expended on the work. This, in a business subject to great risk, with bank interest at 8 and 9 per cent., does not seem to be a very rich result.

We also saw a quartz-crushing machine at work, – for quartz is raised at Ballaarat, though in much less quantity than the wash-dirt. The nature of a quartz-crusher I have before described in speaking of Gympie, the great Queensland gold-field. In Victoria, as I have said, Sandhurst is the great quartz district; – but there are sanguine people who predict a vast wealth of quartz reefs at Ballaarat after the wash-dirt has been all extracted.

(Vol. One, Chapter XXVI)

Vice

Before I leave Ballaarat, I must acknowledge that as it has a philanthropic and humane aspect, so also has it one that is thoroughly vicious and inhuman. When I asked as to the wickedness of the town the excellent mayor bespoke the services of the sergeant of police, and the three of us together inspected the Chinese quarter at night. A more degraded life it is hardly possible to imagine. Gambling, opium-smoking, and horrid dissipation seemed to prevail among them constantly. They have no women of their own, and the lowest creatures of the streets congregate with them in their hovels. But this is far from being the worst of it. Boys and girls are enticed among them, and dwell with them, and become foul, abominable, and inhuman. And yet, so said my friend the policeman, the law can rarely touch them. Their gambling-tables are open. I went into half-a-dozen of these rooms. The sergeant scattered the Chinese, but could do nothing further; – and then in a minute they congregated again and laughed. Though their counters were on all the tables, he could not, he said, prove that they were gambling. It would, however, matter comparatively little what injury they might do to each other by gambling. When a Chinese is thoroughly ruined he destroys himself, – and there is one less about the place. But when I was told that nothing could be done, though children from twelve to fourteen years of age were found in the quarters of these foreigners, – nothing but to take them back to their parents, from whom they would again run away, – I felt surprised that a single 'heathen Chinee' was left alive in the place. 'The parents are as bad as themselves,' said the sergeant, 'and do not care to go after them.'

(Vol. One, Chapter XXVI)

The verandah

In Melbourne there is the 'verandah;' – in Sandhurst there is a 'verandah;' in Ballaarat there is a 'verandah.' The verandah is a kind of open exchange, – some place on the street pavement apparently selected by chance, on which the dealers in mining shares do congregate. What they do, or how they carry on their business when there, I am unable to explain. But to the stranger, or the passer by, they do not look lovely. He almost trembles lest his eyes should be picked out of his head as he goes. He has no business there, and soon learns to walk on the other side of the road. And he hears strange tales which make him feel that the innocence of the dove would not befriend him at all were he to attempt to trade in those parts. I think there is a racing phrase as to 'getting a tip.' The happy man who gets a tip learns something special as to the competence or incompetence of a horse. There are a great many tips in gold mines which fall into the fortunate hands of those who attend most closely, and perhaps with most unscrupulous fidelity, to the business of the verandahs. The knowing ones know that a certain claim is going to give gold. The man who has the tip sells out at a low price, – sells out a certain number of shares, probably to a friend who holds the tip with him. The price is quoted on the share list, and the unfortunate non-tipped sell out also, and the fortunate tipped one buys up all. A claim is not going to give gold, – and the reverse happens. Or a claim is salted; – gold is surreptitiously introduced, is then taken out, and made the base of a fictitious prosperity. The tipped ones sell and the untipped buy. It is easy to see that the game is very pretty; but then it is dangerous. It has certainly become very popular. One is told at Melbourne that all are playing at it, – clergymen, judges, ladies, old ladies and young, married ladies and single, – old men and boys, fathers unknown to their sons, and sons unknown to their fathers, mothers unknown to their daughters, daughters unknown to their mothers, – masters and servants, tradesmen and their apprentices. 'You shall go from one end of Collins Street to another,' a man said to me, 'and you will hardly meet one who has not owned a share or a part of a share.' Gold-mining in Victoria is as was to us the railway mania some twenty-four years ago.[11]

(Vol. One, Chapter XXVII)

Cobb's coaches

We started by one of Cobb's coaches at one o'clock in the day, and reached the little town of Rosedale in Gipps Land at ten the next morning. Cobb's coaches have the name of being very rough, – and more than once I have been warned against travelling by them. They were not fit, I was told, for an effeminate Englishman of my time of life. The idea that Englishmen, – that is, new-chums, or Englishmen just come from home, – are made of paste, whereas the Australian, native or thoroughly acclimatized, is steel all through, I found to be universal. On hearing such an opinion as to his own person, a man is bound to sacrifice himself, and to act contrary to the advice given, even though he perish in doing so. This journey I made and did not perish at all; – and on arriving at Rosedale had made up my mind that twenty hours on a Cobb's coach through the bush in Australia does not inflict so severe a martyrdom as did in the old days a journey of equal duration on one of the time-famous, much-regretted old English mails. More space is allowed you for stretching your legs on the seat, and more time for stretching your legs at the stages. The road of course is rough, – generally altogether unmade, – but the roughness lends an interest to the occasion, and when the coach is stuck in a swamp, – as happens daily, – it is pleasant to remember that the horses do finally succeed, every day, in pull-ing it out again. On this road there is a place called the Glue Pot, extending perhaps for a furlong, as to which the gratified travel-ler feels that now, at any rate, the real perils of travel have been attained. But the horses, rolling up to their bellies in the mud, do pull the coach through. This happens in the darkness of night, in the thick forest, – and the English traveller in his enthusiasm tells the coachman that no English whip would have looked at such a place even by daylight. The man is gratified, lights his pipe, and rushes headlong into the next gully.

(Vol. One, Chapter XXVIII)

Towards Woods Point

At an inn among the mountains, – for here and there one comes upon an inn, though there are no roads, – we found two girls who were desirous of going to a wedding which was to be held in a neighbouring gully. Luckily, or perhaps unluckily, the mounted mailman came up, driving two spare horses before him. So the girls at once borrowed the horses, and the inn afforded one side-saddle. The girl who mounted without the side-saddle rode well, and might have reached the wedding triumphantly; but the other was somewhat at fault, even with the side-saddle. She was bold enough, but had probably never been on horseback before. We had gone on during the trouble of the saddle, as there appeared to be some bashfulness in completing the arrangement; but before long the poor maiden's steed was after us. He had run away with her, and for a moment or two I thought she must have perished among the trees, – but as the beast passed us he shied, and deposited his burden close at the feet of the horse I was riding. She was shaken, for a while speechless, soiled, and wretched; but before long she proclaimed her intention of walking to the wedding. The distance was not above six miles through the woods. The other girl like a true friend dismounted, that she might walk with her companion, and the mailman with his spare horses proceeded on with us to Jericho.

(Vol. One, Chapter XXVIII)

Tasmania – convicts

It will be understood that the lingering English remnants of transported ruffianism would by this time consist chiefly of old men unfit for work. There were 146 English paupers, – convicts who have served their time, but who would be unable to support themselves if turned out, – and there were 10 invalids who would return to their convict work when well. There were also 89 lunatics, of whom only 4 were under sentence. With 506 men to be looked after, 97 officers and constables to look after them, and with only 234 men able to do a day's work, it may well be imagined that the place is not self-supporting. Its net cost is, in round numbers, £20,000; of which, in round numbers again, England pays one-half and the colony the other. It was admitted that when the English subsidy was withdrawn, – for in fact England does pay at present £6,000 a year for general expenses over and above her contribution per man to the establishment at Port Arthur, – that when this should be discontinued, Port Arthur must be deserted.

The interest of such an establishment as this of course lies very much in the personal demeanour, in the words, and appearance of the prisoners. A man who has been all his life fighting against law, who has been always controlled but never tamed by law, is interesting, though inconvenient, – as is a tiger. There were some dozen or fifteen men, – perhaps more, – whom we found inhabiting separate cells, and who were actually imprisoned. These were the heroes of the place. There was an Irishman with one eye, named Doherty, who told us that for forty-two years he had never been a free man for an hour. He had been transported for mutiny when hardly more than a boy, – for he had enlisted as a boy, – and had since that time received nearly 3,000 lashes. In appearance he was a large man and still powerful, – well to look at in spite of his eye, lost as he told us through the misery of prison life. But he said that he was broken at last. If they would only treat him kindly, he would be as a lamb. But within the last few weeks he had escaped with three others, and had been brought back almost starved to death. The record of his prison life was frightful. He had been always escaping, always rebelling, always fighting against authority, – and always being flogged. There had been a whole life of torment such as this; – forty-two years of it; and there he stood, speaking softly, arguing his case well, and pleading while the tears ran down his face for some kindness, for some mercy in his old age. 'I have tried to escape; – always to escape,' he said, – 'as a bird does out of a cage. Is that unnatural; – is that a great crime?' The man's first offence, that of mutiny, is not one at which the mind revolts. I did feel for him, and when he spoke of himself as a caged bird, I should have liked to take him out into the world, and have given him a month of comfort. He would probably, however, have knocked my brains out on the first opportunity. I was assured that he was thoroughly bad, irredeemable, not to be reached by any kindness, a beast of prey, whose hand was against every honest man, and against whom it was necessary that every honest man should raise his hand. Yet he talked so gently and so well, and argued his own case with such winning words! He was writing in a book when we entered his cell, and was engaged on some speculation as to the tonnage of vessels. 'Just scribbling, sir,' he said, 'to while away the hours.'

(Vol. Two, Chapter II)

Tasmanian loyalty

The Tasmanians in their loyalty are almost English-mad. The very regret which is felt for the loss of English soldiers arises chiefly from the feeling that the uniform of the men was especially English. There is with them all a love of home, – which word always means England, – that touches the heart of him who comes to them from the old country. 'We do not want to be divided from you. Though we did in sort set up for ourselves, and though we do keep our own house, we still wish to be thought of by Great Britain as a child that is loved. We like to have among us some signs of your power, some emblem of your greatness. A red coat or two in our streets would remind us that we were Englishmen in a way that would please us well. We do not wish to be Americanised in our ways and thoughts. Well, – if we cannot have a red-coated soldier we will at any rate have a mail-guard with a red coat after the old fashion, and a mail-coachman with a red coat, and a real mail-coach.' And they have the mail-coach running through from Launceston to Hobart Town, and from Hobart Town to Launceston, not in the least like a Cobb's coach, as they are in the other colonies, but built directly after that ancient and most uncomfortable English pattern which we who are old remember; – and they have the coachman and the guard clothed in red, – because red has been from time immemorial the royal livery of England.

The Tasmanians are loyal, but they have terrible doubts of the loyalty of England. Rumours of republican meetings have reached them, of English communism, of international labour meetings, and of opposition to the House of Lords. 'We are English,' they say, 'but you are either French or American. We adhere to our red coats, but you are going to abandon the House of Lords; and oh! – alas that such an idea should be possible! – there are among you some who would abandon the very throne.' I have my own ideas about republicanism, – so called in England, – which are not very favourable to English republicans. I believe them to be few in number and as inferior in general knowledge of their fellow-countrymen as they are in position and influence. I do not think that the Crown is in danger, – believing it to be

much safer than any other crown in the world. And I believe that
the House of Peers has a long life before it. But wise men and
anxious men in Tasmania shake their heads at me, and doubt my
security.

(Vol. Two, Chapter III)

The Chudleigh caves

The Chudleigh caves are one of the wonders of Tasmania – and,
indeed, they are very wonderful. We went there in true guberna-
torial style, with four horses; – for it must be understood that
throughout the colonies, when it is known that the governor is
coming, things are done as they should be. Ours was a private
little party, consisting of four, but we had four horses, and went
to the caves magnificently. We had a very pleasant day, – more
than ordinarily so; but the Chudleigh caves should not be visited
by any one lightly, and I think I may take upon myself to say that
they should not be visited by ladies at all. On this occasion we
were all males.

With our four horses we were driven some sixteen miles, till at
last we were in the middle of thick bush without any vestige of
road. The road had become less like a road by degrees, and the
fields less like fields. Where timber had been cleared away,
wholly or in part, very heavy crops of oats were growing. The
farmers are afraid to trust themselves to wheat because of the
rust, and can hardly live by growing oats, so great is the cost
both of labour and carriage, and so low the price of the grain. On
our journey an old man attached himself to us, who seemed to
have the caves under his peculiar care, and who assured us that
he had shown all the governors over them. He came out upon us
from a public-house, of which he was the proprietor, and promising us that we should have the benefit of his services, followed us
on a wonderful rat-tailed mare with which he jumped over every
obstruction along the road, and made himself very busy, assuring
the governor that no governor could see the caves aright without
him, and taking command of the whole party with that air of
authority which always carries success with it. I think his name

was Pickett. We soon found that we were creatures in Mr Pickett's hand.

We descended from the carriage, Mr Pickett so ordering, but the order was not given till it was impossible for any carriage to proceed farther. We then walked about a mile through the scrub, descending at last into a hole which was the mouth of the cave. Stalactite caves are not uncommon in the world. Those at Cheddar in Somersetshire are very well known, and are very pretty; – much prettier than the caves in Tasmania, as the stones drop into rarer shapes and are brighter and more picturesque. But the caves at Cheddar are nothing to the Chudleigh caves in bigness, blackness, water, dirt, and the enforced necessity of crawling, creeping, wading, and knocking one's head about at every turn. Mr Pickett lighted the candles, told us that we should have to walk about five miles underground, gave us to understand that the water would never be more than up to our middles, that one could do it all in four hours, and that we were about to grope our way through the greatest wonder of the world. Then he led the way gallantly, splashing down into the mud, and inviting his Excellency to take heart and fear nothing. His Excellency took heart and went on. Whether he feared anything, I cannot say. I did, – when I had broken my head for the third time, and especially when I had crawled through a crevice in which I nearly stuck, and as to which I felt almost certain that I should never be able to force my way back again. We were then more than a mile away from the aperture, and innumerable black rivers, little Styxes, dark deceitful Acherons,[12] cold as death, ran between us and the upper air. Pickett was instant with us to go on to the end. We had not seen half the wonders of the place, – which by-the-bye were invisible by reason of the outer darkness. But we were cold to the marrow of our bones, wet through, covered with mud, and assured that, if we did go on, the journey must be made partly on our hands and knees, and partly after the fashion of serpents. At last we rebelled and insisted on being allowed to return. So we waded our way back again. I think that I will never visit another land cave. We had, however, brought fresh clothes. and when we had made a forest toilet, and demolished our chickens and sherry, we were able to smoke the pipe of peace in happiness and contentment under Mr Pickett's auspices. Mr Pickett told us, as we took our leave of him, that he should not enter the caves again till another governor should come to see them.

(Vol. Two, Chapter III)

He visits more convicts

But here, at Rottnest, the aboriginal convicts do work, and work cheerfully. On Sundays they are allowed to roam at will through the island, and they bring home wallabys, and birds, and fishes. At night they are locked up in cells, never less than three together, and are allowed blankets for bedding. It was the nearest approach that I saw to black adult civilisation, – though made through crime and violence. And here I must again express an opinion that the crime and the violence of these men have altogether a different effect on the mind of the bystander than have the same deeds when done by white men. As we condemn them for much in that they are savages, so must we acquit them of much for the same reason. Our crimes are often their virtues; but we make them subject to our laws, – of which they know little or nothing, – and hang them or lock them up for deeds for which they are not criminal in their own consciences, and for the non-performance of which they would be condemned by their own laws. I was astonished to find how large a proportion of these black prisoners had been convicted of murder; – and that the two who were awaiting their trial were both accused of that crime. But these murders were chiefly tribal retributions. A man in some tribe is murdered, or perhaps simply dies. It is then considered necessary that the next tribe should also lose a man, – so that things might be made equal; and some strong young fellow is told off to execute the decision of the elders. Should he refuse to do so, he is knocked about and wounded and ill-treated among his own people. But if he perform the deed entrusted to him, he is tracked down by black policemen, is tried for murder, and has a life-sentence passed against him. When examined as to these occurrences they almost invariably tell the truth; – never endeavouring to screen themselves by any denial of the murder done, or by the absence of sufficient evidence; but appealing to the necessity that was laid upon them. Such an account one of those in the prison, who was to be tried, gave to me in the governor's presence, – which was much as follows, though at the time demanding interpretation, which I hope the reader will not need: – 'Him come,' – him being some old chief in the tribe; – 'him say, "go kill Cracko;"' – Cracko being the destined victim; – 'me no like; him say "must;" me no like very much; him hab spear;' – then there was a sign made of the cruel chief wounding his disobedient subject; – 'then me go kill Cracko.' – 'With a tomahawk?' suggests the governor. The prisoner nods assent, and evidently thinks that the whole thing has been made clear and satisfactory. In very many cases the murderer is acquitted, as the judge very properly refuses to take the prisoner's story as a plea of guilty, and demands that the crime shall be proved by evidence. If the evidence be forthcoming the young murderer is sent to Rottnest with a life-sentence, and, – as I think, – enters on a much more blessed phase of existence than he has ever known before.

In the evening it was suggested that the prisoners should 'have a corroboree' for the amusement of the guests, and orders were given accordingly. At that time I had never seen a corroboree, – and was much interested, because it was said that a special tribe from which sixteen or eighteen of these men came were very great in corroborees. A corroboree is a tribal dance in which the men congregate out in the bush, in the front of a fire, and go through various antics with smeared faces and bodies, with spears and sticks, howling, and moving their bodies about in time; – while the gins, and children, and old people sit round in a circle. I am told that some corroborees are very interesting. I probably never saw a good one, – as I did not find them to be amusing. This corroboree in the Rottnest prison was the best I saw, – but even in that there was not much to delight. When the order was given, I could not but think of other captives who were desired to sing and make merry in their captivity. Here, however, there was no unwillingness, – and when I proposed that five shillings worth of tobacco should be divided among the performers, I was assured that the evening would be remembered as a very great occasion in the prison.

(Vol. Two, Chapter VI)

Perth

Perth I found to be a very pretty town, built on a lake of brackish water formed by the Swan River. It contains 6,000 inhabitants, and of course is the residence of the chief people of the colony, – as the governor is there, and the legislative chamber, and the supreme judge, and the bishop. The governor's house is handsome, as is also the town-hall. The churches, – cathedrals I should call them, – both of the Protestants and Roman Catholics, are large and convenient. On my first arrival I stayed at an inn, – which I did not indeed like very much at first, as the people seemed to be too well off to care for strangers, but which in its accommodation was better than can be found in many towns of the same size in England. I must acknowledge, however, that I was much troubled by musquitoes, and did not think the excuse a good one when I was told that a musquito curtain could not be put up because it was Sunday.

I found that crime of a heavy nature was not common in Perth or the districts round it, though a large portion of the population consisted of men who were or had been convicts. Men were daily committed for bad language, drunkenness, absconding, late hours, and offences of like nature. For men holding tickets-of-leave[13] are subjected to laws which make it criminal for a man to leave his master's employ, or to be absent from his master's house after certain hours, or to allude in an improper manner to his master's eyes. And for these offences, sentences of punishment are given which seem to be heavy, because it is difficult to bear in mind the difference between free men, and prisoners who are allowed partial freedom under certain conditions.

I have heard it said, more than once or twice, in reference not specially to Perth, but to the whole colony, that the ticket-of-leave men are deterred from violence simply by fear, that they are all thieves when they dare to steal, and that the absence of crime is no proof of reformation. The physiognomy, and gait, and general idleness of the men, their habits of drinking when they can get drink, and general low tendencies, are alleged as proof of this. It cannot be supposed that convicts should come out from their prisons industrious, orderly men, fit for self-management. The restraint and discipline to which they have been subject as convicts, independently of their old habits, would prevent this. The Bill Sykes[14] look of which I have spoken, is produced rather by the gaol than by crime. The men are not beautiful to look at. They do spend their money in drink, filling the bars of the public-houses, till the hour comes at which they must retire. But it is much in such a community that they should not return to crimes of violence.

(Vol. Two, Chapter VII)

South Australia – Salt Bush Country

I had not then seen a salt-bush country, though I subsequently passed through such a region in a part of New South Wales, of which I said a few words in speaking of that colony. Here, in the salt-bush of South Australia, there was not a blade of grass when I visited it. The salt-bush itself is an ugly grey shrub, about two feet high, which seems to possess the power of bringing forth its foliage without moisture. This foliage is impregnated with salt, and both sheep and cattle will feed upon it and thrive. It does not produce wool of the best class, – but it is regarded as being a very safe food for sheep, because it rarely fails. At the period of my visit the country was in want of rain; and I was assured that when the rain, then expected, should fall, the surface of the ground would be covered with grass. I can only say that I never saw a country more bare of grass. But for miles together, – over hundreds of square miles, – the salt-bush spreads itself; and as long as that lives the sheep will not be starved. Sometimes this shrub was diversified by a blue bush, a bush very much the same as the salt-bush in form, though of a dull slate colour instead of grey. On this the sheep will not feed. There is also a poisonous shrub which the sheep will eat, – as to which there seemed to be an opinion that it was fatal only to travelling sheep, and not to those regularly pastured on the country.

The run which I visited bears about 120,000 sheep, – and they wander over about 1,200,000 acres. For all these sheep, and for all this extent of sheep-run, it is necessary to obtain water by means of wells, sunk to various depths from fifty to one hundred and twenty feet. The water can always be found, – not indeed always at the first attempt, but so surely that no land in that region need be deserted for want of it. The water when procured is invariably more or less brackish; – but the sheep thrive on it and like it. The wells are generally worked by men, sometimes by horses; but on large runs, where capital has been made available, the water is raised by wind-mills. Such was the case at the place I visited. The water is brought up into large tanks, holding from 30,000 to 60,000 gallons each, and from these tanks is distributed into troughs, made of stone and cement. These are carried out in different directions, perhaps two or three from each tank, and are so arranged that sheep can be watered from either side. If therefore there be three such troughs, the sheep in six different paddocks can be watered from one tank, – the well being so placed as to admit egress to it from various paddocks, all converging on the same centre. In this way 10,000 sheep will be watered at one well. As these paddocks contain perhaps 40 square miles each, or over 25,000 acres, the animals have some distance to travel before they can get a drink. In cold weather they do not require to drink above once in three days; – in moderate weather once in two days; – in very hot weather they will lie near to the troughs and not trouble themselves to go afield in search of food. On the run which I visited there were twenty of these wells, which, with their appurtenances of tanks, and troughs, and wind-mills, had cost about £500 each: – and there had been about as many failures in the search of water, wells which had been dug but at which no water was found; – and these had not been sunk without considerable expenditure.

(Vol. Two, Chapter XII)

Copper versus gold

South Australia is a copper colony. Victoria, New South Wales, and Queensland are pre-eminently golden. Tasmania is doing a little business in gold, but by no means enough to give her importance. Western Australia has lead-mines, though as yet she has derived but little wealth from them; she also is waiting for gold, hoping that it may yet turn up. South Australia is undoubtedly auriferous. Not only have specks of gold been found as in Western Australia, but diggers have worked at the trade, and have lived upon it, and the industry is still continued. At a publican's house I saw bottles of gold, which he made it a part of his trade to buy from diggers. At a certain bank in Adelaide I saw a cabinet with drawers half full of gold, which it was a part of the business of the bankers to buy from publicans, or other intermediate agents. But this was all digger's gold, not miner's gold, – gold got by little men in little quantities from surface-washing. Of gold mines proper there are none as yet in the colony. That there will be such found and worked up in the northern territory, within the tropics, is now an opinion prevalent in Adelaide. Whether there be ground for such hope I have no evidence on which to form an opinion; but should this be the case, the northern territory will probably become a separate colony. Of this, however, I shall have to speak again in another chapter. Up to the time of my visit to Adelaide gold to the value of three-quarters of a million sterling had as yet been found in South Australia. This, of course, is as nothing to the produce of the three eastern colonies, and therefore South Australia is not hitherto entitled to consider herself as a golden land.

But what she has wanted in gold she has made up in copper. And in some respects the copper has, I think, been better than gold, as affording a more wholesome class of labour. There is less gambling in the business, – less of gambling even among the shareholders and managing people, and infinitely less temptation to gamble among the workmen. The fact that the metal must be dealt with in large quantities, that vast weights must be moved, and that heavy machinery must be employed, that no man can find enough to support himself for six months by a stroke of luck and carry it away in his waistcoat pocket, gives a sobriety to the employment which the search after gold often lacks.

(Vol. Two, Chapter XIII)

The telegraph

The telegraph posts and wires by which the Australian colonies are now connected with Great Britain are already an established fact. This line enters the Australian continent from Java, at a point on the northern coast called Port Darwin. At Port Darwin there is a small settlement called Palmerston, around which land had been sold to the extent of 500,000 acres when I was in the colony, and this has been selected as the landing-place of European news. The colonisation of the northern territory is thus begun, – and there can be little doubt but that a town, and then a settlement, and then a colony, will form themselves.

When the scheme of the telegraph was first put on foot the colony of South Australia undertook to make the entire line across the continent, – the submarine line to Java and the line thence on to Singapore and home to Europe being in other hands. It was an immense undertaking for a community so small in number, and one as to which many doubted the power of the colony to complete it. But it has been completed. I had heard, before I left England in 1871, that an undertaking had been given by the government of South Australia to finish the work by January 1, 1872. This certainly was not done, but very great efforts were made to accomplish it, and the failure was caused by the violence of nature rather than by any want of energy. Unexpected and prolonged rains interfered with the operations and greatly retarded them. The world is used to the breaking of such promises in regard to time, and hardly ever expects that a contractor for a large work shall be punctual within a month or two. The world may well excuse this breach of contract, for surely no contractor ever had a harder job of work on hand. The delay would not be worth mention here, were it not that the leading South Australians of the day, headed by the Governor, had been so anxious to show that they could really do all that they had undertaken to perform, and were equally disappointed at their own partial failure.

The distance of the line to be made was about 1,800 miles, and the work had to be done through a country unknown, without water, into which every article needed by the men had to be carried over deserts, across unbridged rivers, through unexplored forests, amidst hostile tribes of savages, – in one of the hottest regions of the world. I speak here of the lack of water, and I have said above that the works were hindered by rain. I hope my gentle readers will not think that I am piling up excuses which obliterate each other. There is room for deviation of temperature in a distance of 1,800 miles, – and Australia generally, though subject specially to drought, is subject to floods also. And the same gentle readers should remember, – when they bethink themselves how easy it is to stick up a few poles in this or another thickly inhabited country, and how small is the operation of erecting a line of telegraph wires as compared with that of constructing a railway or even a road, – how great had hitherto been the difficulty experienced by explorers in simply making their way across the continent, and in carrying provisions for themselves as they journeyed. Burke and Wills[15] perished in the attempt, and the line to be taken was through the very country in which Burke and Wills had been lost. The dangers would of course not be similar. The army of workmen sent to put up the posts and to stretch the wires was accompanied by an army of purveyors. Men could never be without food or without water. But it was necessary that everything should be carried. For the northern portion of the work it was necessary that all stores should be sent round by ships, and then taken up rivers which had not hitherto been surveyed. If the gentle reader will think only of the amount of wire required for 1,800 miles of telegraph communication, and of the circumstances of its carriage, he will, I think, recognise the magnitude of the enterprise.

The colony divided the work, the government undertaking about 800 miles in the centre, which portion of the ground was considered to be most difficult to reach. The remaining distances, consisting of 500 miles in the south and 500 in the north, were let out to contractors. The southern part, which was comparatively easy as being accessible from Adelaide, was finished in time, as was also the middle distance which the government had kept in its own hands. But the difficulties at the northern end were so great that they who had undertaken the work, failed to accomplish it, and it was at last completed by government, – if I remember rightly somewhat more than six months after the date fixed. The line did not come into immediate working order, owing to some temporary fault beyond the Australian borders.

The importance of the telegraph to the colonies cannot be overrated, and the anxiety it created can only be understood by those who have watched the avidity with which news from England is received in all her dependencies.

(Vol. Two, Chapter XIV)

He enlarges his hunting experience

Such a hunt-banquet I never saw before. The spot was some eight or ten miles from Melbourne, close upon the sea-shore, and with a railway-station within a quarter of a mile. It was a magnificent day for a picnic, with a bright sun and a cool air, so that the temptations to come, over and beyond that of hunting, were great. About two hundred men were assembled in a tent pitched behind the house of the master of the festival, of whom perhaps a quarter were dressed in scarlet. Nothing could have been done better, or in better taste. There was no speaking, no drinking, – so to be called, but a violent clatter of knives and forks for about half-an-hour. At about two we were out on a common smoking our cigars in front of the house, and remained there talking to the ladies in carriages till nearly three, when we started. I found the horse provided for me to be a stout, easily-ridden, well-bitted cob; but when I remembered what posts and rails were in this country, I certainly thought that he was very small. No doubt discretion would be the better part of valour! With such a crowd of horses as I saw around me, there would probably be many discreet besides myself, so that I might attain decent obscurity amidst a multitude. I had not bedizened myself in a scarlet coat.

We were upon a heath, and I calculated that there were present about two hundred and fifty horsemen. There was a fair sprinkling of ladies, and I was requested to observe one or two of them, as they would assuredly ride well. There is often a little mystery about hunting, – especially in the early part of the day,

– as all men know who ride to hounds at home. It is not good that everybody should be told what covert is to be drawn first; and even with stag-hounds the officials of the pack will not always answer with full veracity every question put to them by every stranger. On this occasion there seemed to be considerable mystery. No one seemed to know where we were going to begin, and there was a doubt as to the quarry to be chased. I had been told that we were to hunt a dingo, – or wild dog; and there was evidently a general opinion that turning down a dingo, – shaking him I suppose out of a bag, – was good and genuine sport. We do not like bagged foxes at home, – but I fancy that they are unpopular chiefly because they will never run. If a dingo will run, I do not see why he should not be turned down as well as a deer out of a cart. But on this occasion I heard whispers about, – a drag.[16] The asseverations about the dingo were, however, louder than the whispers about a drag, and I went on, believing that the hounds would be put upon the trail of the animal. We rode for some three of four miles over heath-land, nobody around me seeming to be in the least aware when the thing would commence. The huntsman was crabbed and uncommunicative. The master was soft as satin, but as impregnable as plate armour. I asked no questions myself, knowing that time will unravel most things; but I heard questions asked, the answers to which gave no information whatever. At last the hounds began to stir among the high heather, and were hunting something. I cared little what it was, if only there might be no posts and rails in that country. I like to go, but I don't like to break my neck; and between the two I was uncomfortable. The last fences I had seen were all wire, and I was sure that a drag would not be laid among them. But we had got clear of wire fences, – wire all through from top to bottom, – before we began. We seemed to be on an open heath, riding round a swamp, without an obstacle in sight. As long as that lasted I could go as well as the best.

But it did not last. In some three minutes, having ridden about half a mile, I found myself approaching such an obstacle as in England would stop a whole field. It was not only the height but the obduracy of the wooden barrier, – which seemed as though it were built against ever-rushing herds of wild bulls. At home we are not used to such fences, and therefore they are terrible to us. At a four foot and a half wall, a man with a good heart and a good horse will ride; and the animal, if he knows what he is about, will strike it, sometimes with fore as well as hind feet, and come down without any great exertion. But the post and rail in Australia should be taken with a clear flying leap. There are two alternatives if this be not done. If the horse and man be heavy enough and the pace good enough, the top bar may be broken. It is generally about eight inches deep and four thick, is quite rough, and apparently new, – but, as on this occasion I saw repeatedly, it may be broken; and when broken the horse and rider go through unscathed, – carried by their own impetus, as a candle may be fired through a deal board. The other chance is to fall, – which event seemed to occur more often even than the smashing of the rail. Now I was especially warned that if I rode slowly at these fences, and fell, my horse would certainly fall atop of me; whereas if I went fast I should assuredly be launched so far ahead that there would be room for my horse between me and the fence which had upset me. It was not a nice prospect for a man riding something over sixteen stone!

But now had come the moment in which I must make up my mind. Half-a-dozen men were over the rail. Half-a-dozen baulked it. Two fell, escaping their own horses by judicious impetus. One gentleman got his horse half over, the fore quarters being on one side, and the hind on the other, so that the animal was hung up. A lady rode at it with spirit, but checked her horse with the curb, and he, rearing back, fell on her. Another lady took it in gallant style. Of those before me no one seemed to flinch it. For a moment it seemed as though the honour of all the hunting fields in England were entrusted to my keeping, and I determined to dare greatly, let the penalty be what it might. With firm hands and legs, but with heart very low down, I crammed the little brute at the mountain of woodwork. As I did so I knew that he could not carry me over. Luckily he knew as much about it as I did, and made not the slightest attempt to rise with me. I don't know that I ever felt so fond of a horse before.

At that moment, an interesting individual coming like a cannon ball, crashed the top bar beside me, and I, finding that the lady was comfortably arranging her back hair with plenty of assistance, rode gallantly over the second bar. For the next half-hour I took care always to go over second bars, waiting patiently till a top bar was broken. I had found my level, and had resolved to keep it. On one occasion I thought that a top bar never would be broken, – and the cessation was unpleasant, as successful horsemen disappeared one after another. But I perceived that there was a regular company of second-bar men, so that as long as I could get over a rail three feet high I need not fear that I should be left alone. And hitherto the pace had not been quick enough to throw the second-bar men out of the hunt. But soon there came a real misfortune. There was a fence with only one bar, – with only one apparent obstacle. I am blind as well as heavy, and I did not see the treacherous wire beneath. A heavy philanthropist, just before me, smashed the one, and I rode on at what I thought to be a free course. My little horse, seeing no more than I did, rushed upon the wire, and the two of us were rolled over in ignominious dismay. The horse was quicker on his feet than I was, and liking the sport, joined it at once single-handed; while I was left alone and disconsolate. Men and horses, – even the sound of men and horses, – disappeared from me, and I found myself in solitude in a forest of gum-trees.

(Vol. Two, Chapter XVIII)

New Zealand – Maori characteristics

. . . the traditions of the Maori people have been preserved with tenacious fidelity, and the period at which the migration took place is not very remote. They were, for the most part, a brown people, of the Malay race, and seem to have found no human inhabitants before them when they landed. It has been calculated from the succession of chiefs, of whose names tradition has kept the record, that the Maoris landed in New Zealand about the beginning of the fifteenth century. It is perhaps impossible now to fix the date with accuracy. Of all the people whom we have been accustomed to call savages, they were perhaps, in their savage condition as we found them, the most civilised. They lived in houses; had weapons and instruments of their own made of stone; held land for cultivation as the property, not of individuals, but of tribes; cooked their food with fire; stored property so that want and starvation were uncommon among them; possessed a system for the administration of justice, and treated their wives well. But they were greatly addicted to civil wars, and they ate their enemies when they could kill or catch them.

They are an active people, – the men averaging 5 feet 6½ inches in height, and are almost equal in strength and weight to Englishmen. In their former condition they wore matting, now they wear European clothes. Formerly they pulled out their beards, and every New Zealander of mark was tattooed; now they wear beards, – and the young men are not tattooed. Their hair is black and coarse, but not woolly like a negro's, or black like a Hindoo's. The nose is almost always broad, and the mouth large. In other respects their features are not unlike those of the European race. The men, to my eyes, were better looking than the women, – and the men who were tattooed better looking than those who had dropped the custom. The women still retain the old custom of tattooing the under lip. The Maoris had a mythology of their own, and believed in a future existence; – but they did not recognise one Supreme God. Virtue with them, as with other savages, consisted chiefly in courage, and a command of temper. Their great passion was revenge, which was carried on by one tribe against another to the extent sometimes of the annihilation of tribes. The decrease of their population since the English first came among them, has been owing as much to civil war, as to the injuries with which civilisation has afflicted them. They seem from early days to have acquired that habit of fighting behind stockades, – or in fortified pahs,[17] – which we have found so fatal to ourselves in our wars with them. Their weapons, before they got guns from us, were not very deadly. They were chiefly short javelins and stones, both flung from slings. But there was a horror in their warfare to the awfulness of which they themselves seem to have been keenly alive. When a prisoner was taken in war, he was cooked and eaten.

(Vol. Two, Chapter XIX)

Winter

In New Zealand everything is English. The scenery, the colour and general appearance of the waters, and the shape of the hills, are altogether un-Australian, and very like to that with which we are familiar in the west of Ireland and the highlands of Scotland. The mountains are brown and sharp and serrated, the rivers are bright and rapid, and the lakes are deep, and blue, and bosomed among the mountains. If a long-sleeping Briton could be awaked, and set down among the Southland hills, and told that he was travelling in Galway or Cork, or in the west of Ross, he might be easily deceived, though he knew the nature of those counties well, – but he would feel at once that he was being hoaxed if he were told in any part of Australia that he was travelling among Irish or British scenery.

We were unfortunate in the time of the year, having reached the coldest part of New Zealand in the depth of winter. Everybody had told me that it was so, – and complaint had been made to me of my conduct, as though I were doing New Zealand a manifest injustice in reaching her shores at a time of the year in which her roads were all mud, and her mountains all snow. By more than one New Zealander I was scolded roundly, and by those who did not scold me I was laughed to scorn. Did I imagine that because August was summer in England, therefore it was summer at the other side of the world; – or did I think that I should find winter pleasant in Otago, because winter might be preferable to summer in Queensland? I endeavoured to explain that I had had no alternative, – that I must see New Zealand in winter or not see it at all; but one always fails in attempting to make one's own little arrangements intelligible to others, and I found it better to submit. I had come at the wrong time; – was very sorry for it, but would now make the best of it. Perhaps the roads would not be so very bad. I was assured that they could not possibly be worse.

Nevertheless, as I had come to see scenery, I determined to see it as far as my time and strength would allow. I had learned that Lake Wakatip was the great object to be reached, – Wakatipu is the proper name, but the abbreviated word is always used. From

Invercargill I could certainly get to Wakatip, as the coach was running, and from Wakatip I might possibly get down to Dunedin, – but that was doubtful. If not, I must come back to Invercargill. I hate going back, and I made up my mind that if the mud and snow were no worse than British mud or British snow, we would make our way through.

(Vol. Two, Chapter XX)

An accident

On the fifth day, – the worst of all, for the snow fell incessantly, the wretched horses could not drag us through the mud, so that I and the gentleman with me were forced to walk, and the twelve miles which we accomplished took us five hours, – we reached the town of Tuapika, whence we were assured there would run a well-appointed coach to Dunedin. Tuapika is otherwise called Lawrence, – and it may be as well here to remark that in this part of New Zealand all towns have two names. The colonists give one, – sometimes, as in the case of Tuapika, taking that of the natives, – and the government gives another. We had come through Dunedin alias Clyde, through Teeviot alias Roxburgh, through Beaumont which had some other name which I have forgotten, and at last reached Tuapika alias Lawrence. The rivers and districts have been served in the same way, and as the different names are used miscellaneously, the difficulty which travellers always feel as to new localities is considerably enhanced. At Tuapika we found an excellent inn, and a very good dinner. In spite of the weather I went round the town, and visited the Athenæum or reading-room. In all these towns there are libraries, and the books are strongly bound and well thumbed. Carlyle, Macaulay, and Dickens[18] are certainly better known to small communities in New Zealand than they are to similar congregations of men and women at home. I should have liked Tuapika had it not snowed so bitterly on me when I was there.

On the following day we got on board the well-appointed coach at six in the morning. It certainly was a well-appointed coach, and was driven by as good a coachman as ever sat upon a box; but the first stage, which took us altogether six hours, was not memorable for good fortune. There was a lower new road and an upper old road. The former was supposed to be impracticable because of the last night's snow, and the man decided on taking the hills. As far as I could see we were traversing a mountain-side without any track; but there was a track, for on a sudden, as we turned a corner, we found ourselves in a cutting, and we found also that the cutting was blocked with snow. The coach could not be turned, and the horses had plunged in so far that we could with difficulty extricate them from the traces and pole-straps. The driver, however, decided on going on. Shovels were procured, and for two hours we all worked up to our hips in snow, and did at last get the coach through the cutting. But it was not practicable to drive the horses down the hill we had ascended, and we therefore took them out and brought it down by hand, – an operation which at any rate kept us warm.

(Vol. Two, Chapter XX)

Maori superstition

On the contrary they have forced many among us to learn theirs. They have doubtless been aided in this by the action of the missionaries, who felt, as has been common with those who have based the progress of civilisation chiefly on religious teaching, that they could retain a more exclusive hold on the natives by learning their language than by teaching to them the language of the settlers. The effect has been greatly to increase the difficulty of amalgamating the races. Those difficulties have been overwhelming, and no amalgamation is now possible.

The Maoris, with all the teaching that has been lavished on them, seem never to have overcome the incubus of barbarous superstition. The 'tapu,' before we came, was with them all powerful. Doubtless the power has been weakened, but it has not been got rid of even by Christian Maoris. The 'tapu' makes a thing sacred, so that it should not be touched; – sacred, or perhaps accursed. Priests are 'tapu.' Food is very often 'tapu,' so that only sacred persons may eat it, and then must eat it without touching it with their hands. Places are frightfully 'tapu,' so that no man or woman may go in upon them. Chiefs are 'tapu,' – particularly their heads. Dead bodies in some circumstances are 'tapu.' Indeed there was no end to the 'tapu,' and it is easy enough to see how strongly the continuance of such superstition must have worked against civilisation.

The desire of accumulating property, combined with the industry for doing so, is perhaps of all qualifications for civilisation the most essential. But the Maoris had, and still have, an institution terribly subversive both of the desire and of the power to collect wealth. This is called 'muru,' and consists in the infliction of punishment for faults, or accidents, – or even for faults or accidents committed by others. Sometimes it is enforced in the way of compliment, – and a Maori in such cases would consider himself to be slighted if he were not half-ruined by a 'muru.' Those who perform the 'muru' visit the afflicted one, eat up all his provision, and take away all his moveables. The expedition that thus performs justice is called a 'taua.' If a man's wife runs away, a 'taua' of his own friends visits him as a mark of condolence, another 'taua' of his wife's friends visits him to punish him for not taking better care of her. A third 'taua' on behalf of the Lothario comers,[19] because he also has got into a mess, – and between the three the unhappy victim is denuded of everything.

– – – –

It is with pain that I write as I do about a gallant people, whose early feelings towards us were those of kindness and hospitality, and as to whom I acknowledge that they have nearly had the gifts which would have enabled us to mix with them on equal terms. And I feel grieved that I cannot participate more cordially than I do with the sympathies of those who have been stirred by a certain romantic element in the Maori character to build up in their own imaginations the fiction of a noble race. More than one such has pointed out to me in glowing language the poetry of the Maori story, and has pointed out to me that it required but a New Zealand Walter Scott to make the Maoris equal to the Highlanders. I cannot but answer to this that the blood of the Highlander is to be found at present wherever the English language is spoken, and that among all mankind no man is less likely to melt away than he. But the Maoris are going. No doubt the story of the Maori may be told with poetry. Such an attempt is not in my way; but as far as I have told it, I have endeavoured to tell it with truth.

(Vol. Two, Chapter XXV)

Parliamentary debate

I was often asked in New Zealand whether the line of parliamentary debate in that colony did not contrast favourably with that which I had heard in the Australian parliaments. I am bound to say that at Wellington I heard no word to which any Speaker of a House could take exception, and that this propriety of language was maintained while very hard things were being said by members, one of another. This is, I think, as it should be. The life necessary for political debate cannot be maintained without the saying of hard things; but the use of hard words makes debate at first unbearable, and after a time impracticable. But I thought that the method of talking practised in the New Zealand House of Representatives was open to censure on another head. I have never in any national debating assembly, – not even at Washington, – seen so constant a reference to papers on the part of those who were speaking as was made in this debate. It seemed as though barrows full of papers must have been brought in for the use of gentlemen on one side and on the other. From this arises the great evil of slowness. The gentleman on his legs in the House, – when custom has made that position easy to him, – learns to take delight in delaying the House while he turns over one folio after another either of manuscript which has been arranged for him, or of printed matter which he has marked for reference. And then, to show how very much at home he is, while gentlemen are gaping around him, he will look out for new references, muttering perhaps a word or two while his face is among the leaves, – perhaps repeating the last words of his last sentence, and absolutely revelling in the tyranny of his position.

But while doing so, he is unconsciously losing the orator's power of persuasion. I doubt whether Demosthenes often looked at his papers, or Cicero when he was speaking, or Pitt.[20] Judging from what I have seen from the stranger's gallery at home, I should say that a New Zealand minister had learned to carry to an absurdity a practice which is authorised, and no more than authorised, by the usage of our House of Commons. A Speaker, on observing such fault, can hardly call the offender to order, – but he might have the power of putting out the gas.

I cannot conclude my remarks about the Wellington Assembly and the debate which I heard there, without saying that the four Maori members discreetly split their votes, two supporting, and two voting against, the ministry.

(Vol. Two, Chapter XXVI)

Kauri trees

The kauri gum exudes from the kauri tree, but is not got by any process of tapping, or by taking the gum from the tree while standing. The tree falls and dies, as trees do fall and die in the course of nature; – whole forests fall and die; – and then when the timber has rotted away, when the centuries probably have passed, the gum is found beneath the soil. Practice tells the kauri gum seekers where to search for the hidden spoil. Armed with a long spear the man prods the earth, – and from the touch he knows the gum when he strikes it. Hundreds of thousands of tons probably still lie buried beneath the soil; – but the time will come when the kauri gum will be at an end, for the forests are falling now, not by the slow and kind operation of nature, but beneath the rapid axes of the settlers.

I was taken out from Auckland by a friend to see a kauri forest. Very shortly there will be none to be seen unless the searcher for it goes very far a-field. I was well repaid for my trouble, for I doubt whether I ever saw finer trees grouped together; and yet the foliage of them is neither graceful nor luxuriant. It is scanty, and grows in tufts like little bushes. But the trunks of the trees, and the colour of the timber, and the form of the branches are magnificent. The chief peculiarity seems to be that the trunk appears not to lessen in size at all till it throws out its branches at twenty-five or perhaps thirty feet from the ground, and looks therefore like a huge forest column. We saw one, to which we were taken by a woodsman whom we found at his work, the diameter of which was nine feet, and of which we computed the height up to the first branches to be fifty feet. And the branches are almost more than large in proportion to the height, spreading out after the fashion of an oak, – only in greater proportions.

These trees are fast disappearing. Our friend the woodman told us that the one to which he took us, – and than which he assured us that we could find none larger in the forest, – was soon to fall beneath his axe. When we met him he was triumphing over a huge monster that he had felled, and was splitting it up into shingles for roofing houses. The wood as it comes to pieces is yellow and resinous with gum, and on that account, – so he told us, – was super-excellent for shingles. The trees are never cut down for their gum, which seems to be useless till time has given it a certain consistency. Very soon there will not be a kauri tree left to cut down in the neighbourhood of Auckland.

(Vol. Two, Chapter XXVIII)

Maketu and after

At Maketu I walked up among their settlements, and shook hands with men and women, and smiled at them, and was smiled upon. At the inn they came and sat alongside of me, – so near that the contiguity sometimes almost amounted to an embrace. The children were noisy, jovial, and familiar. As far as one could judge, they all seemed to be very happy. There was a European schoolmaster there, devoted to the Maori children, – who spoke to me much of their present and future condition. He had great faith in their secular learning, but had fears as to their religious condition. He was most anxious that I should see them in school before I departed on the next morning, and I promised that I would do so. Though I was much hurried, I could not refuse such a request to a man so urgent in so good a cause. But in the morning, when I was preparing to be as good as my word, I was told that the schoolmaster had got very drunk after I had gone to bed, had smashed the landlord's windows, and had been carried away to his house by two policemen, – greatly, I hope, to the sorrow of those Maori scholars. After this little affair, it was not thought expedient that I should trouble him at an early hour on the following morning. I cannot but remark here that I saw very much more of drunkenness in New Zealand than in the Australian colonies; – and I will remark also, for the benefit of those who may ever visit these lakes, that there is a very nice little inn at Maketu.

On the following day we rode thirty-five miles, to Ohinemutu, through a very barren but by no means unpicturesque country. The land rises and falls in rapid little hills, and is tossed about in a wonderful fashion; – but there is no serious ascent or descent. The first lake seen is Roto Iti, at the end of which we had to swim our horses across a river, passing over it ourselves in a canoe, – as we had done also at Maketu. And here at the end of the lake, we found a very fine Maori house, or whare, – I believe the word is properly so spelt, but it consists of two syllables. And by the whare was a huge war-canoe, capable of carrying some sixty men at the paddles. These, as far as I could learn, were the property of the tribe, rather than of any individual. The whare was a long, low room, with high pitched roof, with an earthen floor, and ornamented with grotesque and indecent carvings. I may, however, as well say that I doubt whether I should have discovered the indecency had it not been pointed out to me. I don't think any one lived in the whare, – the chief of the tribe, as is usual, preferring his own little hut. No doubt had I wished to stay there, I might have slept on one of the mats with which a portion of the floor is covered.

Roto Iti, as I saw it, was very pretty, but I did not stop to visit the farther end of it, where, as I was told, the chief beauty of it lay. It may be as well to state that Roto is the Maori word for lake. We went on to Ohinemutu, passing a place called Ngae, on the lake Roto Rua, – whence, according to the Maori legend, a Maori damsel, hearing the flute of her lover in the island Mokoia, swam off to him. As the distance is hardly more than a mile, and as the Maoris are all swimmers, the feat did not seem to me to be very wonderful, – till I heard that the flute was made out of the tibia of a man's leg. At present there is a telegraph station at Ngae, and I found an unfortunate telegraphist living in solitude, inhabiting a small office on the lake side. Of course one took the opportunity of telegraphing to all one's friends; – but as visitors to Roto Rua are as yet but very scarce, I can hardly think that the station can pay its expenses.

On the farther side of Roto Iti I had seen great jets of steam at a distance. At Ohinemutu, on Roto Rua, I came to the first hot springs which I saw closely, and I must own that at first they were not especially pleasing. Before reaching the spot, we had to take our horses through the edge of the lake up to their bellies, at a place where the water was so impregnated with sulphur as to be almost unbearable on account of the stench. I had known the smell of sulphur before, – but here it seemed as though the sulphur were putrid. Ohinemutu itself is a poor little Maori village, which seems to have collected itself round the hot springs, close on the borders of the lake, with a view to the boiling of potatoes without the trouble of collecting fuel. Here was a little inn, – or accommodation-house, as it is colonially called, – kept by a European with a half-caste wife, at which the traffic must be very small indeed. He appeared to be the only white inhabitant of the place, and I cannot say that I thought him happily placed in regard to his neighbours or neighbourhood. At Ohinemutu there is nothing pretty. The lake itself has no special loveliness to recommend it. But close upon its edge, there are numerous springs of boiling water, – so close that some of them communicate with the lake, making the water warm for some distance from the shore. There were half-a-dozen pools within a couple of hundred yards of the inn, in which you could boil potatoes or bathe at your will, choosing the heat which you thought desirable. Close beside the gate was one pool which is always boiling. My companion told me that a Maori man had come to him at that spot, desiring to be enlisted in the Maori Contingent. He was bound to refuse the recruit as being too old, – whereupon the disappointed man threw himself into the pool and was boiled to death. Along the path thence to the bathing-pool mostly frequented by the Maoris, there were various small jets here and there, some throwing up a little water, and others a little stream, – very suggestive of accidents in the dark. Such accidents are not at all uncommon, the thin crust of earth not unfrequently giving way and letting through the foot of an incautious wanderer into a small boiling cauldron below. Farther on there is the small square pool, round and in which Maoris are always clustering; – on which no European would, I should imagine, ever desire to encroach, for the Maoris are many, and the waters are not much. Above and around this, flat stones have been fixed on the earth over steam-jets, – and here the Maoris squat and talk, and keep themselves warm. They seem to become so fond of the warmth as hardly to like to stir out of it. A little to the left, there is a small land-locked cove of the lake in which canoes were lying, and into which a hot spring finds its way, – so that the water of the whole cove may perhaps average ninety degrees of heat. Here on the following morning I bathed, and found myself able to swim without being boiled. but on the previous evening, about nine, when it was quite dark, I had bathed in another pool, behind the inn. Here I had gone in very light attire to make my first experience of these waters, my friend the Captain accompanying me, and here we had found three Maori damsels in the pool before us. But this was nothing, – nothing, at least, in the way of objection. The night was dark; and if they thoroughly understood the old French proverb which has become royally English, why should we be more obstinate or less intelligent? I crept down into the pool, and as I crouched beneath the water, they encouraged me by patting me on the back. The place was black, and shallow, but large enough for us all. I sat there very comfortably for half-an-hour while they conversed with the Captain, – who was a Maori scholar. Then I plunged into a cold river which runs into the lake a few yards from the hot spring, and then returned to the hot water amidst the renewed welcomings of the Maori damsels. And so I passed my first evening among the geysers, very pleasantly.

(Vol. Two, Chapter XXIX)

Farewell to the Maoris

During one long day a wild cat was the only animal we saw after leaving the neighbourhood of the place from which we started. On that night we slept at a Maori pah, which we did not reach till dark, – and before reaching it we had to pass through a dense wood in darkness so thick that I could not see my hand. I mention the fact in order that I may express my wonder at the manner in which my friend the Captain made his way through it. That night I had a small Maori hut all to myself, – one in which were deposited all the tokens of recent Maori habitation. There was a little door just big enough for ingress, – hardly big enough for egress, – and a heap of fern-leaves, and a looking-glass, and a bottle which looked like perfumery, – and the feeling as of many insects. In the morning two old women cooked some potatoes for us, – and I rode away, intending never to spend another night among the Maoris.

They are certainly more highly gifted than other savage nations I have seen. They are as superior in intelligence and courage to the Australian Aboriginal as they are in outward appearance. They are more pliable and nearer akin in their manners to civilised mankind than are the American Indians. They are more manly, more courteous, as also more sagacious than the African negro. One can understand the hope and the ambition of the first great old missionaries who had dealings with them. But contact with Europeans does not improve them. At the touch of the higher race they are poisoned and melt away. There is scope for poetry in their past history. There is room for philanthropy as to their present condition. But in regard to their future, – there is hardly a place for hope.

(Vol. Two, Chapter XXIX)

The Colonies

Here, in England, we naturally regard the colonies chiefly as the recipients of our redundant population. In that respect they are invaluable to us. We may probably be justified in saying that our great increase of people has been given to us in order that we might populate such lands. But we have much redundant population for which they are not fitted. The penniless young man who wants a genteel position, and who bases his claim to that condition of things on his education, will not generally find his claim allowed. If he go out with his position assured to him by interest it may be well with him, otherwise he will descend into the lowest grade of servitude, and will probably find himself a shepherd. The same fate in a different form will be the fate of ladies who emigrate hoping to earn by their talents and acquirements that bread which a too crowded market makes it difficult for them to find here. For their wares, excellent as they are, the market is also crowded there. Such are not the emigrants that Great Britain should be most urgent to send.

But for men who can and will work with their hands, for women who can cook and be generally useful about a household, for girls who are ready to learn to cook and to be generally useful, these colonies are a paradise. They will find the whole condition of life changed for them. The slight estimation in which labour is held here will be changed for a general respect. The humbleness, the hat-touching, the servility which is still incidental to such work as theirs in this old country, and which is hardly compatible with exalted manhood, has found no footing there. I regard such manhood among the masses of the people as the highest sign of prosperity which a country can give.

(Vol. Two, Chapter XXXI)

SOUTH AFRICA

Introduction

It was in April of last year, 1877, that I first formed a plan of paying an immediate visit to South Africa. The idea that I would one day do so had long loomed in the distance before me. Except the South African group I had seen all our great groups of Colonies, – among which in my own mind I always include the United States, for to my thinking, our Colonies are the lands in which our cousins, the descendants of our forefathers, are living and still speaking our language. I had become more or less acquainted I may say with all these offshoots from Great Britain, and had written books about them all – except South Africa. To 'do' South Africa had for some years past been on my mind, till at last there was growing on me the consciousness that I was becoming too old for any more such 'doing.' Then, suddenly, the newspapers became full of the Transvaal Republic.[1] There was a country not indeed belonging to Great Britain but which once had been almost British, a country, with which Britain was much too closely concerned to ignore it, – a country, which had been occupied by British subjects, and established as a Republic under British authority, – now in danger of being reconquered by the native tribes which had once peopled it. In this country, for the existence of which in its then condition we were in a measure responsible, the white man there would not fight, nor pay taxes, nor make himself conformable to any of these rules by which property and life are made secure. Then we were told that English interference and English interference only could save the country from internecine quarrels between black men and white men. While this was going on I made up my mind that now if ever must I visit South Africa. The question of the Confederation of the States was being mooted at the same time, a Confederation which was to include not only this Republic which was so very much out of elbows, but also another quiet little Republic of which I think that many of us did not know much at home, – but as to which we had lately heard that it was to receive £90,000 out of the revenue of the Mother Country, not in compensation for any acknowledged wrong, but as a general plaster for whatever little scratches the smaller community, namely the Republic of the Orange Free States,[2] might have received in its encounters with the greater majesty of the British Empire. If a tour to South Africa would ever be interesting, it certainly would be so now. Therefore I made up my mind and began to make enquiries as to steamers, cost, mode of travelling, and letters of introduction. It was while I was doing this that the tidings came upon us like a clap of thunder of the great deed done by Sir Theophilus Shepstone.[3] The Transvaal had already been annexed! The thing which we were dreaming of as just possible, – as an awful task which we might perhaps be forced to undertake in the course of some indefinite number of months to come, had already been effected. A sturdy Englishman had walked into the Republic with five and twenty policemen and a Union Jack and had taken possession of it. 'Would the inhabitants of the Republic like to ask me to take it?' So much enquiry he seems to have made. No; the people by the voice of their parliament declined even to consider so monstrous a proposition. 'Then I shall take it without being asked,' said Sir Theophilus. And he took it.

That was what had just been done in the Transvaal when my idea of going to South Africa had ripened itself into a resolution. Clearly there was an additional reason for going. Here had been done a very high-handed thing as to which it might be the duty of a Briton travelling with a pen in his hand to make a strong remonstrance. Or again it might be his duty to pat that sturdy Briton on the back, – with pen and ink, – and hold his name up to honour as having been sturdy in a righteous cause. If I had premeditated a journey to South Africa a year or two since, when South Africa was certainly not very much in men's mouths, there was much more to reconcile me to the idea now that Confederation and the Transvaal were in every man's mouth.

(Vol. One, Chapter I)

Federation

The binding together of a colonial group into one great whole is regarded as a preparation for separation from the mother country. It is as though we at home in England were saying to our children about the world; – 'We have paid for your infantine bread and butter; we have educated you and given you good trades; now you must go and do for yourselves.' There is perhaps no such feeling in the bosom of the special Colonial Minister at home who may at this or the other time be advocating this measure; but there must be an idea that some preparation for such a possible future event is expedient. We do not want to see such another colonial crisis as the American war of last century between ourselves and an English-speaking people. But in the Colonies there is a sort of loyalty of which we at home know nothing. It may be exemplified to any man's mind by thinking of the feeling as to home which is engendered by absence. The boy or girl who lives always on the paternal homestead does not care very much for the kitchen with its dressers, or for the farmyard with its ricks, or the parlour with its neat array. But let the boy or girl be banished for a year or two and every little detail becomes matter for a fond regret. Hence I think has sprung that colonial anger which has been entertained against Ministers at home who have seemed to prepare the way for final separation from the mother country.

Federation, though generally unpopular in the Colonies, has been welcomed in the Eastern Province of South Africa, because it would be a means of giving if not entire at any rate partial independence from Capetown domination. If Federation were once sanctioned and carried out, the Eastern Province thinks that it would enter the union as a separate state, and that it would have such dominion as to its own affairs as New York and Massachusetts have in the United States.

But there would be various other States in such a Federation besides the two into which the Cape Colony might be divided, and in order that my readers may have some idea of what would or might be the component parts of such a union, I will endeavour to describe the different territories which would be included, with some regard to their population.

(Vol. One, Chapter IV)

Capetown – The Capital

I had always heard that the entrance into Capetown, which is the capital of the Cape Colony, was one of the most picturesque things to be seen on the face of the earth. It is a town lying close down on the seashore, within the circumference of Table Bay so that it has the advantage of an opposite shore which is always necessary to the beauty of a seashore town; and it is backed by the Table Mountain with its grand upright cliffs and the Lion with its head and rump, as a certain hill is called which runs from the Table Mountain round with a semicircular curve back towards the sea. The 'Lion' certainly put me in mind of Landseer's lions, only that Landseer's lions lie straight. All this has given to Capetown a character for landscape beauty, which I had been told was to be seen at its best as you enter the harbour. But as we entered it early on one Sunday morning neither could the Table Mountain nor the Lion be seen because of the mist, and the opposite shore, with its hills towards The Paarl and Stellenbosch, was equally invisible. Seen as I first saw it Capetown was not an attractive port, and when I found myself standing at the gate of the dockyard for an hour and a quarter waiting for a Custom House officer to tell me that my things did not need examination, – waiting because it was Sunday morning, – I began to think that it was a very disagreeable place indeed. Twelve days afterwards I steamed out of the docks on my way eastward on a clear day, and then I could see what was then to be seen, and I am bound to say that the amphitheatre behind the place is very grand. But by that time the hospitality of the citizens had put me in good humour with the city and had enabled me to forget the iniquity of that sabbatical Custom House official.

But Capetown in truth is not of itself a prepossessing town. It is hard to say what is the combination which gives to some cities their peculiar attraction, and the absence of which makes others unattractive. Neither cleanliness, nor fine buildings, nor scenery, nor even a look of prosperity will effect this, – nor will all of them combined always do so. Capetown is not specially dirty, – but it is somewhat ragged. The buildings are not grand, but there is no special deficiency in that respect. The scenery around is really fine, and the multiplicity of Banks and of Members of Parliament, – which may be regarded as the two most important institutions the Colonies produce, – seemed to argue prosperity. But the town is not pleasing to a stranger. It is as I have said ragged, the roadways are uneven and the pavements are so little continuous that the walker by night had better even keep the road. I did not make special enquiry as to the municipality, but it appeared to me that the officers of that body were not alert.

(Vol. One, Chapter V)

He learns discretion

Wherever I go I visit the post-office, feeling certain that I may be able to give a little good advice. Having looked after post-offices for thirty years at home I fancy that I could do very good service among the Colonies if I could have arbitrary power given to me to make what changes I pleased. My advice is always received with attention and respect, and I have generally been able to flatter myself that I have convinced my auditors. But I never knew an instance yet in which any improvement recommended by me was carried out. I have come back a year or two after my first visit and have seen that the things have been just as they were before. I did not therefore say much at Capetown; – but I thought it would have been well if they had not driven the public to buy stamps at a store opposite, seeing that as the Colony pays salaries the persons taking the salaries ought to do the work; – and that it would be well also if they could bring themselves to cease to look at the public as enemies from whom it is necessary that the officials inside should be protected by fortifications in the

shape of barred windows and closed walls. Bankers do their
work over open counters, knowing that no one would deal with
them were they to shut their desks up behind barricades.

But I am bound to say that my letters were sent after me with
that despatch and regularity which are the two first and greatest
of post-official virtues. And the services in the Colony generally
are very well performed, and performed well under great difficulties. The roads are bad, and the distances long, and the transit is
necessarily rough. I was taken out to see such a cart as I should
have to travel on for many a weary day before I had accomplished my task in South Africa. My spirit groaned within me as
I saw it, – and for many a long and weary hour it has since
expanded itself with external groanings though not quite on such
a cart as I saw then. But the task has been done, and I can speak
of the South African cart with gratitude. It is very rough, – very
rough indeed for old bones. But it is sure.

(Vol. One, Chapter V)

Parliament

I cannot finish these remarks without saying that the most sensi-
ble speech I heard in the House was from Mr Saul Solomon. Mr
Solomon has never been in the Government and rarely in opposition, but he has been perhaps of as much use to the Colony as
any living man. He is one who certainly should be mentioned as
a very remarkable personage, having risen to high honours in an
occupation perhaps of all the most esteemed among men, but for
which he must have seemed by nature to be peculiarly ill
adapted. He is a man of very small stature, – so small that on first
seeing him the stranger is certainly impressed with the idea that
no man so small has ever been seen by him before. His forehead
however is fine, and his face full of intelligence. With all this
against him Mr Solomon has gone into public life, and as a
member of Parliament in the Cape Colony has gained a respect
above that of Ministers in office. It is not too much to say that he
is regarded on both sides as a safe adviser; and I believe that it
would be hardly possible to pass any measure of importance

through the Cape Legislature to which he offered a strenuous opposition. He reminded me of two other men whom it has been my privilege to know and who have been determined to seize and wear parliamentary honours in the teeth of misfortunes which would have closed at any rate that profession against men endowed with less than Herculean determination.[4] I mean Mr Fawcett[5] who in our own House at home has completely vanquished the terrible misfortune of blindness, and my old friend John Robertson[6] of Sydney, – Sir John I believe he is now, – who for many years presided over the Ministry in New South Wales, leading the debates in a parliamentary chamber, without a palate to his mouth. I regard these three men as great examples of what may be done by perseverance to overcome the evils which nature or misfortune have afflicted.

(Vol. One, Chapter VI)

The Knysna

Perhaps the ugliest collection of ruined huts I ever visited was 'Sweet Auburn, loveliest village of the plain.'[7] But the pretty English villages will have a parson, a doctor, an officer's widow, a retired linen-draper, and perhaps the Dowager Squiress, living in houses of different patterns, each standing in its own garden, but not so far from the road as to stand in its own ground. And there will be an inn, and the church of course, and probably a large brick house inhabited by some testy old gentleman who has heaps of money and never speaks to any body. There will be one shop, or at the most two, the buying and selling of the place being done in the market-town two miles off. In George the houses are all of this description. No two are alike. They are all away from the road. They have trees around them. And they are quaint in their designs, many of them having been built by Dutch proprietors and after Dutch patterns. And they have an air of old fashioned middle class comfort, – as though the inhabitants all ate hot roast mutton at one o'clock as a rule of their lives. As far as I could learn they all did.

There are two churches, – a big one for the Dutch, and a little one for the English. Taking the village and the country round, the Dutch are no doubt in a great majority; but in George itself I heard nothing but English spoken. Late on a Sunday evening, when I had returned from the Knysna, I stood under an oak tree close to the corner of the English church and listened to a hymn by star light. The air was so soft and balmy that it was a pleasure to stand and breathe it. It was the longest hymn I ever heard; but I thought it was very sweet; and as it was all that I heard that Sunday of sacred service, I did not begrudge its length. But the South Africans of both colours are a tuneful people in their worship.

The comfort of the houses, and the beauty of the trees, and the numbers of the gardens, and the plentiful bounty of the green swards have done much for George; – but its real glory is in the magnificent grouping of the Outiniqua mountains under which it is clustered. These are altogether unlike the generality of South African hills, which are mostly flat topped, and do not therefore seem to spring miscellaneously one from another, – but stand out separately and distinctly, each with its own flat top. The Outiniquas form a long line, running parallel with the coast from which they are distant perhaps 20 miles, and so group themselves, – as mountains should do, – that it is impossible to say where one ends and another begins. They more resemble some of the lower Pyrenees than any other range that I know, and are dark green in colour, as are the Pyrenees.

The Knysna, as the village and little port at the mouth of the Knysna river are called, is nearly 60 miles from George. The rocks at the entrance from the sea are about that distance, the village being four or five miles higher up. We started with four mules at 6.30, – but for the natural wickedness of the animals it would have been at 5.30, – and went up and down ravines and through long valleys for 50 miles to a place called Belvidere on the near side of the Knysna river. It would be hard to find 50 miles of more continuously picturesque scenery, for we were ever crossing dark black streams running down through the close ravines from the sides of the Outiniqua mountains. And here the ravines are very thickly wooded, in which respect they differ much from South African hill sides generally. But neither would it be easy to find 50 miles more difficult to travel. As we got nearer to the Knysna and further up from the little streams we had crossed, the ground became sandy, – till at last for a few miles it was impossible to do more than walk. But the mules, which had been very wicked in the morning, now put forth their virtues, and showed how superior they could be under stress of work to their nobler half-brother the horse.

(Vol. One, Chapter VII)

He meets Kafir chiefs

When I was at King Williamstown I was invited to hold a conference with two or three Kafir Chiefs, especially with Sandilli, whose son I had seen at school, and who was the heir to Gaika, one of the great kings of the Kafirs, being the son of Gaika's 'great wife,' and brother to Makomo the Kafir who in the last war had done more than Kafir had ever done before to break the British power in South Africa. It was Makomo who had been Sir Harry Smith's[8] too powerful enemy, – and Sandilli, who is still living in the neighbourhood of King Williamstown, was Makomo's younger but more royal brother. I expressed, of course, great satisfaction at the promised interview, but was warned that Sandilli might not improbably be too drunk to come.

On the morning appointed about twenty Kafirs came to me, clustering round the door of the house in which I was lodging, – but they declined to enter. I therefore held my levee out in the street. Sandilli was not there. The reason for his absence remained undivulged, but I was told that he had sent a troop of cousins in his place. The spokesman on the occasion was a chief named Siwani, who wore an old black coat, a flannel shirt, a pair of tweed trousers and a billycock hat, – comfortably and warmly dressed, – with a watch-key of ordinary appearance ingeniously inserted into his ear as an ornament. An interpreter was provided; and, out in the street, I carried on my colloquy with the dusky princes. Not one of them spoke but Siwani, and he expressed utter dissatisfaction with everything around him. The Kafirs, he said, would be much better off if the English would go away and leave them to their own customs. As for himself, though he had sent a great many of his clansmen to work on the railway, – where they got as he admitted good wages, – he had never himself received the allowance per head promised him. 'Why not appeal to the magistrate?' I asked. He had done so frequently, he said, but the Magistrate always put him off, and then, personally, he was treated with very insufficient respect. This complaint was repeated again and again. I, of course, insisted on the comforts which the Europeans had brought to the Kafirs, – trousers for instance, – and I remarked that all the royal princes around me were excellently well clad. The raiment was no doubt of the Irish beggar kind but still admitted of being described as excellent when compared in the mind with red clay and a blanket. 'Yes, – by compulsion,' he said. 'We were told that we must come in and see you, and therefore we put on our trousers. Very uncomfortable they are, and we wish that you and the trousers and the magistrates, but above all the prisons, would go – away out of the country altogether.' He was very angry about the prisons, alleging that if the Kafirs did wrong the Kafir Chiefs would know how to punish them. None of his own children had ever gone to school, – nor did he approve of schools. In fact he was an unmitigated old savage, on whom my words of wisdom had no effect whatever, and who seemed to enjoy the opportunity of unburdening his resentment before a British traveller. It is probable that some one had given him to understand that I might possibly write a book when I returned home.

When, after some half hour of conversation, he declared that he did not want to answer any more questions, I was not sorry to shake hands with the prominent half dozen, so as to bring the meeting to a close. But suddenly there came a grin across Siwani's face, – the first look of good humour which I had seen, – and the interpreter informed me that the Chief wanted a little tobacco. I went back into my friend's house and emptied his tobacco pot, but this though accepted, did not seem to give satisfaction. I whispered to the interpreter a question, and on being told that Siwani would not be too proud to buy his own tobacco, I gave the old beggar half a crown. Then he blessed me, as an Irish beggar might have done, grinned again and went off with his followers. The Kafir boy or girl at school and the Kafir man at work are pleasing objects; but the old Kafir chief in quest of tobacco, – or brandy, – is not delightful.

(Vol. One, Chapter XI)

Natal – Bishop Colenso[9]

In 1853 Dr Colenso was appointed Bishop of Natal, and by the peculiarity of his religious opinions has given more notoriety to the Colony, – has caused the Colony to be more talked about, – than any of its Governors or even than any of its romantic incidents. Into religious opinion I certainly shall not stray in these pages. In my days I have written something about clergymen but never a word about religion. No doubt shall be thrown by me either upon the miracles or upon Colenso. But when he expressed his unusual opinions he became a noted man, and Natal was heard of for the first time by many people. He came to England in those days, and I remember being asked to dinner by a gushing friend. 'We have secured Colenso,' said my gushing friend, as though she was asking me to meet a royal duke or a Japanese ambassador. But I had never met the Bishop till I arrived in his own see, where it was allowed me to come in contact with that clear intellect, the gift of which has always been allowed to him. He is still Bishop of Natal, and will probably remain so till he dies. He is not the man to abandon any position of which he is proud. But there is another bishop – of Maritzburg – whose tenets are perhaps more in accord with those generally held by the Church of England. The confusion has no doubt been unfortunate, – and is still unfortunate, as has been almost everything connected with Natal. And yet it is a smiling pretty land, blessed with numerous advantages; and if it were my fate to live in South Africa I should certainly choose Natal for my residence. Fair Natal, but unfortunate Natal! Its worldly affairs have hitherto not gone smoothly.

(Vol. One, Chapter XIV)

He takes a walk

In the evening I went out, still alone, for a walk and without a guide, found my way to the public park and the public gardens. I cannot say that they are perfect in horticultural beauty and in surroundings, but they are spacious with ample room for improvement, well arranged as far as they are arranged, and with a promise of being very superior to anything of the kind at Capetown. The air was as sweet, I think, as any that I ever breathed. Through them I went on, leaving the town between me and the sea, on to a grassy illimitable heath on which, I told myself, that with perseverance I might walk on till I came to Grand Cairo. I had my stick in my hand and was prepared for any lion that I might meet. But on this occasion I met no lion. After a while I found myself descending into a valley, – a pretty little green valley altogether out of sight of the town, and which as I was wending along seemed at first to be an interruption in my way to the centre of the continent. But as I approached the verge from which I could look down into its bosom, I heard the sound of voices, and when I had reached a rock which hung over it, I saw beneath me a ring, as it might be of fairy folk, in full glee – of folk, fairy or human, running hither and thither with extreme merriment and joy. After standing awhile and gazing I perceived that the young people of Fort Elizabeth were playing kiss-in-the-ring. Oh, – how long ago it was since I played kiss-in-the-ring, and how nice I used to think it! It was many many years since I had even seen the game. And these young people played it with an energy and an ecstasy which I had never seen equalled. I walked down, almost amongst them, but no one noticed me. I felt among them like Rip Van Winkle. I was as a ghost, for they seemed not even to see me. How the girls ran, and could always have escaped from the lads had they listed, but always were caught round some corner out of the circle! And how awkward the lads were in kissing, and how clever the girls in taking care that it should always come off at last, without undue violence! But it seemed to me that had I been a lad I should have felt that when all the girls had been once kissed, or say twice, – and when every girl had been kissed twice round by every lad, the thing would have become tame, and the lips unhallowed. But this was merely the cynicism of an old man, and no such feeling interrupted the sport. There I left them when the sun was setting, still hard at work, and returned sadly to my dinner at the club.

(Vol. One, Chapter X)

Durban

Natal has had many hardships to endure and Durban perhaps more than its share. But there it is now, a prosperous and pleasant seaport town with a beautiful country round it and thriving merchants in its streets. It has a park in the middle of it, – not very well kept. I may suggest that it was not improved in general appearance when I saw it by having a couple of old horses tethered on its bare grass. Perhaps the grass is not bare now and perhaps the horses have been taken away. The combination when I was there suggested poverty on the part of the municipality and starvation on the part of the horses. There is also a botanical garden a little way up the hill very rich in plants but not altogether well kept. The wonder is how so much is done in these places, rather than why so little; – that efforts so great should be made by young and therefore poor municipalities to do something for the recreation and for the relief of the inhabitants! I think that there is not a town in South Africa, – so to be called, – which has not its hospital and its public garden. The struggles for these institutions have to come from men who are making a dash for fortune, generally under hard circumstances in which every energy is required; and the money has to be collected from pockets which at first are never very full. But a colonial town is ashamed of itself if it has not its garden, its hospital, its public library, and its two or three churches, even in its early days.

I can say nothing of the hotels at Durban because I was allowed to live at the club, – which is so peculiarly a colonial institution. Somebody puts your name down beforehand and then you drive up to the door and ask for your bedroom. Breakfast, lunch, and dinner are provided at stated hours. At Durban two lunches were provided in separate rooms, a hot lunch and a cold lunch, – an arrangement which I did not see elsewhere. I imagine that the hot lunch is intended as a dinner to those who like to dine early. But, if I am not mistaken, I have seen the same faces coming out of the hot lunch and going in to the hot dinner. I should imagine that these clubs cannot be regarded with very much favour by the Innkeepers as they take away a large proportion of the male travellers.

(Vol. One, Chapter XV)

A travelling incident

We were apparently quite full but heard at starting that there was still a place vacant which had been booked by a gentleman who was to get up along the road. The back carriage, which was of the waggonette fashion, uncovered, with seats at each side, seemed to be so full that the gentleman would find a difficulty in placing himself, but as I was on the box the idea did not disconcert me. At last, about half way, at one of the stages, the gentleman appeared. There was a lady inside with her husband, with five or six others, who at once began to squeeze themselves. But when the gentleman came it was not a gentleman only, but a gentleman with the biggest fish in his arms that I ever saw, short of a Dolphin. I was told afterwards that it weighed 45 pounds. The fish was luggage, he said, and must be carried. He had booked his place. That we knew to be true. When asked he declared he had booked a place for the fish also. That we believed to be untrue. He came round to the front and essayed to put it on the foot-board. When I assured him that any such attempt must be vain and that the fish would be at once extruded if placed there, he threatened to pull me off the box. He was very angry, and frantic in his efforts. The fish, he said, was worth £5, and must go to Maritzburg that day. Here Apollo[10] shewed, I think, a little inferiority to an English coachman. The English coachman would have grown very red in the face, would have cursed horribly, and would have persistently refused all contact with the fish. Apollo jumped on his box, seized the reins, flogged the horses, and endeavoured to run away both from the fish and the gentleman.

But the man, with more than colonial alacrity, and with a courage worthy of a better cause, made a successful rush, and catching the back of the vehicle with one hand got on to the step behind, while he held on to the fish with his other hand and his teeth. There were many exclamations from the folks behind. The savour of the fish was unpleasant in their nostrils. It must have been very unpleasant as it reached us uncomfortably up on the box. Gradually the man got in, – and the fish followed him! Labor omnia vincit improbus.[11] By his pertinacity the company seemed to become reconciled to the abomination. On looking round when we were yet many miles from Pieter Maritzburg I saw the gentleman sitting with his feet dangling back over the end of the car; his neighbour and vis-a-vis, who at first had been very loud against the fish, was sitting in the same wretched position; while the fish itself was placed upright in the place of honour against the door, where the legs of the two passengers ought to have been. Before we reached our journey's end I respected the gentleman with the fish, – who nevertheless had perpetrated a great injustice; but I thought very little of the good-natured man who had allowed the fish to occupy the space intended for a part of his own body. I never afterwards learned what became of the fish. If all Maritzburg was called together to eat it I was not asked to join the party.

I must not complete my record of the journey without saying that we dined at Pinetown, half way, and that I never saw a better coach dinner put upon a table.

The scenery throughout from Durban to Pieter Maritzburg is interesting and in some places is very beautiful. The road passes over the ridge of hills which guards the interior from the sea, and in many places from its altitude allows the traveller to look down on the tops of smaller hills grouped fantastically below, lying as though they had been crumbled down from a giant's hand. And every now and then are seen those flat-topped mountains, – such as is the Table mountain over Capetown, – which form so remarkable a feature in South African scenery, and occur so often as to indicate some peculiar cause for their formation.

Altogether what with the scenery, the dinner, Apollo, and the fish, the journey was very interesting.

(Vol. One, Chapter XV)

Pieter Maritzburg

On arriving at Pieter Maritzburg I put up for a day or two at the Royal Hotel which I found to be comfortable enough. I had been told that the Club was a good club but that it had not accommodation for sleeping. I arrived late on Saturday evening, and on the Sunday morning I went, of course, to hear Bishop Colenso preach. Whatever might be the Bishop's doctrine, so much at any rate was due to his fame. The most innocent and the most trusting young believer in every letter of the Old Testament would have heard nothing on that occasion to disturb a cherished conviction or to shock a devotional feeling. The church itself was all that a church ought to be, pretty, sufficiently large and comfortable. It was, perhaps, not crowded, but was by no means deserted. I had expected that either nobody would have been there, or else that it would have been filled to inconvenience, – because of the Bishop's alleged heresies. A stranger who had never heard of Bishop Colenso would have imagined that he had entered a simple church in which the service was pleasantly performed, – all completed including the sermon within an hour and a half, – and would have had his special attention only called to the two facts that one of the clergymen wore lawn sleeves, and that the other was so singularly like Charles Dickens as to make him expect to hear the tones of that wonderful voice when ever a verse of the Bible was commenced.

Pieter Maritzburg is a town covering a large area of ground but is nevertheless sufficiently built up and perfected to prevent that look of scattered failure which is so common to colonial embryo cities. I do not know that it contains anything that can be called a handsome building; – but the edifices whether public or private are neat, appropriate, and sufficient. The town is surrounded by hills, and is therefore, necessarily, pretty. The roadways of the street are good, and the shops have a look of established business. The first idea of Pieter Maritzburg on the mind of a visitor is that of success, and this idea remains with him to the last. It contains only a little more than 4,000 white inhabitants, whereas it would seem from the appearance of the place, and the breadth and length of the streets, and the size of the

shops, and the number of churches of different denominations, to
require more than double that number of persons to inhabit it.
Observation in the streets, however, will show that the deficiency is made up by natives, who in fact do all the manual and
domestic work of the place. Their number is given as 2,500; but
I am disposed to think that a very large number come in from the
country for their daily occupations in the town. The Zulu adher-
ents to Pieter Maritzburg are so remarkable that I must speak
separately of them in a separate chapter. The white man in the
capital as in Durban is not the working man, but the master, or
boss, who looks after the working man.

I liked Pieter Maritzburg very much, – perhaps the best of all
South African towns. But whenever I would express such an
opinion to a Pieter Maritzburger he would never quite agree with
me. It is difficult to get a Colonist to assent to any opinion as to
his own Colony. If you find fault, he is injured and almost
insulted. The traveller soon learns that he had better abstain from
all spoken criticism, even when that often repeated, that dreadful
question is put to him, – which I was called upon to answer
sometimes four or five times a day, – 'Well, Mr Trollope, what
do you think of ——,' – let us say for the moment, 'South
Africa?' But even praise is not accepted without contradiction,
and the peculiar hardships of a Colonist's life are insisted upon
almost with indignation when colonial blessings are spoken of
with admiration. The Government at home is doing everything
that is cruel, and the Government in the Colony is doing everything that is foolish. With whatever interest the gentleman himself is concerned, that peculiar interest is peculiarly ill-managed
by the existing powers. But for some fatuous maddening law he
himself could make his own fortune and almost that of the
Colony. In Pieter Maritzburg everybody seemed to me very
comfortable, but everybody was ill-used. There was no labour, –
though the streets were full of Zulus, who would do anything for
a shilling and half anything for sixpence. There was no emigration from England provided for by the country. There were not
half soldiers enough in Natal, – though Natal has luckily had no
real use for soldiers since the Dutch went away. But perhaps the
most popular source of complaint was that everything was so

dear that nobody could afford to live. Nevertheless I did not hear that any great number of the inhabitants of the town were encumbered by debt, and everybody seemed to live comfortably enough.

(Vol. One, Chapter XVI)

An English farmer

We rode up to many farms at which we were of course received with the welcome due to the Governor, and where in the course of the interview most of the material facts as to the farmer's enterprise, – whether on the whole he had been successful or the reverse, and to what cause his success or failure had been owing, – would come out in conversation. An English farmer at home would at once resent the questionings which to a Colonial farmer are a matter of course. The latter is conscious that he has been trying an experiment and that any new comer will be anxious to know the result. He has no rent to pay and does not feel that his condition ought to remain a secret between him and his landlord alone. One man whom we saw had come from the East Riding of Yorkshire more than twenty years ago, and was now the owner of 1,200 acres, – which however in Natal is not a large farm. But he was well located as to land, and could have cultivated nearly the whole had labour been abundant enough, and cheap enough. He was living comfortably with a pleasant wife and well-to-do children, and regaled us with tea and custard. His house was comfortable, and everything no doubt was plentiful with him. But he complained of the state of things and would not admit himself to be well off. O fortunati nimium sua si bona norint Agricolæ.[12] He had no rent to pay. That was true. But there were taxes, – abominable taxes. This was said with a side look at the Governor. And as for labour, – there was no making a Zulu labour. Now you could get a job done, and now you couldn't. How was a man to grow wheat in such a state of things, and that, too, with the rust so prevalent? Yes; – he had English neighbours and a school for the children only a mile and a half off. And the land was not to say bad. But what with the taxes and what with the Zulus, there were troubles more than enough. The Governor asked, as I thought at the moment indiscreetly, but the result more than justified the question, – whether he had any special complaint to make. He had paid the dog tax on his dogs, – 5s. a dog, I think it was; – whereas some of his neigbours had escaped the imposition! There was nothing more. And in the midst of all this the man's prosperity and comfort were leaking out at every corner. The handsome grown-up daughter was telling me of the dancing parties around to which she went, and there were the pies and custards all prepared for the family use and brought out at a moment's notice. There were the dining room and drawing room, well furnished and scrupulously clean, – and lived in, which is almost more to the purpose. There could be no doubt that our Yorkshire friend had done well with himself in spite of the Zulus and the dog tax.

An Englishman, especially an English farmer, will always complain, where a Dutchman or a German will express nothing but content. And yet the Englishman will probably have done much more to secure his comfort than any of his neighbours of another nationality. An English farmer in Natal almost always has a deal flooring to his living rooms; while a Dutchman will put up with the earth beneath his feet. The one is as sure to be the case as the other. But the Dutchman rarely grumbles, – or if he grumbles it is not at his farm. He only wants to be left alone, to live as he likes on his earthen floor as his fathers lived before him, and not to be interfered with or have advice given to him by any one.

(Vol. One, Chapter XVI)

Dutch and German farmers

One Hollander whom we visited was very proud indeed of what he had done in the way of agriculture and gave us, not only his own home-grown oranges, but also his own home-grown cigars. I had abandoned smoking, perhaps in prophetical anticipation of some such treat as this. Others of the party took the cigars, – which, however, were not as good as the oranges. This man had planted many trees, and had done marvels with the land round his house. But the house itself was deficient, – especially in the article of flooring.

Then we came to a German farmer who had planted a large grove about his place, having put down some thousands of young trees. Nothing can be done more serviceable to the country at large than the planting of trees. Though there is coal in the Colony it is not yet accessible, – nor can be for many years because of the difficulty of transport. The land is not a forest-land, – like Australia. It is only on the courses of the streams that trees grow naturally and even then the growth is hardly more than that of shrubs. Firewood is consequently very dear, and all the timber used in building is imported. But young trees when planted almost always thrive. It has seemed to me that the Governments of South Africa should take the matter in hand, – as do the Governments of the Swiss Cantons and of the German Duchies, which are careful that timber shall be reproduced as it is cut down. In Natal it should be produced; and Nature, though she has not given the country trees, has manifestly given it the power of producing them. The German gentleman was full of the merits of the country, freely admitting his own success, and mitigating in some degree the general expressions against the offending Native. He could get Zulus to work – for a consideration. But he was of opinion that pastoral pursuits paid better than agriculture.

We came to another household of mixed Germans and Dutch, where we received exactly the same answers to our enquiries. Farming answered very well, – but cattle or sheep were the articles which paid. A man should only grow what corn he wanted for himself and his stock. A farmer with 6,000 acres, which is the ordinary size of a farm, should not plough at the most above 40 acres, – just the patches of land round his house. For simply agricultural purposes 6,000 acres would of course be unavailable. The farming capitalists in England who single-handed plough 6,000 acres might probably be counted on the ten fingers. In Natal, – and in South Africa generally, – when a farm is spoken of an area is signified large enough for pastoral purposes. This may be all very well for the individual farmer, but it is not good for a new country, such as are the greater number of our Colonies. In Australia the new coming small farmer can purchase land over the heads of the pastoral squatters who are only tenants of the land under Government. But in South Africa the fee of the land has unfortunately been given away.

(Vol. One, Chapter XXI)

The Zulus – Cetywayo[13]

... a young lady read to me a diary which had just been made by a Zulu who had travelled from Natal into Zulu-land to see Cetywayo, and had returned not only in safety but with glowing accounts of the King's good conduct to him. The diary was in the Zulu language and my young friend, if I may call her so, shewed her perfect mastery over that and her mother tongue by the way in which she translated it for me. That the diary was an excellent literary production, and that it was written by the Zulu in an extremely good running hand, containing the narrative of his journey from day to day in a manner quite as interesting as many published English journals, are certainly facts. How far it was true may be a matter of doubt. The lady and her family believed it entirely, – and they knew the man well. The bulk of the white inhabitants of Pieter Maritzburg would probably not have believed a word of it. I believed most of it, every now and then arousing the gentle wrath of the fair reader by casting a doubt upon certain details. The writer of the journal was present, however, answering questions as they were asked; and, as he understood and spoke English, my doubts could only be expressed when he was out of the room. 'There is a touch of romance there,' I would say when he had left us alone. 'Wasn't that put in specially for you and your father?' I asked as to another passage. But she was strong in support of her Zulu, and made me feel that I should like to have such an advocate if ever suspected myself.

The personal adventures of the narrator and the literary skill displayed were perhaps the most interesting features of the narrative; – but the purport was to defend the character of Cetywayo.

(Vol. One, Chapter XVII)

He observes the Zulus

I should have added, however, that he always wears his rags with a grace. The Zulu rags are perhaps about equal to the Kafir rags in raggedness, but the Zulu grace is much more excellent than the Kafir grace. Whatever it be that the Zulu wears he always looks as though he had chosen that peculiar costume, quite regardless of expense, as being the one mode of dress most suitable to his own figure and complexion. The rags are there, but it seems as though the rags have been chosen with as much solicitude as any dandy in Europe gives to the fit and colour of his raiment. When you see him you are inclined to think, not that his clothes are tattered, but 'curiously cut,' – like Catherine's gown.[14] One fellow will walk erect with an old soldier's red coat on him and nothing else, another will have a pair of knee breeches and a flannel shirt hanging over it. A very popular costume is an ordinary sack, inverted, with a big hole for the head, and smaller holes for the arms, and which comes down below the wearer's knees. This is serviceable and decent, and has an air of fashion about it too as long as it is fairly clean. Old grey great coats with brass buttons, wherever they may come from, are in request, and though common always seem to confer dignity. A shirt and trousers worn threadbare, so ragged as to seem to defy any wearer to find his way into them, will assume a peculiar look of easy comfort on the back and legs of a Zulu. An ordinary flannel shirt, with nothing else, is quite sufficient to make you feel that the black boy who is attending you, is as fit to be brought into any company as a powdered footman. And then it is so cheap a livery! and over and above their dress they always wear ornaments. The ornaments are peculiar, and might be called poor, but they never seem amiss. We all know at home the detestable appearance of the vulgar cad who makes himself odious with chains and pins, – the Tittlebat Titmouse[15] from the counter. But when you see a Zulu with his ornaments you confess to yourself that he has a right to them. As with a pretty woman at home, whose attire might be called fantastic were it not fashionable, of whom we feel that as she was born to be beautiful, graceful, and idle, she has a right to be a butterfly, – and that she becomes and justifies the quaint trappings which she selects, so of the Zulu do we acknowledge that he is warranted by the condition of his existence in adorning his person as he pleases. Load him with bangle, armlet, ear-ring and head-dress to any extent, and he never looks like a hog in armour. He inserts into the lobes of his ears trinkets of all sorts, – boxes for the conveyance of his snuff and little delights, and other pendants as though his ears had been given to him for purposes of carriage. Round his limbs he wears round shining ornaments of various material, brass, ivory, wood and beads. I once took from off a man's arm a section of an elephant's tooth which he had hollowed, and the remaining rim of which was an inch and a half thick. This he wore, loosely slipping up and down and was apparently in no way inconvenienced by it. Round their heads they tie ribbons and bandelets. They curl their crisp hair into wonderful shapes. I have seen many as to whom I would at first have sworn that they had supplied themselves with miraculous wigs made by miraculous barbers. They stick quills and bones and bits of wood into their hair, always having an eye to some peculiar effect. They will fasten feathers to their back hair which go waving in the wind. I have seen a man trundling a barrow with a beautiful green wreath on his brow, and have been convinced at once that for the proper trundling of a barrow a man ought to wear a green wreath. A Zulu will get an old hat, – what at home we call a slouch hat, – some hat probably which came from the corner of Bond Street and Piccadilly three or four years ago, and will knead it into such shapes that all the establishments of all the Christys[16] could not have done the like. The Zulu is often slow, often idle, sometimes perhaps hopelessly useless, but he is never awkward. The wonderfully pummelled hat sits upon him like a helmet upon Minerva or a furred pork pie[17] upon a darling in Hyde Park in January. But the Zulu at home in his own country always wears on his head the 'isicoco,' or head ring, a shining black coronet made hard with beaten earth and pigments, – earth taken from the singular ant hills of the country, – which is the mark of his rank and virility and to remove which would be a stain.

I liked the Zulu of the Natal capital very thoroughly. You have no cabs there, – and once when in green ignorance I had myself carried from one end of the town to another in a vehicle, I had to pay 10s. 6d. for the accommodation. But the Zulu, ornamented and graceful as he is, will carry your portmanteau on his head all the way for sixpence. Hitherto money has not become common in Natal as in British Kafraria, and the Zulu is cheap. He will hold your horse for you for an hour, and not express a sense of injury if he gets nothing; – but for a silver threepence he will grin at you with heartfelt gratitude. Copper I believe he will not take, – but copper is so thoroughly despised in the Colony that no one dares to shew it. At Maritzburg I found that I could always catch a Zulu at a moment's notice to do anything. At the hotel or the club, or your friend's house you signify to some one that you want a boy, and the boy is there at once. If you desired him to go a journey of 200 miles to the very boundary of the Colony, he would go instantly, and be not a whit surprised. He will travel 30 or 40 miles in the twenty-four hours for a shilling a day, and will assuredly do the business confided to him. Maritzburg is 55 miles from Durban and an acquaintance told me that he had sent down a very large wedding cake by a boy in 24 hours. 'But if he had eaten it?' I asked. 'His Chief would very soon have eaten him,' was the reply.

(Vol. One, Chapter XVII)

White man's rule

The white ruler of the black man feels all this, and knows that without some spur or whip he cannot do his work at all. His is a service, probably, of much danger, and he has to work with a frown on his brow in order that his life may be fairly safe in his hand. In this way he is driven to the daily practice of little deeds of tyranny which abstract justice would condemn. Then, on occasion, arises some petty mutiny, – some petty mutiny almost justified by injustice but which must be put down with a strong hand or the white man's position will become untenable. In nineteen cases the strong hand is successful and the matter goes by without any feeling of wrong on either side. The white man expects to be obeyed, and the black man expects to be coerced, and the general work goes on prosperously in spite of a small flaw. Then comes the twentieth case in which the one little speck of original injustice is aggravated till a great flame is burning. The outraged philanthropist has seen the oppression of his black brother, and evokes Downing Street, Exeter Hall, Printing House Square, and all the Gospels.[18] The savage races from the East to the West of the Continent, from the mouth of the Zambesi to the Gold Coast, all receive something of assured protection from the effort; – but, probably, a great injustice is done to the one white ruler who began it all, and who, perhaps, was but a little ruler doing his best in a small way. I am inclined to think that the philanthropist at home when he rises in his wrath against some white ruler of whose harshness to the blacks he has heard the story forgets that the very civilization which he is anxious to carry among the savage races cannot be promulgated without something of tyranny, – some touch of apparent injustice. Nothing will sanctify tyranny or justify injustice, says the philanthropist in his wrath. Let us so decide and so act; – but let us understand the result. In that case we must leave the Zulus and other races to their barbarities and native savagery.

(Vol. One, Chapter XVIII)

Langalibalele[19]

There are three hundred and twenty thousand Natives in Natal, with hundreds of thousands over the borders on each side of the little Colony, and it is essential that all these should believe Great Britain to be indomitable. If Langalibalele had been allowed to be successful in his controversy every Native in and around Natal would have known it; – and in knowing it every Native would have believed that Great Britain had been so far conquered. It was therefore quite essential that Langalibalele should be made to come. And he did more than refuse to obey the order. A messenger who was sent for him, – a native messenger, – was insulted by him. The man's clothes were stripped from him, – or at any rate the official great coat with which he had been invested and which probably formed the substantial part of his raiment. It has been the peculiarity of this case that whole books have been written about its smallest incidents. The Langalibalele literature hitherto written, – which is not I fear as yet completed, – would form a small library. This stripping of the great coat, or jazy* as it is called, – the word ijazi having been established as good Zulu for such an article, – has become a celebrated incident. Langalibalele afterwards pleaded that he suspected that weapons had been concealed, and that he had therefore searched the Queen's messenger. And he justified his suspicion by telling how a pistol had been concealed and had been fired sixteen years before. And then that old case was ripped up, and thirty or forty native messengers were examined about it. But Langalibalele after taking off the Queen's messenger's jazy turned and fled, and it was found to be necessary that the Queen's soldiers should pursue him. He was pursued, – with terrible consequences. He turned and fought and British blood was shed. Of course the blood of the Hlubi tribe had to flow, and did flow too freely. It was very bad that it should be so; – but had it not been so all Zululand, all Kafirland, all the tribes of Natal and the Transvaal would have thought that Langalibalele had gained a great victory, and our handful of whites would have been unable to live in their Colony.

Then Langalibalele was caught. As to matters that had been done up to that time I am not aware that official fault of very grave nature has been found with those who were concerned; but the trial of Langalibalele was supposed to have been conducted on unjust principles and before judges who should not have sat on the judgment seat. He was tried and was condemned to very grave punishment, and his tribe and his family were broken up. He was to be confined for his life, without the presence of any of his friends, in Robben Island, which, as my reader may remember, lies just off Capetown, a thousand miles away from Natal, – and to be reached by a sea journey which to all Zulus is a thing of great terror. The sentence was carried out and Langalibalele was shipped away to Robben Island.

(Vol. One, Chapter XVIII)

---

* I have seen it asserted that this word comes from 'jersey' – a flannel undershirt. But I seem to remember the very sound as signifying an old great coat in Ireland, and think that it was so used long before the word 'jersey' was introduced into our language.

Later thoughts

Have we not stretched our arms far enough? Do not we already feel that the efforts demanded from us are so excessive as to produce a sense of fear lest our means should be inadequate? If it be our duty to civilize the world at large, should we not pause a little as we do it? Having absorbed the Transvaal in 1877, and Cyprus in 1878, should we now in 1879 add Zululand to Affghanistan? The task grows to such an extent that a new acquisition will be required to satisfy the ambition of each three months. We are already beginning to hear that scruples in such a matter are absurd, – as indeed we have seemed to think, – and that Egypt ought to be made our own very shortly. Any question of abstract justice in such matters seems to have been thrown altogether to the winds. We are powerful, we are energetic, we are tenacious; but may it not be possible that we shall attempt to clutch more than we can hold? When once the subject peoples shall have begun to fall from our grasp, the process of dropping them will be very quick.

When we annexed the Transvaal there was a reason. A European people were holding it, and they, though not English or at that time English subjects, were an offshoot from an English colony. It was a Dutch community with English mixed through them. And to the native imagination, though a difference between Dutch and English was felt and acknowledged, they were both white. For the protection of the Dutch, for the protection of ourselves, for the protection of civilisation in South Africa generally, the annexation of the Transvaal was a necessity. All that is required of us in reference to Zululand is to fix a boundary. I am far from being blind to the difficulty of doing this, but I think it may be done by some measure short of annexing another entire country which will also require that a further boundary shall be fixed on the further side of it! We are to go to war with the Savage we are told because he is not as yet altogether civilized. If that is to be accepted as a reason there can be no end to our wars while there is an untamed Native left in Africa.

I have no fear myself that Natal will be overrun by hostile Zulus; – but much fear that Zululand should be overrun by hostile Britons. We have begun unfortunately; and, annoyed by that, are probably being hurried into excessive energy and unnecessary expense; but I cannot bring myself to fear that any number of Zulus will prevail long against British troops.

[From *South Africa,* abridged edition (1879), Chapter XI]

Mail to Newcastle

The mail cart from the capital to Newcastle took two and a half days on the journey, and was on the whole comfortable enough. One moment of discord there was between myself and the sable driver, which did not, however, lead to serious results. On leaving Pieter Maritzburg I found that the vehicle was full. There were seven passengers, two on the box and five behind, – the sixth seat being crowded with luggage. There was luggage indeed everywhere, above, below and around us, – but still we had all of us our seats, with fair room for our legs. Then came the question of the mails. The cart to Newcastle goes but once a week; and though subsidiary mails are carried by Zulu runners twice a week over the whole distance, – 175 miles, – and carried as quickly as by the cart, the heavier bulk, such as newspapers, books, &c., are kept for the mail conveyance. The bags therefore are, in such a vehicle, somewhat heavy. When I saw a large box covered with canvas brought out I was alarmed, and I made some enquiry. It was, said the complaisant postmaster's assistant who had come out into the street, a book-post parcel; somewhat large as he acknowledged, and not strictly open at the ends as required by law. It was, he confessed, a tin box and he believed that it contained – bonnets. But it was going up to Pretoria, nearly 400 miles, at book-parcel rate of postage, – the total cost of it being, I think he said, 8s. 6d. Now passengers' luggage to Pretoria is charged 4s. a pound, and the injustice of the tin box full of bonnets struck my official mind with horror. There was a rumour for a moment that it was to be put in among us, and I prepared myself for battle. But the day was fine, and the tin box was fastened on behind with all the mails, – merely preventing any one from getting in or out of the cart without climbing over them. That was nothing, and we went away very happily, and during the first day I became indifferent to the wrong which was being done.

But when we arrived for breakfast on the second morning the clouds began to threaten, and it is known to all in those parts that when it rains in Natal it does rain. The driver at once declared that the bags must be put inside and that we must all sit with our legs and feet in each other's lap. Then we looked at each other, and I remembered the tin box. I asked the conscientious mail-man what he would do with the bag which contained the box, and he immediately replied that it must come behind himself, inside the cart, exactly the place where my legs were then placed. I had felt the tin box and had found that the corners of it were almost as sharp as the point of a carving knife. 'It can't come here,' said I. 'It must,' said the driver surlily. 'But it won't,' said I decidedly. 'But it will,' said the driver angrily. I bethought myself a moment and then declared my purpose of not leaving the vehicle, though I knew that breakfast was prepared within. 'May I trouble you to bring a cup of tea to me here,' I said to one of my fellow victims. 'I shall remain and not allow the tin box to enter the cart.' 'Not allow!' said the custodian of the mails. 'Certainly not,' said I, with what authority I could command. 'It is illegal.' The man paused for a moment awed by the word and then entered upon a compromise. 'Would I permit the mail bags to be put inside, if the tin box were kept outside?' To this I assented, and so the cart was packed. I am happy to say that the clouds passed away, and that the bonnets were uninjured as long as I remained in their company. I fear from what I afterwards heard that they must have encountered hard usage on their way from Newcastle to Pretoria.

The mail cart to Newcastle was, I have said, fairly comfortable, but this incident and other little trifles of the same kind made me glad that I had decided on being independent. Three of my fellow passengers were going on to Pretoria and I found that they looked forward with great dread to their journey, – not even then expecting such hardships as did eventually befall them.

(Vol. One, Chapter XIX)

Transvaal – the Boers

The reader will probably perceive that these charges indicate an absence of that civilization which is produced in the world by the congregated intelligences of many persons. Had Shakespeare been born on a remote South African farm he would have been Shakespeare still; but he would not have worn a starched frill to his shirt. The Dutch Boer is what he is, not because he is Dutch or because he is a Boer, but because circumstances have isolated him. The Spaniards had probably reached as luxurious a mode of living as any European people when they achieved their American possessions, but I have no hesitation in saying that the Spaniards who now inhabit the ranches and remote farms of Costa Rica or Columbia are in a poorer condition of life than the Dutch Boers of the Transvaal. I have seen Germans located in certain unfortunate spots about the world who have been reduced lower in the order of humanity than any Dutchmen that I have beheld. And I have been within the houses of English Free Settlers in remote parts of Australia which have had quite as little to show in a way of comfort as any Boer's homestead.

Such comparisons are only useful as showing that distance from crowded centres will produce the same falling off in civilization among one people as among another. The two points of interest in the matter are, – first the actual condition of these people who have now become British subjects, and secondly how far there is a prospect of improvement. I am now speaking of my journey from Natal up to Pretoria. When commencing that journey, though I had seen many Dutchmen in South Africa I had seen none of the Boer race; and I was told that those living near to the road would hardly be fair specimens of their kind. There was very little on the road to assist in civilizing them and that little had not existed long. From what I afterwards saw I am inclined to think that the impressions first made upon me were not incorrect.

The farmers' houses generally consisted of two main rooms, with probably some small excrescence which would serve some of the family as a sleeping apartment. In the living room there would be a fire-place, and outside the house, probably at thirty or forty yards' distance, there would be a huge oven built. The houses would never be floored, the uneven ground being sufficiently solid and also sufficiently clean for the Dutchman's purposes. There would seldom be a wall-paper or any internal painting of the woodwork. Two solid deal tables, with solid deal settees or benches, – not unfrequently with a locker under them, – would be the chief furniture. There might be a chair or two, but not more than one or two. There would always be a clock, and a not insufficient supply of cups, saucers, and basins. Knives, forks, and spoons would be there. The bedroom of course would be a sanctum; but my curiosity, – or diligence in the performance of the duty on which I was intent, – enables me to say that there is always a large bedstead, with a large feather bed, a counterpane, and apparently a pair of sheets. The traveller in Central America will see but little of such decencies among the Spanish farmers there.

Things in the Boer's house no doubt are generally dirty. An earthen floor will make everything dirty, – whether in Ireland or in the Transvaal. The Boer's dress is dirty, – and also, which is more important, that of the Boeress. The little Boerlings are all dirty; – so that, even when they are pretty, one does not wish to kiss them. The Boers are very prolific, marrying early and living a wholesome, and I think, a moral life. They are much given to marrying, the widow or the widower very speedily taking another spouse, so that there will sometimes be three or four families in the one house. The women have children very early in life, – but then they have children very late also; which seems to indicate that their manner of living is natural and healthy. I have heard them ridiculed for their speedy changes of marital affection, but it seems to me natural that a man or a woman living far apart from neighbours should require the comfort of a companion.

I am quite convinced that they are belied by the allegation which denies to them all progress in civilization. The continued increase in the number of British and German storekeepers in the country, who grow rich on their trade with the Boers, is sufficient of itself to tell one this. Twenty years since I am assured that it was a common thing for a Boer to be clad in skins. Now they

wear woollen clothing, with calico. I fancy that the traveller
would have to travel very far before he found a skin-clad Boer.
No doubt they are parsimonious; – it might perhaps be more fair
to call them prone to save. I, personally, regard saving as a
mistake, thinking that the improvement of the world generally is
best furthered by a free use of the good things which are earned,
– and that they who do not themselves earn them should, as a
rule, not have them. It is a large question, which my readers
would not thank me to discuss here. But there are two sides to it,
– and the parsimony of the Boer who will eat up the carcase of a
wild beast till it be rotten so that he need not kill a sheep, and
may thus be enabled to stock a farm for his son, will have its
admirers in Great Britain, – if not among fathers at any rate
among sons. These people are not great consumers, as are our
farmers. They wear their clothes longer, and stretch their means
further; but that the Boer of to-day consumes very much more
than his father there can be no doubt; – and as little that his sons
and daughters will consume more.

(Vol. Two, Chapter I)

Pretoria

Down many streets of the town, – down all of them that are on
the slope of the descent, – little rivulets flow, adding much to the
fertility of the gardens and to the feeling of salubrity. Nothing
seems to add so much to the prettiness and comfort of a town as
open running water, though I doubt whether it be in truth the
most healthy mode of providing for man the first necessary of
life. Let a traveller, however, live for a few days but a quarter of
a mile from his water supply and he will learn what is the
comfort of a rivulet just at his door-step. Men who have roughed
it in the wilderness, as many of our Colonists have had to do,
before they have settled themselves into townships, have learned
this lesson so perfectly that they are inclined, perhaps, to be too
fond of a deluge. For purposes of gardening in such a place as
Pretoria there can be no doubt about the water. The town

gardens are large, fertile, and productive, whereas nothing would grow without irrigation.

The streets are broad and well laid, with a fine square in the centre, and the one fact that they have no houses in them is the only strong argument against them. To those who know the first struggling efforts of a colonial town, – who are familiar with the appearance of a spot on which men have decided to begin a city but have not as yet progressed far, the place with all its attributes and drawbacks will be manifest enough. To those who have never seen a city thus struggling into birth it is difficult to make it intelligible. The old faults of old towns have been well understood and thoroughly avoided. The old town began with a simple cluster of houses in close contiguity, because no more than that was wanted. As the traffic of the day was small, no provision was made for broad spaces. If a man could pass a man, or a horse a horse, – or at most a cart a cart, – no more was needed. Of sanitary laws nothing was known. Air and water were taken for granted. Then as people added themselves to people, as the grocer came to supply the earlier tanner, the butcher the grocer, the merchant tailor his three forerunners, and as a schoolmaster added himself to them to teach their children, house was adjoined to house and lane to lane, till a town built itself after its own devise, and such a London and such a Paris grew into existence as we who are old have lived to see pulled down within the period of our own lives. There was no foresight and a great lack of economy in this old way of city building.

– – – –

In such towns the smallness of the houses is not the characteristic which chiefly produces the air of meanness which certainly strikes the visitor, nor is it their distance from each other, nor their poverty; but a certain flavour of untidiness which is common to all new towns and which is, I fear, unavoidable. Brandy bottles and sardine boxes meet the eye everywhere. Tins in which pickled good things have been conveyed accumulate themselves at the corners. The straw receptacles in which wine is nowadays conveyed meet the eye constantly, as do paper shirt-collars, rags, old boots, and fragments of wooden cases. There are no dust holes and no scavengers, and all the unseemly relics of a hungry and thirsty race of pioneers are left open to inspection.

And yet in spite of the mud, in spite of the brandy bottles, in spite of the ubiquitous rags Pretoria is both picturesque and promising. The efforts are being made in the right direction, and the cottages which look lowly enough from without have an air of comfort within. I was taken by a gentleman to call on his wife, – an officer of our army who is interested in the gold fields of the Transvaal, – and I found that they had managed to gather round them within a very small space all the comforts of civilized life. There was no front door and no hall; but I never entered a room in which I felt myself more inclined to 'rest and be thankful.' I made various calls, and always with similar results. I found internal prettinesses, with roses and weeping willows outside which reconciled me to sardine boxes, paper collars, and straw liquor-guards.

(Vol. Two, Chapter IV)

The 'Zoutpan'

We went north from Pretoria and crossing through the spurs of the Magaliesberg range of hills found ourselves upon a plain which after a while became studded with scrub or thorn bushes. Close to the saltpan, and still on the plain, we came to the residence of a Boer who gave us water, – the dirtiest that ever was given to me to drink, – with a stable for our horses and sold us mealies for our animals. As one of our party was a doctor and as the Boer's wife was ill, his hospitality was not ill repaid. A gentle rise of about 200 feet from the house took us to the edge of the pan, which then lay about 300 feet below us, – so as to look as though the earthwork around the valley had been merely thrown out of it as earth might be thrown from any other hole. And this no doubt had been done, – by the operation of nature.

The high outside rim of the cup was about 2¼ miles round, with a diameter of 1,500 yards; and the circle was nearly as perfect as that of a cup. Down thence to the salt lake at the bottom the inside of the bowl fell steeply but gradually, and was thickly covered with bush. The perfect regularity of shape was, to the eye, the most wonderful feature of the phenomenon. At the bottom to which we descended lay the shallow salt lake, which at the time of our visit was about half full, – or half covered, I might better say, in describing the gently shelving bottom of which not more than a moiety was under water. In very dry weather there is no water at all, – and then no salt. When full the lake is about 400 yards across.

Some enterprising Englishman had put up a large iron pan 36 feet by 20, and 18 inches deep, with a furnace under it, which, as everything had been brought out from England at a great cost for land transit, must have been an expensive operation. But it had been deserted because the late Government had been unable to protect him in the rights which he attempted to hire from them. The farmers of the neighbourhood would not allow themselves to be debarred from taking the salt, – and cared nothing for the facts that the Government claimed the privilege of disposing of the salt and that the Englishman had bought the privilege. The Englishman therefore withdrew, leaving behind him his iron pan and his furnace, no doubt with some bitter feelings.

It is probable, I believe, that another Englishman, – or a Scotchman, – will now commence proceedings there, expecting that Downing Street will give better security than a Republican President. In the meantime our friend the Boer pays £50 per annum to the Government, and charges all comers some small fine per load for what they take. Baskets are inserted into the water and are pulled up full of slush. This is deposited on the shore and allowed to drain itself. On the residuum carbonate of soda rises, with a thick layer, as solid cream on standing milk; – and below this there is the salt more or less pure, – very nasty, tasting to me as though it were putrid, – but sufficing without other operation for the curing of meat and for the use of cattle.

(Vol. Two, Chapter IV)

Gold and its perils (i)

It is only now and then, – and I may say that the nows and thens
are rare, – that we find a gold-seeker who has retired into a
settled condition of wealth as a result of his labours among the
Gold Fields. But great towns have sprung up, and tradesmen
have become wealthy, and communities have grown into compact forms, by the expenditure which the gold-seekers have
created. Melbourne is a great city and Ballarat is a great city, not
because the Victorian gold-diggers have been rich and successful;
– but because the trade of gold-finding creates a great outlay. If
the gold-diggers themselves have not been rich they have enriched the bankers and the wine-merchants and the grocers and
the butchers and the innkeepers who have waited upon them.
While one gold-digger starves or lives upon his little capital,
another drinks champagne. Even the first contributes something
to the building up of a country, but the champagne-drinker
contributes a great deal. There is no better customer to the
tradesmen, no more potent consumer, than the man who is
finding gold from day to day. Gold becomes common to him, and
silver contemptible.

I say this for the purpose of showing that though the gold
trade of the Transvaal has not as yet been remunerative, –
though it may perhaps never be truly remunerative to the gold-
seekers, – it may nevertheless help to bring a population to the
country which will build it up, and make it prosperous. It will do
so in the teeth of the despair and ruin which unsuccessful speculations create. There is a charm and a power about gold which is
so seductive and inebriating that judgment and calculation are
ignored by its votaries. If there be gold in a country men will
seek it though it has been sought there for years with disastrous
effects. It creates a sanguine confidence which teaches the gold-
dreamer to believe that he will succeed where hundreds have
failed. It despises climate, and reconciles the harshness of manual
labour to those who have been soft of hand and luxurious of
habit. I am not now intending to warn the covetous against the
Gold Fields of South Africa; – but am simply expressing an
opinion that though these gold regions have hitherto created no

wealth, though henceforth they should not be the source of fortune to the speculators, they will certainly serve to bring white inhabitants into the country.

Gold and its perils (ii)

The Limpopo is an unfortunate river as much of its valley with a considerable district on each side of it is subjected by nature to an abominable curse, – which population and cultivation will in the course of years probably remove but which at present is almost fatal to European efforts at work within the region affected. There is a fly, – called the Tsetse fly, – which destroys all horses and cattle which come within the regions which it selects for its own purposes. Why it should be destructive to a party of horses or to a team of oxen and not to men has I believe to be yet found out. But as men cannot carry themselves and their tools into these districts without horses or oxen, the evil is almost overpowering. The courses of the fly are so well known as to have enabled geographers to mark out on the maps the limits of the Tsetse country. The valley of the Limpopo river may be taken as giving a general idea of the district so afflicted, the distance of the fly-infested region varying from half a dozen to 60 and 80 miles from the river. But towards the East it runs down across the Portuguese possessions never quite touching the sea but just reaching Zululand.

Tatin is to the north west of this region, and though the place itself is not within the fly boundary, all ingress and egress must have been much impeded by the nuisance. The first discovery there of gold is said to have been made by Mauch. There has been heavy work carried on in the district and a quartz-crushing machine was used there. When I was in the Transvaal these works had been abandoned, but of the existence of gold in the country around there can be no doubt. In 1868 the same explorer, Mauch, found gold at a spot considerably to the south east of this, – south of the Limpopo and the Tsetse district, just north of the Olifant's river and in the Transvaal. Then in 1871 Mr Button found gold at Marabas Stad, not far to the west of Mauch's discovery, in the neighbourhood of which the mines at Eesteling

are now being worked by an English Company. On the
Marabas-Stad gold fields a printed report was made by Captain
Elton[20] in 1872, and a considerable sum of money must have
been spent. The Eesteling reef is the only one at present worked
in the neighbourhood. Captain Elton's report seems to promise
much on the condition that a sufficient sum of money be raised to
enable the district to be thoroughly 'prospected' by an able body
of fifty gold-miners for a period of six months. Captain Elton no
doubt understood his subject, but the adequate means for the
search suggested by him have not yet been raised. And, indeed, it
is not thus that the gold fields have been opened. The chances of
success are too small for men in cold blood to subscribe money
at a distance. The work has to be done by the gambling energy
of men who rush to the spot trusting that they may individually
grasp the gold, fill their pockets with the gold, and thus have in a
few months, perhaps in a few days or hours, a superabundance of
that which they have ever been desiring but which has always
been so hard to get!

(Vol. Two, Chapter V)

Pretoria to the diamond fields

On the 1st of October I and my friend started from Pretoria for
the Diamond Fields, having spent a pleasant week at the capital
of the Transvaal. There was, however, one regret. I had not seen
Sir Theophilus Shepstone though I had been entertained at his
house. He, during the time, had been absent on one of those
pilgrimages which Colonial Governors make through their do-
mains, and would be absent so long that I could not afford the
time to wait his return. I should much have liked to discuss with
him the question of the annexation, and to have heard from his
own lips, as I had heard from those of Mr Burgers, a description
of what had passed at the interviews between them. I should
have been glad, also, to have learned from himself what he had
thought of the danger to which the Dutch community had been
subject from the Kafirs and Zulus, – from Secocoeni and Cetywayo, – at the moment of his coming. But the tale which was not

told to me by him was, I think, told with accuracy by some of those who were with him. I have spoken my opinion very plainly, and I hope not too confidently of the affair, and I will only add to that now an assurance of my conviction that had I been in Sir T. Shepstone's place and done as he did, I should have been proud of the way I had served my country.

We started in our cart with our horses as we thought in grand condition. While at Pretoria we had been congratulated on the way in which we had made our purchases and travelled the road surmounting South African difficulties as though we had been at the work all our lives. We had refilled our commissariat chest, and with the exception that my companion had shied a bottle of brandy, – joint property, – at the head of a dog that would bite him, – not me, – as we were packing the cart, there had been as yet no misfortune. Our Cape-boy driver had not once been drunk and nothing material had been lost or broken. We got off at 11 A.M.; and at half past one P.M., – having travelled about fifteen miles in the normal two and a half hours, – we spanned out and shared our lunch with a very hungry-looking Dutchman who squatted himself on his haunches close to our little fire. He was herding cattle and seemed to be very poor and hungry. I imagined him to be some unfortunate who was working for low wages at a distance from his home. But I found him to be the lord of the soil, the owner of the herd, and the possessor of a home-stead about a mile distant. I have no doubt he would have given me what he had to give if I had called at his house. As it was he seemed to be delighted with fried bacon and biscuits, and was aroused almost to enthusiasm over a little drop of brandy and water.

On our road during this day we stopped at an accommodation house, as it is called in the country, – or small Inn, kept by an Englishman. Here before the door I saw a flying flag intended to represent the colours of the Transvaal Dutch Republic. The Englishman, who was rather drunk and very civil, apologized for this by explaining that he had his own patriotic feelings, but that as it was his lot in life to live by the Boers it was necessary that he should please the Boers. This was, however, the only flag of the Republic which I saw during my journey through the country, and I am inclined to think that our countryman had mistaken the signs of the time. I have however to acknowledge in his favour that he offered to make us a present of some fresh butter.

We passed that night at the house of a Boer, who was represented to me as being a man of wealth and repute in the country and as being peculiarly averse to English rule, – Dutch and republican to his heart's core. And I was told soon after by a party who had travelled over the same road, among whom there were two Dutchmen, that he had been very uncourteous to them. No man could have been more gracious than he was to us, who had come in as strangers upon his hospitality, with all our wants for ourselves, our servants and our horses. I am bound to say that his house was very dirty, and the bed of a nature to make the flesh creep, and to force a British occupant of the chamber to wrap himself round with further guards of his own in the shape of rugs and great coats, rather than divest himself of clothes before he would lay himself down. And the copious mess of meat which was prepared for the family supper was not appetising. But nothing could be more grandly courteous than the old man's manner, or kinder than that of his wife. With this there was perhaps something of an air of rank, – just a touch of a consciousness of superiority, – as there might be with some old Earl at home who in the midst of his pleasant amenities could not quite forget his ancestors. Our host could not speak a word of English, – nor we of Dutch; but an Englishman was in the house, – one of the schoolmasters of whom I have spoken before, – and thus we were able to converse. Not a word was said about the annexation; – but much as to the farming prospects of the country. He had grown rich and was content with the condition of the land.

He was heartily abused to us afterwards by the party which contained the two Dutchmen as being a Boer by name and a boor by nature, as being a Boer all round and down to the ground. These were not Hollanders from Holland, but Dutchmen lately imported from the Cape Colony; – and as such were infinitely more antagonistic to the real Boer than would be any Englishman out from Europe. To them he was a dirty, ignorant and arrogant Savage. To him they were presumptuous, new-fangled, vulgar upstarts. They were men of culture and of sense and of high standing in the new country, – but between them and him there were no sympathies.

I think that the English who have now taken the Transvaal will be able, after a while, to rule the Boers and to extort from them that respect without which there can be no comfort between the governors and the governed; – but the work must be done by English and not by Dutch hands. The Dutch Boer will not endure over him either a reforming Hollander from Europe, or a spick-and-span Dutch Africander from the Cape Colony. The reforming Hollander and the spick-and-span Dutch Africander are very intelligent people. It is not to be supposed that I am denying them any good qualities which are to be found in Englishmen. But the Boer does not love them.

Soon after starting from our aristocratic friend's house one of our horses fell sick. He was the one that kicked, – a bright bay little pony, – and in spite of his kicking had been the favourite of the team. We dined that day about noon at a Boer's house, and there we did all that we knew to relieve the poor brute. We gave him chlorodyne and alum, – in accordance with advice which had been given to us for our behoof along the road, – and when we started we hitched him on behind, and went the last stage for that day with a unicorn team. Then we gave him whisky, but it was of no use. That night he could not feed, and early the next morning he laid himself down when he was brought out of the stable and died at my feet. It was our first great misfortune. Our other three horses were not the better or the brighter for all the work they had done, and would certainly not be able to do what would be required of them without a fourth companion.

The place we were now at is called Wonder Fontein, and is remarkable, not specially for any delightfully springing run of water, but for a huge cave, which is supposed to go some miles underground. We went to visit it just at sunset, and being afraid of returning in the dark had not time to see all of it that is known. But we climbed down into the hole, and lit our candles and wandered about for a time. Here and there, in every direction, there were branches and passages running under ground which had hitherto never been explored. The son of the Boer who owned the farm at which we were staying, was with us, and could guide us through certain ways; – but other streets of the place were unknown to him, and, as he assured us, had never yet been visited by man. The place was full of bats, but other animals we saw none. In getting down, the path was narrow, steep, low and disagreeable enough; – but when once we were in the cave we could walk without stooping. At certain periods when the rains had been heavy the caves would become full of water, – and then they would drain themselves when the rains had ceased. It was a hideously ugly place; and most uninteresting were it not that anything not customary interests us to some extent. The caves were very unlike those in the Cango district, which I described in the first volume.

At Wonder Fontein there were six or seven guests besides the very large family with which the Boer and his wife were blessed, and we could not therefore have bedrooms apiece; – nor even beds. I and my young friend had one assigned to us, while the Attorney General of the Colony, who was on circuit and to whom we had given a lift in our cart to relieve him for a couple of days of the tedium of travelling with the Judge and the Sheriff by ox waggon, had a bench assigned to him in a corner of the room. In such circumstances a man lies down, but does not go to bed. We lay down, – and got up at break of day, to see our poor little horse die.

(Vol. Two, Chapter VI)

Griqualand West – River diggings

I was taken up to Barkly 'on a picnic' as people say; and a very nice picnic it was, – one of the pleasantest days I had in South Africa. The object was to shew me the Vaal river, and the little town which had been the capital of the diamond country before the grand discovery at Colesberg Kopje had made the town of Kimberley. There is nothing peculiar about Barkly as a South African town, except that it is already half deserted. There may be perhaps a score of houses there most of which are much better built than those at Kimberley. They are made of rough stone, or of mud and whitewash; and, if I do not mistake, one of them had two storeys. There was an hotel, – quite full although the place is deserted, – and clustering round it were six or seven idle gentlemen all of whom were or had been connected with diamonds. I am often struck by the amount of idleness which persons can allow themselves whose occupations have diverged from the common work of the world.

When at Barkly we got ourselves and our provisions into a boat so that we might have our picnic properly, under the trees at the other side of the river, – for opposite to Barkly is to be found the luxury of trees. As we were rowed down the river we saw a white man with two Kafirs poking about his stones and gravel on a miner's rickety table under a little tent on the beach. He was a digger who had still clung to the 'river' business; a Frenchman who had come to try his luck there a few days since. On the Monday previous, – we were told, – he had found a 13 carat white stone without a flaw. This would be enough perhaps to keep him going and almost to satisfy him for a month! Had he missed that one stone he would probably have left the place after a week. Now he would go on through days and days without finding another sparkle. I can conceive no occupation on earth more dreary, – hardly any more demoralizing than this of perpetually turning over dirt in quest of a peculiar little stone which may turn up once a week or may not. I could not but think, as I watched the man, of the comparative nobility of the work of a shoemaker who by every pull at his thread is helping to keep some person's foot dry.

After our dinner we walked along the bank and found another 'river' digger, though this man's claim might perhaps be removed a couple of hundred yards from the water. He was an Englishman and we stood awhile and talked to him. He had one Kafir with him to whom he paid 7s. a week and his food, and he too had found one or two stones which he shewed us, – just enough to make the place tenable. He had got upon an old digging which he was clearing out lower. He had, however, in one place reached the hard stone at the bottom, in, or below, which there could be no diamonds. There was however a certain quantity of diamondiferous matter left, and as he had already found stones he thought that it might pay him to work through the remainder. He was a most good-humoured well-mannered man, with a pleasant fund of humour. When I asked him of his fortune generally at the diggings, he told us among other things that he had broken his shoulder bone at the diggings, which he displayed to us in order that we might see how badly the surgeon had used him. He had no pain to complain of, – or weakness; but his shoulder had not been made beautiful. 'And who did it?' said the gentleman who was our Amphytrion[21] at the picnic and is himself one of the leading practitioners of the Fields. 'I think it was one Dr ——,' said the digger, naming our friend whom no doubt he knew. I need not say that the doctor loudly disclaimed ever having had previous acquaintance with the shoulder.

The Kafir was washing the dirt in a rough cradle, separating the stones from the dust, and the owner, as each sievefull was brought to him, threw out the stones on his table and sorted them through with the eternal bit of slate or iron formed into the shape of a trowel. For the chance of a sievefull one of our party offered him half a crown, – which he took. I was glad to see it all inspected without a diamond, as had there been anything good the poor fellow's disappointment must have been great. That halfcrown was probably all that he would earn during the week, – all that he would earn perhaps for a month.

(Vol. Two, Chapter VIII)

Kimberley

You stand upon the marge and there, suddenly, beneath your feet lies the entirety of the Kimberley mine, so open, so manifest, and so uncovered that if your eyes were good enough you might examine the separate operations of each of the three or four thousand human beings who are at work there. It looks to be so steep down that there can be no way to the bottom other than the aerial contrivances which I will presently endeavour to explain. It is as though you were looking into a vast bowl, the sides of which are smooth as should be the sides of a bowl, while round the bottom are various marvellous incrustations among which ants are working with all the usual energy of the ant-tribe. And these incrustations are not simply at the bottom, but come up the curves and slopes of the bowl irregularly, – half-way up perhaps in one place, while on another side they are confined quite to the lower deep. The pit is 230 feet deep, nearly circular, though after awhile the eye becomes aware of the fact that it is oblong. At the top the diameter is about 300 yards of which 250 cover what is technically called 'blue,' – meaning diamondiferous soil. Near the surface and for some way down, the sides are light brown, and as blue is the recognised diamond colour you will at first suppose that no diamonds were found near the surface; – but the light brown has been in all respects the same as the blue, the colour of the soil to a certain depth having been affected by a mixture of iron. Below this everything is blue, all the constructions in the pit having been made out of some blue matter which at first sight would seem to have been carried down for the purpose. But there are other colours on the wall which give a peculiar picturesqueness to the mines. The top edge as you look at it with your back to the setting sun is red with the gravel of the upper reef, while below, in places, the beating of rain and running of water has produced peculiar hues, all of which are a delight to the eye.

As you stand at the edge you will find large high-raised boxes at your right hand and at your left, and you will see all round the margin crowds of such erections, each box being as big as a little house and higher than most of the houses in Kimberley. These are the first recipients for the stuff that is brought up out of the mine. And behind these, so that you will often find that you have walked between them, are the whims by means of which the stuff is raised, each whim being worked by two horses. Originally the operation was done by hand-windlasses which were turned by Kafirs, – and the practice is continued at some of the smaller enterprises; – but the horse whims are now so general that there is a world of them round the claim. The stuff is raised on aerial tramways, – and the method of an aerial tramway is as follows. Wires are stretched taught from the wooden boxes slanting down to the claims at the bottom, – never less than four wires for each box, two for the ascending and two for the descending bucket. As one bucket runs down empty on one set of wires, another comes

up full on the other set. The ascending bucket is of course full of
'blue.' The buckets were at first simply leathern bags. Now they
have increased in size and importance of construction, – to half
barrels and so upwards to large iron cylinders which sit easily
upon wheels running in the wires as they ascend and descend
and bring up their loads, half a cart load at each journey.

As this is going on round the entire circle it follows that there
are wires starting everywhere from the rim and converging to a
centre at the bottom, on which the buckets are always scudding
through the air. They drop down and creep up not altogether
noiselessly but with a gentle trembling sound which mixes itself
pleasantly with the murmur from the voices below. And the
wires seem to be the strings of some wonderful harp, – aerial or
perhaps infernal, – from which the beholder expects that a louder
twang will soon be heard. The wires are there always of course,
but by some lights they are hardly visible. The mine is seen best
in the afternoon and the visitor looking at it should stand with his
back to the setting sun; – but as he so stands and so looks he will
hardly be aware that there is a wire at all if his visit be made, say
on a Saturday afternoon, when the works are stopped and the
mine is mute.

When the world below is busy there are about 3,500 Kafirs at
work, – some small proportion upon the reef which has to be got
into order so that it shall neither tumble in, nor impede the work,
nor overlay the diamondiferous soil as it still does in some
places; but by far the greater number are employed in digging.
Their task is to pick up the earth and shovel it into the buckets
and iron receptacles. Much of it is loosened for them by blasting
which is done after the Kafirs have left the mine at 6 o'clock. You
look down and see the swarm of black ants busy at every hole
and corner with their picks moving and shovelling the loose blue
soil.

But the most peculiar phase of the mine, as you gaze into its
one large pit, is the subdivision into claims and portions. Could a
person see the sight without having heard any word of explana-
tion it would be impossible, I think, to conceive the meaning of
all those straight cut narrow dikes, of those mud walls all at right
angles to each other, of those square separate pits, and again of

those square upstanding blocks, looking like houses without doors or windows. You can see that nothing on earth was ever less level than the bottom of the bowl, – and that the black ants in traversing it, as they are always doing, go up and down almost at every step, jumping here on to a narrow wall and skipping there across a deep dividing channel as though some diabolically ingenious architect had contrived a house with 500 rooms, not one of which should be on the same floor.

(Vol. Two, Chapter VIII)

The great civilizer?

Who can doubt but that work is the great civilizer of the world, – work and the growing desire for those good things which work only will bring? If there be one who does he should come here to see how those dusky troops of labourers, who ten years since were living in the wildest state of unalloyed savagery, whose only occupation was the slaughter of each other in tribal wars, each of whom was the slave of his Chief, who were subject to the dominion of most brutalizing and cruel superstitions, have already put themselves on the path towards civilization. They are thieves no doubt; – that is they steal diamonds though not often other things. They are not Christians. They do not yet care much about breeches. They do not go to school. But they are orderly. They come to work at six in the morning and go away at six in the evening. They have an hour in the middle of the day, and know that they have to work during the other hours. They take their meals regularly and, what is the best of all, they are learning to spend their money instead of carrying it back to their Chiefs.

Civilization can not come at once. The coming I fear under any circumstances must be slow. But this is the quickest way towards it that has yet been found. The simple teaching of religion has never brought large numbers of Natives to live in European habits; but I have no doubt that European habits will bring about religion. The black man when he lives with the white man and works under the white man's guidance will learn to believe really what the white man really believes himself. Surely we should not expect him to go faster. But the missionary has endeavoured to gratify his own soul by making here and there a model Christian before the pupil has been able to understand any of the purposes of Christianity. I have not myself seen the model Christian perfected; but when I have looked down into the Kimberley mine and seen three or four thousand of them at work, – although each of them would willingly have stolen a diamond if the occasion came, – I have felt that I was looking at three or four thousand growing Christians.

Because of this I regard Kimberley as one of the most interesting places on the face of the earth. I know no other spot on which the work of civilizing a Savage is being carried on with so signal a success. The Savages whom we have encountered in our great task of populating the world have for the most part eluded our grasp by perishing while we have been considering how we might best deal with them. Here, in South Africa, a healthy nation remains and assures us by its public tendency that when protected from self-destruction by our fostering care it will spread and increase beneath our hands. But what was to be done with these people? Having found that they do not mean to die, by what means might we instruct them how to live? Teach them to sing hymns, and all will be well. That is one receipt. Turn them into slaves, and make them work. That is another receipt. Divide the land with them, and let them live after their own fashions; – only subject to some little control from us. That was a third. The hymns have done nothing. The slavery was of course impossible. And that division of land has been, perhaps not equally futile, but insufficient for the growing needs of the people; – insufficient also for our own needs. Though we abuse the Kafir we want his service, and we want-more than our share of his land. But that which no effort of intelligence could produce has been brought about by circumstances. The Diamond Fields have been discovered and now there are ten thousand of these people receiving regular wages and quite capable of rushing to a magistrate for protection if they be paid a shilling short on Saturday night.

(Vol. Two, Chapter IX)

Diamonds (i)

I was soon sick of looking at diamonds though the idea of holding ten or twenty thousand pounds lightly between my fingers did not quite lose its charm. I was however disgusted at the terms of reproach with which most of the diamonds were described by their owners. Many of them were 'off colours,' stones of a yellowish hue and therefore of comparatively little value, or stones with a flaw, stones which would split in the cutting, stones which could not be cut to any advantage. There were very many evil stones to one that was good, so that nature after all did not appear to have been as generous as she might have been. And these dealers when the stones are brought to them for purchase, have no certain standard of value by which to regulate their transactions with their customers. The man behind the counter will take the stones, one by one, examine them, weigh them, and then make his offer for the parcel. Dealing in horses is precarious work, – when there is often little to shew whether an animal be worth £50, or £100, or £150. But with diamonds it must be much more so. A dealer offers £500 when the buyer has perhaps expected £2,000! And yet the dealer is probably nearest to the mark. The diamonds at any rate are bought and sold, and are sent away by post at the rate of about £2,000,000 in the year. In 1876 the registered export of diamonds from Kimberley amounted in value to £1,414,590, and reached 773 pounds avoirdupois in weight. But it is computed that not above three quarters of what are sent from the place are recorded in the accounts that are kept. There is no law to make such record necessary. Any one who has become legally possessed of a diamond may legally take it or send it away as he pleases.

Diamonds (ii)

Nevertheless there is a stain sticking to the diamonds, – such a stain as sticks to gold, which tempts one to repeat the poet's caution:-

Aurum irrepertum, et sic melius situm
Cum terra celat, spernere fortior,
    Quam cogere humanos in usus.[22]

It would be untrue to say that he who works to ornament the world is necessarily less noble than the other workman who supplies it with what is simply useful. The designer of a room-paper ranks above the man who hangs it, – and the artist whose picture decorates the wall is much above the designer of the paper. Why therefore should not the man who finds diamonds be above the man who finds bread? And yet I feel sure that he is not. It is not only the thing procured but the manner of procuring it that makes or mars the nobility of the work. If there be an employment in which the labourer has actually to grovel in the earth it is this search for diamonds. There is much of it in gold-seeking, but in the search after diamonds it is all grovelling. Let the man rise as high as he may in the calling, be the head of the biggest firm at Kimberley, still he stands by and sees the grit turned, – still he picks out the diamonds from the other dirt with his own fingers, and carries his produce about with him in his own pocket. If a man be working a coal mine, though he be himself the hardest worked as well as the head workman in the business, he is removed from actual contact with the coal. But here, at Kimberley, sharp prying eyes are wanted, rather than an intelligence fitted for calculations, and patience in manipulating dirt than skill in managing men or figures.

And the feeling engendered, – the constant recollection that a diamond may always be found, – is carried so far that the mind never rests from business. The diamond-seeker cannot get out of his task and take himself calmly to his literature at 4 P.M. or 5 or 6. This feeling runs through even to his wife and children, teaching them that dirt thrice turned may yet be turned a fourth time with some hope of profit. Consequently ladies, and children, do turn dirt instead of making pretty needle-work or wholesome mud pies. When I heard of so much a dozen being given to young bairns for the smallest specks of diamonds, specks which their young eyes might possibly discover, my heart was bitterly grieved. How shall a child shake off a stain which has been so early incurred? And when ladies have told me, as ladies did tell me, – pretty, clever, well-dressed women, – of hours so passed, of day after day spent in the turning of dust by their own fingers because there might still be diamonds among the dust, I thought that I could almost sooner have seen my own wife or my own girl with a broom at a street crossing.

There is not so much of this now as there was, and as years roll on, – if the diamonds still be to be found, – there will be less and less. If the diamonds still be there in twenty year's time, – as to which I altogether decline to give my opinion, – a railway will have been carried on to Kimberley, and planks will have been carried up, and perhaps bricks from some more favoured locality, and possibly paving stones, so that the town shall be made to look less rowdy and less abominable. And pipes will be laid on from the Vaal river, and there will be water carts. And with the dust the flies will go into abeyance. And trees will have been planted. And fresh butter will be made. And there will be a library and men will have books. And houses will have become pleasant, so that a merchant may love to sit at home in his own verandah, – which he will then afford to have broad and cool and floored. And as the nice things come the nasty habits will sink. The ladies will live far away from the grit, and small diamonds will have become too common to make it worth the parents' while to endanger their children's eyes. Some mode of checking the Kafir thieves will perhaps have been found, – and the industry will have sunk into the usual grooves. Nothing, however, will tend so much to this as the lessening of the value of diamonds. The stone is at present so precious that a man's mind cannot bear to think that one should escape him.

(Vol. Two, Chapter IX)

The Orange Tree Free State – Bloemfontein

It stands isolated in the plain, – without any suburb except the native location which I have named, – with as clearly defined a boundary on each side as might be a town built with a pack of cards, or one of those fortified citadels with barred gates and portcullises which we used to see in picture books. After travelling through a country ugly, dusty and treeless for many weary hours the traveller at last reaches Bloemfontein and finds himself at rest from his joltings, with his bones not quite dislocated, in the quiet little Dutch capital, wondering at the fate which has led him to a spot on the world's surface, so far away, apparently so purposeless, and so unlike the cities which he has known.

I heard of no special industry at Bloemfontein. As far as I am aware nothing special is there manufactured. It is needful that a country should have a Capital, and therefore the Orange Free State has Bloemfontein. I was told that some original Boer named Bloem first settled there by the side of the stream in which water runs when there has been rain, and that hence has come the name. But the little town has thriven with a success peculiarly its own. Though it would seem to have no raison d'etre just there where it stands, – though it has been encouraged and fostered by no peculiar fertility, adorned with no scenic beauty, enriched by no special gifts of water or of metals, even though the population has not grown beyond that of the suburb of some European town, still it carries its metropolitan honours with a good air, and shocks no one by meanness, dirt, or poverty. It certainly is not very grand, but it is grand enough. If there be no luxury, everything is decent. The members of the Volksraad are not carried about in gorgeous equipages, but when they have walked slowly to their Chamber they behave themselves there with decorum. There is nothing pretentious in Bloemfontein, – nothing to raise a laugh at the idea that a town with so small a population should call itself a capital.

It is a town, white and red, built with plastered walls or of brick, – with a large oblong square in the centre; with four main streets running parallel to each other and with perhaps double that number of cross streets. The houses are generally but one storey high, though this is not so invariably the case as at Kimberley. I do not remember, however, that I was ever required to go up-stairs, – except at the schools. The supply of water is I am assured never-failing, though in dry weather it has to be drawn from tanks. A long drought had prevailed when I reached the place, and the bed of the riverlet had been dry for many days;

but the supply of water seemed to be sufficient. Fuel is very scarce and consequently dear. This is of the less importance as but little is wanted except for the purpose of cooking.

At one extreme end of the town are the public buildings in which the Volksraad is held and the judges sit. Here also are the offices of the President and the Secretary. Indeed all public business is here carried on. The edifice has but the ground floor with a clock tower rising from the centre. It is long and roomy and to my eye handsome in its white neatness. I have heard it laughed at and described as being like a railway station. It seems to be exactly that which such a Capital and such a Republic would require. The Volksraad was not sitting when I was there and I therefore could only see the beautiful arm-chairs which have lately been imported at a considerable expense for the use of the Members; – £13 10s. a chair I think I was told! It is impossible to conceive that gentlemen who have been accommodated with such chairs should wilfully abandon any of the dignity attached to them. For a central parliament the chairs may be fitting, but would be altogether out of place in a small provincial congress. Except the churches and the schools there are not any public buildings of much note in Bloemfontein, – unless the comfortable residence of the President may be so called. This belongs to the State but is not attached to the House of Parliament.

My residence when I was at Bloemfontein was at the Free State Hotel, and I do not know that I was ever put up much better. Two circumstances militated against my own particular comfort, but they were circumstances which might probably recommend the house to the world at large. I was forced to take my meals in public at stated hours; – and I had a great deal too much put before me to eat. I am bound, however, to say that all I had given to me was good, though at that time it must have been very difficult to supply such luxuries. The butter had to be bought at 5s. 6d. a pound, but was as plentiful as though the price had been only a shilling, – and it was good which I had not found to be the case elsewhere in South Africa. What was paid for the peas and beans and cauliflowers I don't know; but I did know that the earth around was dry and parched and barren everywhere, – so that I was almost ashamed to eat them. These details may be of interest to some readers of my pages, as the place of which I am speaking is becoming at present the sanitorium to which many an English consumptive patient is sent. Such persons, at any rate when first reaching Bloemfontein, are obliged to find a home in an hotel, and will certainly find one well provided at the Free State. It commended itself to me especially because I found no difficulty in that very serious and often troublesome matter of a morning tub.

Bloemfontein is becoming another Madeira, another Algiers, another Egypt in regard to English sufferers with weak chests and imperfect lungs. It seems to the ignorant as though the doctors were ever seeking in increased distance that relief for their patients which they cannot find in increased skill. But a dry climate is now supposed to be necessary and one that shall be temperate without great heat. This certainly will be found at Bloemfontein, and perhaps more equably so through the entire year than at any other known place. The objection to it is the expense arising from the distance and the great fatigue to patients from the long overland journey. Taking the easiest mode of reaching the capital of the Free State the traveller must be kept going six weary days in a Cobb's coach, being an average of about thirteen hours a day upon the road. This is gradually and very slowly becoming lightened by the opening of bits of the railway from Fort Elizabeth; but it will be some years probably before the coaching work can be done in less than five days. The road is very rough through the Catberg and Stromberg mountains, – so that he who has made the journey is apt to think that he has done something considerable. All this is so much against an invalid that I doubt whether they who are feeble should be sent here. There can I imagine be no doubt that the air of the place when reached is in the highest degree fit for weak lungs.

(Vol. Two, Chapter XII)

Native Territories – Sapena

We walked up the hill with Mr Daniel and had not been long among the huts when we were accosted by one Sapena and his friends. Now there is a difficulty with these people as to the next heir to the throne, – which difficulty will I fear be hard of solving when old King Maroco dies. His son by his great wife married in due order a quantity of wives among whom one was chosen as the 'great wife' as was proper. In a chapter further on a word or two will be found as to this practice. But the son who was the undoubted heir died before his great wife had had a child. She then went away, back to the Bechuanas from whom she had come, and among whom she was a very royal Princess, and there married Prince Sapena. This marriage was blessed with a son. But by Bechuana law, by Baralong law also, – and I believe by Jewish law if that were anything to the purpose, – the son of the wife of the heir becomes the heir even though he be born from another father. These people are very particular in all matters of inheritance, and therefore, when it began to be thought that Maroco was growing old and near his time, they sent an embassy to the Bechuanas for the boy. He had arrived just before my visit and was then absent on a little return journey with the suite of Bechuanas who had brought him. By way of final compliment he had gone back with them a few miles so that I did not see him. But his father Sapena had been living for some time with the Baralongs, having had some difficulties among the Bechuanas with the Royal Princess his wife, and, being a man of power and prudence, had become half regent under the infirm old Chief. There are fears that when Maroco dies there may be a contest as to the throne between Sapena and his own son. Should the contest amount to a war the Free State will probably find it expedient to settle the question by annexing the country.

Sapena is a well built man, six feet high, broad in the shoulders, and with the gait of a European. He was dressed like a European, with a watch and chain at his waistcoat, a round flat topped hat, and cord trowsers, and was quite clean. Looking at him as he walks no one would believe him to be other than a white man. He looks to be about thirty, though he must be much older. He was accompanied by three or four young men who were all of the blood royal, and who were by no means like to him either in dress or manner. He was very quiet, answering our questions in few words, but was extremely courteous. He took us first into a large hut belonging to one of the family, which was so scrupulously clean as to make me think for a moment that it was kept as a show hut; but those which we afterwards visited, though not perhaps equal to the first in neatness, were too nearly so to have made much precaution necessary. The hut was round as are all the huts, but had a door which required no stooping. A great portion of the centre, – though not quite the centre, – was occupied by a large immoveable round bin in which the corn for the use of the family is stored. There was a chair, and a bed, and two or three settees. If I remember right, too, there was a gun standing against the wall. The place certainly looked as though nobody was living in it. Sapena afterwards took us to his own hut which was also very spacious, and here we were seated on chairs and had Kafir beer brought to us in large slop-bowls. The Kafir beer is made of Kafir corn, and is light and sour. The Natives when they sit down to drink swallow enormous quantities of it. A very little sufficed with me, as its sourness seemed to be its most remarkable quality. There were many Natives with us but none of them drank when we did. We sat for ten minutes in Sapena's house, and then were taken on to that of the King. I should say however that in the middle of Sapena's hut there stood a large iron double bedstead with mattress which I was sure had come from Mr Heal's establishment in Tottenham Court Road.[23]

Round all these huts, – those that is belonging to the royal family and those no doubt of other magnates, – there is a spacious courtyard enclosed by a circular fence of bamboo canes, stuck into the ground perpendicularly, standing close to each other and bound together. The way into the courtyard is open, but the circle is brought round so as to overlap the entrance and prevent the passer-by from looking in. It is not, I imagine, open to every one to run into his neighbour's courtyard, – especially into those belonging to royalty. As we were going to the King's Palace the King himself met us on the road surrounded by two or three of his councillors. One old councillor stuck close to him always, and was, I was told, never absent from his side. They had been children together and Maroco cannot endure to be without him. We had our interview out in the street, with a small crowd of Baralongs around us. The Chief was not attired at all like his son's wife's husband. He had an old skin or korass around him, in which he continually shrugged himself as we see a beggar doing in the cold, with a pair of very old trowsers and a most iniquitous slouch hat upon his head. There was nothing to mark the King about his outward man; – and, as he was dressed, so was his councillor. But it is among the 'young bloods' of a people that finery is always first to be found.

(Vol. Two, Chapter XIII)

Conclusion

South Africa is a country of black men, – and not of white men. It has been so; it is so; and it will continue to be so. In this respect it is altogether unlike Australia, unlike the Canadas, and unlike New Zealand. And, as it is unlike them, so should it be to us a matter of much purer gratification than are those successful Colonies. There we have gone with our ploughs and with our brandy, with all the good and with all the evil which our civilization has produced, and throughout the lands the native races have perished by their contact with us. They have withered by commune with us as the weaker weedy grasses of Nature's first planting wither and die wherever come the hardier plants, which science added to nature has produced. I am not among those who say that this has been caused by our cruelty. It has often been that we have struggled our very best to make our landing on a shore an unmixed blessing to those to whom we have come. In New Zealand we strove hard for this; – but in New Zealand the middle of the next century will probably hear of the existence of some solitary last Maori. It may be that this was necessary. All the evidence we have seems to show that it was so. But it is hardly the less sad because it was necessary. In Australia we have been successful. We are clothed with its wools. Our coffers are filled with its gold. Our brothers and our children are living there in bounteous plenty. But during the century that we have been there we have caused the entire population of a whole continent to perish. It is impossible to think of such prosperity without a dash of suffering, without a pang of remorse.

In South Africa it is not so. The tribes which before our coming were wont to destroy themselves in civil wars have doubled their population since we have turned their assagais to ploughshares. Thousands, ten thousands of them, are working for wages. Even beyond the realms which we call our own we have stopped the cruelties of the Chiefs and the no less fatal superstitions of the priests. The Kafir and the Zulu are free men, and understand altogether the privileges of their freedom. In one town of 18,000 inhabitants, 10,000 of them are now receiving 10s. a week each man, in addition to their diet. Here at any rate we have not come as a blighting poison to the races whom we have found in the country of our adoption. This I think ought to endear South Africa to us.

(Vol. Two, Chapter XVII)

NOTES

(These notes are not intended to be exhaustive, but merely to provide some additional information.)

THE WEST INDIES AND THE SPANISH MAIN

[1] *Atrato.* The ship on which Trollope sailed for the West Indies from Southampton on 17 November 1858.

[2] Don Pedro Badan Caldéron de la Barca. A Trollope joke: Pedro Caldéron de la Barca (1600–81) was the great Spanish dramatist.

[3] Mr Anthony Trollope Ben Jonson. The joke continues through another literary reference (Jonson 1572–1637). Trollope had an exhaustive interest in Jacobean drama.

[4] 'Mens sana in corpore sano.' A sound mind in a sound body (Juvenal, *Satires*).

[5] Poblada! Bushy.

[6] White Creoles. Those born and naturalised in the West Indies, but of European descent.

[7] They'd have read me out. i.e., expelled her from her church through a 'reading out' of the sentence of expulsion.

[8] Ernulphus (1040–1124). Bishop of Rochester. The curse against him appears in Vol. iii of *Tristram Shandy* by Laurence Sterne (1713–68).

[9] Maria . . . Sterne. The reference is to his *A Sentimental Journey Through France and Italy* (1768) in which Maria is reintroduced. She had first appeared in Vol. ix of *Tristram Shandy*.

[10] Jacob's ladder. Seen by the patriarch Jacob in a vision (Genesis 28:12).

[11] Trash-houses. Buildings on a sugar plantation where the stalks from which the juice has been expressed are stored for fuel. (OED)

[12] *Filibustering.* Spanish for freebooting. Specifically, lawless American adventurers who sought to instigate revolts and exploit for gain areas of Central and South America (for example Cuba in 1851 and Nicaragua in 1855).

[13] Clive . . . Warren Hastings. The first (1725–74) avenged the Black Hole of Calcutta at the battle of Plassey (1757). His conduct in India was the subject of an investigation, as was that of Warren Hastings (1732–1818), who was impeached in 1788 and acquitted in 1795.

[14] Thalberg and Soyer. Sigismund Thalberg (1812–71), born in Geneva, outstanding pianist of his generation: Alexis Soyer (1809–58), French gastronomist,

came to London, made chef to the Reform Club, culinary adviser on the Irish famine (1847) and in the Crimea (1855).

[15] Fanny Grey. I have been unable to trace this reference.

[16] Circean circle.   Enchanted into a trap, as the sorceress Circe turned Odysseus's companions into swine and held them captive (*Odyssey*, Book x).

[17] Charybdis pools.   Whirlpool on the Sicilian coast, paired with Scylla in classical mythology; if you avoid one you may fall into the other.

[18] No Leander feat.   Leander of Abydos swam the Hellespont to visit his lover Hero.

[19] Elysium.   Paradise of Happy Lands according to the Greek poets.

[20] Happy valley of Rasselas.   *Rasselas, Prince of Abyssinia* (1759) by Dr Johnson (1709–84). Rasselas resides in the happy valley, which he leaves in order to travel and gain experience of life.

[21] 'O, si sic omnes!'.   O, if everything were like this!

[22] Knickerbocker and Rip van Winkle.   Diedrich Knickerbocker, the pseudonym taken by Washington Irving (1783–1859) in his burlesque *A History of New York* (1809): Rip van Winkle appeared in Irving's *The Sketch Book* (1819–20).

[23] The Anti-Corn-Law League.   Formed after much agitation in 1839 to get the tax on grain abolished. The Laws were repealed in 1846.

[24] A rose by any other name ...   *Romeo and Juliet* Act II, scene ii.

[25] Cortes.   Hernando Cortes (1485–1547), first European to view the Pacific.

[26] Queen Pomare. Presumably Aimatta Pomare IV (1827–77) of Tahiti.

[27] Hood's Whims and Oddities.   *Whims & Oddities: in Prose and Verse* were published in 1826–7. They were by Thomas Hood (1799–1845).

[28] 'That patient merit of the unworthy takes' *Hamlet* Act III, scene ii.

[29] Pelion or Ossa.   Adding difficulty to difficulty. In mythology when the giants tried to reach heaven, they placed Mount Pelion on Mount Ossa as a scaling ladder.

[30] 'Aurum irrepertum et sic melius situm!' Undiscovered gold (better thus placed while earth hides it). (Horace, *Odes*, iii.)

[31] Bicher.   Scots dialect, sometimes bicker (beaker), bowl or dish for holding liquid, drinking cup.

[32] Boaz.   The tiny Bermudan isle which housed the convict settlement set up in the 19th century.

NORTH AMERICA

[1] My mother wrote a book about the Americans.   Frances Trollope's *The Domestic Manners of the Americans*, which became something of a best-seller in its time, was published on 19 March 1832.

[2] I should think that I had cause to be proud of my work.   Despite his admiration for much of what he saw, Trollope is highly critical of women, spoilt

children, hotels and many aspects of American life, so much so that he apologises for what he has written at the end of his second volume.

³ De Tocqueville.   Alexis de Tocqueville (1805–59) visited America and produced a classic study *La démocratie en Amérique* (1835, 1840).

⁴ The tea that had been sunk there.   A reference to the Boston Tea Party of 16 December 1773 when colonists threw a cargo of tea into Boston Harbour as a protest against the duties imposed on tea by the English Parliament. It effectively sparked the American War of Independence.

⁵ *Chef d'oeuvre.*   A masterpiece.

⁶ A Sybarite.   A self-indulgent person, intent on luxurious living (from Sybaris, Southern Italy), a city of the Ancient Greeks noted for its effeminacy and luxury.

⁷ Mr Murray.   The publisher of Albemarle Street, celebrated for publishing Lord Byron and, in the 19th century, for a series of guidebooks. Trollope's irony here derives perhaps from his own dealings – or rather non-dealings – with John Murray (see Introduction, p. xvii).

⁸ Longfellow, Emerson, Hawthorne.   Leading American men of letters at the time of Trollope's visit. Longfellow (1807–82), poet, particularly celebrated for *The Song of Hiawatha* (1858); R. W. Emerson (1803–82), philosopher, lecturer, mystic having, like Longfellow, an international reputation; Nathaniel Hawthorne (1804–64), author of *The Scarlet Letter* (1850), the major fictional treatment of American Puritanism.

⁹ *De rigueur.*   Required by fashion or etiquette.

¹⁰ *Ad nauseam.*   To a disgusting degree.

¹¹ Mr Gladstone.   William Ewart Gladstone became Chancellor of the Exchequer in 1859 and reduced the duty on French wines, which were probably re-exported to America.

¹² Sir Edmund Head.   Head (1805–68) was Governor General of Canada between 1854 and 1861.

¹³ Phlegethon.   The river of liquid fire in Hades, the underground abode of the dead in Greek mythology.

¹⁴ Fremont.   John Fremont (1813–90) American explorer who became a General in the Northern Army. A controversial figure, he was relieved of his command. He became a Presidential candidate in 1864 but withdrew.

¹⁵ Hercules . . . cleanse the stables of the southern king.   The legendary Greek hero had twelve labours imposed upon him by the Argive king: the fifth was to cleanse the Augean stables, which had not been cleaned out for thirty years. It is a favourite Trollope analogy.

¹⁶ Bull's Run.   The most important early battle of the Civil War occurred on 21 July 1861. See James M. McPherson, *Battle Cry of Freedom: The Civil War Era* (Oxford, 1988), 339 ff.

¹⁷ Cord of logs.   A unit of wood cut for fuel in a stack 4×4×8 feet.

¹⁸ *Ars celare artem* [ars est celare artem].   True art conceals the means by which it is achieved. (Ovid, *Ars Amatoria.*)

¹⁹ Hugger-mugger.   Keeper of secrets, one who hushes up or is stealthy.

[20] Ginger is hot in the mouth . . . cakes and ale.   *Twelfth Night* Act II, scene iii, one of Trollope's favourite quotations, and used three or four times in *North America*.

[21] The Maine Liquor Law.   Introduced in 1851 by Neal Dow, mayor of Portland, it imposed prohibition, and there were many riots against it.

[22] The 'Mayflower'.   The ship which left Plymouth in December 1602 carrying the Puritan Pilgrim Fathers to America.

[23] *O fortunatus sua si bona norint!*   O how lucky they are if only their realised it! (Virgil, *Georgics*.)

[24] Miss Faithfull.   Emily Faithfull (1835–95), set up the Victoria Press in 1860. She was one of the founders of the Women's Printing Society.

[25] Braggadocio.   Boasting, arrogant pretension.

[26] Washington.   George Washington (1732–99), first President of the United States, the capital being named after him and becoming the seat of government in 1800.

[27] Palmyra, ruined city of great commercial, religious and historical importance, 150 miles NE of Damascus.

[28] La Fayette Squire.   So named after the Marquis de la Fayette (1757–1834), one of the heroes of the American War of Independence: ironically, in his old age, a society acquaintance of Trollope's mother.

[29] General Jackson.   Andrew Jackson (1767–1845) American President from 1828 to 1836.

[30] Trollope's guess has not been fulfilled.

[31] Sub dio.   In view of the context, probably sub divo – under the open sky.

[32] Any great sum of money.   In fact the bazaar was a terrible failure, and Mrs Trollope faced debts which could not be repaid.

[33] Their march into Russia.   A reference to Napoleon's fatal Russian campaign of 1812.

[34] Hector and Ajax.   The first, one of the Trojan heroes in Homer's *Iliad*, slain by Achilles, the second the giant son of Telemon in the same poem, driven mad by the fact that the dead Hector's armour was bestowed on Ulysses instead of himself.

[35] Sloughs of despond.   In John Bunyan's *The Pilgrim's Progress* (1678), Christian has to cross the Slough of Despond, a dangerous bog, in order to reach the Wicket Gate.

[36] Mr Seward.   William Henry Seward (1801–72), Lincoln's Secretary of State, a strong abolitionist and anti-slavery campaigner. Trollope wrote in *An Autobiography* that Seward was 'a wise man' and that he was instrumental in preventing war between America and England at the time of the Trent incident.

[37] Mr Cameron . . . Mr Stanton.   Simon Cameron (1799–1889) Secretary of State for War in 1860, later transferred to Moscow by Lincoln: Edwin Stanton (1814–69) succeeded him at the War Department in January 1862.

[38] Augean stables . . .   American Hercules. See note 15 p. 245.

[39] Danae's golden shower.   Danae was the Argive princess, seduced by Zeus, then hidden in a golden shower. She was the mother of Perseus.

[40] Cakes and ale ... See note 20 p. 246.

[41] It is not better to rule in hell than serve in heaven. 'Better to reign in hell than serve in heaven' (Milton, *Paradise Lost*, Book I, 261).

[42] Lord Derby ... no definite arrangement. A passing Trollopian political glance: Lord Derby was Prime Minister 1858–9 and again 1866–8.

[43] That Van Wyck committee! Charles Henry Van Wyck (1824–95) American senator whose committee investigated corruption and financial mismanagement during the Civil War.

[44] The death of Hector ... Homer also sang of it. i.e. in *Iliad*, Book xxii.

AUSTRALIA AND NEW ZEALAND

[1] Mrs Beecher Stowe with her memories of sunny duchesses. Harriet Beecher Stowe (1811–96), author of *Uncle Tom's Cabin*, wrote a series of letters, *Sunny Memories of Foreign Lands* (1854) describing her stay in England, Scotland and Europe. She was much fêted. Trollope is being ironic.

[2] Gin. A female Australian aboriginal; a native woman or wife. (OED)

[3] Arcadian shepherd life ... Tityrus ... Phyllis. The names of shepherd and shepherdess who represent simple rustic love: they are found in Virgil's *Eclogues*.

[4] Corin ... Touchstone. *As You Like It* Act III, scene ii.

[5] Hoggetts ... wethers. Yearling sheep ... castrated male sheep.

[6] As Edwards and Joyce note, Sir James Martin was Prime Minister of New South Wales for three periods, the last from December 1870–May 1872, but did not hold that office again.

[7] Lowther or Chatsworth. The first is Lowther Castle south of Penrith near Ullswater. The second is the palatial seat of the Duke of Devonshire in Derbyshire, 8 miles West of Chesterfield, the park with gardens being 10 miles in circumference.

[8] Scott in prose, and Byron in verse. Sir Walter Scott (1771–1832), author of the Waverley novels, and Lord Byron (1788–1824) the Romantic poet.

[9] *Life in the Bush*. This sequence is based on Trollope's stay with his son Frederic at Mortray (20 October–12 November 1871).

[10] 'A joy for ever'. 'A thing of beauty is a joy for ever' is the opening line of John Keats' *Endymion* (1818).

[11] The railway mania some twenty-four years ago. The reference is obviously to the late 1840s. The great age of railway speculation ended with the disgrace of George Hudson, the so-called 'railway king' in 1849.

[12] Little Styxes, dark deceitful Acherons. Rivers in Hades in Greek mythology, over which Charon ferried the dead.

[13] Tickets-of-leave. Licences giving convicts their liberty under certain conditions before their prison sentence has expired.

[14] The Bill Sykes look. Bill Sikes, house-breaker and murderer of Nancy in Dickens' *Oliver Twist* (serialised 1837–9).

[15] Burke and Wills. Richard O'Hara Burke (1820–61) and William John Wills

(1834–61). These explorers were lost south of Cooper's Creek, as Edwards and Joyce point out in their *Australia*, and in fact only a small section of the line ran near there.

[16] A drag. Strong-smelling lure for hounds (in place of the fox, etc).

[17] Fortified pahs. Strongly protected native camps.

[18] Carlyle, Macaulay, and Dickens. Major nineteenth-century writers: Carlyle (1795–1881), historian and critical, social and political commentator on his times: Lord Macaulay (1800–59), major essayist and historian, and Charles Dickens (1812–70); one of the great novelists of the Victorian period, he reached the widest public.

[19] Lothario comers. Lothario is taken from a character in Rowe's play *The Fair Penitent* (1703), and is equated with deception in love, rakish behaviour.

[20] Demosthenes ... Cicero ... Pitt. Demosthenes (385–322 BC) the great Athenian orator; Cicero (106–43 BC), Roman orator, statesman and man of letters, subject of a life by Trollope, published in 1880. Pitt (1759–1806), English statesman, became Prime Minister at the age of twenty-four.

SOUTH AFRICA

[1] The Transvaal Republic. Developed by the Boers originally in 1856, undermined by the natives in 1877, and hence taken over by the British, who reduced the natives' threat and restored the economy.

[2] Orange Free States. In South Africa, lying between the Vaal and the Orange rivers. Annexed by the British in 1848, granted independence in 1854 but later made common cause with the Boers before annexation again in 1900. Dutch was the official language.

[3] Sir Theophilus Shepstone   (1817–93). South African statesman who occupied the Transvaal with twenty-five policemen in January 1877 and declared it to be under British control. He continued the administration there until 1879.

[4] Herculean determination.   In classical mythology, Hercules had to perform twelve labours of strength. (See p. 245.)

[5] Mr Fawcett   (1833–84) Blinded in a shooting accident by his father, he became Liberal member for Brighton in 1865, displaying great courage and eloquence throughout his parliamentary career and earlier.

[6] John Robertson   (1816–91), distinguished Australian statesman.

[7] 'Sweet Auburn, loveliest village of the plain.'   The opening line of 'The Deserted Village' (1770) by Oliver Goldsmith (1730–74) in which he deplores the increase in trade and the depopulation of the countryside.

[8] Sir Harry Smith (1787–1860), distinguished soldier and statesman, Governor of the Cape of Good Hope.

[9] Bishop Colenso   (1814–83), Bishop of Natal, got into serious trouble because of his rejection of the historical truth of the *Pentateuch*, though he returned to Natal in 1865. In his *Clergyman of the Church of England* (1866) Trollope's final

essay is on 'The Clergyman who subscribes for Colenso'. While it harks back to the old 'truths' it rejects literalism in Biblical interpretation.

[10] Apollo.   The sun god of Greek mythology, often represented as charioteer, hence the ironic reference here.

[11] Labor omnia vincit improbus.   Never-ending work conquered all things (Virgil, *Georgics*).

[12] O fortunati nimium sua si bona norint Agricolae.   O lucky farmers, if only they realised how happy they are. (See note 23, p. 245.)

[13] Cetewayo.   King of the Zulus in 1872, his militaristic instincts were checked by the British. With the outbreak of the Zulu War in 1879 Cetewayo was defeated at Ulandi, removed, but restored to his kingdom in 1883. He died in 1884.

[14] Catherine's gown.   See *The Taming of the Shrew* Act IV, scene iii, l. 140 (for Catherine read Katherina).

[15] Tittlebat Titmouse.   The shopman in Samuel Warren's *Ten Thousand a Year* (1839).

[16] All the Christys.   A reference to the London firm of auctioneers of works of art founded in 1766.

[17] A helmet upon Minerva or a furred pork pie.   Minerva was the Roman goddess of wisdom. She was also identified with Athene, Greek goddess of war, and is represented as being helmeted for battle. A pork pie hat has a flat crown and no brim, or else the brim is turned up all round.

[18] Downing Street, Exeter Hall, Printing House Square ... i.e. invokes the government, the great religious and humanitarian meeting-place of the day and the power of the press as epitomised by the *Times*.

[19] Langalibalele. Chief of the Amahlubi tribe in Natal, he led a rebellion in 1873. He refused to return captured guns, was banished to Robben Island, returned to Natal in 1886, died in 1889.

[20] Captain Elton.   James Frederic Elton (1840–77), African explorer, reported on the gold and diamond fields in 1871.

[21] Amphytrion.   i.e. The real host, wo provides the feast, as Zeus did when he visited Alcmene. She was the wife of Amphytrion, but by Zeus she became the mother of Hercules.

[22] Aurum irrepertum, et sic melius ... see p. 244.   It is stronger to spurn undiscovered gold (better thus placed while earth hides it) than to gather it for human uses.

[23] Mr Heal's establishment ... This was founded in 1810 and moved to Tottenham Court Road in 1840 where it still stands. It specialised in bedding, supplied same for the British in the Crimean War and throughout the Empire.

FURTHER READING

Apart from the Penguin abridged *North America* (ed. Mason) and *Australia* (ed. Edwards and Joyce) already referred to, the travel books (excluding *New Zealand*) were issued in paperback (without annotation) by Alan Sutton in the 1980s. Trollope's novels are available in World's Classics, Oxford University Press, where the series is nearing completion. The Trollope Society has issued eighteen titles so far, and will publish the complete fiction by the end of the decade. *The Complete Short Stories* ed. Betty Breyer, in five volumes (Pickering & Chatto, 1990–1) is readily available. N. John Hall's edition of *The Letters of Anthony Trollope* (Stanford University Press, 1983) is invaluable for any student of Trollope. The recent biographies have contributed greatly to my understanding of Trollope. These are: R. H. Super, *The Chronicler of Barsetshire: A Life of Anthony Trollope* (University of Michigan Press, 1988); Richard Mullen, *Anthony Trollope: A Victorian in His World* (Duckworth, 1990); N. John Hall, *Trollope: A Biography* (Oxford University Press, 1991); Victoria Glendinning, *Trollope* (Hutchinson, 1992).

ELEPHANT PAPERBACKS

Literature and Letters
Stephen Vincent Benét, *John Brown's Body*, EL10
Isaiah Berlin, *The Hedgehog and the Fox*, EL21
Anthony Burgess, *Shakespeare*, EL27
Philip Callow, *Son and Lover: The Young D. H. Lawrence*, EL14
James Gould Cozzens, *Castaway*, EL6
James Gould Cozzens, *Men and Brethren*, EL3
Clarence Darrow, *Verdicts Out of Court*, EL2
Floyd Dell, *Intellectual Vagabondage*, EL13
Theodore Dreiser, *Best Short Stories*, EL1
Joseph Epstein, *Ambition*, EL7
André Gide, *Madeleine*, EL8
John Gross, *The Rise and Fall of the Man of Letters*, EL18
Irving Howe, *William Faulkner*, EL15
Aldous Huxley, *After Many a Summer Dies the Swan*, EL20
Aldous Huxley, *Ape and Essence*, EL19
Aldous Huxley, *Collected Short Stories*, EL17
Sinclair Lewis, *Selected Short Stories*, EL9
William L. O'Neill, ed., *Echoes of Revolt: The Masses,
    1911–1917*, EL5
Ramón J. Sender, *Seven Red Sundays*, EL11
Wilfrid Sheed, *Office Politics*, EL4
Tess Slesinger, *On Being Told That Her Second Husband Has
    Taken His First Lover, and Other Stories*, EL12
B. Traven, *The Bridge in the Jungle*, EL28
B. Traven, *The Carreta*, EL25
B. Traven, *The Cotton-Pickers*, EL32
B. Traven, *General from the Jungle*, EL33
B. Traven, *Government*, EL23
B. Traven, *March to the Montería*, EL26
B. Traven, *The Night Visitor and Other Stories*, EL24
B. Traven, *The Rebellion of the Hanged*, EL29
Anthony Trollope, *Trollope the Traveller*, EL31
Rex Warner, *The Aerodrome*, EL22
Thomas Wolfe, *The Hills Beyond*, EL16

Theatre and Drama
Robert Brustein, *Reimagining American Theatre*, EL410
Robert Brustein, *The Theatre of Revolt*, EL407
Irina and Igor Levin, *Working on the Play and the Role*, EL411
Plays for Performance:
    Aristophanes, *Lysistrata*, EL405
    Pierre Augustin de Beaumarchais, *The Marriage of Figaro*,
        EL418
    Anton Chekhov, *The Seagull*, EL407
    Fyodor Dostoevsky, *Crime and Punishment*, EL416
    Euripides, *The Bacchae*, EL419
    Georges Feydeau, *Paradise Hotel*, EL403
    Henrik Ibsen, *Ghosts*, EL401
    Henrik Ibsen, *Hedda Gabler*, EL413
    Henrik Ibsen, *The Master Builder*, EL417
    Henrik Ibsen, *When We Dead Awaken*, EL408
    Heinrich von Kleist, *The Prince of Homburg*, EL402
    Christopher Marlowe, *Doctor Faustus*, EL404
    The Mysteries: Creation, EL412
    The Mysteries: The Passion, EL414
    Sophocles, *Electra*, EL415
    August Strindberg, *The Father*, EL406

ELEPHANT PAPERBACKS

American History and American Studies
Stephen Vincent Benét, *John Brown's Body*, EL10
Henry W. Berger, ed., *A William Appleman Williams Reader*, EL126
Andrew Bergman, *We're in the Money*, EL124
Paul Boyer, ed., *Reagan as President*, EL117
Robert V. Bruce, *1877: Year of Violence*, EL102
George Dangerfield, *The Era of Good Feelings*, EL110
Clarence Darrow, *Verdicts Out of Court*, EL2
Floyd Dell, *Intellectual Vagabondage*, EL13
Elisha P. Douglass, *Rebels and Democrats*, EL108
Theodore Draper, *The Roots of American Communism*, EL105
Joseph Epstein, *Ambition*, EL7
Lloyd C. Gardner, *Spheres of Influence*, EL131
Paul W. Glad, *McKinley, Bryan, and the People*, EL119
Daniel Horowitz, *The Morality of Spending*, EL122
Kenneth T. Jackson, *The Ku Klux Klan in the City, 1915–1930*, EL123
Edward Chase Kirkland, *Dream and Thought in the Business Community, 1860–1900*, EL114
Herbert S Klein, *Slavery in the Americas*, EL103
Aileen S. Kraditor, *Means and Ends in American Abolitionism*, EL111
Leonard W. Levy, *Jefferson and Civil Liberties: The Darker Side*, EL107
Seymour J. Mandelbaum, *Boss Tweed's New York*, EL112
Thomas J. McCormick, *China Market*, EL115
Walter Millis, *The Martial Spirit*, EL104
Nicolaus Mills, ed., *Culture in an Age of Money*, EL302
Nicolaus Mills, *Like a Holy Crusade*, EL129
Roderick Nash, *The Nervous Generation*, EL113
William L. O'Neill, ed., *Echoes of Revolt: The Masses, 1911–1917*, EL5
Glenn Porter and Harold C. Livesay, *Merchants and Manufacturers*, EL106
Edward Reynolds, *Stand the Storm*, EL128
Geoffrey S. Smith, *To Save a Nation*, EL125
Bernard Sternsher, ed., *Hitting Home: The Great Depression in Town and Country*, EL109
Athan Theoharis, *From the Secret Files of J. Edgar Hoover*, EL127
Nicholas von Hoffman, *We Are the People Our Parents Warned Us Against*, EL301
Norman Ware, *The Industrial Worker, 1840–1860*, EL116
Tom Wicker, *JFK and LBJ: The Influence of Personality upon Politics*, EL120
Robert H. Wiebe, *Businessmen and Reform*, EL101
T. Harry Williams, *McClellan, Sherman and Grant*, EL121
Miles Wolff, *Lunch at the 5 & 10*, EL118
Randall B. Woods and Howard Jones, *Dawning of the Cold War*, EL130

European and World History
Mark Frankland, *The Patriots' Revolution*, EL201
Lloyd C. Gardner, *Spheres of Influence*, EL131
Gertrude Himmelfarb, *Victorian Minds*, EL205
Thomas A. Idinopulos, *Jerusalem*, EL204
Ronnie S. Landau, *The Nazi Holocaust*, EL203
Clive Ponting, *1940: Myth and Reality*, EL202